THE DARK RISE

The Dark Rise

SHASTA JORDAN

Line After Line Edits

CONTENTS

| 1 |

Chapter

At the beginning of his life's greatest undertaking, Caneon had great plans to use the city library as central command. Being the place where he worked made it almost perfect. There was a storage room in the back behind the stacks that no one utilized. Years ago, it was a place to view microfiche, but the library converted to digital media with the onslaught of millennials; the viewer forgotten on a table like a discarded toy.

The room seemed a perfect fit, but a voice in his head repeatedly said no. Eventually, he caved to caution and set up shop in his own front room. It's wasn't like there was a line of people waiting to visit him and the house was built in a more genteel era. Back when civilized people kept the front room formal for visitors and the family room in the back of the house was for actual family.

He gave up his privacy along with the front room. It was a sacrifice to be sure. But the dedicated space was so important to the work.

The little voice in his head had proven shrewd. Mere months after he began his group, the head librarian decided to use that back-storage room as a kid's reading nook. It was the latest library gimmick with the sole purpose of increasing patronage. What a sad world they lived in, that people needed to be sold on reading.

It was well worth the invasion of these selected strangers when all was said and done. And after a little over a year of weekly visits the awkwardness had finally reached a bearable level.

The doorbell clanging through the house set his nerves to jangling. He jerked from his chair with every intention of giving a significant piece of his mind to whomever he found on the other side of the door. Drew and Trina barged in before he made it. No surprise there. Annoyance, yes, but no surprise.

Them being teenagers factored into both feelings. They were single to none the worst group of patrons he had to manage on a daily basis. He would take a gaggle of terrible twos over pubescent people every day.

Not that Drew was technically a teen at twenty years of age. Perhaps it was his relationship with the younger Trina that tricked one into categorizing him that way. Or maybe the boy just acted younger than his peers. Growing up without a mother may have stunted his maturity. Caneon didn't have a large sampling to compare against.

Drew was a necessary evil no matter what his age or lack of social etiquette. In the years of watching library computer users like a hawk, he had yet to see anyone as savvy with the machines as Drew. He could make them dance and sing if he wanted to.

One particularly slow day, Caneon had watched the kid do just such a thing for fun. That was two full days before he convinced the younger man to join his elite little group. It would have been only one day before, but he had needed the extra twenty-four hours to convince himself he could survive the addition of someone so unformed.

Dealing with the boy on a weekly basis hadn't turned out to be such a dreaded disaster. Mostly, he was a laid-back kid who did what he was told. Drew should by all rights be attending a college somewhere that could accommodate his high IQ. Over the last year, Caneon had come to realize the boy's genius went well beyond the tech he adored.

Drew could unearth anything he wanted on any given device no matter how shielded people thought it was. It had taken Caneon a long time to get past the nightmares of men with guns and badges busting down his door.

These days he was cool as a cucumber. The amount of information Drew had found them far outweighed the consequences should they ever get caught. At least in his mind. He was certain he wouldn't be the one they incarcerated. No one who spoke with him for five minutes would believe he had hacked anything.

He barely managed to check his email, and social media left a nasty taste in his mouth. His mother had been an archeologist and his father an English Literature professor. He had been raised to read actual books with pages and put true value on the ways and objects of the past.

It made him a bit of a freak with his peers and he knew it but didn't care. Let the average thirty-year-old's spend their lives attached to their electronic devices. Caneon was indubitably far above average.

Drew's talents made anything the boy did or said worth handling, even the constant smell of pizza grease and burnt cheese that lingered around him like bad cologne. The girlfriend on the other hand was a gum chewing, bubble blowing, slang talking nightmare who served no real purpose. Sure, on occasion she dug something out of the ether, but those times did not balance the amount of disturbance she caused. Drew undoubtably would have found the information first if she hadn't been distracting him.

Caneon had tried several times to banish her, but she refused to acknowledge his sovereignty over his own house. Like the proverbial penny she just kept showing up. Barring an obscene use of violence to physically throw her out he had no options but to suffer her presence. It was the current bane of his existence.

The two in question sashayed back to their workspace making themselves at home while he found his way to his books. This placed him and the teenagers on opposite sides of the work area which was by no means a coincidence.

He had arranged everything with Lynea's help to promote the most productive environment possible. Months of routine and the hard-fought establishment of personal space had solidified each person's dominion.

Neatly arrayed pens, notebooks, erasers, staplers, and an assortment of other office products they regularly helped themselves to in order to catalog and track their findings resided on a table near the front door. This was Lynea's domain of which she was uncontested queen. It was fastidiously well kept, and she permitted no waste. One of the many things he appreciated about her. The years of being a soccer mom had trained her in ways he wouldn't have comprehended before she came along.

Within reach of the table, two filing cabinets were packed with reports and papers for reference. This was also part of Lynea's providence, but she had them so well trained at this point she almost never had to reprimand them for misfiling. The woman would have made a fierce librarian. He had a sneaking suspicion her teenage children would be far above their peers when it came to manners and good behavior.

As she took up a stack of papers left for her, it crossed his mind to wander as he did from time to time what her home was like. He had met both of her children at the library in a peripheral fashion. They seemed to have the potential to become productive adults;

somewhat entitled but still acceptable. The husband remained a mystery.

She never talked about any of them with the group, and he had chosen to respect that. After all he didn't want anyone prying into his personal life. Whatever her home was like, he didn't think she was happy there, but he was horrible at interacting with people. Maybe she was ecstatic. People were a mystery.

Caneon's gaze drifted to the long folding table taking up most of the far wall. Drew was sprawled in a chair at one end in front of the computer Caneon had bought for the group. Being a novice in such matters, he had driven Drew to the store, set the kid free to gather whatever was needed, and swiped the credit card at the end of the ordeal. It was not a pleasant memory but the amount of data they had pulled from the device had made it worth every second of agony.

At the moment, Drew was happily clacking away at the keys of said computer with Trina looking over his t-shirt clad shoulder. A bubble proceeded to grow from out of her lips reaching dangerous proportions before bursting in a shower of pink goo all over her face. She giggled and Caneon cringed. He would find flecks of sticky pink goo on everything from now until what felt like eternity.

On the table next to his own personal set of millennials sat stylishly colored boxes of drives and wires. Trina moved past those to their printer and grabbed a paper as it came through. In their work area, she did her one useful job, highlighted whatever had caught Drew's attention and dropped it into a basket near the middle of the table for Megan.

Their resident demonologist slash goth aficionado, and her de facto assistant Tyrone would read through it at some point in the night. Their job was to fit it into context or file as irrelevant but possibly useful later. Other than his own, it was easily the most important part of the work.

Megan had slipped in quietly, as usual. She was already engrossed in whatever she'd dug out from amongst her stacks of books and folders. She kept the pieces of the puzzle that appeared most relevant close to her, for reference, as she sorted through incoming papers. It all looked like chaos, but he was convinced she had the capacity to tell you exactly where to find any piece of information you requested, should she want to.

She was a strange duck, flaunting her rebellion for the world to see. Her dyed black hair and multiple piercings screamed; I am not like you! He had never known anyone before who relished being the one thing that was not like the others. To so completely disregard the rules of society made him uneasy in parts of him he dared not look at too deeply. As a result, she made him highly uncomfortable and he tried to spend as little time with her as possible.

There was no doubt she was a brilliant mind. Her grasp of demonology and the history of the occult were unparalleled in her age group. He had checked into her college record. Every teacher who had ever taught her raved, gushed, and rambled on about her skills and intelligence. It was emotionally uncomfortable to read but informative, so he pushed through.

He found her need to try and connect with him off putting. Had it been a purely personal choice, her attempts at socializing would have been enough for him to sever their interactions. The professional in him wouldn't allow it. She was a conducive assistant, finding patterns while he pursued further information.

Tyrone helped her immensely with that. He would spend hours walking back and forth, pinning pieces of information up along the timeline for everyone to see. It kept his athletic body constantly in motion. Building that timeline was without contest the most vital part of the project. You could have a million interesting facts, but they meant nothing without context.

Tyrone was the worlds' largest worker bee, hovering between the board and Megan. Always comparing new information that came in to parts of the timeline they had already verified. It was a dance that sometimes distracted Caneon from his own work. The big dark-skinned man dancing around the little black-haired girl so studiously. It was overtly obvious to all that he was infatuated with her. Caneon speculated they were sleeping together but it had no relevance in his life, so he would never bother to find out.

His own desk sat next to the big timeline board. As much as they received from the internet, there were still so many things you could only find in the pages of a real book. He used the connections he had built up over the years to beg, borrow or steal pages and or whole books that were too old, obscure, or rare to be found on Drew's computer.

That meant they contained more of the early pieces of the time-line, making them invaluable but far harder to search. He would concede that Drew and his computer created more volume than he ever could. What do they say though? Quality not Quantity?

He had his own legal cabinet next to him which contained books he allowed no one other than himself to touch. He valued them to the degree he kept the cabinet locked at any time the group wasn't working with them. They were unspeakably old and completely ir-replaceable. No one else in this room could be trusted to treat them the way they deserved. One did not let the children play with the good china after all.

He was happy to immerse himself in one such book once his group was all present. It relieved him of the necessity of chatting with each member as they made themselves at home. For the length of time required to finish the research, this was their work area and not his personal private space. He had to keep reminding himself of that fact. It wasn't without effort.

A muffled bang echoed through the room. Searching for the source of the sound, his eyes were drawn to the teenage girl constantly marring his inner peace. For reasons he didn't fully comprehend, just having her in the same room chafed on his nerves, leaving them raw.

Trina glanced up then promptly returned her attention to some crinkled paper spread out in front of her. Her hands furiously resumed marking on it with a yellow highlighter. He hated the way she crumpled things up just to carry them in her pockets. How was a person supposed to find anything useful amidst all those folds and creases? Infuriated, covered the way those untidy pieces of paper made him feel.

Normally, he would keep his distance from her and her paper, but there was something in her smirk that drew him across the room. Curiosity was his only real vice, and he allowed himself to give in. It was after all a relatively harmless sin no matter what they said about the cat. She was frantically smoothing the page as he came to rest over her shoulder, and he couldn't contain the self-gratified smile twitching at his lips.

There weren't many yellow marks on the page, so he was trying to deduce what could possibly have put such a satisfied grin on her face when he realized she was referencing her paper with one of his books. One of his precious, never to be crinkled, always to be protected books. The obnoxious little brat must have stolen it when his back was turned.

He was two seconds from a full out temper when she realized who was standing behind her and desperately snapped the book shut. Her startled lurch and the mask of fright on her face almost soothed his pique, almost.

"What in the name of all that is holy do you think you are doing with *that* book?" His clenched teeth served to smother some of the volume but not all. Everyone in the room froze as if a picture were about to be taken. It was no secret he felt his books were far more valuable than any person on the planet-barring himself, of course.

"I... I just. I was using it…I mean…" Her voice strangled itself into silence. He raised just one brow in that way he had seen his father do countless times to recalcitrant students. "I only meant to borrow it." She found her voice, but he had to lean in to hear the words mumbled into the table.

This created the sensation of leaning completely over her and he started to feel like a bird of prey closing in on a helpless bunny. Accepting the fact, she was most assuredly not helpless let alone cute and furry. He was however dangerous in his own way and he knew it.

"Borrow it? Borrow it?" He was pushing her into the table with his presence by this point and obtained great satisfaction in it. She deserved to be terrified. The book she had so carelessly borrowed was one of only twelve copies of a translation of a scroll that no longer existed. Her carelessness could have caused something of true value to cease to exist.

"Dude, chill. I'm sorry." Her voice was a bare whisper and he only heard her because he was literally braced directly above her. He knew the apology shouldn't have any effect on him, but the fact he had never in an entire year heard her say those two words put some weight behind it. He straightened up, allowing her to sit erect, without moving far enough away to let the pressure off the back of her chair.

"Do you really think that is going to make it ok? Have your parents raised such a spoiled child that you believe yourself entitled to steal people's belongings at will?" He made sure to nudge the back of her chair enough to push her stomach into the table.

"No. I did the same things you do. I promise…I was careful. I just wanted.…...I just wanted to compare this article this guy wrote. It seemed kinda important?" The last was most definitely a question, but he gave it no regard due to its lack of context.

He did however calm down enough to become conscious of a pair of thin cloth gloves on her hands meant to keep oils and dirt off the book's pages. The tome itself was sitting on a protective cloth exactly as it would have been if he had pulled it out himself.

"You are extremely lucky nothing has happened to this book while you had custody of it." He stepped back from her chair allowing her to move so she could pull in a full breath. As far as he could see it looked like she had indeed been careful. That didn't excuse the theft. "I will not indulge your childish whims. You will never touch my books again without express permission. I do not care how important you believe yourself and your findings to be. It is Megan's job to cross reference articles and bring anything she finds worthy to me. Do you understand what I'm telling you?"

"Yeah." Her face was a shade of pink and he suspected tears were causing the glossy sheen in her eyes. Her feelings weren't going to sway him. The brat should have thought of the consequences before she acted. That was the problem with teenagers today. They never thought actions through.

"Good." He retreated another step as he gestured for her to wrap the book in the protective cloth. "Now return my book and get back to helping Drew with his work or leave. I really don't care which. No, that's not true, I would prefer you leave." She handed up the book and he turned to walk back to his desk only to find Tyrone blocking his path.

"Can I help you with something?" It wouldn't do to get into a confrontation with the big man. He was after all a trained mixed martial arts fighter. Thankfully, Tyrone simply stepped aside with a glower. Feeling his breathe rush out, Caneon realized he'd been holding it unconsciously. Who could fault him? The man was intimidating.

Walking back to his area, he chose not to look left or right. It mattered not what the others thought of either his confrontation with Trina or his exchange with Tyrone. This was his house, and he would behave as he saw fit. If they didn't care for his methods of dealing with the girl, well they knew where the door was, as the saying went.

There was a strained pressure in the air for quite some time afterwards; it had even him squirming in his seat. He was relieved to hear Megan get up and head into the kitchen for coffee. That simple act cut the tension and everyone else returned to their normal noise level almost at once. Only then did he realize he'd never put the purloined book back into the cabinet.

It was perched conspicuously on the corner of his desk. Seeing it there, he couldn't seem to distract himself from it. What had she been cross referencing? He had skimmed through the text a few days ago and found little of significance. He had in fact been ready to send it back to its actual owner.

Hating himself for giving any credibility to her thievery, he scanned the room for the crinkled piece of paper he had observed earlier. The niggly feeling in his gut was pushing him. He needed to follow up on the little he had read over her shoulder before becoming distracted by anger.

Something about the young man's claim that the Mexica people, as they were once called, had fled their mythical homeland, Aztlan, to escape a blood thirsty tyrant god did fit well with the remainder of his groups findings.

Most of the tidbits they had scraped together focused on Europe and Asia. It was a trend he had never questioned because the majority of vampiric legends came from those regions. This was the first hint of the race they were looking for having a presence in the Americas.

It was glaringly logical given a little thought. There had been people here the entirety of that time, but the written word wasn't nearly as prevalent as on the European continent. The population of the Americas at the time was predominantly nomadic with a culture that passed history down orally from one generation to the next.

It was no giant leap to conclude some of the creatures they were looking for had found a home amongst these nomadic tribes. Who better to live with than people coming and going so often they wouldn't have time to notice oddities and voice inquiries? If you were trying to hide what you were they would provide an ideal cover. If you intended to live as a god, they were simple people, easily convinced. This region was going to require more research.

He pulled the book closer. Inside was a description of a pyramid temple in the jungles of Mexico dedicated to the god of sun, his mother the earth, and his siblings, the stars, and the moon. The author described the temple as the center of a great city now abandoned and falling into ruin. He surmised its inhabitants had died of disease based on bodies he found littering the streets and laying untended in homes and places of business.

The writer, an explorer sent from the Aztec nation searching for their homeland of Aztlan, was repulsed by the treatment of those left behind. The bodies being untended would prohibit their souls from traveling on to live with the gods. His most plausible theory being his ancestors fled in such terror the only ones remaining were incapable of leaving.

He dedicated many months to walking the streets and tending the bones. It became his life's work to care for the ancestors he had found, and he documented it painstakingly. The pages of detailed burial records were much of the reason Caneon had set the book aside as unhelpful.

The author knew none of the names of the bodies he cared for, so he recorded exacting descriptions of where they were found and the remains of their apparel. It was an excruciating read, even for him. Buried amid that were just as exacting details of the temple.

Our intrepid young explorer tried many times to find entrance with each failed attempt meticulously recorded. His fruitless searches for any type of doorway left him venting frustration on the pages. A series of anger laden entries became interspersed with his descriptions.

He was driven to the point of climbing to the apex of the pyramid hoping to drop into what he was sure would be an open center. No such opening existed, and he nearly fell to his death scaling the lichen covered stone. That was the last of his tries at the temple.

His self-determined duty to the dead was finally complete. He wrestled with how unwilling he'd become to walk away from the city. It was certain in his mind that he had found Aztlan, and he knew it was imperative he return to his people and report the finding. His heart refused to say goodbye even for a time.

He became obsessed with the conviction that someone was inside the temple. Trapped. He was convinced to try once again to uncover a way in. His lack of success failed to deter him. Shortly after this his descriptions turned from eloquent and detailed to rambling and crazed.

Demons haunted a hellish dreamscape he could not escape, slicing his body and reveling as his blood spilled in a dance of violence and carnality. In the daylight he felt eyes on him always. He was being hunted, a stalking game. A voice spoke to him soothingly in quiet times, pleading for him to leave this place and return home. As his feet reached the edges of the city, his body would not obey his will and turned back to the temple. His last entries were broken and muddled.

The scrolls were found with his desiccated body decades later, trapped in a cave in the middle of the jungles of northern Mexico. There was no city to be found within miles and the scrolls were believed to be the ramblings of a dying man deprived of food and water.

Looking up from his reading, Caneon had to give the brat credit. She was on to something here and she had found it somewhere he had overlooked. Galling as it was to admit, she had done well. The descriptions of the young adventurer were so close to others they had found and fit into their timeline too well to be coincidence.

"Megan, put this on the timeline." Caneon handed over the book reluctantly not wanting to publicly applaud that Trina had gotten something right. Megan took the book just the way he'd trained her. She would care for it the way it deserved. The others gathered round her to read over her shoulder. He forced himself not to pry them away from the fragile pages. They had a right to know what had been found, he supposed.

"Trina, what else do we know about the Aztecs?" She jumped when he spoke which made him feel a little guilty considering what she had found, but he refused to give in to the feeling. Thievery was still thievery, after all.

She turned her chair his way, causing him to hope there was a diatribe of information heading his way. He braced himself to hear her out.

"They were nomadic, um, until they settled in the valleys of Mexico, like, founding the city that Mexico City now sits upon. Aztec myths say they were, like, lead from a place called by their, like, god of sun or something. He brought them to where they settled in Mexico, I guess. They were farmers and fierce hunters with, um, their own kind of government. They sacrificed in blood to their god, and by the time the Spanish came they had, like, conquered most of what is, like, modern day Mexico." Her voice was rushed, and he knew she was uncomfortable reciting facts while he stared at her. Most teenagers were.

"Anything else about this city? Aztlan?" That was where his interest lay. Where they ended up was obviously far away from what they left behind. He wanted to go where they started. The tingling making its way through his body assured him, that was the place he would find answers to his questions.

"Umm...No, not really. It is supposed to be somewhere in, like, northern Mexico, but nobody has really found it or at least nobody has, like, been able to prove they've found it." She turned to grab the crumpled paper off the desk behind her. "This, um, guy claims to have found a pyramid like temple he believes could be it. But it was just, like, him and some friends exploring when they found it and, like, they haven't been able to lead anyone back to the site." She was staring down at the paper as she talked. Something about this man's story was calling to her as well. Damn the bad luck.

Megan looked up from the book she'd finished skimming through. Her ability to speed read was almost as invaluable as her knowledge of ancient languages. "The Aztecs worshiped a whole slew of gods. The one they credit with leading them from Aztlan is Huitzilopochtli, the Sun. He came to be when his mother, a goddess herself, is impregnated by a ball of feathers while cleaning the temple. Her daughter the goddess of the moon and her sons, the gods of the stars, plot to kill her once they figure out she's preggo.

"As they decapitate her, Huitzilopochtli pops out fully formed and slays them. Quite dramatic. Somewhere after that he leads all seven tribes away from Aztlan and into what is now Mexico City. He was their hero. The Aztecs spent centuries giving blood sacrifice in honor of him. Or maybe to him. There's a lot of debate about when blood sacrifices began and what they were supposed to symbolize. Meaning, nobody really knows why they started doing it." Her black lips curved up in a disconcerting smile as she caught his eyes. He quickly shifted his focus.

"Bring me that paper, Trina. I think we need to contact the man you found." If the descriptions of the city matched, then that would lend credence to both stories. This of course raised the question of why no one else had managed to find this city over the centuries, but the jungle was a mysterious place that guarded its secrets.

"Um. He lives in Arizona. That's all I've really been able to, like, find from the report." She handed the paper to Drew instead of him and he clenched his hands to keep from lunging. Granted, the kid could probably find more information than him, but that wasn't the point. He had specifically asked for the paper, and she had specifically ignored him.

"Drew get me a name and address. A cell number as well. I need to hear this man's story for myself." Getting up from his desk he walked into the back room to cool down. It wouldn't do to go ranting at the brat, again.

"You ok?" Lynea snuck up behind him in her quite way. The woman walked like a ninja for no reason he could fathom. Maybe years of sneaking up on misbehaving children?

"Yes, I'm just irritated." She was the only person in the group who was comfortable enough to have followed him, which made her the only one he could possibly talk to. "I do not understand teenage insolence and I have even less tolerance for it!" His hands shook with the frustration he was struggling to hold in.

"That I understand. I would lay down my life for my kids, but there are days I could happily smack them silly." She chuckled under her breath and he caught a glimpse of a younger more relaxed woman. She must have been something in her day.

"How do you stop yourself?" He was asking as much to get an answer as to keep her talking. Most of the time she was all business. This softer side was a rare gift.

"Just like you did. I rant and rave and then, walk away.... quickly!" Her laugh this time was full and boisterous. She understood the struggle he was having with the youngest members of his group. He grasped that from the gleam in her eyes. A calm filled him knowing that in this very small window of time someone understood him. It wouldn't last and that made it precious.

"We should probably get back out there before they destroy all of the work we've done." He turned to walk back into the work room only to find her stifling laughter. "What is so funny?"

"Nothing. I guess I'm just in a silly mood." Her smile suggested more to the story, but he was certain she was not going to explain. Whatever it was, one could be sure he was the brunt of the joke. Shaking his head, he brushed past her, through the hall and out into the work area. Women made no sense at all.

Drew had the information he requested ready and waiting on his desk along with Trina's crumpled paper. If she was going to stick around, he was going to have to talk to her about neatness. Some things could not be overlooked, no matter how one tried.

For now, it was more important to collaborate this story. Reading through the article Trina had printed off didn't get him nearly enough information. Yes, the descriptions were similar, and both temples were in the same general area, but it wasn't enough to conclude anything definitively. If you were going to prove the existence of mythological creatures, you needed more than coincidence.

According to the newspaper article there were four members in the hiking party. The young man, Trenton Cole, his sister Aleece, her fiancé and a family friend had all gone to Mexico with the express purpose of exploring the jungle for lost architecture. Finding the temple and surrounding city had been a dream come true. A dream they claimed had conveniently appeared out of the mist in front of them.

They explored extensively during the day mapping with GPS as they went. Night fall pushed them to leave the ruins and return to their hotel with plans of returning the next day. They had every intention of sharing their find with authorities after they'd satisfied their own curiosity.

Only they were unable to relocate the site when they tried to go back. The coordinates marked took them to an anonymous spot in the jungle. No amount of searching revealed either the city or the path they had cut the day before. Authorities accused the group of fabricating the find to gain attention and sent them home with a scolding.

Caneon felt to the depths of his bones that these modern-day explorers were telling the truth. He wanted desperately to speak to all four of the group in depth. There wasn't much chance they were willing to come to him, so a trip to Arizona was in order. No way was he going to trust this kind of conversation to a telephone. Sometimes you had to look someone in the eyes when they told their tale.

"Drew, can you get me a plane ticket to Arizona, leaving tomorrow, please?" He was already mentally packing his suitcase and writing the letter he would need to send to his bosses about an extended leave of absence. Who knew where this could take him?

"You're going alone?" The incredulity in Drew's voice pulled him out of his thoughts.

"Yes. Is there a problem with that?" He couldn't imagine why the kid would care. It's not like he could afford to go. He wasn't angling for Caneon to pay for the ticket, so he could go on some grand adventure, was he?

"No. It's just um, you're just not um..." His courage seemed to desert him along with his words. All Caneon could think was pluck it up boy. You're never going to be a man if you can't learn to speak for yourself. Maybe Drew gleaned some of that off his face because he straightened his spine and started again. "You aren't very *good* with people you know."

It was the kind of statement that hung in the air with nowhere to go. What exactly was he supposed to do with that? He already knew he wasn't good with people. That's why he had Lynea. What was the kids point?

"I think he's trying to say one of *us* might have a better chance getting them to talk. I'll bet they've had a lot of negative attention to their story. The article proves there was unfavorable media attention. It won't make them feel they should trust strangers asking questions." Lynea's reasonable voice explained so quietly he almost didn't take offense. He suspected she had used that tone for exactly that reason. The woman was rather good at managing people.

"Great. You can go with me. Everyone loves to talk to you." That would teach her to try and manipulate him. He was no schoolboy to be pushed around.

"Ok, I will." The underlying excitement in her voice took the air right out of his sails. With much to do and no one left in the room he wanted to talk to he took his leave of them all. Let them find their own way out just like they came in.

| 2 |

Chapter

Warm air rushed her face exiting the airport in Phoenix next to Caneon. The summer like heat was a shock having just left the chill of early spring at home. Lynea had read the temperature here could top 115 degrees in the actual summer. She shuddered at the idea. Thank everything, they were traveling while the weather was mild.

Standing on the sidewalk, she scrolled through their itinerary for the name of the hotel she had booked. She'd tried to pick somewhere affordable but not sleazy. Not that she had enough experience with low end accommodations to tell the difference.

Caneon stopped talking to her on the plane when she told him where they were staying. Maybe that meant he felt it was below him. Maybe it meant he was out of things to say. She was never completely sure where he stood.

A taxi pulled up to the curb and she quickly claimed it. After fighting the luggage cart to the trunk area, she gratefully left her baggage in the driver's hands. Caneon made a face at the cart and she imagined he was sneering at the number of suitcases. He had brought only one carry on with him and vocally protested at all the extra work it had taken to check her bags in and then out. Let him pout. She needed every bit of it to make herself presentable. First impressions were of vital importance.

Sliding into the back seat, she worked on her tablet while she waited for Caneon and the driver to join her. She had put together a file full of pertinent information Drew and Trina had found for her on the members of the Mexico expedition. It wasn't as thorough as she would have liked, but it would do. They were certainly talented at info gathering.

Those two where the cutest and they really did make a great team. The lovey dovey could get too sweet sometimes like an unwanted sugar high, but all young couples were that way. She almost got drawn into a memory of a time when her and her husband Jared were happy like that. What a waste of time that would be. Yanking herself back to the present with purpose she focused in on the tablet.

Caneon slid into the seat next to her mere seconds before the driver took his place behind the wheel. She gave him the address then handed Caneon his paper copy of the file she was perusing on her tablet.

"I still don't see why we can't go straight to this Trenton's house?" Caneon grouched as he took the file.

"How is he going to take us seriously if we show up looking like this?" She asked as she gestured to her own state of disarray.

"What's wrong with how we look?" He genuinely seemed mystified and she felt a little sorry for him. Being careful not to let that show on her face for the sake of their precariously balanced friendship, she answered.

"We look like travel stained hobos with our wrinkles, plane hair and smeared makeup." It was a statement of fact on her part.

"I don't wear makeup"

She fought hard to hold down the disgruntled sigh. How could one person be so out of touch? "I know that. I was referring to myself. So, even if you don't care about your appearance, I'm not standing on his doorstep surrounded by luggage looking like this. I am going to the hotel first. You are an adult. You can do whatever makes you happy."

"I'll wait for you, of course. Otherwise what would be the purpose of you coming. I just don't see the need." He was obsessively cleaning under his nails again which she knew was a sign he'd become agitated.

Holding back the urge to pat his shoulder comfortingly because it would not comfort him, she folded her hands in her lap. Best not to let them stray. "I'll be as quick as possible. I promise." That was the best she could do for him.

He nodded as he turned to look out the window. His way of saying the conversation was over. The view as she glanced out her own window was breathtaking. If she gazed past the buildings, the mountains could be seen in contrast to the unbelievably blue sky. She'd never known so many shades of blue could be meshed together at the same time. It was as if the horizon never stopped.

Breathless from the eye feast, she barely noticed as the taxi pulled into the parking lot and stopped next to the lobby door. As she stepped out of the taxi, the heat hit her again in direct contrast to the coolness of the air-conditioned cab. How did people adjust to their climate always fluctuating like that?

She left the driver and bell boy to load her luggage onto the cart, so she could enter the cooled air of the lobby. It took her no time at all to confirm her reservation with the front desk and have room keys in hand. She passed one over to Caneon as he reached her side. Turning, she found the bell boy waiting with her luggage cart and headed towards the elevator.

They were in adjoining rooms on the third floor, so it was a quick ride up, then they were walking down a fashionably decorated hallway. She happily noted as they made their way down the hall that they were far enough from the elevator to not have constant foot traffic outside their doors. She was pleased the staff had heeded her instructions.

Leaving Caneon at his door, she proceeded to the next one down and dug in her purse as the bell boy unloaded the cart. She dismissed him with a generous tip and a nudge out the of room. The door closed succinctly between them she could finally enjoy a few moments of blissful peace.

One of the main reasons she needed this stop at the hotel was simply to orient her mind to her new surroundings. She loved to travel and over the years her and Jared and the kids had taken multiple vacations to locales all around the world. Every single one had been magical, but she needed this moment in the beginning of each to set her mind. A mental recalibration to allow her to put aside the routines of home and adapt to the new.

Of course, she was never going to admit that emotional need to the man in the next room. He had no empathetic bones in his body. It would have been all the ammunition he needed to bully her into skipping the hotel entirely. Thinking of him reminded her, she had a limited time before he would be banging on her door. She quickly set about righting her appearance to be ready for a first meeting.

Sure enough, as she finished the touch up on her eyeliner the knob on the door that separated the two rooms began to rattle. Did he really think she wanted him to have that kind of access to her room? Not in this lifetime. He was a good enough guy under all the rough edges, but she had no interest in allowing anymore men to have influence over her life. She would just inform him he needed to use the public door in the hallway from now on.

A fist almost landed squarely in her face as she opened the door. He quickly aborted the knock as she appeared before him. Looking put out and more rumpled then he had when they entered the hotel, she knew he had spent the time working himself into a nervous frenzy.

"Can we go now?" His voice dropped an octave on the last word. She could tell he was at the limit of his patience. Good thing she was ready.

"Yes. Let me grab my purse and I'll meet you in the hall." His face relayed such a look of exasperation she could readily tell he didn't understand the need to close the door between the rooms. The one thing she never thought she would need to worry about on this trip was him invading her personal space. That was a common ground they shared.

Motioning for him to follow her into her room she closed and locked the door he had just come through. Boundaries needed to be maintained. Grabbing her purse from the table by the door she headed out the doorway to the hall leaving him no choice but to follow. It was a matter of minutes and they were standing on the curb outside the hotel while a taxi pulled up.

Once she had given the driver the address to Trenton's home, she decided they should use the drive to go over their game plan for the interview. She had set up the meeting, so they were expected; although Caneon's impatience meant they were going to be at least twenty minutes early. It couldn't be helped. They would have to hope the brother and sister wouldn't be too offended.

"We need to focus on getting as detailed information as possible about the temple and where it is located." Caneon stated in his usual arrogant way.

"I disagree. We need to connect with them first. Ask about their trip. Why they were in Mexico and what took them out exploring into the jungle. They have to trust us first." Lynea knew this was why she was here. Caneon's version of this interview would be an interrogation.

"That's a waste of time. It doesn't matter what happened before they saw the temple."

"It matters if you want to know that they are telling you the whole truth. If you go straight to the parts of the story everyone else called bunk their defenses will go up."

"But we believe them." He seemed completely flummoxed.

"They don't know that. The sister, Aleece, lost her job and her fiancé broke off the engagement to distance himself from the fall out. They have plenty of reason to be distrustful." Lynea tried to be gentle with the rebuke but she was worn out from the travel and her patience was thin. "Trenton is a geography teacher and the school district he works for told him he had to disavow the story or lose his position. The world has not been nice to them over this."

"Your telling me I have to let you take the lead." The scrunched skin around his mouth conveyed his displeasure at the idea.

"Yes. That's what I'm telling you." Lynea waited patiently for the arguments. None came. That made her anxious. What was he planning?

Turning in her seat to stare at him, she could see he had gotten lost in thought. She was probably safe then. Content to let him stew while she set up the game plan in her own mind, she did nothing to gain his attention. Quicker than she was prepared for, the taxi was pulling into a quiet neighborhood tucked behind a strip mall.

It was middle class all the way; likely built in the sixties. Most of the houses were sedately painted brick with lawns of artistically arranged cactus and rock. It was far removed from the lush greenery she loved. The taxi pulled onto the concrete driveway of a home that stood out from its well-maintained neighbors only because of the golden yellow someone had painted it.

Reluctantly, she paid the driver, and they were forced to climb out into the heat once again. Walking up to the door took her breathe away a little. She wasn't sure if it was a sign she was getting old or if the dry air was searing her lungs shut. It felt like the latter. Ringing the bell, she hoped for the inhabitants to answer quickly. She was melting like a middle-aged snow woman.

A pretty strawberry blonde opened the door just as Caneon pushed his way to the front to ring the bell a second time. Ironic considering how annoyed he always got at Drew and Trina for doing that. Lynea moved to enter the cloud of cool air she could feel seeping out of the door only to find Caneon blocking her way. He had frozen like a statue. What the heck?

"HI. My name is Lynea Marks, and this is Caneon James. I talked to Trenton on the phone earlier. We have a meeting with him. I'm sorry we are a bit early. Is this an okay time or do you need us to come back?" Lynea's mind wasn't completely on her introduction. She was busy pushing herself around Caneon who was standing there staring at the poor woman like some demented creeper. At this point they were going to be lucky not to get the door slammed in their faces.

"I'm Trenton's sister, Aleece. You must be the people who were interested in the Mexico trip. He said you were coming by later. To be honest, I'm not interested in whatever article you're writing. That whole thing is over for me." Her attention kept being drawn back over her shoulder. Had they caught her in the middle of something or was she hoping someone would appear and save her?

Breaking past Caneon, Lynea stood in front of him hoping to distract Aleece from his odd behavior. They were going to have a long and stern talk when they got a private moment. In the meantime, there was some damage control that needed to be taken care of.

"I understand that. Completely. Of course, we're not here to pressure you into anything you're not comfortable with. If we could just come in for a few minutes we would be happy to explain why we are here." Lynea, trying like a crazy person to look relaxed, reached back and pinched the closest of Caneon's body parts she could find. It felt like an arm.

"Yeah. You can come in. Trenton wants to talk to you and it's his house." She stepped to the side and gestured towards the interior. Hoping Caneon had retrieved his senses, Lynea walked through the entrance. After the glare of the sun, her eyes were slow to adjust. Partially blinded, Lynea was hesitant to move too far into the room for fear of tumbling over the couch and further damaging their first impression.

"Go ahead and sit wherever you want. I'll get my brother." The young woman left them to sort it out in the dark as she walked through an arch into what seemed like a hallway. Lynea was quickly able to distinguish enough shapes that she felt confident walking around a table and sitting on the couch. To her immense relief Caneon was right behind her and took a seat to her left.

"What was that on the doorstep? "She hissed under her breath.

"Nothing." His pink stained cheeks belied that word. She could see again. Thank goodness. She took in the comfortable but cheap furniture covered in mismatched southwest designs. The siblings had obviously meshed two households to live together. Maybe when the sister's engagement broke off?

"Liar." She knew there weren't going to be any answers offered up sitting here but she couldn't help jabbing at him. She was rewarded with a glare as Aleece came back through the archway with a man who was clearly her brother on her heels.

Lynea stood quickly and offered her right hand to shake while elbowing Caneon with her left. At this point he couldn't be trusted to remember his etiquette. Trenton shook her hand and introduced himself then shook the hand Caneon had lacklusterdly held out. Niceties aside they sat. Lynea and Caneon on the couch, Trenton on the love seat to their right and Aleece in the chair to their left.

"What can I do for you?" Trenton's tone was courteous. In his early thirties, he came across as rugged and outdoorsy. His blonde hair was sun bleached and the tanned skin was a`la natural. At six feet plus, he could have been imposing but the charming smile and laid-back way he relaxed on the couch had Lynea feeling at home with a friend.

"We have been doing research on odd happenings, like what you experienced in Mexico. Our group found your story on the internet and were hoping to learn more." Lynea figured the more honest she was with them the more open they would be with her.

"It's not a story" Aleece squawked. Blue eyes cut sharply Lynea's way as the sister moved forward on her chair. Lynea realized she's already stumbled. The brothers easy air had lulled her into forgetting the sister's wariness.

"NO. Of course not. A bad choice of words. I'm sorry." Flustered Lynea wasn't sure how to move forward without stepping on another landmine. She could feel her face heating and desperately hoped her cheeks weren't turning red.

"Aleece." The one word combined with a brotherly look had the younger woman sitting back into her chair. The more laid-back pose did nothing to disguise the anger festering underneath.

"We believe everything you saw and heard was real. If you would allow us, we would like to give you a chance to prove it." Caneon's voice was surprisingly full of confidence and not his usual arrogance. He was looking Aleece in the eye and for reasons Lynea could not fathom the woman was relaxing and starting to smile. No one opened to Caneon like that.

"How?" Leaning forward the brother looked a lot warier than his sister.

"You take us to Mexico and show us where the city is. We will find a way to get inside. Once we do we will take pictures and video to document the find." Caneon was still staring at the sister but Lynea could see that he'd caught the brother's interest.

"Who's footing the bill?" Trenton asked

"I am. A few of our associates will be joining us if that's ok with you. All you need to pay for is food and drink. Are you interested?" Caneon's offer put Lynea in a state of shock. He never paid for anything he didn't have to. Not to mention no one had planned on going to Mexico. This was supposed to be a simple interview not the beginning of an adventure flick.

"Yes!" Aleece was perched on the seat of her chair ready to jump up and pack at a moment's notice it seemed.

"Don't you think we should talk about this?" Turning to his sister Trenton shut them out of the conversation.

"No. I want to go. It's my chance to prove to Devon that he's a stupid ass. I'm going. Whether or not you want to is up to you." The resolve in her eyes made it clear she wouldn't be swayed.

"For you, I'll go." Turning back to us he met Caneon's eyes defiantly. "We are in, but I swear if you are screwing with us or this is some kind of set up, I will personally break at least one of your bones."

"I assure you my intentions are above board." Caneon sat back with a self-satisfied smile and a side glance at the sister. Lynea made sure her mouth wasn't hanging open. This manly show of standing up to the brother was so not the Caneon that she had come to know. What was up with him?

"Wait a minute." Lynea shook off her state of shock. "We haven't cleared this with anyone else. Don't you think we should contact the others first? They have lives that will need to be rearranged. I have a life that will need to be rearranged. Not everyone can just jump on a plane."

Caneon shrugged off her protest and turned back to Aleece. A wise woman knew when to fight and when to battle it out later. In the car without an audience. Lynea considered herself a wise woman. In the meantime, perhaps it was best to go with the flow.

"When do you want to leave?" Trenton asked. Someone should see to the practicalities and Lynea was looking for a lifeboat of normalcy in a world gone topsy-turvy. Arranging travel, she could do.

"It will take us at least a day maybe two to arrange travel for the rest of our group. Also, I will need to arrange for rooms in whatever village is closest to our destination, so I'll need that information from your last trip." She set her anxieties aside as she mentally checked off her travel to do list. Her mind was quickly set to making sure everything would be ready.

"I'll just take a quick sec and get our travel details for you." Trenton unfolded his body from the loveseat and went back through the arch he'd first used to enter.

Without a purpose Lynea felt lost, so she pulled out her phone and started checking her calendar. She would need to make sure Jared was aware of their son Tanner's baseball schedule, so he could be at the game. It looked like Lydee, their daughter, had a band concert next week. She would need to have a ride home after practice.

Hopefully, Jared wouldn't be too distracted by his lovely assistant to take care of things at home since Lynea would be extending her trip. A thrill chased up her spine at the idea of throwing all the responsibility on Jared and heading off on her own. It had been too long since she'd put her needs before his.

Trenton reentered the room and she looked up to realize while she had been lost in thought Aleece had moved over to the loveseat and started a hushed conversation with Caneon. Wishing she hadn't been so distracted, she wondered what that conversation had entailed. Now she would never know. Caneon wasn't one to share.

"Here you go." Trenton handed her a sheet of notebook paper with all the pertinent information written on it. He had lovely penmanship. "I'll need to arrange a few things for work. I'll text you when I know better what time I can get out of here."

"Of course. You have my number." Standing Lynea had to practically yank Caneon up by the arm. He seemed content to stay and visit with the sister. If he were anyone other than Caneon she would think he had a crush. Even crazier it seemed to be reciprocated.

"Don't take too long. I would like to depart tomorrow." Caneon resisted Lynea's attempts to rush him out the door. "Lynea is a wiz with travel, so it should be no problem"

"Of course. That should work for us." Aleece jumped in to agree.

Feeling ganged up on, Lynea hurried out the door. With relief, she found the Uber she had ordered on her phone waiting for them. Moving quickly, so that her companion didn't fall behind she jumped in the back seat of the SUV. She had fumbled this meeting from the word go and Caneon had saved the day. Nobody was going to let her live this down.

"What where you and the sister talking about in there?"

"Hmm. Oh...mostly Mexico. She wanted to know if I had ever been. When I told her I hadn't, she was sharing some of the things she loves about the country. It sounds quiet fascinating. I can't wait to experience it myself." His eyes had gone dreamy. No doubt now. He was falling for Aleece. Megan was going to be crushed.

The young woman thought she kept her feelings a secret but Lynea watched people. She had witnessed that dreamy look in Megan's eyes when Caneon talked. The way she paid attention to every word while the rest of them fought to stay awake. How she glowed when he praised her. No one was that devastated by criticism unless they were emotionally entangled. The poor girl didn't seem to realize he was oblivious.

This trip had just gotten awkward. Or more awkward maybe. Watching Caneon fawn over some girl was already making Lynea uncomfortable. Having to watch Megan be wrecked by it was going to take it to another level.

"What did you just get us into?" She could finally voice her pique.

"I got us an escorted trip directly to where we want to go. You should be thanking me." Caneon glared at her from his side of the car.

"Maybe I would be if you hadn't committed us all without asking anyone. Our friends have jobs and lives. They can't just drop them on a whim." Lynea could feel the temperature rising under her skin.

"They don't have to accompany us if it's too difficult for them. This is the discovery of a lifetime. If that's important to them then they will do what needs to be done to be there." He was glowering as he turned his back on her. Silence held sway for the rest of the drive.

Out the car window, she could see the hotel loom above them as they pulled in. Lynea was relieved to pay the driver with her phone allowing her to leave Caneon behind. He could find his own way to his room. She needed time to contact the others, arrange a spur of the moment trip to Mexico and regain her balance. Her dinner was going to be room service. He could fend for himself.

| 3 |

Chapter

Three days later the last of the group finally found themselves in Mexico. Tyrone had required every second of that time to push his clientele off on other personal trainers. He hoped like hell they were faithful enough to come back once he was able to get home. He was crazy to be giving up the money and running off to Mexico. It would go from crazy to downright stupid if he came home to find himself without an income.

His mama's nurse had agreed to live in while he was gone so she was taken care of. Physically anyways. She loved the woman who cared for her like family, but he still felt like he should be there holding her hand. After all the years of hard work and sacrifice so he could succeed, she deserved that. Which was exactly why his life over the last two years had become work, mama, and the research group.

He had told her all about the group over the months he had spent working with them. Most of the time it was the only interesting thing he had to talk about. So, she knew every piece of the puzzle they had managed to scrounge up.

Sometimes, he felt like finding the answer was the only thing she kept holding on to life for. One last mystery to solve on the way out. The cancer had gotten so bad most of her days where spent with the morphine drip on high, but she turned it down to listen to him go on about finding vampires.

Which is exactly why he should have stayed at home tending to the woman who gave him life. But a moment of stubbornness on her part had him setting off to Mexico to find her those answers. He was a good boy who had always tried to please the mama who worked so hard raising him up alone.

So, he was in Mexico praying to God each day to keep her alive long enough he could give her this one last thing. Even if he didn't really understand why it was so important to her.

Sweat trickled down Tyrone's back as he stood in the heat outside the airport waiting for Lynea and this Trenton guy to come get them. Trina couldn't convince her parents to let her miss school, so it was just him, Drew and beautiful Megan melting in the tropic swelter.

They should have expected there would be nowhere to wait with air-conditioning. While him and Drew had grumbled about it, Megan had stoically trudged to the parking area with her bag bumping along behind her. His apathetic angel. If only she would acknowledge he was a male person.

Before mama had become completely bed ridden she had met Megan. She had called the younger woman sweet and sensitive. The woman who raised him had always been able to see people for who they really were. No matter what affectation they put out there for the world to see. It was her superpower.

The air was heavy with moisture while the sun beat down on them through the thatched roof on the pavilion they were using for shelter. He ached to rub the moisture off his skin, but his shirt was already dripping. If he didn't think of it as sweat, then it wasn't, right?

Megan didn't sweat. She glistened in her loose black tank top and short denim cutoffs with the studded belt that was her favorite. The wisps of bangs that clung to her forehead only enhanced the spiky look of her hairdo.

She was bouncing on the balls of her feet and he knew it was her excitement at seeing Caneon again. What she saw in that man, he couldn't understand. He wished he could but seriously the guy was weird. Tyrone needed a way to show her not weird guys could be attractive too.

A van came at them leaving dust in its wake. It was painted a fresh white that didn't quite hide the dents and dings resulting from dirt road driving. Plastered along the side was the name of the resort they were staying at. La Casita Del Sol. The house of the sun. That sounded hyped up.

It pulled alongside them and a Hispanic guy in his twenties jumped out of the passenger side to open the sliding door. He smiled a little too big and long, setting Tyrone's hackles up. In his experience guys who looked like that were about to boost something or stick you.

Despite his unease, he followed Drew and Megan to the back of the van where he stowed his luggage. Megan was fighting to lift hers while pushing it onto the top of the already unsteady pile. Images of her crushed under the weight of toppled luggage had him warily lending a hand to heft it up. He'd learned early on not to 'help' Megan or she'd light off like a firecracker. That girl was independent in all caps.

Still she wasn't crazy unreasonable, so he earned a smile, and thanks for his efforts with the luggage. That was going to feed the need in him for a few months. She was an addiction he had, no doubt, but he hadn't found the cure yet. Maybe he never wanted to.

The ride to the hotel was bumpy. Because of the delay to help load Megan's luggage he found the only seat left was in the back. He felt little to none of the anemic air conditioning the entire ride. It wasn't the first time in his life he had gone without things others took for granted. No doubt, it wouldn't be the last.

The resort finally came into view and he found himself pleasantly surprised. Admittedly, it was just a glorified hacienda. He had seen them often during his only year at Arizona State University before he blew his knee out and his football scholarship disappeared. It was nestled prettily into the hillside amongst the palm trees and foliage. Not necessarily the ideal picture on the postcard as the stucco was chipping and the landscaping was looking overgrown, but it would do.

They filed into the front lobby to find a small desk in an alcove to the right where a woman waited presumably to check them in. Directly in front of them was an arch, and through it Tyrone could see a tiled bar with stools in bright colors marching neatly down the front. Lining the back wall was a mirror where open air shelves were filled with neatly lined bottles of alcohol.

Before they could turn to the woman at the desk, Lynea strolled through the arch to greet them. She was carrying a margarita and dressed in a loosely flowing dress that took ten years off. How had he never realized what a stunner she must have been in her youth? The control she always maintained over herself and her emotions kept him from seeing anything but her carefully maintained facade of upper-class middle-aged housewife.

Vacation was agreeing with her. Maybe it was just being away from her ass of a husband. He had met the man twice at the gym while he was working. Both times Jared had treated him like an over paid towel boy. No, that man did not deserve a woman as loyal as Lynea.

Stepping forward he took her free hand and placed a gallant kiss on the top of it. Just a light brush of lips against skin so she didn't get the wrong impression, but every woman deserved to know when she was looking lovely. Mama had made sure he appreciated that.

"You look spectacular." He smiled at her as he stepped back. No reason to make her feel pushed.

"Why thank you." Her flushed cheeks and the glimmer in her eyes were his reward. Women were marvelous creatures. "Your rooms are ready. Here are your keys. I'm sorry you and Drew have to share. The budget didn't allow for singles. Megan, you are rooming with me" She pulled them out of a hidden pocket in her dress and handed them over.

"Um, that's cool." Drew stammered. Maybe Tyrone wasn't the only one to be swept off his feet a little at this new relaxed Lynea.

"Yeah that's okay with me too. I can hang with the kid." He smiled with just a little bit of extra charm. She would never compare to his angel, but he could enjoy a small amount of flirting.

Megan grabbed her key from Lynea and headed for the stairs without a word. He could only hope that the extra stomp in her step was a bit of jealousy. If only he could be smooth with her, the woman he cared about, his life would be different.

"I thought you were going to come get us from the air strip." That had been his understanding of the plan and Lynea didn't usually vary a plan once it was formed.

"I was, but Fernando offered to go instead. It was too good to refuse." She smiled in the loose way people do after a couple of margaritas.

"Gotcha. I'm ready to set this duffel bag down for a while, so I'm headed to the room." Tyrone gave her arm a playful pat and headed up the stairs after Megan. Unintentionally making her jealous was well and good, but he didn't want her thinking he had any real interest in the older woman.

He was at the top of the stairs when he heard Drew coming up behind him. Glancing over his shoulder at his new roomie he slowed his walk so the kid could catch up. By the time they made it to their room, the two of them were in lock step.

A tussle erupted as they pushed and shoved to enter the door first. Tyrone gained the upper hand and moved in. Then immediately stopped; Saltillo tile was covering almost every surface and the ones spared that treatment were covered in fabrics so bright as to stun the eyes. It took a minute to adjust. Like walking onto the sun.

"Lynea wanted me to tell you we are all supposed to meet in the um bar at 5 so we can plan or something." Drew was walking to the double bed on the left as he spoke. Gliding over to the other bed, Tyrone grunted his response as he dropped his bag to the floor and his body to the bed simultaneously. He needed a siesta. When in Mexico right?

Hours later he pried his eyes open to find the light had softened into the beginnings of a tropical twilight. Peering at the digital numbers on his watch revealed he had less than ten minutes to freshen up and get downstairs. There was no time to call. Damn it. He shot a quick text off to his mama's caretaker as a check in.

A fresh t-shirt and wet cloth to the face was all he needed before he descended to the first-floor bar. Walking into the room he easily spotted his friends taking up the entirety of the back area. Since the room was no more than ten feet wide and the bar took up a good four feet of that they were sitting at the large booth in the corner with spillover at the bar and still talking easily.

Sauntering up to the seat left in the booth he dropped down next to a blonde man he didn't know. Assuming this was Trenton, he sized him up as he would any opponent. Newcomers always needed to be thoroughly assessed. He needed to know what it would take to protect his people if it came to that.

"Hey, you must be Tyrone." Trenton held his hand out and Tyrone shook it. Just because he didn't trust the man didn't mean he was going to forget all the manners his mama had worked so hard to instill in him.

"Yeah that's me. Trenton, right?"

"Guilty. We were just waiting for you, so I guess we can get started. Lynea and Caneon have filled us in over the last couple of days, while we've waited for everyone to get here. I'm trying to wrap my mind around the whole vampire thing. It's way out there you know." His easy laugh and self-depreciating head shake took most of the sting out of the disbelief.

"I'm still waiting to see it myself but bro I have read a lot of stuff that makes me think this is legit." Tyrone could respect the honesty of holding back trust, but they were going out into the jungle together. People needed to be all in.

"Alright guys, tomorrow is a big day. We all need to be on the same page or things are liable to go sideways." Lynea set her drink down and scooted it out of easy reach. Message received. It was time to set fun aside. "Drew, why don't you tell everyone how you plan on finding the city."

"So, um I have this friend who I met online on this site I'm not supposed to tell you guys about. He collects satellite images trying to prove government conspiracies and stuff like that. I asked him to search up the coordinates and dates you guys gave Lynea from your last trip." He pulled out two pictures from a folder and placed them on the table as he talked. "These are the images he captured the day Trenton's group was here."

Leaning forward Tyrone could see a lot of greenery viewed from above. It didn't look all that interesting until he focused in. Just peeking out of the trees was the glimpse of what his untrained brain thought was a pyramid. Holy crap. He was seeing now.

He felt Trenton's body tense with the process of drawing in breath as he caught hold of the same sight.

"It's there. It's really there." The breathy words left the man's mouth on an exhale. Maybe the dude hadn't been all that positive about what he had seen that trip. The mind can play crazy tricks on you.

"Yeah, dude, It's really there." Drew's voice reverberated with excitement. "So, assuming we aren't dealing with a bunch of mystic hoodoos I'm, um, guessing it's a shield." Pointing to the second paper brought everyone's attention to the picture of the exact same trees without a pyramid in sight. "This one is from the day you tried to take authorities back to the site."

"I think there is someone, um, living in the city and they are using a shield to cover their tracks. So, in theory all we need to do is find a way to disrupt the shield." The kid sat back like the cat eating the canary.

"Are we left to assume that you have found a way to do just that?" Caneon's eyebrow was twitching in irritation.

"Yeah, of course." Drew's duh dude look did nothing to soothe Caneon. The kid seemed to realize he was close to being choked and wiped his face clear. "Right, you want me to explain. OK."

"Another guy I know sent me some schematics for how to build like a frequency generator. We just turn it on, and it should disrupt whatever frequency the shield is resonating with. That makes us a hole. Easy peasy." The big ole grin on his face directly contrasted the skepticism plastered across every other face at the table.

"Let me get this straight. We walk out into the jungle with some crazy device you built off the internet. Then we turn it on and if a miracle happens and we don't all blow up; it will turn off this advanced shield that has been standing for who knows how many centuries. After that the invisible city appears and bang we are in?" The sneer on Megan's face clearly transmitted her lack of confidence.

"Yep. That's it." Nothing was putting a dent in Drew's pride at his accomplishment.

"Does anyone have a better plan?" The strawberry blonde sitting next to Caneon put her two cents in. That must be Aleece. She was pretty in a cookie cutter barbie kind of way. Could that be attraction he was reading in Caneon's body language? He almost didn't dare hope.

Everyone sat in silence for several heartbeats. As crazy as the kid's plan was it was going to carry the day. Tyrone had learned months ago not to bet against Drew. He lost his mama before he was old enough to really know her and his old man was venom spitting mean. The kid had developed this quiet strength that kept his back bone straight even in the scariest of messes.

"I'm in." He wasn't scared to be the first one to back his boy's plan.

"Me too." Leave it to his angel to go all in despite her reservations. He respected her level of loyalty.

As the others chimed in, they all started to giggle and grin in that way people do when they know they've committed to something insane. All you can do is laugh because there is no point in feeling the fear. There was no turning back now.

"Perfect. I suggest everyone get a good meal and then a good night's sleep. We are going to need our A game tomorrow." Leave it to Lynea to mother everyone. Most of the group would ignore her but Tyrone had learned in his youth how to manage his time for optimum performance. Years of juggling football practice, honor roll and a part time job would do that.

Off to the right he could see the bartender wiping nonexistent messes off the bar. He caught the man's eye and signaled. Rising to his full height he met the guy at the bar and ordered himself a chimichanga and some tacos. His stomach had just reminded him about the skipped lunch. He wasn't the type of guy who missed meals on the regular.

Others in the group began ordering food and someone got a round of drinks headed their way. Maybe it was the adventure they were starting or the vacation destination, the barriers drifted away leaving none of their usual awkwardness. Laughter and conversation filled the room. He wasn't sure exactly when it had happened, but these dysfunctional people had become his.

A smile settled on his face. Time slipped by in the way it does when you're enjoying good food and drinks with people you enjoy. Pushing his now empty plate aside he downed the last of his beer and took his leave. Lynea was right. No matter what they found in that jungle they needed to be in top form. Besides, mama kept strange hours, so he needed to take the chance to call her.

| 4 |

Chapter

Drew watched Tyrone leave the quaint little bar and knew he should join him. There were still last-minute checks to make on the device, but he couldn't pull himself away. The comradery flowing through the room held him as tight as any rope. Maybe, it was being in a country where he was old enough to have a beer with them. Maybe, it was the plan he'd come up with on his own. It didn't matter. They were treating him as an equal.

Lynea told a joke that had everyone busting up and Megan elbowed him in her inability to contain her body movements. He didn't even care there would be a bruise tomorrow. It would be a mark of honor. Caneon wasn't glaring at him which was huge. That might have more to do with the strawberry blonde the man kept staring at. It didn't matter. He would enjoy it.

It was way past any decent hour when Lynea finally called it quits. She had indulged in a few to many margaritas and Megan helped her up the stairs. He followed behind them in case they tipped the wrong way. Not wanting to miss a moment, he'd nursed the two beers that had been passed his way. Years of dodging his dad's drunken fists only to suffer through the worse apologies the next morning had made him leery of alcohol.

Thankfully, the women made it into their room without major incident. Once he was in his own, he couldn't calm the antsy tingling running up and down his legs, driving him to move. There was a lot of pressure to have his device work. Deciding to take it into the lobby and work with it some more he grabbed the bag it was in and headed out.

Downstairs he found the lobby and bar closing for the night. Outside there was a veranda that still had lights on, so he grabbed a table and set to work. Lost in the tweaking and fiddling he failed to note the time until the haze on the horizon revealed the sun was coming up. Crap. Lynea was going to fry him if she found out he'd pulled an all-nighter.

Brilliant light shot through his closed eyelids as someone yanked back the curtains above his bed. Turning toward the wall, he tried to pull his blankets up to block out the offending sun.

"Rise and shine princess." Tyrone chuckled as he easily twisted the blankets away from Drew, leaving him with no protection in the morning light.

"I dote wanna." Drew mumbled trying to use his arm in place of the blanket.

"Don't care." Drew could hear Tyrone rustling around near the bathroom and curiosity had him lifting his head. Only to nearly drown as a wall of water slammed into him.

"Now you've showered as well. Perfect." Tyrone set down the ice bucket he had used with a happy thump.

Wide awake and not just a little bit pissed Drew mopped the excess water off himself as best he could. Standing up, he found a towel shoved in his face by a meaty black fist. Jerking it out of Tyrone's grasp, he wiped down his face and hair. Pulling the sopping shirt over his head he threw it at the man to blame for its wetness.

His satisfaction was stolen when a chuckling Tyrone caught it easily and took it into the bathroom to ring it out in the sink. The big guys cheerful humming provided a soundtrack to Drew fumbling through his bag for a clean one. There was no winning this war though, so he yanked it down over his chilled chest as he let the irritation go. That wasn't even close to being in the top ten worst ways he had been woken up.

Checking around the room, he gathered his belongings and stuffed them haphazardly into his bag while Tyrone looked on in amusement. His tablet was the last thing to be unceremoniously dumped into his backpack. It was an old model that he barely used anymore but that was no reason to leave it behind.

"Don't you need to check in with your mom or something?" Drew hoped to distract the man so there would be no further pranks headed his way.

"Already done. Mama is doing fine. Thanks for asking." Tyrone smiled that easy way he had.

Shaking his head Drew hid his own smile. Spending time with the big guy was like chilling with a Xanax. He mellowed the mood right out. Drew had never felt that from another person before. Slipping his shoes on he headed down to join everyone at the rental van.

Knowing that they could be in the jungle for a couple of days, they had opted not to pay for rooms they weren't using and would take the luggage with them.

"Everyone already loaded up. You're the last man in so you get the backseat." Tyrone breezed past him with a cocky strut, ruffling Drew's hair as he passed.

A headache started to pulse through his skull, and Drew piled the regret onto his decision to waste the night working. Important as the device was it couldn't run itself. If he bungled something because he was sleep deprived there would be no forgiveness.

Inside the van he found himself crammed into the middle seat between Trenton and Lynea. Normally there wasn't anything wrong with either of them, but today he wasn't feeling the love.

Lynea had dark glasses covering half her face and the part he could see was sallow. That big bag had better be her throw up plan because he was not sacrificing his sneaks. Trenton had pulled his ball cap down over his eyes and slouched against the window. He might be asleep or dead. Drew wasn't going to poke him and find out.

They were not in ideal shape to head off into the jungle. Luckily Caneon looked his usual stiff bodied self behind the wheel and Aleece was perkily riding shot gun. They would get there safe.

Tyrone and Megan shared the middle seat which normally would have had his man sitting pretty. Except she was laser focused on the two people chatting up front. A competition was brewing there. Crappy prize though.

Deciding to get whatever catch up sleep he could Drew tipped his head back against the seat and let his mind slip away. It quickly became obvious the jarring of his body wouldn't allow him to relax. It didn't matter. He didn't have the energy to move.

The van lurching to a stop hours later jerked him upright. Moving his stiff muscles slowly so they didn't bind, he elongated his body in degrees. Confident his legs would now hold him he shuffled out of the van and into the warm sunlight.

His stomach was way off so he didn't trust it when it screamed lunch time. Lynea pulling an ice chest out of the back supported his body's assessment. He went with it. Moving to help her, he quickly grabbed a handle. Under a nearby tree, she opened it up and started handing sandwiches out. Collapsing nearby he scarfed down his food.

Hunger assuaged; the rest of his senses kicked into gear. A hum was growing louder the longer they sat there, but he swore he couldn't hear it with his ears. It was running through his body leaving goosebumps on his skin. Looking down he could see the hair standing straight up on his arm.

Longings took control of his mind. To be near someone. Someone lonely who needed him. She was frightened and cold. Left alone. Trapped and abused. He could save her.

Smacking the back of his head on the tree he was propped against he struggled to clear his thoughts. A dark fog creeped in making it hard to see or hear anything but the voice. Her voice. She intended him harm. She didn't want him to know that. Anger filled her to see it in his mind.

She pushed at his walls. Reaching into places he kept sacred, she pulled deep on his strings. He faded, relinquishing control. Going to her. No. She wouldn't drag him under like that. He had survived the darkness that was his father. He would not lose himself now. Digging his fingernails into his palms until blood trickled from the cuts, he bought a moment of clarity.

"Wake up Drew!" Lynea was inches from his nose shaking him like a limp doll. He locked onto her hazel eyes and tugged on the lifeline. She stopped shaking him. Before his fuddled mind could register it, she reared back and slapped him with all her strength. Listing to the side, he would have fallen had his body not kicked back in gear. Nothing ever felt better than his hand landing in the cool grass just where he needed it to.

Chaos reigned all around him as the others tried to figure out why this motherly woman had hauled off on him. He wanted to defend her, but the wind wasn't back in his lungs yet. Focusing in on her, he was dismayed to see tears making tracks down her cheeks.

"Thank you." The croak that eked out of his throat hurt deeply. It didn't matter. He needed her to be okay.

She nodded her head at him only seconds before she was shoved out of the way by well-meaning hands looking for injury. Megan was in his face only seconds before Tyrone picked her up and set her aside. The fury emanating from her tiny frame meant the big guy would pay dearly later.

Pushing past the pain, he lurched forward and sucked in a deep breath. He could do this. Summoning the remnants of his courage he pushed his feet under him and tottered to a fully erect position. Tyrone hovering like a new mother with both arms extended, acting as bumper pads, made him want to laugh. Nope there wasn't oxygen for that. One simple message so the buzzing voices would subside for a blessed moment.

"I'm ok. I had a nightmare." That was it. All that he had in him expended; he gave up his manly pride and leaned against his friend. Tyrone did an admirable job of making it look less wimpy than it was. No way was he admitting to anyone that he thought someone had tried to take control of his body. That was too crazy even for this group.

"I'm so sorry Drew." Lynea was hovering at his side her hands fluttering like hummingbirds looking for a place to land. Reaching up he grasped hold of one with the scraps of strength returning to his body. His heart wanted to squeeze it reassuringly. The weak grip he managed didn't get the job done.

"It's good. I'm good. Really. Damn, you pack a wallop." Turning his face, he showed off the aching cheek where an imprint of her hand had to be clear as day. It wasn't the hardest he'd ever been hit but she'd spun his head. He was a little bit impressed. Forcing an up-turn of his lips, he hoped they took it as a grin. Their pinched faces relayed his failure.

Working harder to stand on his own, he fought to let Lynea off the guilt hook. She had acted quickly to pull him out of whatever that crazy had been. There was no reason for her to be ashamed. Even if it was the worlds creepiest space out she had helped him break free. Now how did he let everyone else in on it without sounding like a stupid kid afraid of the boogie man?

"How close are we to the GPS coordinates?" Pushing away from Tyrone, he forced himself to stand on his own two legs. Working through the awkward moment was the best plan he could come up with.

"It's about a twenty-minute hike that way." Trenton pointed over his shoulder to indicate where they would need to go.

"Perfect. I'll just grab my bag and we can be off." Drew tested the process of walking with a few tentative steps before he got too far away from Tyrone. Falling on his face wasn't going to help anyone feel better. Finding them trustworthy, for the most part, he made his way to the back of the van.

Grabbing his black duffel, he turned to walk back to where Trenton waited. Everyone else was hurriedly cleaning up the lunch debris so he didn't feel like he needed to move quickly. Lynea and Megan slid the cooler into the back of the van with minimal strug-gle. Megan headed off to keep watch over Caneon and Aleece and Lynea moved to join him.

"I am so sorry. I need you to know that. I don't know what over-came me. You were staring at me and there was so much fear in your eyes, and I knew what I had to do. It's crazy I know. Slapping you like that. I can't explain why I did it." Her shoulders slumped and the hitch in her breathing clued him in to impending tears.

"I was petrified. Terrified. Can't move, can't breathe scared. I've never had night terrors or anything before. You woke me out of it. No worries. We are totally chill." She was the only one he would admit even that much to. Mom's had like a vow of confidentiality right. Like priests and doctors and stuff.

She reached up and laid her hand on his throbbing cheek. Her hand was cool on his skin. Like maybe she was healing him with her mom touch. For a fraction of a second he imagined how it would have felt to have a mom do that for him as a child. The miracle of kisses filled with loving goodness was unknown to him.

"Thank you for taking care of me." He placed his hand over hers and then moved them away from his face. It wouldn't do to get caught up in wishing for what he never had.

Stepping away from her, he returned to his original plan to move forward. Trenton had been joined by several of the others. Drew picked up his pace to avoid being last. He could do without everyone staring at him again. For any reason.

After he stepped up to the group, Trenton headed off into the jungle. Him and Tyrone had taken the lead. They both carried wicked looking machetes they took turns swinging in an arc. Slicing through the air, they severed leaves and tree limbs alike with lethal grace. Drew imagined if a person were to step out of the jungle and into their path. It was gruesome.

Even with the blades clearing the way it was a treacherous hike. Roots and vines clogged the ground waiting to entangle a carelessly placed foot. He was grateful to feel the fugue of earlier fading. It was taxing every bit of energy he had to keep moving forward. His focus zeroed down until nothing existed but the next step.

Abruptly he found himself nose to back with Aleece who had been walking in front of him. Peering around her to the front of the party he tried to decipher why they had stopped. He couldn't see a thing other than leaves and people's heads.

Jostling past Aleece, he made his way through the crowd between him and Trenton. The closer he got the more confused he was as to why they had stopped. There was nothing around them. At all. Just a whole lot of the same plants and trees they had been fighting through for almost half an hour.

"Why have we stopped?" Caneon asked the question on everyone's minds. He stood next to Tyrone trying vainly to see the GPS device in Trenton's hand.

"We're here." Trenton held the device up so the little flag symbol directly in the middle was in plain view. Drew's experience with this kind of thing was nil so he trusted that meant they had arrived.

"I don't see anything." Caneon was so pissed his body was vibrating with it. Come on dude. Nobody expected to be able to see it. That's why they brought the device. Sometimes Drew didn't understand adults.

"Give me a second and I'll have the device up and running." Settling the bag onto the ground Drew set to work pulling it out.

"Shouldn't we be able to feel around for buildings or something? A shield would hide it, but it's still there right?" Aleece made her way to the front of the group. "That's the big thing everyone said when we came out here last time. Not about the shields but how we should be standing in the middle of buildings no matter how well they are hidden."

"Where were you standing when you marked the coordinates?" Caneon trying to act charming was almost creepy.

"Right in the middle of everything. We thought we would hit something, literally, before we ever got to the mark." Trenton looked confused. "When I put this in here we were standing between two buildings, staring straight at the temple. The ground under our feet was brick." He looked down as if to verify that was not what he was standing on now.

"It's possible that whatever is powering the shield is also scrambling your GPS. Sending false readings. I knew that was a possibility" Drew threw over his shoulder as he finished up his work.

"Wait. Are you saying we came all the way out here with the possibility that we are in the wrong place?" Caneon lost all pretense at charming. "Didn't you think that was something we might find pertinent?" He was fairly hissing the words.

"Chill man. Even if we are off base, we should be close enough to see the shields when I start the devise."

"What if your device doesn't operate properly? What then? Do we walk around with our hands in front of us searching in the proverbial dark?" Caneon seethed. Aleece had placed her hand on his arm placatingly. It calmed him enough to speak lucidly again. Now Megan looked like she was eating lemons.

"The device is legit. It'll work." To emphasis his point he reached down and flipped the switch. The air became charged almost immediately. Drew could feel it vibrate around him. He had to fight to keep his teeth from chattering.

As the sensation grew, his skin felt like it was trying to climb off his body. Tingles and prickles started building in his hands and legs. Much more of this and he was going to scratch himself bloody to make it stop. Frantically probing around them, he prayed to see a building, a wall, a freaking glimpse of anything remotely man made.

Then to the left more than five feet away a shimmer in the trees caught his eye. Further into the jungle, past the point Trenton had stopped, there was movement. Walking toward it, he kept his eyes trained on the spot afraid to lose it if he glanced away.

Pushing through a particularly thick patch, he became nervous when it slipped from sight. Fearing he would pull the last frond away and find nothing more than another bunch of jungle he held his breath. As his arm moved the obstacle, a wondrous sight was revealed.

Through the trees, less than twenty feet away, was a road undulating like they were viewing it through water. His device must be too weak to fully penetrate the shield. It didn't matter because they could see it and that meant they could move through it.

Turning to yell at his friends, he was surprised to find them bunched up directly behind him. Six sets of eyes stared at him expectantly. It seemed he was the leader now. OK, then. Setting his shoulders firmly in place, he strode across the remaining distance with all the confidence he wished he were feeling.

Reaching the undulating window, he stretched his arm out to touch it, expecting to feel liquid. Instead he experienced a blast of heat followed by a gush of cool air as his hand broke through to the other side. He couldn't be sure thanks to the fluctuations, but it felt like the ambient air inside the shield was cooler than the air around them.

Shoving all his determination into one big effort, he lunged forward. The rush of heat was harsh as it passed over his body. On the other side was refreshing relief from the sweltering mugginess they had marched through all day.

Marveling at the scenery around him he was astounded to find himself in a magnificently preserved ancient Aztec city. Directly in front of him was a road marching straight between buildings to a temple reigning supreme over it all. The hand-cut stacked-stone buildings were a display of beautiful craftsmanship. Hanging from windows and doorways where tatters of intricately woven cloth clearly once used as coverings.

The others joined him in staring dumbly around. Sure, they all said they believed but, like him, no one had planned on finding anything. Except maybe Caneon. The true believer who had never really converted Drew. He had been sure that the best they could hope for was overgrown and crumbled rock.

"We found it." Aleece's voice was hushed. Apparently even she was shocked, and she had been here before. "We found it!" The screech of excitement was accompanied by a strange little happy dance involving skipping and foot kicking. It was enough to make Drew smile. When she pulled Caneon into it the look on his face had more than just Drew laughing out loud.

Riding the rush of adrenaline from their find, they spared scant seconds to divide into twos and threes before scattering into the buildings to explore. The possibilities were as unknown as the city they had broken into.

| 5 |

Chapter

Megan fumed as she trudged up the road with Drew and Tyrone in tow. Everyone else had dashed off without a thought for her. To be stuck with the kids was humiliating. She was a grown woman with loads to offer the world, but everyone kept pigeonholing her because of her fashion choices. It was discrimination. That's what it was.

She was the one who had toiled countless hours away researching. It was her sweat that had put together the pieces of this puzzle. She was the glue that made everything fit and they brushed her off when it came time for the important work.

Well, she would show them. She would find the evidence Caneon needed. She could do that. She had the training. Wasn't she the one who had a degree in demon studies? Yes, she was. Aleece couldn't do that for him.

With purpose renewed, Megan began to take in the world around her. Caneon had to be in heaven with all the artifacts laying around. She slowed her pace to study the open rooms to her left and right. One doorway gave her a glimpse of a rough wooden dining table with plates of thin stone set out for a meal. Another showed her a work bench with hand-made tools hanging on pegs above it.

Nothing of paper or cloth seemed to have weathered well. Leather book bindings flapped in the slight breeze. Slightly askew, they perched precariously from shelves nearly empty of the papers that should have filled them. Tattered remnants of blankets clung to pieces of straw filled lumps that must have once been mattresses.

For all their uniqueness none of these things were the find Caneon was looking for. Knowing his ultimate goal, she chose not to linger over the detritus of a long-ago nation. Today they were hunting for something far more interesting.

They spent hours wandering the streets, inspecting the buildings for signs of something more than day to day living. To no avail. Feeling weary, Megan was ready to return to the group and try again tomorrow. She had lost sight of the boys. Frustrated at having to find them she quickly searched the area nearest her.

When they didn't turn up and she couldn't get them to answer her calls, anxiety started to set in. It was only a couple of hours ago that Drew had his little episode. What if he had collapsed somewhere? Tyrone better not have taken him back without telling her. Her feet picked up speed as she rushed around the next corner hoping to see them.

All that greeted her were more empty buildings. Moving forward she worked to cover ground swiftly. Her breath coming in short gasps as she struggled to keep up the pace. She needed to find her friends. Why the sensation of malicious eyes on her?

Slick sweat had her clothes sticking to her skin in the rapidly cooling air. Pausing to catch her wind she realized the sky was darkening above her. How had time slipped away from her so easily? She should be back to the others by now.

Her eyes darted around the horizon frantically searching for a landmark she could recognize, no luck. She was lost. The darkening sky had obliterated the outline of the temple that had loomed above them all day. Without it she had no idea which way to turn. Fear spiked in her veins. She couldn't spend all night out here, alone.

A shadow shifted alongside the building across from her. Straining, she was desperate to make out a shape.

"Drew? Tyrone? Is that you?" Her words echoed emptily back to her. Maybe it was nothing. Off to her left she caught movement again. "This isn't a joke guys!"

A scrape of noise to her right had her jumping to the left, pivoting her head to see all the angles. Her body ached to move but her mind froze her in place. Going out into the gathering darkness could land her smack into the arms or paws of whatever or whoever was out there.

Moving cautiously, she edged her way along the road keeping the building at her back. She reached the corner, and there was a decision to make. A low chuckle, less than ten feet behind her, propelled her forward.

Crossing the alleyway as quickly as possible she felt the air shift around her. Something had passed close by. Trying to still her heart, she fought to believe it was all in her mind. There was nothing in the dark. Right?

Something more substantial than the wind brushed the back of her neck. Goose bumps rose on her arms as she pushed down the instinct to run. She would not be the girl jumping at shadows. Forcing her feet to maintain some dignity, she worked to put distance between herself and whatever wasn't out there. A howl in a nearby ally was all it took to ditch the charade and sprint for her life.

The need to breathe forced her to give her lungs a break. Stopping in the shelter provided by two walls, she struggled once again to orient herself. The buildings all looked the same in the dark.

Would she even know if she had passed the same one twice? She needed to calm herself and think rationally.

A cloth flapping in a window frame had her skittering to the left. What she needed was to get off these streets and back to her people. The million-dollar question was, which way took her towards them, and which took her farther away?

The distinct sound of claws on stone pressed her into motion once again. Passing by alleys in the dark she swore there where whispers in the gloom. Hands reaching out towards her dissipated into shadow as she careened past. No more time for stopping as she was hounded from one alley to the next.

Her brain ran through the horror movie ways she was about to die as her legs kept her moving. Anything but standing still. She couldn't give the shadows time to coalesce into something solid. Desperate, she howled for help between gulping sobs. Tears burned their way down her face washing her eyeliner into black trails down her cheeks.

The darkness crept up on her as she ran, stealing the light from her eyes. She was soon fumbling along in complete blackness. Unable to see two steps in front of her, she had no choice but to slow her pace. It wouldn't help to stumble and break a leg.

Panting with fear and exertion, she happened upon a wall she could feel her way along. Her throat ached from the struggle of breathing and yelling for help. Her body was screaming at her to stop and rest. She didn't dare cede to that demand. Like an animal stalked by a predator she knew that any cession of movement meant her downfall.

Like a mirage in the desert, light appeared in the distance. Honing-in on the beacon of safety she worked her way forward. The closer she got the more the darkness receded allowing her to move faster and faster. Practically at a run, she burst out of the buildings and into the clearing where her friends waited.

Startled faces turned towards her expectantly. Relief pushed back at the embarrassment trying to work its way into her emotions. She was alive and safe. No one should judge her for what she had done to get that way.

"Where have you been?" Tyrone roared at her as he lurched up from his spot near the fire. "We searched everywhere for you! Why would you walk off without telling us where you were going?"

He looked fearsome. Any other time she might have dealt with his concern for her. Right now, she was pissed.

"Where was I? How about where were you two? I was lost and screaming for help! That is where I was. Lost! Thanks so much for coming back to the comfort of your fire without finding me." Megan's voice cracked as her volume increased.

"Let's take a minute to calm down." Trenton moved toward Megan with all the caution one would give a wild animal. "Come sit down by the fire and warm up." As his coat settled around her Megan felt the residual warmth from his body seep into her freezing limbs.

She let him lead her to the fire in a semi trance. Adrenaline was wearing off and her body was starting to shake. Her legs wobbled underneath her, casting doubt on whether they could carry her to the fire. Trenton wrapped his arm around her waist and lifted just slightly.

Her arm brushed against something heavy on his hip as he settled her. A worry for another time. The shift in her body weight put all the hard work on him. All she had to do was hold on a few steps more.

Once she was settled near the fire the silence that had held them all inert was broken by multiple voices inquiring about her misadventure. Her eyes drank in the shelter they provided with their love and concern. Each face another brick in the wall she was building around her unsteady emotions.

She would not break down in front of them. Her family had ingrained in her long ago how to hide her soft underbelly for the sake of appearances. Emotions were to always be private things. In a world of cutthroat business practices and political leanings there was no room for missteps. Gathering her armor around herself she prepared to brush off the onslaught of questions.

"Are you OK?" Lynea's soft voice pierced the other voices. She was sitting across the fire from where Trenton had settled Megan. Her voice shouldn't have carried that far. Maybe hers was the only question Megan wanted to answer.

"Yeah. I am now. Thanks for not heading back to the van without me." Megan's hands shook as she contemplated the horror she would have been trapped in without the light of the fire.

"Your welcome, but we couldn't have left if we wanted to." Lynea's lips twisted as she answered.

"What do you mean?" Megan grasped the chance to shift the focus to anything else.

"When we all gathered back here Tyrone and Drew told us you were missing immediately. We figured the best thing we could do was get help." Lynea was at her matter of fact best.

"Caneon and I volunteered to go back to the van and use the CB radio in it to call for help." Aleece scuffed her feet in the dirt at her feet. "We should have been able to make it there in a half hour." She shook her head in confusion as her voice drifted into silence.

"It was getting dark as you walked back into camp." Lynea prompted.

"Yeah, we just walked and walked for over an hour and then we were back here. I swear we kept a good eye on the compass." Aleece shrugged. "Nobody was willing to have another go at it in the dark, so we started a fire. Trenton and the guys had just come back from searching for you again."

"We scoured the parts of the city where we had seen you last. I swear we inspected every nook and cranny." Tyrone burst into the conversation his eyes pleading for forgiveness. "I don't know how you didn't hear us yelling for you."

"It doesn't make sense. You should have heard me too. Not that it matters now. I saw the fire and found you. No harm no foul." Megan wanted nothing more at this point than to be left alone with her emotions. She wasn't one to share. "I vote we get some sleep and tackle it in the morning."

For a heartbeat no one moved. There wasn't one of them who wanted to acknowledge that something beyond their explanation was going on here. That didn't mean anyone was anxious to close their eyes and be vulnerable in this place.

"I suggest we keep a watch tonight. There are seven of us so, two-person teams with the night split into three shifts. I think Megan deserves to take the night off. Does that work for everybody?" Trenton looked around expectantly. After a chorus of mumbled "yeahs" and a brief team picking shuffle, they settled as comfortably as they could around the fire.

Megan bunched and bundled her day pack into the world's most uncomfortable pillow. Tucking Trenton's coat under her chin like a child warding off the boogie man she hoped he didn't come to take it back. It was no bed at The Ritz but the warmth of the fire and the sound of her friends breathing brought her comfort.

Her muscles ached from the tension still trapped in them. As they tried to relax, a shaking rose up from deep inside that she couldn't control. She became desperately afraid she was going to start sobbing right there in the middle of everyone.

The first and most painful lesson she had learned in her families' mansion was no matter the cost you don't cry. Crying was for losers and the Garvin's were assuredly not losers. They excelled at all they did. Politics, business, marriage. They shone as beacons of success to inspire all who knew them. Of the life lessons she had tossed aside over the years since they disowned her this one kept coming back to stick.

She reached across her body and pinched the underside of her forearm until the pain eclipsed the anxiety coursing through her. Breathing deeply to dispel the physical pain she finally felt her body go slack. Afraid that the others might have noticed her minor battle with herself she glanced around the fire.

All she saw were closed eyes and rhythmically rising chests. Aleece was straight across the fire with her back to Megan so she could keep watch. Trenton must have situated himself on this side of the fire but there was no way to confirm it without turning over. That would draw way too much attention. She had no choice but to hope his back was turned like Aleece's, but she was glad he was on first watch.

When she closed her eyes, the full expectation was she would spend the night replaying the terror in the dark. Braced for the inevitable onslaught she instead found herself cocooned in warmth and safety. Her last thought as she drifted off was *How odd.*

The warmth of morning touched her face long before her body was ready to rise. She had never been a morning person. No amount of behavior modification from her dad had ever changed that. Of course, she had never wanted it to. Here it was different. The others were already rustling around so she figured they weren't going to let her lay around.

She couldn't blame them. There was a lot to do today. They had to escape this crazy haunted city. With that thought flashing through her mind she found a spurt of motivation to get herself up and moving.

On her feet she saw that her group members had been busy. All that was left of their makeshift camp were the remnants of the fire and a neat row of packs ready to go. She found Trenton off to the edge of camp talking with Caneon.

They didn't notice her as she approached. One of the benefits of being so short was not invading the average person's line of sight. They were talking in hushed tones, so she couldn't make out enough to decipher their conversation. It was something they didn't want anyone else to hear though. The second they caught sight of her they clammed up like crooks in a cop shop.

"Here's your coat back." She handed the article of clothing to Trenton with a smile. It had been gentlemanly of him to go without last night, so she could stay warm. She snuck a quick look at Caneon hoping to find even the scarcest hint of jealousy. Nope. Turns out Aleece was her sign it was time to move on.

"It was my pleasure." A boyish smile spread across Trenton's face as he took the coat from her extended hand. She was caught for a second by the sight. "Did you need something else?" He tilted his head just a little to the left as he asked the question.

"NO. No, I'm good. Thanks. Really, it was cool of you to let me borrow it." Megan gave herself a mental shake before fleeing back to the group. Stupid, stupid. Just because Caneon had turned into a dead end didn't mean she needed to run full tilt down a different road. Nope. She was going to be happily uncoupled. Maybe forever.

By this point Lynea and the rest had donned their packs. They milled near the point where the group had breached the shield the day before, waiting for the others. Once Megan had her pack in place, she felt more settled. They were heading home.

Caneon had found his city. There was no proof here that anything they had been theorizing about was real. Maybe he would come back some other time with a bigger group. The shield alone should get him funding to launch a dig like his mother used to. That should keep him happy for a while. She would not be coming back.

In fact, she was pretty sure she was done with the research group once they got home.

This trip had proved one thing. She wasn't as adventurous as she liked to think she was. Traveling the world from the comfort of five-star hotels and paid cars was not the same as hiking into the jungle. Right now, she would give anything for a concierge and a hot bath.

"I've been thinking about it and I think I know what our problem is." Drew got everyone's attention. "We were so hyped to go through the shield yesterday that we left the sound wave generator on the outside. It must have run out of juice or something. So, the shield is no longer disrupted. We kinda figured we could walk on out whenever we wanted." This had several heads bobbing along.

"So, I think the shield is a lot more advanced than any of us could have planned on. I mean, what if the city is here but not exactly here. Like an umbrella keeps the rain off you. Simple. That's the kind of shield we thought we were dealing with. What if the umbrella could throw you out of sync with the rain? Put you in a bubble maybe. The rain would essentially just go through you." Confusion was passed from one glance to the other like a flu.

"You lost us." Caneon barked impatiently.

"OK...Like what if you tried to reach out of the bubble and touch the rain? You're not existing in the same space as the rain anymore, so your hand would just glide along the edge of the bubble." The kid looked way too satisfied with his explanation considering all the glazed looks he was getting.

"So, we are in a bubble?" Skepticism dripped from Caneon's voice.

"Kind of. Yeah." Drew was nodding his head manically. "So, we can't just walk out. The edges of the bubble will push us to the side. We need to disrupt the shield like we did to get in here."

"How exactly do we do that?" Tyrone wasn't hiding his disbelief any better than Caneon.

"The other device created an alternating sound wave to disrupt it. I spent my time on watch modifying my cell phone to do something similar." He held up his phone for everyone to see. "The problem is going to be the size of the disruption. Only one or two people will um make it through. So, I'll go first. When I'm on the other side I'll do whatever to the other device and start it up and you all can follow."

Megan figured this sounded like an even crazier plan than the one that had gotten them stuck here. She wasn't the one in charge though. If the others went along for the ride, then so would she. Apparently, no one was keen on staying where they were because "OK" and "Let's do it" floated on the air.

Drew headed to what he claimed was the exact spot where he broke the shield the day before. He must have marked it in some way only he could tell. Megan would never have been able to pick it out, but he appeared super confident. His fingers danced across the touch screen of his phone doing who knows what. Eventually he smiled, and the others pressed around him. His arm shot up in the air holding his phone and a low-pitched buzzing resonated from it.

Megan raised her hands to cover her ears as the noise infiltrated her mind. Her brain was vibrating so hard it was going to break her skull. The longer it continued the greater her desire to press her arms around her head. The sensation became untenable. Her feet moved her backward long before her brain sent the signal. But nothing happened to the shield.

There was no ripple of movement or thinning like there had been last time. They all moved further and further away. Eyes trained steadily on Drew's phone and the unchanging air around it.

Megan took the time to glance at Drew. He was sweating like he'd ran a marathon, and his skin was chalky. She estimated less than thirty seconds before he passed out. Still no change in the shield. This wasn't going to work.

It took all her will power to drop her arms and move back towards that sickening noise. She did it for her friend who was hurting himself trying to break them free. Her feet picked up speed as she focused solely on Drew. He needed to turn off that sound. Now.

She lost reasonable thought within a few steps of him. The uneven ground had her barreling into him full tilt. If she had been thinking clearly, she would have applied some brakes to the motion. Instead she tackled him Sunday night football style. They both went down in a tangle of limbs.

The phone went flying out of his hands and crashed against an invisible barrier. Little pieces shot back at them like shrapnel. Head ducked, Megan was all about the cessation of the gruesome noise and the relief flooding her skull.

She was shocked to feel blood trickle down her neck and along her arms. A quick inspection told her it came from little wounds covering most of her body. Cuts from the wreckage that was Drew's phone.

His lanky body had her pinned to the ground. He wasn't moving. Her heart lurched with fear. What if she had acted too late? Frantically her fingers sought a pulse point. An arm. His neck. Anywhere that would tell her his heart still beat.

His arm twitched next to her left shoulder. She pulled her right arm free enough to reach over and wrap her hand around his wrist. A steady rhythm was her reward for the effort. Relief dulled her senses and held her in its grip.

Someone tugging at her clothes brought her back to focus. Tyrone was standing over them like a dark angel with the suns brilliance back lighting him. As he reached for her she had the oddest sense of déjà vu. She must have smacked her head as they fell.

Hands pushed and pulled at her and Drew's bodies until she felt his weight lift. She turned her head to the side, so she could see him being laid carefully on the ground next to her. A stabbing pain shooting up her neck into her skull had her quickly turning back. This brought her sight line back to Tyrone who was now running his eyes over every inch of her. He better be checking for injuries.

The smile on his face came off more relieved friend than perv. And that was a good thing. Right. Nobody looked happy when blood was gushing, or bones were sticking out. Well, maybe crazy serial killer types but Tyrone wasn't one of those.

"Are you okay to stand?" He offered a hand which she ignored.

"Yeah. I think so." She struggled to pull herself up only to lose her wind midway.

He braced his hand under her elbow and had her upright with the slightest flex of his biceps. Vertical again, she found herself staring into the same circle of concerned faces as the night before. This was becoming a bad habit.

Lynea had Drew sitting up with his head between his knees. He was still the color of chalk but conscious was a vast improvement. Wobbling the two steps to him, Megan plopped her unsteady butt down next to him. She wasn't as ready to be vertical as she had assumed.

"Are you okay kiddo?" She leaned over until her head was practically resting on his arm. "Sorry about the rough landing."

"It didn't work." His voice shook with defeat. "We can't get home"

Afraid that the shaky voice was an indicator of tears, Megan pulled back from the poor kid. Dealing with that was way out of her skill set. Best to give him privacy to pull himself back together. He was right though. They were trapped. The thought almost had *her* in tears. Despite the appearance she put out to the world, she had never thought of herself as a pessimist. Until now.

| 6 |

Chapter

Caneon couldn't pry his eyes from the spot where the kids' cell phone had shattered. Stuck in the middle of the jungle in Mexico was not how his story was supposed to end. He had great things to accomplish still. What kind of universe would allow this to happen to him?

"We obviously aren't getting out of here today." Trenton's voice jarred Caneon out of his reverie. How unhelpful that guy was, to stand around and state the obvious. Was the man trying to cause panic?

"What do we do?" Tyrone was looking to Trenton like he expected the man to have an answer. This puzzled Caneon to no end. Why would Trenton know what to do? He was a geography teacher not Indiana Jones.

"We emptied our packs last night for dinner. That means we need to find food here in the city. Shelter as well. We should look for a larger building further into the city. That will keep out any weather or wild animals." Trenton finished his hero speech to resolute nods from the group.

"What kind of food, exactly, do you expect us to find in a centuries old, abandoned city? Half of these buildings are on the verge of collapse. We can't just pick one and hope for the best." Caneon was determined to be the voice of reason here.

"I saw several different types of fruit yesterday while we were exploring. We should harvest those. As for meat, I was thinking we could practice some of the trapping skills I learned a lifetime ago in boy scouts. Since you're the historian maybe you should be the one to assess the buildings and find us a sturdy one." Trenton finished with an uplifted brow. Was that a challenge or a question? Caneon hated interpreting body language. Just say what you mean already.

"I'm a librarian not a carpenter. How am I supposed to know what's safe?" Caneon huffed.

"You seemed to know which ones were crumbling to the ground, so I just assumed. Take Aleece with you then. She worked as a carpenter's apprentice during summer breaks to pay for school." Turning away from Caneon he motioned Tyrone over for a private conversation. How dismissive and rude could the man be?

Steaming mad from the slight, Caneon snatched his pack off the ground where he had tossed it to help Drew and Megan. He would go and find them the best shelter there could possibly be in this crumbling city. That would teach Trenton not to dismiss him.

"Are you ready?" Aleece's voice startled him out of his snit. "Caneon?"

"Yes. Let's go." Let the group follow Trenton for now. They would see who the true leader was soon enough.

It took them two days to settle into their new home and none of it was devoted to exploring the temple. Caneon and Aleece found a four- room building that was small by modern standards but spacious compared to those surrounding it.

The largest of the rooms was the main hub. Much to Caneon's annoyance Drew had been quick to point out that he could lay on the floor with his feet touching one wall then stretch his arms above his head and almost touch the other wall. The world was full of critics.

It barely fit them all at one time, so they ate in shifts. This pleased Caneon since it meant he didn't have to deal with making polite conversation over the top of everyone talking. The weathered wooden table that originally occupied the space only fit four at a time, anyways. How barbaric to be forced to stand while eating.

They split the other three rooms between them for sleeping. Caneon was furious to find himself cohabitating with Trenton. Did the man have to intrude on everything in his life? The upside was no one felt safe enough to close their eyes unprotected, so they had continued with Trenton's idea to keep watch. Caneon was still blessed with bouts of alone time.

For the sake of better sleep, they had modified the schedule so that two people split the night between themselves and the others slept. It wasn't perfect but so far no one had died. Caneon hadn't been forced to take a night watch yet. Tonight, would be the first.

Tyrone and Trenton had found some old traps that, once refurbished, were sturdy enough to function. So far, they had outsmarted a rabbit and an iguana. Caneon felt they were exorbitantly happy with themselves. Not a single soul among them was enthused to eat lizard. Everyone exerted tremendous effort not to think about the cooked meat as they consumed it.

Excursions around the edge of their side of the city had produced numerous types of fruits. Caneon had looked forward to having this chance to shine. Surely his advanced intelligence would make him more successful than his peers at foraging. In the end, bananas and mangoes topped the most gathered list because everyone recognized them.

Drew ruined it when he came back from his foraging excursion with the most exotic variety. He had researched edible plants and animals before he came exploring. So, he was now the expert gatherer, and everyone was looking to him for advice.

Caneon was growing increasingly frustrated. This was his project. All the years he had sacrificed to get them here were quickly forgotten. He was relegated to errand boy while everyone else scored homeruns for the team.

He eavesdropped on the others enough to know they were giving up faith of getting back to civilization. Drew tried to keep hope alive by talking incessantly about the shield being inconsistent. That there might be a problem with its power supply. He believed the shield would at some point lose energy on its own. This is how he explained Trenton's original group getting in and out of the city like they did.

He had set up some kind of system that he checked every day. It would let him know if the shield got weak enough to walk through it. The others wanted to buy in. You could see the desperation and longing on their faces as he talked. But the longer it dragged on the more they avoided him when he began with his theories. His optimism was too bright.

Caneon fully acknowledge the irony of himself being Drew's staunchest and possibly last supporter. Before this ill-fated trip, he didn't think the kid had a lot of practical skills outside the computer. But the young man had proven to be so much more than a talented hacker. If someone was going to figure out how to escape this trap, it was Drew.

That was exactly why Caneon needed to recruit him for a side trip. The shield could go down at any time. When it did they would all rush at the chance to escape. Without the information they had come for. Forty-eight hours had been wasted already focused solely on food and shelter. They needed to be exploring before they lost their chance.

Drew thought he had this shield figured out and they could come back when they wanted. Aleece and her brother had thought the same thing. Whatever had created this shield was beyond their level of intelligence. If they left without finding it, they may never get the chance to try again.

The deserted city hid the answers he had spent his life hunting. A part of his soul would die if he had to return without obtaining them. None of the others shared his viewpoint. Every one of his suggestions to send teams out had been shut down without consideration. He needed to take the matter into his own hands.

Drew was only ever alone when he went to appraise his warning system. Caneon waited until then to approach him. As the younger man set out into the jungle, Caneon angled away from the building down another road. He caught glimpses of the kid as they passed intersections, but he made sure to stay on his parallel route until they left the buildings behind.

Once they were into the greenery Caneon cut across the distance between them until he was able to step out of the trees and into Drew's path.

"Oh my g..." Drew startled and tripped on a root behind him when Caneon appeared out of nowhere. Arms wind milling he stutter stepped several times before he was able to get his feet solidly planted once more. Caneon reached his hand out with the intent of helping the boy gain his balance. Drew steadied himself and slapped Caneon's arm away. "I got it. What in the heck are you doing out here? And why are you sneaking up on me?"

"I apologize. Scaring you wasn't my intention. I merely wanted to have a private conversation." The contrition he felt was mitigated by the boys overly dramatic reaction. It's not like he had been holding a weapon.

"What do you want?" Drew's petulant scowl urged Caneon to cut to the chase.

"I want to explore the temple." Caneon's words did nothing to ease the kids scowl. "I know Trenton and the others have rejected the proposal. I'm also quite sure the answers we came looking for are concealed there. Why endure all of this only to go home empty handed?"

"What are you suggesting?" Drew let the scowl slip for a second and Caneon took that as an invitation to push harder.

"You and I fill a knapsack with provisions and proceed directly to the temple. No side trips or investigations. We search the area thoroughly. If we find nothing by nightfall, then we return to the group." Caneon infused his voice with as much confidence as he could muster.

"One, day trip? That's it? You'll settle in to help make our time here as bearable as possible if I do one day trip?" Drew's eyebrows nearly met his hairline he was so skeptical.

"I'm not promising I'll never bring it up again if that's what you're asking. After all we could be here for months or even years. But I will promise to set it aside for a bit of time. Yes." Caneon didn't dare hope it had been this easy.

"OK. Then I'll go with you dude. This once. If we get stuck here long enough, Trenton is gonna want to go up there anyways, so yeah. But just you and me this time. Sure. It's a little late to be going today. You have second watch, right?"

"Yes, that's correct."

"OK. We'll go when your watch is over. Just have your pack ready and with you. We can sneak out at first light." Drew stared at him until he nodded his head in acquiesce. "Great. See ya."

The kid started off into the jungle once more, leaving Caneon to make his own way back. It was a short walk spent planning the next day's adventure. He passed Lynea and Megan as he reached the buildings once more. From the look of things, they were headed out foraging. They waved at him nonchalantly but didn't slow to talk.

He was grateful not to be interrupted. Important events where afoot. Closer to their makeshift home he caught a glimpse of Aleece walking towards him with a bucket they had cobbled together. She must have been to the spring to get water.

Hurrying towards her, he hoped to engage in conversation. She intrigued him from first sight. Her beauty was of course part of the attraction, but more than her glossy hair and sky-blue eyes kept him captivated.

The lilt of her voice soothed a part of him that he had only recently realized was constantly ruffled. Her smile lit up his mind like fireworks. Nothing about her grated on him like other people did. It made her his most treasured person.

"Can I help you with that?" Smiling in a way he hoped was casual he indicated the bucket full of water in her arms.

"Thank you Caneon, but I've got it." She smiled, and his brain sparked. He didn't want her to stop so he fell into step beside her.

"How are you today?" With anyone else he would have asked the question as a social conformity, but he truly cared about her welfare.

"I'm doing good. I took the time to wash up a little while I was at the spring. It was amazing!" She twisted her head to lock gazes with him for a moment. "Where are you coming back from?"

"Oh. I uh was talking with Drew really quick." He stumbled as his brain tried to create a plausible conversation topic other than the truth.

"Yeah? About what? I didn't think the two of you got along." Her nose crinkled in confusion. He had been afraid she was going to ask that. He hated the idea of lying to her. What would she think of him if she found out later? Did he dare tell her the truth?

"Can you keep a secret?" His pulse quickened with fear that she would say no.

"Is it going to put anyone in danger if I don't tell?" She would have to ask that. He couldn't find a way to say no without lying.

"Maybe. But only me and Drew. Nobody else will be involved in our excursion." They approached the building quickly. He hoped reaching it would put an end to this increasingly uncomfortable conversation.

"Caneon." She reached out and grabbed his arm effectively bringing them both to a halt. "What are you plotting?" She stared into his eyes so intently he felt like she could read the truth there without him saying a word. Sighing, he resigned himself to trusting her.

"Drew and I are departing for the temple at dawn." His gaze searched her face for signs of acceptance.

"By yourselves?" She yipped.

"Yes. It's best that way. The two of us can move rapidly there and back. I must grasp this chance before it slips away. The proof I require is inside that structure. I can feel it." He stated emphatically.

"Then I'm coming with you." She stated.

Caneon's watch that night dragged on into oblivion. His mind wouldn't focus on anything other than the sluggish movements of his watch hands. There was no danger of his falling asleep with the adrenaline pushing his body to move, but he was confident that an elephant could have snuck up on him he was so distracted.

By the time light started to filter through the window coverings, he had repacked his knapsack three times. Each one had involved a full inventory with adjustments as his mind assessed possible scenarios they might face. One more time through and his bag would burst.

There was no more blessed sight than Drew's lanky frame emerging from the room he shared with Tyrone. Gesturing for silence, he moved past Caneon and into the predawn light outside.

The temptation to exit without Aleece was strong. He had no desire to put her in harms' way.

Megan's account of a dark presence watching her while she was lost in the city was chilling. It was also most likely nothing more than a figment of her fear fueled imagination. The human brain understands on a subliminal level that what could be hiding out there is dangerous.

When it came to Aleece though, he was reticent to trust in that explanation. What if there truly was an ominous being stalking them? They had witnessed no additional incidents but that only proved the creature, if there was one, was intelligent enough not to approach them as a unit. Safety in numbers was a real thing. If you applied that truth, the three of them might not be sufficient numbers to keep it away.

Aleece emerged from her room before he could act on his deliberations. He gestured her out into the morning air. He deposited a note onto the workbench they used to prepare food before following her through the door. The last thing he craved was panic and disorder when the others discovered they were missing and assumed the worst.

Joining his companions, he took the lead. It was best if they were far away from here before the others awoke. It would take only one early riser to put the whole plan in jeopardy.

After he felt comfortable with the distance between them and anyone who might stop them, he slowed his pace to a more sustainable level. As deep as his desire to see the temple was, he didn't want to arrive too exhausted to explore.

"So, do we know what we are looking for once we get there?" Aleece had fit so comfortably into his world he was stunned at the reminder she hadn't been around long enough to know their end goal.

"Anything that proves vampires were real." Drew used his duh tone of voice. Caneon found it beyond irritating.

"What exactly does that look like?" Aleece's eyebrows where furrowed. "There's not going to be a book labeled 'vampires are real, but that's not what you call us.'"

Drew shrugged and moved ahead. Apparently, the kid found it a waste of time to discuss the issue. Truth be told none of them could be sure of what evidence they would find. It just seemed obvious that proof of something like vampires would stand out. A -you'll know it when you see it- kind of situation.

Aleece was still watching him expectantly. Since he had no easy answer for her, he took his cue from the younger man. Shrugging helplessly, he picked up the pace. Apparently, even her beautiful voice could cause anxiety.

Minutes passed quickly as morning bloomed around them. By the time they reached the bottom of the temple there was no hint of the sunrise left in the sky. Towering above them the structure loomed ominous and overwhelming.

They had mere hours to search an area that would have taken archeologists years to explore. Truth was they barely had enough time to map the perimeter of the building let alone plumb its depths. Caneon stood in awe of the stone structure rising above him. His mind couldn't wrap around the momentous task he had set for them. How do you eat an elephant? One bite at a time.

"Let's start at the top." Caneon moved towards the steps that scaled the side of the building in front of them.

"Why?" Drew had pulled his backpack around so that he could access the inner pouch.

"It appears to be the prominent part of the temple. Therefore, it should house the most important aspects." Caneon stated.

"Right. But we um both know if you want to hide something you do it in the basement." Drew's face was a mask of teenage rebellion. How long did it take one to grow out of that?

"Assuming we knew where the entrance to the basement was located, I might agree with you. We don't. Consequently, we will start at the top." Caneon resumed his movement toward the stairs but the kid didn't budge.

"I have another idea." Reaching into his pack he pulled out an electronic device. "Maybe I can use this to track the source of the shield. I bet we find that, and we find your proof."

"Didn't you break that?" Caneon was confused. Did young people nowadays carry around spare devices for emergencies?

"That was my phone. This is a tablet. Big difference man." Drew had that condescending look he got when he talked about technology around Caneon. He was sure it was designed specifically to make him feel stupid.

"What is that going to do for us?" Aleece broke into the tension.

"I've calibrated it to read the frequency the shield is vibrating on. It's how I've been monitoring the shield strength. It will be crude, but the readings should get stronger as we get closer to the source."

"So, a giant game of hot/cold?" Aleece was giggling for some reason Caneon couldn't fathom. He'd never heard of this game.

Caneon walked away from the two of them as Drew grinned back. There was nothing he despised more than inside jokes. If everyone didn't understand the reference it was simply rude to mention it. Why did so many people not understand this concept?

The closer he paced to the temple the farther into the background his companion's conversation faded. A serenity entered his mind flowing from there into all corners of his body. Sensations of floating and warmth pulled him closer to the temple steps. He thought he should call out to Aleece or maybe even Drew, but the calm pushed him along faster than he could act.

| 7 |

Chapter

Tyrone swatted at the hands shaking him awake. Sleep clung like cobwebs as he fought to return to the real world. His dreams had been dark and dangerous. An exquisite woman calling to him from deep in the city. His body longed to return to her embrace.

The voice demanding answers fought to pull him out of her clutches. As he drew closer to consciousness, a terrible sense of foreboding filled him. Determination to break her bonds filled his mind, giving him the strength to rouse.

"Where did your friends go with my sister?" Trenton roared in his face. He had the sense this wasn't the first time the other man had asked the question.

"What? Bro, I got no clue what you're talking about." Tyrone moved to sit as he pulled away from Trenton's grasp.

"Your friends. They left camp this morning and took my sister with them. Don't pretend you didn't know about it. You and the kid practically live in each other's pockets." Trenton's voice rose to earth moving volumes.

"Chill for a second. I haven't heard a thing about them leaving. You are yelling at the wrong man." Glancing over at Drew's sleeping mat, Tyrone took in the lack of personal effects. Drew had packed everything before leaving. Where could they have gone that the guy would have found that necessary?

"You really don't know?" Trenton deflated. The confusion on Tyrone's face must have conveyed he was equally in the dark.

"No man. I'm sorry. Who all is gone? My friends wouldn't have gone somewhere without letting us know." Tyrone's mind was playing catch up after the abrupt awakening.

"I don't know. Caneon woke me up to tell me it was dawn. I got up and went about my routine. It was strange that he didn't come in to sleep, but he's a different kind of guy, so I blew it off." Trenton gave himself a mental shake. Rubbing his face, he stood and began pacing.

Throwing his feet to the side of his mat, Tyrone made short work of putting his sneakers on. His body surged up, propelling him across the narrow space to the door. After a year of working with the man, he knew Caneon would never leave without a note of some kind.

In the main living area Lynea and Megan huddled near the table. They were engrossed in whatever Lynea was holding and failed to notice the men entering the room. Tyrone suspected Trenton's yelling had woken them. It looked like they had found the note.

"Where did they go?" He crossed the distance to look over Lynea's shoulder.

"To the temple." She flashed her eyes up at him before returning to the note. "Caneon thought we were wasting the trip, so he talked the other two into helping him."

He reached around to grab the note from her. Reading through the words for himself he ignored the fight glinting in her eyes.

Their friends had headed into danger by themselves. There was no time for worrying about manners.

"We can't let them go in there alone." Megan snatched the note back from him with a defiant glower. "Pack your stuff. Quickly."

"Yes ma'am." Mama had taught him to be respectful. Plus, he agreed with her. Caneon and the others were headed into the mouth of a lion with water guns to protect themselves. He reversed direction to return to his room. Trenton's back disappeared through the doorway next to his own. Guess he wasn't the only one on board.

Returning to the main room he found the women had geared up as well. This was the weakest looking rescue party he had ever seen. It was all they had, so it was going to have to be enough.

Trenton joined them and they were out the door without a word. There was still the hope that they would catch up with the others before they entered the temple. His lungs burned as his legs pumped to keep up with the pace Trenton set.

The man was clearly worried about his sister's welfare, so Tyrone understood the push to move faster. He wanted to find them as well, but they weren't going to be able to sustain this reckless pace. The women had already dropped behind the men's longer strides. He had a moment of indecision before he let his own legs slow to their pace.

Hopefully, the man who was now a good twenty feet ahead of them would notice the growing distance and wait for them. If not, they were all headed to the same place. They would catch up eventually. Trenton never glanced back, let alone slowed. So be it.

The dash to the temple went faster than Tyrone would have thought. He hadn't believed they were camped all that close to the imposing structure. Standing at the base was Trenton. He was shielding his eyes from the sun as he scoured the side of the building visible to them.

"Do you see them?" Tyrone was fighting to see clearly through the glare.

"No. Nothing." Trenton's shoulders slumped.

"This is a big building. Let's split up and search. We yell if we find anything." Lynea took charge in her usual way. He had enjoyed spending time with the relaxed version of this woman but right now they needed this talent of hers.

"OK. I'll go up. Tyrone go left. Ladies take the right. We make a circle and meet on the other side." Trenton ascended the stairs without waiting to see if the others would consent. Shrugging at the women, Tyrone started off in his assigned direction. Why argue with a logical plan?

Dirt and bits of rock sprinkled his head as he rounded the corner. Up above he could see Trenton shimmying along a crumbled ledge. Hopefully, the man was part mountain goat. Tyrone would hate to have to catch him.

A scuffling sound to his left pulled his eyes away from Trenton's daring feats. There was nothing to see but shadowed alley ways amid abandoned buildings. Tyrone went back to scouring the walls of the temple looking for any sign that someone had opened a hidden door.

Minutes later the scuffling sound returned on his left. They had seen few wild animals since finding themselves trapped. That didn't mean there wasn't a big cat stalking out there. It would go a long way towards explaining Megan's story of being stalked.

Thinking of her focused his concern on her and Lynea. Perhaps it hadn't been such a great idea to split up. They didn't know what was trapped in this city with them. Caneon and Drew believed it was a sentient being. They hadn't stated it flat out, but he had caught their drift.

Maybe he should turn around and catch up with his friends. They could circle the base of the temple together and then catch up with Trenton. Looking up he could no longer see the other man above him. The scuffling grew louder as his feet ground to a halt.

His about face was laced with a healthy amount of respect. He was a big man in prime fighting shape. Against a human opponent he gave himself more than good odds. Panthers and Jaguars could be as big as he was. Easy. Plus, they sported teeth and claws the likes of which he couldn't compete with. He had been in the ring enough to know when not to pick a fight.

The sound grew louder as it moved closer to his position. His feet sped up. If it managed to get in front of him he would be forced to turn and race for the far side of the temple. His mind was racing through the possible escape routes he might find that way.

Suddenly, he heard the scuffling from directly behind him. Twisting his torso to gain a better vantage he caught sight of a sleek black cat. There was no lag time between the glimpse and his feet hitting full speed. Ahead of him another cat stalked out of an alley way. Since when did they hunt in pairs? He was left with no choice but to veer onto a side street.

With the way open before him he burst into a full run. He had never been so glad that he had kept up with his conditioning even after football was no longer a part of his life. The constant wind sprints meant he had a minuscule chance of finding somewhere to hide before they caught him.

The soft shuffle of paws scraping on cobblestone kept his adrenaline levels at all-time highs. As an alley appeared to his left he darted down it. There was always the danger of getting caught in a dead end, but he hoped to twist and turn enough for the predators behind him to lose track of their prey.

He dove to the right or left at random intervals with nothing more than blind faith. It was sometime before he took in the lack of noise behind him. Slowing only enough to ensure he didn't trip and kill himself, he glanced over his shoulder. Nothing.

There was a building to his left with a wooden door hanging haphazardly from rotting leather hinges. He fought to pull the door open far enough to fit his burly chest through. Several painful scrapes later he was on the right side. His arms bulged as he manhandled the door back into place. A table near the door toppled on its side became an impromptu door stop with his exhausted body acting as extra weight behind it.

His labored breathing made hearing anything on the other side of the door next to impossible. He could only pray the cats weren't passing close enough to pick up the noise. His head rested on the weathered wood while he strained to catch the slightest indication his pursuers were still tracking him.

Minutes ticked by in strained anticipation. His mind produced images of his mangled body being ripped into equal pieces for them to share. What a lovely dinner he would make.

As soon as he was sure the panthers weren't going to tear around the corner and pounce on the door he fought to regain his footing. The muscles in his legs shook with the effort to hold him. He was kind of glad no one was around to see him wobble over to a chair and plop down like an old man.

What was he supposed to do now? His frantic run through the ruins had left him turned around. He could orient on the temple but the idea of wandering the streets with the cats still prowling made his stomach churn. Calling for help would likewise run the risk of attracting the wrong attention.

Resigned to being stuck where he was for the time being, he settled in to wait. It wasn't long before the drop came. His adrenaline fed system had exhausted his resources. There was no choice in the matter as his eyelids slammed closed.

A chill wind brought him straight back to his feet. Standing in the room with him was the woman from his dreams. She was stunning in her beauty. Improbably tall and willowy with hair the color of live fire and enormous eyes of diamond, she took his breath away.

"Who are you?" The words seeped from his lips.

"They called me Sorche. You may do the same." She glided towards him while her dark dress flowed around her legs. As she leaned down, her slender fingers brushed his chin lightly, bringing all his senses to high alert.

"How did you get in here?" He could see that his blockade was intact. It was unfeasible to imagine this magnificent creature crawling through the lone window.

"You called me, and I came. It's simple really." She smirked at his ignorance. He didn't want her to find him ignorant.

"Of course. How kind of you to come to my aid." The words fell from his lips as he pressed them to the hand she offered.

"What a sweet boy you are. We are going to have such a grand time." Laughing she drew his hand up to her face and placed the palm against her sumptuous lips. Pain arced up his arm as she nipped his skin. Warm blood trickled into his palm only to be lapped up by her tongue.

"How can I serve you?" He drowned in her cold stare as the words tumbled out of his mouth. Down he fell until all he could sense was her hand on his skin. From across an endless chasm he felt his body move. She was taking him somewhere and he had no power to control it. Standing on the ledge of the chasm he screamed into its dark depths.

| 8 |

Chapter

Megan stood on the far side of the temple with Lynea, waiting impatiently for Tyrone to appear. The man had the longest legs ever. He should have made it around twice as fast as they had. She knew he had slowed his pace on the trip here. Her inner voices warred over whether that was condescending or thoughtful.

Her foot began to tap emphatically. Patience had never been her strong suit. Before she became the black sheep, her parents praised that trait. A go-getter they called her. Don't let anyone force you to wait on their timetable they said.

She pulled her mind away from the memories. The focus needed to be on getting everyone safely back to camp. There was something dark out here waiting for them to slip up. When they got Caneon and his flunkies back to safety she was going to take a layer of skin off their backs.

"Where is he?" Lynea's voice was strained. So, Megan wasn't the only one worried about his delay.

"I don't know. Tyrone should definitely have beat us." Megan scanned the corner of the building once more.

"Maybe he found something?"

"Yeah it's possible. Maybe he yelled, and we didn't hear him. Should we walk his way a bit? Just to see if he's around the corner or something?" Movement was what Megan craved.

"What if Trenton comes and we aren't here? We could all end up lost." Leave it to Lynea to be obnoxiously practical.

"What if Tyrone is right around the corner hurt? You know Trenton is armed right?" Megan could play the what if game, too.

"Having a gun doesn't solve everything. To the corner, no farther. I'll stay here so I can see you and Trenton. If you don't see Tyrone, come back. Deal?"

"Sure." Megan didn't plan on doing that, but Lynea didn't need that information right now.

The walk to the corner put Megan's nerves on end. The closer she came to going around it, the surer she became of finding his mangled body on the ground. She braced for the trauma of seeing a friend like that. Her entire being exhaled when the ground was empty as far down as she could see.

Her eyes traveled the length of the building then back to Lynea. There was no doubt the woman would be first class furious if she took one step around the corner. Was it worth having to soothe those rumpled feathers to look for clues?

Megan's heart traveled back over the many ways Tyrone had looked out for her. Small things like coffee she didn't have to ask for or new gloves when hers had holes. There wasn't a time over the last year that Tyrone had known of a need and not tried to fill it for her. Of course, it was worth pissing Lynea off.

Seconds after she left Lynea's sight line she heard the woman yell. The rebel soul she nurtured took a small amount of pleasure in tweaking her elder. It's not like she couldn't run back to Lynea if needed.

Moving quickly to keep Lynea's pique at a minimum she made it more than halfway down the wall with no sign of Tyrone. There was only one corner between her and where they started. She couldn't fathom any reason for him to have gone that way. He knew they would be waiting for him on this side.

A strange shuffling noise among the buildings had her hightailing it back to her mother hen. They could explore further once Trenton joined them. No one should be out here alone. It was idiotic and emotional of her to have forgotten that.

Lynea's worried face was a welcome sight.

"Don't you do that again! You said you would stay in sight!" Lynea was shouting as she closed the last few feet.

"Yeah. I get it. I thought I might find something." Megan sulked. Why did she feel guilty? The woman needed to lighten up.

"Did you?"

"No."

Shaking her head, Lynea turned and headed back to their rendezvous point. Megan was left to trail behind her like a scolded puppy. Trenton made his way down the staircase just as they reached the bottom.

"Did you find anything up there?" Lynea queried.

"No. Not a sign of them anywhere." Trenton scanned the area. "Where's Tyrone? Did he find something?"

"That's a good question." Lynea said as she glanced at Megan like the younger woman might be hiding the answer.

"I have no idea either. Maybe he found a door?" She was throwing out any idea to take the heat off herself.

"Did you see something to make you think a part of the wall was really a door?" The hope in Trenton's voice made her feel stupid.

"No." She darted her eyes to the ground, so she didn't have to see his defeat.

"What do we do now?" Trenton was looking to Lynea.

"We go back to camp. This wandering off isn't helping anyone. We return to a safe place and wait for them to come back to us. Along the way we search for Tyrone. He can't have gone too far." Lynea nodded her head once as if she were agreeing with herself.

Megan hesitated to contradict her. The older woman was already pissed. Tyrone's generosity to all of them pushed to the front of her mind though. If they had light, finding him needed to be their priority.

"I'm ok with leaving the temple. Caneon and them probably couldn't get in either. For all we know they are sitting back at camp trying to figure out where we went. Tyrone on the other hand is a problem. We need to find him." Megan looked between the other two hoping for support.

"You're probably right. Let's find Tyrone." Trenton stated.

"We search the immediate area only. Then we go back to camp. No one leaves our eye line." Lynea conceded with a pointed look Megan's way.

Megan took the lead since it had been her idea. Just like a few minutes ago there were no signs of Tyrone along the building for most of the wall. It was only as they came within the last twenty feet of the corner that they could see scuff marks in the dust.

The cobblestones were too clean further out to decipher which direction he had gone but it was clear he hadn't walked along the wall any farther than that. They made semi circles away from the wall trying to find any other evidence of his passing.

In the end it came down to none of them being skilled at tracking. They had no clue what they were looking for, so they found nothing. Big surprise. He might as well have vanished into thin air.

Defeated, the trio headed back to camp. Their only hope was finding him sitting in the main room laughing about his adventures with the others.

The distance back dragged on longer than the way up had. Megan's mind drifted over the moments before they had split up. It hadn't occurred to her they should stick together. Tyrone was a trained fighter. He could take care of himself.

But he hadn't. He'd ran into something that was bigger than him. She had known there was something out there. From day one she had known it wasn't safe. She should have stopped him from going off on his own. If he wasn't at camp that was on her.

The sun was losing its strength as they entered the obviously empty building. Bags were placed dejectedly on the floor. No one stated the palpable absence of their friends.

| 9 |

Chapter

The knot's in Drew's stomach cinched tighter as he trailed behind Caneon. Their trio had traipsed up the steps of the temple and through a mysterious hidden door on the second tier like a zombie parade. A countless blur of stone corridors had been trod through the day until his feet ached.

They hadn't followed willingly the whole time. This place had a creep factor of 12. Nothing they tried had slowed down the train they were on.

Aleece had pried and pulled at their mindless leader but he didn't register her presence. Drew planted himself like a pillar in the man's path. Caneon walked around him like sidestepping a wooden post. They worked together to turn him around and five seconds later he righted his path.

The choice to abandon Caneon or follow where he led was an easy one to make. No matter how self-righteous the dude could be. He was still one of them. And you don't leave your friends behind. So, they followed.

The ominous atmosphere of the stone temple made conversation stilted. Aleece gave it a go occasionally but stuttered to a halt every time. He didn't mind the silence. It gave him time to observe. At some point they would return to civilization. How many people could say they had roamed the insides of an Aztec temple no one else had ever been in?

As far as he could tell the floor slanted downward, meaning they were headed into the depths of what felt like a tomb. He had expected fancy stonework and carvings. All they had seen so far was cobwebs. This place was a boring box. So, uniform in fact, there were no landmarks to build a return trail on. He was hoping all trails upward would lead out.

There was a stale feel to the air around them, so he figured no one had disturbed the dust on the floors in a very long time. The taste in his mouth from inhaling the stuff recalled mold and dirt. No surprise but gross.

He wasn't a claustrophobic person as a rule, but this place created the sensation of being buried alive. His dreams of treasure hunting were being dashed on the ground under Caneon's steadily shuffling feet. There wasn't anything to find here but creepy crawlies and possible cave ins.

"Aleece." He half muttered half whispered her name. No reason to disturb whatever might be resting in this place.

"What?" Her chipper voice had him cringing.

"Should we go back?" He moved closer to keep from raising his voice.

"You know we can't turn him around." She flipped her hand at Caneon's back.

"I know. It's just…" Drew didn't want to admit he was becoming tempted to leave the other man behind. Whatever had him in this trance wasn't leading them anywhere good.

"I won't go back without him." Aleece nailed his thoughts in one try. They must have registered on his face. Trina told him he wore his emotions on his face for the world to see.

"Yeah, I get that. Neither would I. It's just…this feels like a trap. You know?" He ran his hands through his hair in exasperation. She was not stupid. She had to have figured that out on her own.

"Yeah. I know. But what choice do we have?" She glanced back over her shoulder to grimace at him.

There didn't seem to be much to say after that. The silence stretched taut between them. He could leave and save his own skin but was that the right move? It didn't seem like the answer should be 'yes'. It didn't seem like the answer should be 'no' either. Which choice could he live with?

Caneon turned to the left as he reached an intersecting hallway. As Aleece followed, the devil on his shoulder whispered this is the time to tuck tail and run. By the time she realized he wasn't behind her he could be halfway back to the door.

Maybe he could leave Caneon to his fate. Maybe. The guy was a royal pain in the ass. Aleece was too sweet to suffer whatever was waiting for them. He probably couldn't save her, or himself, but he couldn't desert her. There. Choice made. Now to focus on survival.

Aleece glanced back as Caneon stopped in front of a door. It was the first one they had seen since they entered the temple. Standing eight feet tall and made of stone, Drew couldn't see a way to open it. There were no hinges in sight for it to swing on nor a handle to pull.

Caneon was shaking his head and looking around like a sleep-walker released from a bad dream. So, they had arrived. Now was the time to run for the hills. Whatever was beyond that sealed door wouldn't be anything they could turn back from.

Faced with the option to walk away, Drew found himself inextricably drawn forward. As he moved close to it, he could see in the dim light what looked like a keypad to the right. It was roughened stone like the rest, but the nine-key configuration was unmistakable.

What was a modern thing like a keypad doing in an ancient Aztec temple no one had been in for centuries? The puzzle of it had him shuffling nearer. On each of the keys was a hieroglyphic type figure. Did that mean there was a password to open it?

Within seconds of the thought entering his head, he could think of nothing other than figuring it out. He ruffled around in his backpack until he found a note pad and pencil. Placing a sheet of paper against a key, he used the pencil to rub across the rough surface. Moving on to the next key, he worked his way through them until he had all nine transferred onto his paper in order.

Stepping back from the keypad, he used his flashlight to study each symbol through the dust floating in its beam. The squiggles and dots made no sense to him. He growled in frustration. Aleece's finger traced one of the symbols as she leaned in for a closer look.

On his other side Caneon crept forward to catch his own glance. The older man quickly snatched the paper from his hands. That was rude even by his standards. Drew reared back to protest only to realize it would be pointless. Caneon was lost in what he was studying. He wouldn't comprehend anything Drew yelled at him.

"What do you think?" Turning to his less rude companion Drew hoped they could work the problem out together.

"No clue. I'm a legal secretary. Ancient languages, as beautiful as they are, make no sense to me." Aleece shrugged her petite shoulders and turned back to watching Caneon.

"Do you see a pattern?" It looked like he was stuck with Caneon to help him solve this puzzle.

"Huh? Oh, Yes I do." Caneon never lifted his head from the paper. Thanks for sharing dude.

"Care to explain to the rest of us?" Drew wasn't giving up. The silence went on so long he began to think the other man had forgotten they were alive.

"Caneon?" Aleece finally spoke up to get his attention.

"Yes?" He looked up at her. Progress.

"Can we get through the door?" She smiled sweetly, and Drew watched Caneon pull himself together to answer. The power of a woman at her best.

"Absolutely. It's a pass phrase. Each symbol is a word or sequence of words." Caneon beamed proudly at her smiling face.

"Great. Punch it in. Let's get this show on the road." Drew found himself bouncing in place. What was everyone waiting for?

"I don't know the phrase." Caneon said it like everyone should already have known that. What good was knowing it was a phrase if you didn't know the phrase? Drew resisted the urge to punch something.

"Can we figure it out?" Aleece was trying to play peacemaker again. She had a habit of doing that. Drew wasn't in the mood.

Pissed off at the delay and Caneon's showboating Drew walked over to the pad and started jabbing at the keys randomly. Anything to keep from reeking violence on the know-it-all behind him. His fingers moved from key to key with fluid grace in a random pattern that didn't feel all that random. The sound of a familiar feminine laughter echoed in his mind.

He didn't bother to hide his surprise when the door retracted into the ceiling above them. That should not have worked. Aleece gasped behind him as Caneon came to stand on his right. Inside, the room slowly lit up.

Surrounded by the gloom of the stone temple it took him ages to register what was illuminating in front of him. Screens were mounted side by side on the far side of the room shining bright blue.

Under them where control consoles the likes of which he'd only seen in sci-fi movies.

There was no human way to logic out the use of most of the knobs and buttons, let alone the images flickering under the translucent panels. Along the wall to their left marched a line of what most closely resembled computer servers.

Stepping into the room, he had to see what was off to their right. A thin crystalline barrier stretched the entire breadth of the wall floor to ceiling. Glowing cords and wires wound their way around the edges in a serpentine manner. In the middle of the enclosure was a stone bed like an altar. Laying atop the alter was the most stunning creature.

Drawn closer by his curiosity he assumed she was sleeping. Even prone he could tell she had to be well over six feet tall. Her slender body was clothed in robes of sky blue with an exquisite gold embroidery winding through it. Holding his own hand out he imagined her long fingers would almost double the length of his.

Her hair seemed to move as he watched it. Multiple shades of brown wavered in and out of his focus. As he neared the glass wall, he realized her hair wasn't moving at all. The colors of each strand were changing before his eyes creating the illusion of movement. This close he was able to get a look at her face. Her cheek bones stood out in stark relief to her slender chin. Her delicate nose seemed to disappear above her full mouth.

He watched the rise and fall of her chest to be sure she was alive. What was she? There was enough about her that was alien for him to be sure she wasn't strictly human. How did she get here?

"Drew. Maybe you should come back over here." Aleece was standing next to Caneon by the doorway when he looked back.

"Why? She's an alien. A legit alien" His voice was full of awe even to his own ears.

"Yeah I can see that. Which is why I think maybe we should just go." He could hear her fear resonating through the room.

"No way. This is big. She's it Caneon. The thing we've been searching for." Excitement was bubbling up in him. They had done it. For real.

"Maybe. Drew, she brought us to this destination through dubious means. Perhaps she desired to be found. It isn't prudent to search further without alerting the others." Caneon was always taking the fun out of everything. Prudent was the last thing he wanted to be with an alien laying in front of him. Besides, she was asleep.

"Go tell them. I'll hang here." Let the scaredy cats run for it. You couldn't pry him away with a bulldozer.

"I don't think that's a good idea. We should stick together." Aleece wasn't going to leave him. Whatever.

Ignoring them for the moment, Drew began to explore the consoles nearest the enclosure. There had to be a manual or something right? Even if it were in the alien language he saw scrolling on the screens he was confident he could decipher enough to get an idea of how this thing worked.

He was probably the first human to have seen this. How cool was that. Nothing on the right-side screamed instructions, so he turned to search on the left. As he passed by the woman her head turned and eyes of amethyst locked onto his own.

Stunned into silence by the brilliant purple color of the iris, he barely registered how large they were. Staring at her like this, they engulfed his view. A humming began inside his skull. He surged to the side in a fight to break the link he could feel her working to build between them.

His struggle caused his hand to land on the panel he had just walked away from, and a whirring filled the room. At first, he thought it was an escalation of the hum. Caneon yelling at Aleece to get out of the room made him think of the panel he'd hit. Glancing down, his hand was squarely in the middle of a screen scrolling through the same type of hieroglyphics on the keypad outside.

Jerking his palm away from the symbols did nothing to stop whatever he had set in motion. His eyes darted back to the alien in time to see the barrier dissolve into thin air. The woman inside pushed herself into an upright position facing him. She rose to her full height and his head tilted way back to look up at her.

The colors in her hair began to shift wildly producing shades of brown and copper he hadn't known existed. Her amethyst eyes captured his once again. This time she simply moved towards him. As she glided his way, he looked down to see if her feet were actually moving.

"What have you done?" Her voice vibrated through the room and into his skull.

"I...I don't..um. I'm not sure." He couldn't find the words to explain with the air in the room pushing on his chest.

"I was not meant to come out of stasis. Because of this the shield will fall." The accusation in her gaze convinced him this wasn't the good thing he thought it was.

"I didn't mean to." As an apology it sucked. He wasn't making a very good impression on the first alien he had ever met.

"Who are you?" Aleece hadn't left the room after all. He didn't know whether to cheer or groan.

"My name is Naelah. Who asks?" As she turned her gaze to Aleece, Drew found himself free to move. He retreated behind Caneon without hesitating.

"I'm Aleece. These are my friends. Caneon and Drew." She pointed at each of the men as she said their names with no reaction from the alien.

"Why have you woken me?" Naelah seemed to believe they had a purpose here. Her questions didn't make sense. She was the one who had drawn them to this room. What game was she playing?

"We didn't wake you on purpose. You scared me, and I fell on the controls." Drew tried to feel brave answering from behind Caneon's shoulder.

"This will not do." She seemed distressed. If he wasn't busy being scared, Drew might be tempted to feel sorry for her. He watched her walk over to the consoles and tap on various screens. When she turned back there was defeat on her face. "I've been in stasis too long. The bed will no longer support me. Without my consciousness to provide energy and direction there is no way to renew the shield. She will be free." Naelah swayed before straightening her spine.

"I'm unsure that we are understanding you correctly. Were you maintaining the shield from inside there?" Caneon gestured to the alter and now open enclosure.

"I was." She turned her brilliant eyes towards him. There was pleading all over her slim face. What did she think they could do for her?

"And it was acting as a prison of sorts for someone else?" Aleece was quick to piece together puzzles.

"Correct."

"Why?" Drew's curiosity momentarily overrode his fear.

"To keep everyone safe until my people can return." She looked down her nose at him. Proving it was all about attitude.

"Who are your people?" Caneon was practically salivating over the question.

"The Valdan." Apparently, that was all the answer she felt they needed. Personally, Drew would have liked a boatload more detail.

There wasn't time to ask more as she glided around them and out the door. It was all the three of them could do to keep up with her long-legged pace. Watching her hair undulate in the low light of the hall Drew realized certain sheens were glowing as they came and went. It was hypnotizing to watch.

The rush of fresh air on their faces came as a shock. He knew the trip into that alien room had taken them twice as long. Angling to see around Naelah he glimpsed cut outs in the walls ahead of them. That must be the source of the rain he smelled swirling around.

Glancing out one as they walked past, he had a clear view down onto the city streets they had trekked that morning. How had they gotten so high up into the temple? He was certain they hadn't entered any type of elevator since finding Naelah.

"Where are we going?" Drew strained his leg muscles to draw close to the tall woman.

She twisted slightly to look back at him in surprise. Perhaps she had forgotten about them tagging along behind her. He felt like they came in way below her standard of being worthy of conversation.

"I am going to the apex of the temple to track Sorche." She resumed her saunter.

"Who or what is Sorche?" Drew was fully aware the continued questioning put him on shaky ground. He couldn't help himself. There were things they needed to know.

She decided not to grace him with an answer. He was left to stalk along behind her in the hopes of finding the answer for himself. Glancing back, he could see that Caneon and Aleece were lagging. That or they were pulling back on purpose. He didn't have time to figure out which. The alien being took precedence.

They approached a door similar to the one in the basement. Naelah pushed a code into the pad next to it and it glided upward. From his viewpoint he couldn't be 100%, but it didn't look like the same one he had used on the other door. Why would she have multiple codes? He was niggling on the idea that someone other than her had led them into the depths of the temple. But why?

Inside the room, he found himself once again surrounded by technology beyond his understanding. Chestnut copper hair settled around her as she took a seat at one of the consoles. A soft whirring resonated from the machines along the far wall as she manipulated the controls that had leapt off the screens in a 3D interactive light show. He moved himself into an optimal position to watch everything she did.

Moving as stealthily as he could manage, he wrangled the tablet out of his pack. The camera on it was three generations old and glitchy as all get out, but it was something. A longing for his decimated phone rose up. Not to be distracted, he started recording everything he could.

When Naelah glanced at his device and showed no reaction he became bolder. He moved around the room, working to steadily record every aspect. The world was going to need evidence of this epic day. He was going to own the internet.

Caneon and Aleece had stationed themselves outside the room. They could see through the door, but neither ventured close enough to get a real look at what was going on. He tried to motion them in, but they shook off his signals.

Whatever. It was their loss. He found himself back at Naelah's side and recording over her shoulder. Her head was tipped to study the images in front of her. He couldn't make any meaning out of the symbols she was absorbed with.

"What is this?" The question was out before he could filter.

"Tracking coordinates."

"For this Sorche?" He wasn't going to lose the roll once she answered.

"Yes. It appears she is still within the city. Perhaps she in unaware the shield has fallen."

"It's already down?" The good news was, they were all going home.

"Unfortunately. It is only a matter of time until she realizes nothing stops her from satiating her appetites." Naelah's shoulders slumped in a wholly human way.

"What appetites?" The chill chasing down Drew's spine had everything to do with memories of a dark voice in his head as they approached the city.

There was no response from his alien companion. He was quickly coming to expect the lack of sharing. Without answers, there was little for him to do but record over her shoulder. Abruptly, she rose from the chair. He fumbled not to drop the tablet while shuffling out of her path.

She was on her way out the door before he had righted himself. Two steps later, he grabbed his pack and shoved the tablet into it as he moved after her. His life was quickly becoming a frustrating game of catch up.

Caneon and Aleece were exactly where he had last glimpsed them. Coming through the door he could see Naelah's receding back. Caneon reached to grab his arm as he rushed past, but the man was slow and easy to dodge. Drew was on the alien woman's heels a quick sprint later.

Guilt had him looking back to see his friends trailing along a fair distance behind. They weren't appreciating the importance of what had been found. Caneon should have been rejoicing to have her at his fingertips. This was his proof. Why was he holding back?

"Naelah." Drew needed to get her attention.

"Yes." She slowed only slightly to acknowledge him.

"Where are we going?" His friend's reticence was giving him doubts about his blind faith.

"To stop Sorche." That explained nothing to him. He recognized the door they were approaching as the one they had originally used to enter the temple. Perhaps the others would feel better once they were out in the city again.

They descended the steps and arrived at the foot of the temple before they paused. He relished the chance to catch his breath. She moved quicker than anyone he'd ever tried to keep up with. Scouring the jungle around them she seemed unsure of which way to go.

"Can I help? You seem lost." He wasn't sure what he could do, but the compulsion to help was there.

"I've lost her signal." Naelah retreated into her own thoughts with the cryptic statement. Signal?

"Why did we stop?" Aleece and Caneon had decided to be a part of the team it seemed. About time.

"I don't really know." Drew looked to the alien woman for help, but she was still tuned out.

"Perhaps we should return to our comrades." Caneon didn't need to state that they should ditch the alien in the process. The dude really needed to get a poker face.

"She said earlier that this Sorche she is looking for has appetites. What if they include drinking blood?" Drew was hoping to pull the older man back in with the vampire connection.

"Her appetite *is* for human blood. How do you know of such things?" Naelah had him pinned with her amethyst eyes.

"We have myths. From ancient civilizations. We call them vampires." Drew shuddered as he realized what they had set free.

"Vampires? I've never heard of such a thing." She searched inside his skull with her eyes.

"It's a common name several civilizations have used for a species of beings that survive on human blood. Modern civilization has long written them off as a mythical construct created to explain fears of death and dead bodies based on lack of scientific knowledge." Caneon stepped forward to engage her. At least his favorite pet project would keep Drew from being the only human in this conversation. Yay for history.

"I see. Are there other names for these creatures?"

"Several. As well as creatures that are similar to this with intrinsic differences in either physical capabilities or appearance." Caneon was showing the enthusiasm he reserved solely for his favorite study.

"Interesting. I would like to study these myths. Can you accommodate this?"

"Yes, of course but not here. The research is at my home." Caneon visibly quivered at the idea of teaching this creature. Naelah locked eyes with Caneon then nodded her agreement before turning toward their base camp.

Drew felt a cold breeze skitter across his skin. They had been sharing this city with a lethal creature that had nothing to do with the mythical movies he'd gorged on. She was real, she was alien, and she could have taken them down. Why hadn't she?

He followed Naelah as she glided towards the camp they had naively left undefended this morning. He hoped like hell they would find everyone sitting around the fire ready to rip them a new one for disappearing all day.

| 10 |

Chapter

Lynea spent the afternoon tidying camp while she surreptitiously kept an eye on the road into the city. Being unable to find their friends at the temple didn't mean there had been trouble. Losing Tyrone did.

Trenton had insisted leaving camp put more of them at risk. She couldn't refute the logic of it, but it was unbearable to leave Tyrone to fend for himself. Megan had come unglued at the idea and stocked off into the jungle alone.

Leave it to that contrary girl to decide to have deep feelings for the man now that he was in trouble. A year of fawning after her in silent hope had gotten him nowhere. When he returned to camp Lynea was going to pull him aside and let him in on this new development. It was guaranteed Megan would never tell him how she felt.

Megan's obvious fear of being alone pushed her back to camp before she went far. Her experience that first night had left a deeply set panic. Lynea spent her nights listening to the nightmares play out.

When she finally spotted Tyrone stalking towards them her heart leaped into action in her chest. The relief momentarily blinded her to the fiery beauty keeping pace behind him. Once she took notice, there was no pulling her eyes away.

The woman drifted along the road as if it was a sheet of glass. Her hair shimmering in waves of undulating reds and yellows. Like fire flickering about her head the movement was beyond anything Lynea had ever witnessed in colors made by man or god. The woman topped Tyrone's 6'4" frame although she lacked his musculature. Her slenderness created a sense of elongation Lynea's mind was rejecting.

Despite the fragility of her appearance Lynea sensed power emanating from her. Bile choked her throat as she braced to face the woman at close distance. Megan bolted from the building behind Lynea yelling Tyrone's name. Trenton emerged from the trees across the clearing at the sound of yelling.

Megan reached her goal as everyone converged on the space around their makeshift firepit. Tyrone never hesitated as he pulled his arm back and landed a punch in Megan's face that would undoubtedly leave things bruised if not broken.

The girl crumpled to the ground at his feet without a sound. He stepped over her like a rock in his path and took up position between her body and the other two humans. Lynea couldn't move as she fought to process the insanity.

Trenton had no such problem as he rushed towards the larger man. Tyrone sidestepped his punch and countered with a two-fisted hack to Trenton's back as forward momentum carried him past. Tumbling over Megan's inert body, Trenton managed to pull himself into a roll that left him eating dirt, several feet beyond Tyrone's grasp.

The MMA fighter had resumed his defensive position with no hesitation. Peering closer, Lynea took stock of blankness on a face she knew to carry a smile and lack of feeling in usually expressive eyes. Combined with his behavior it wasn't a leap to conclude he wasn't in control of himself. What could she do to break him out of it?

As Trenton circled the man looking for a weak point, Lynea studied the strange woman who accompanied him. The icy stare locked on her own brought a wobble to her knees. This was no one to take lightly. But Megan, and Tyrone's lives were at stake. Bracing her treacherous body, she moved warily as she vied for a better view of Megan. Her priority was to ensure the girl was still breathing.

The woman glanced between the two humans, keeping an eye on both but showing no sign of concern. A ring of sorts was extracted from a fold in her black dress and slipped onto her finger. Drifting forward she bent down to grab Megan's wrist.

Lynea's angle gave her a glimpse of sharp metal before the woman ran the ring along the inside of Megan's wrist and blood began to flow. In horrified transfixion she watched as the woman placed her mouth along the cut and suckled. Vampire. Unholy Hell.

The sounds of two men exchanging body blows filtered through the shock. Glancing over, she watched Tyrone lift Trenton up by the shirt and fling him back at least fifteen feet. Baskets scattered as he landed amongst them. His head drifted from side to side as he struggled to rise.

"Tyrone stop!" Lynea was certain he was beyond reasoning, but she couldn't continue to watch her friends hurt each other. His gaze never left his foe. Resuming his defensive posture like an automaton, his body stayed in motion to remain between Trenton and the woman.

Yelling had Lynea swiveling around to stare at the road. Coming towards them were Caneon, Drew, and Aleece. Her feet turned to join her friends, but her mind redirected them. She needed to be brave and dislodge that woman from Megan's arm.

She reached the two women with little resistance since Trenton had resumed his attack on Tyrone. Their would-be champion was running on fumes. She needed to move quickly. Darting up to the two women, she reached Megan's side as the evil creature raised her head. The diamond eyes moved past her and landed beyond her shoulder.

Knowing the woman's distraction wouldn't last long, she slapped Megan across the face. Wake up damn it. Grasping her un-injured wrist, Lynea began to tug her away from the blood sucking creature. Megan roused enough to pull back. It was anti-productive. Bracing her feet, Lynea jerked harder. The younger woman raised her head. One glance from Lynea's face to the leech's blood slicked lips had Megan scrambling in the right direction.

As they cleared the woman's reach, Drew threw himself into the fray. He hit her fiery head with his backpack pushing her away from Tyrone. She drew herself to her full height. Rearing back, she back-handed the kid with enough force to knock him off his feet. He had the presence of mind to move the second he hit the ground and the kick she sent his way flew past him.

Scurrying further away, he scrambled to his feet. He prepared to reengage with only the slightest sway. Lynea couldn't stand there and do nothing, as the kid fought her battle. Racing for Trenton's pack, she went for the gun he kept there when it wasn't on his hip.

As she dumped its contents onto the ground the shiny metal was nowhere to be found. Lynea choked back her frustration. Where was it? She knew he didn't have it, or he would have used it already.

Reaching into the side pockets, she came up empty again. Frustration strangled her ability to think. Where could it be?

"Are you looking for his gun?" Aleece had come to kneel beside her in the dirt.

"Yes! Do you know where it is?" Lynea grabbed the other woman's arms in desperation.

"No. It should be in his pack." Tears leaked from Aleece's eyes.

Megan staggered up to them and dropped into the dirt as her strength waned. She glanced at the strewn contents of the bag, then between the two women kneeling before her. "You want the gun."

"Yes!" Lynea choked on the word.

"I dropped it in the jungle. When I saw Tyrone." Megan's words had barely tapered off before Aleece was running in the direction Megan's arm pointed.

"How could you do that? She'll never find it in time. We need to help." Lynea was lifting Megan to her feet without giving her time to process the statement. "Let's go."

They hobbled along in the deadliest game of three-legged race ever. Megan relied more on Lynea with each step. If they didn't find the weapon soon she was going to be forced to choose between who to protect.

"Near that tree. I was standing right there." Megan indicated which one with a flick of her wrist before she slid to the base of one closer to her. "The ammunition should be with it. I had it loaded."

Lynea sprinted to the specified place. There was a glint of sun off metal in the tangled vegetation. Tearing at the ferns and vines woven over the spot she feared she'd never pull it free. She landed on her backside when the flora finally gave way. Her breath clogged in her throat as she inspected the weapon. Aleece was there reaching over her shoulder as she concluded everything was intact.

"I'm trained with this. Thank you, ladies. Lynea you should stay here with Megan. Find the rest of the ammo. I'll come back for you when it's safe." Rushing off Aleece didn't wait to hear protest or acceptance.

Lynea's heart tore at being forced to abandon one or the other of her friends. Megan was too feeble to be left alone. The battle taking place in the clearing could be heard from where they perched. She dug through the vegetation once more and came out with the box of bullets. Trenton cried out in pain. Drew howled a battle cry.

They were fighting for their lives while she sat helplessly by. Megan's breathing had grown steadier. Lynea stood, ready to take the box to Aleece.

Two shots rang out in the humid air. Birds screeched as animals fled the noise. Then silence reigned. Unable to withstand the curiosity, she made her way to the clearing. Standing at the corner of their makeshift home was Aleece, the gun clenched in her hands. It's muzzle still pointed where she had shot.

Following the trajectory, Lynea was horrified to be staring at Tyrone's chest as blood soaked his shirt from the mortal wounds. His face conveyed neither pain nor fear. The disconnection remained, and Lynea hoped it would hold on until death claimed him. That seemed somehow merciful. Over his shoulder, the woman who held his leash was showing all the furious emotion he lacked.

She scooped him up like a child with a broken toy and stalked into the jungle. It felt disgusting to allow her to claim him that way. No one moved to stop the injustice. Drew's face was frozen in tear stained disbelief as Lynea met his eyes. He shook his head slightly. She wasn't sure if he was conveying disbelief or discouraging her from following.

Caneon came up alongside Aleece. Her arms were still frozen in place. He pried the gun from her grasp and handed it off to her brother who'd joined them. Trenton appeared to have taken the worst end of the fight. His face was already beginning to swell and bruise. He would be lucky to see out of his left eye by morning. Scrapes ran up his arms and face from hitting the ground, and he moved with the kind of caution that meant at least one rib was broken.

"What happened?' Lynea had to know what had gone so terribly wrong.

"He stepped in front of the bullets. Didn't even hesitate." Trenton's voice was muffled as it left his throat.

"I didn't mean to." Tears spilled from Aleece's eyes. "I didn't want to."

She crumpled into her brother's arms as Caneon awkwardly patted her back. The man was still hopeless at other people's emotions. Lynea turned to go back for Megan. There was no reason to leave her laying helpless on the jungle floor.

The younger woman had passed out propped against a tree. Lynea was grateful to find Drew had followed her into the jungle. The kids face didn't look much better than Trenton's, but he picked Megan up with ease. They emerged into the clearing to find an alien woman similar in appearance to Tyrone's companion. Lynea's heart plummeted into her feet.

"She's not evil, like the other one." Drew's voice was hushed.

"What?" Lynea couldn't make sense of the words.

"Her name is Naelah. We found her in the temple." He continued forward to the others. Choosing to trust her friend, Lynea moved forward cautiously.

"Where did you go?" Caneon was posing the question to the alien woman as Drew placed Megan onto a nearby bench. "We needed your help. I thought you wanted to find this Sorche woman."

"That was the objective. Unfortunately, she had already taken a Thrall. With his blood, as well as that of the young woman, she is much stronger than I currently am. The likelihood of her defeating me was high." Naelah stated.

"One of our friends is dead. Others are injured. You should have helped." Drew spat the words at her.

"Her thrall is most likely within her capabilities to heal. The others are within mine. Once I have done this, I will require your assistance to find and stop Sorche."

"Because we were so successful this time? Lady, you are crazy." Trenton winced as he shifted.

"We will need to recruit others to our cause. This is where your assistance will be valuable." She looked down her nose at each member of their group. No one met her eyes. Especially Lynea.

Was she ready to go further down the rabbit hole? She had already experienced more than imaginably possible. Her family would be expecting her home any day now. Could she put them off to help her friends chase blood sucking alien monsters?

"If Sorche is allowed to remain free she will awaken others like her. They will enslave humanity once again." Her voice contained a deeper note of reverberation.

Lynea gagged at the images of carnage sifting through her mind. Blood and gore took a back seat to depravity and horror. She fought the bile climbing up her throat at the vision of her children living in such a world.

"I'll help." She had to do what she could to protect them. It was a mother's right. "What do you need?"

"There are others like me living in your world. I've received reports of them over the centuries. You will help me to navigate your society and find them."

"I'm in. For Tyrone." Drew's young shoulders squared up ferociously. Lynea couldn't help comparing him to her own son, Tanner. She would do what she could to get him back to his own family.

"Can she really heal him?" Aleece's voice scraped out of her throat.

"I believe that to be so. The weapon you utilized is unfamiliar. There may be facets of it that I can't account for." Naelah's head tilted to the side as she regarded Aleece.

"If he lives, can you free him from this thrall?" Her head tilted up as she met the alien woman's amethyst eyes.

"If he desires to be free then there is the possibility of breaking the binds placed upon him." She inclined her head forward slightly.

"Then me and my brother will help you. On the condition you help us find and free Tyrone." Aleece locked eyes with her brother who nodded.

"I would be remiss if I exited my own adventure before it had reached its conclusion." Caneon interjected.

"I'm not going home until Tyrone does." Megan struggled to sit as she spoke.

"Very well. We have an accord. Perhaps we should sit as I avail you of my people's history. The knowledge will be required to proceed." Naelah took her own advice and moved to a bench near Megan. The others followed suit. "I belong to an alien race originating on a planet far outside of your universe. We call it Valda. For reasons you needn't be privy too, we colonize uninhabited planets to ensure the continuation of our species. Earth was selected thousands of years ago for that purpose. Preliminary surveys gave no suggestion of sentient life."

"We were therefore quite taken aback to find humans dotting the planet upon our arrival. Word was sent back to Valda that others should not be sent. An avert and avoid order was put into effect. Protocol dictated we were to move to a secondary site in another galaxy. Alas, factions within our leadership found that planet undesirable. A vote was taken, and we remained here." She paused to scan the group. "Interaction with the humans was inevitable. There was zero chance that we would not influence evolution. It was decided that both species would be best served if we acted as leaders and guides to the fledgling race. With little choice but to follow our leaders we spread out among the world and began settlements."

"Civilizations flourished. Protocols aside we found success. Those in leadership positions congratulated themselves. That was premature."

Naelah paused to glower into the rapidly darkening jungle. Like a switch had been pushed everyone shuffled at once. Stretching and wandering the immediate area to ease stiff muscles. Caneon gathered wood he then tossed into the firepit and Lynea found herself impressed by his willingness to help with the menial chores. She moved to ignite the fire, so they could use its light to pretend to fight off the dark. The glow pulled Naelah's attention back to the group and just like that everyone returned to their seats.

"I am unclear on when or how the deviance began. Perhaps, only those involved in it have that knowledge. We were dispersed so thinly there was inadequate communication. Empires were formed and enslaved under our noses. Those engaging in blood taking gained a power we had failed to anticipate."

"In a bid to stop Valdan's from engaging in base activities our leaders made the practice punishable by death. They were naïve to believe they had the ability to enforce such a decree. The Dark Ones, as we called them for their dark tendencies, took extreme measures to eradicate all leaders of the Valdan. For a time, we believed they would see us all dead or turned to their ways."

"The humans turned the tide. Slaves revolted against their oppressors. In the centuries since we had arrived they had multiplied exponentially. Sheer numbers brought down numerous Dark Ones. To our detriment, they failed to distinguish between us. Several Valdan were killed needlessly. A twofold plan was formed."

"Scientists took one of our ships and retreated to a cloaked location. There they engaged in an effort to negate the effects human blood had on Valdan physiology. In the interim, we lured Dark Ones to remote places and used our stasis pods to channel our life forces into impenetrable shields such as the one surrounding this city." Her voice trailed off as she stared into the flames.

"Wait a minute." Drew's complaint broke into the story pulling Lynea out of the ambience Naelah had created. "I'm trying to be patient because I want the entire story, but you're skimming over crazy things. Like how you could personally know anything about something that happened thousands of years ago or even hundreds. Or what does drinking blood do to change Valdan into Dark Ones. I need more."

He was right. Her story had holes you could drive through. She was so obviously other than human. It simply hadn't occurred to Lynea to question the fantastic parts. Now that Drew was asking questions though, she couldn't help thinking they should be asking more. Could this woman be trusted? Who was going to verify or dispute anything she said?

"I request your forgiveness. In my desire to keep things concise, I have neglected to be clear. Valdan have a significantly longer life span than humans. Even without the stasis pods we can attain an age beyond the thousand-year mark. With them the length of time we can extend that is increased expeditiously. Every Valdan or Dark One on the planet came here on the colony ships."

"As for the blood, it chemically changes the Valdan body. This magnifies abilities Valdan already possess; turning an ability to min-imally influence the human mental process into the ability to hold someone in Thrall against their will. It corrupts the Valdan mind as well. Creating a physical dependence in the blood that distorts and warps the Valdan until there sole focus is driven by that addiction. For the sake of expedience, we can discuss the particulars at a later time. Perhaps as we travel. Is that sufficient?"

"Yeah, I guess. Wow. OK." Drew's voice stuttered to a stop.

"The intention was to find a cure or barring that a means to eradicate Dark Ones without massive loss of life. Should the scientists fail to succeed, they were meant to wipe the planet clean. One of these three options should have come to pass by now. We must determine what went amiss. Sorche can't be truly stopped until we have deciphered that piece of information."

"Do you know where the scientists retreated?" Caneon asked.

"No. The location was known only to those who embarked on the mission."

"You mentioned allies. Where are they?" Trenton was all but laying on the bench by this point. Lynea felt pretty wilted herself and no one had pummeled her half to death.

"You said you could heal them." She was tired of story time. It was action time.

"You are correct. I am remiss once again." Rising from her perch on the bench Naelah moved to stand over Trenton. Her hand slipped into the folds of her robe. When it emerged, there was a device attached to the palm. She slid this along the side of Trenton's face. Like a magic eraser the bruises and swelling were wiped away. Lynea's breath hitched.

He was sitting tall within moments of her running the device along his side. Stretching his arms above his head a smile crept across his face when nothing glitched. Side twists followed by a full body stretch finally seemed to satisfy him all things were back to normal. Naelah shifted to Megan only to pull back.

"This one has been corrupted. I was unaware there had been a blood exchange." Naelah looked to Caneon as she spoke.

"Is there nothing you can do for her?" He seemed genuinely concerned. Lynea was surprised. She'd been under the impression he considered the younger woman to be nothing more than a useful assistant. Good for him, getting attached to people and caring about their welfare.

"Sorche has begun the process of making her Thrall by injecting her own blood into this human's system. Eventually, should she have enough time her body will cleanse the foreign contaminate. Until such time she'll feel sickly."

"Enough time?" Lynea couldn't let the omission slide.

"Without Sorche obtaining close enough proximity to feed on her again as well as inject further contamination."

"Perfect. We can do that. How long?" Lynea snapped.

"Two days. Possibly three. It's dependent on the human's immune system."

"Great. Let's hope you're as tough as you think you are, Megan. The two of us have learned quite enough for one night. Come on roomy, let's get you inside." Lynea pulled the younger woman up from the bench and half carried her to their room. No one else left the circle of light.

| 11 |

Chapter

Megan scrambled over the jagged rocks as flames scorched her heels. Heat boiled the sweat on her face as it formed, creating blisters on her already blackened skin. Darting to the left, she gained a foot of blessed relief. A lukewarm breeze across her skin felt like heavenly relief. Pushing her aching muscles, she clambered up the peak in front of her.

There was no time to take in the charred vistas around her as the heat rose behind her. Twisting to the right she threw her battered body down the incline. The reckless move gained her blessed seconds of cool air. Ratcheting quickly to the left, she rolled to the bottom, once there she was off and running before the flames caught her.

A flash of blue caught her eye. Desperation drove her towards it. Water was her only hope of survival. Straining forward she prevented her body from flinging itself headfirst into the blue depths. Why would this oasis be here?

Fearing a trick, she sliced her knees and palms as she dropped beside the kiddie pool sized oval of water. Dipping her bloodied hands into the cool depths brought only relief. With that small assurance her control faded. She dived into its depths with no direction but down.

Her breath burned in her lungs as it was consumed. Still her legs propelled her. The fire within held no torment compared to the fire above. As her vision began to fade she embraced the quick end to her suffering. Here in the dark depths, she would find peace.

A hand grasped hold of her ankle before that desired peace could take hold. She had been found. Struggling against the malignant hold, she thrashed and churned to return to the dark. Not to be out done the grip tightened as her body was drawn upwards. Defeat eventually stilled her struggles.

Her face broke the cool water as her lungs filled of their own accord. She certainly hadn't given them permission to resume this retched existence. As she floated listlessly on the surface, oxygen filled her blood, restoring her brain's ability to function. Although the air was warm, and the sky was smothered in ashy clouds, there was no searing heat to indicate flame nearby. Paddling her way to shore, she searched for the person who had pulled her from her relief.

There sitting on the blackened rocks as if they were the softest sand was Tyrone. His smile had never been so dear. Her bruised body protested the necessary effort to pull it free of the waters grasp. On dry land again, she mustered the energy to make her way to her friend.

"What are you doing here?" She couldn't find the grace to make the seat look comfortable like he did.

"I was going to ask you the same thing. Please don't tell me she's taken you over as well." He reached across to grasp her hand with a boldness he's never shown before.

"Who? What do you mean?" She wanted to enjoy the reprieve of sitting with him, but his presumptions pushed at her.

"Sorche. This is where she keeps those she thralls. The constant torment keeps us too weak to fight. Just my theory. Like psyching your partner out before a big match." He shrugged as his gaze wandered off to the side.

"Last I checked Lynea was tucking me into bed like a kid. The rest were talking to the other alien chick. Naelah. You think Sorche took over my mind like she did yours. Hey, you punched me." Megan's hand came to rest on her bruised cheek.

"Did I? Sorry." He didn't look all that sorry.

"You beat Trenton to a pulp. I thought you were gonna kill him." She squeezed the large hand still encasing her own. The response she was expecting never came. He barely registered she was there.

"Yeah, I kinda felt that. Weird." He turned to stare into her eyes. "I don't think you're here for good. FIGHT HER!"

Megan bolted up into a sitting position. Her lungs squeezed shut as she hacked nonexistent ash from them. Her hands trembled as they smoothed her heated skin. Jerking her feet out of the bedroll she made her way around Aleece's sleeping body and over to Lynea.

"Wake up, Lynea" She shook the woman's shoulder hard enough it made her own teeth rattle.

"What the heck? Megan?? What are you doing out of bed? Is everything OK?" Lynea was freeing herself from the blankets of her bedroll as she fired questions.

"I saw Tyrone."

"You what? Where? Take me." She had her shoes on before Megan could stop her.

"Not like that. In my dream." Megan felt scorched anew under Lynea's scowl.

"A bad dream. You woke me up for a bad dream. What are you twelve?" Her shoes were flipped off her feet in succinct order as she laid down and turned her back on Megan.

"No, 23. Lynea, it was real. My dream."

"Go back to sleep." Lynea threw the words over her shoulder before pulling the blankets around her chin.

"I was in this horrible place where everything was on fire. Then he saved me. He told me to fight her and I woke up here. It sounds crazy but there is gobs of research to prove people can communicate in dreams. Under the right circumstances it's reproducible. What if the blood Naelah says is in mine created a connection of some kind?"

"Go on." Lynea was flipped onto her back now but her arm covered her eyes, so Megan couldn't be sure if she were still trying to go back to sleep. Better make this fast.

"I don't really remember the woman with Tyrone, but I think her hair looked like fire, right? He said he was trapped there. It was a horrible place, Lynea. Horrible like it was on fire. We need to save him."

"Did he tell you how? Or where he is?"

"No. He did say something about the place distracting him, so he wouldn't fight. I don't know. It was all bizarre." Her excitement was gone now that she'd realized how little help the conversation had really been. Why hadn't she asked questions? Lynea would have.

"Go back to bed Megan. We'll talk about it with the others in the morning."

Megan crept back into her bedroll in defeat. She could have saved Tyrone and she'd screwed it all up. Just like everything else in her life. Turns out her father was right about her.

| 12 |

Chapter

Caneon settled on the same bench he had used last night. Naelah's story still circled around his mind as he labored diligently to process it. There had always been certainty that a species or mutation had created the vampire legends. It was logically sound reasoning. What hadn't entered the equation was the possibility they weren't extinct.

His entire quest had been built on the carefully researched evidence of a creature long gone from this world. Daydreams had clearly defined the end result for him. Accolades would be presented after the grand adventure was lived. Groundbreaking research that changed the face of history would ensue. It was a story he could dine out on for decades. No one ever died in those fantasies.

This creature they had unearthed was ghastly. She would change the way the world worked. Forever. His name would always be attached to the atrocities her and her kind committed. Like Columbus and smallpox, he would go down in history as the bringer of death. Whether he intended it or not.

The only hope was put the creature back in her box before too much damage could be done. If they could retrieve Tyrone in the process, then more the better. What they could not do was fail.

Trenton dropped into the space beside him, jarring his thoughts into chaos. The man had no concept of personal boundaries or social etiquette. It was a frustration that he simply didn't have the patience for today.

"We need to head for the Navajo nation. I've been there before. The alien man Naelah was talking about last night who lives there is our best bet for good info." Trenton leaned forward to steeple his fingers before him.

"I disagree. Alaska is a better choice. Quelis sounds like a standout warrior. That is entirely what we need to fight this opponent." Caneon wasn't stunned to find they disagreed fundamentally.

"You're both wrong. Lihah, in Egypt sounds like she is wise and bad ass. That should be our target." Aleece's natural fragrance drifted around Caneon as she sat. He breathed it in and felt the nerves Trenton had ruffled settle back into place.

"I agree that Lihah sounds like a great ally, but Egypt is a prohibitive distance away. Both of the others being on the North American Continent make them more accessible and therefore better options." He patted her hand to take the sting out of it.

"I understand the obstacles. She's still the most experienced at dealing with Dark Ones. It's worth the effort." She patted his hand. Some of those nerves she'd soothed went on high alert.

Naelah joined them in her stately way, creating a timely distraction. He was very much afraid his response to Aleece would have crushed anything beautiful blooming between them.

"Have you come to a conclusion on our destination? We can linger here no longer."

"We are at a standstill. Which ally do you feel it most beneficial to reach first?" Caneon felt that the decision should have been hers alone. He had argued as much last night. She in turn had refused based on her lack of understanding of their society. Like that mattered. He didn't understand most of society and he functioned just fine.

"If the only factor were the person themselves I would seek out Lihah. She is easily the most qualified."

"Ha! I told you." Aleece jabbed her finger in his face for emphasis. Jerking back from the offending digit he struggled not to swat it away.

"Yes, you did. But she clearly stated there are other factors." Caneon fought to place a check on his temper.

"Well, if easiest to get to is the leading factor, we obviously head for Molab. It's a cake walk from here to New Mexico." Trenton had to throw his two cents in. Per usual.

"What are we talking about?" Lynea plopped down across from them with a blue enamel cup in her hand.

"Where to go next. After you took Megan to bed we discussed possible allies. Now we're picking who should be first." Trenton moved to sit next to her as he talked. Caneon hoped the man wasn't getting fresh. Lynea was married. If she was going to stray from that commitment she should choose a better candidate.

"I see. Well, continue. I'll play catch up as I drink my watered-down coffee." The pucker of her face as she took a sip was testament to its flavor.

"I believe we've reached an impasse. Without a deciding vote we're clearly talking in circles." Caneon looked to the others for input. None was forth coming.

"Hey guys. What's up?" Drew's demeanor was unusually cheery this morning. He must have enjoyed an unbroken sleep cycle. Caneon was jealous.

"They can't decide where to go." Lynea scooted over to give the kid room on her bench.

"Easy. We split. Half to Alaska and Half to Egypt. Then we meet in New Mexico where we plan a kick ass strategy." His crooked grin almost had Caneon smiling back. He really did make it sound easy.

"Who goes where smart guy?" Trenton was scowling at the younger male.

"Aleece, Caneon and Naelah to Egypt. Lihah sounds like the type who won't deal with humans. Plus, her shields are up so Naelah is the only one who can find her. Then me, you, Lynea and Megan go to Alaska. If Megan's up for travel. Quelis shouldn't be too hard to find if he lives near human towns like she said." The kid nodded once liked he'd settled the whole thing. The arrogance of youth.

Caneon struggled to find the flaw in the plan. Other than the obvious question of how they were going to get a six-and-a-half-foot tall alien woman past people without attracting undue attention there didn't seem to be much wrong with the idea.

"It could work." Caneon was loath to concede that much.

"It's brilliant! Great job Drew." Aleece gave him an air high five which he returned from across the fire pit.

"It does cover all the bases." Trenton crossed his feet out in front him.

"Great. Let's do it. I'll wake Megan up." Lynea dumped the dregs from her cup into the ashes left from last night's fire before heading inside. The others scattered as they worked to break down camp.

The trek back to the van was somber. Megan was too weak to walk on her own. The others took turns as her human crutch. It was a slow and tiring process that doubled the time it had taken them to hike in. Finding the white van sitting undisturbed where they had left it felt like a minor miracle.

Caneon threw his bag into the open back doors then claimed his spot in the driver's seat. He wasn't ceding that to Trenton's take over. It took longer than it should have for them to settle Megan into one of the rear seats. She had become unresponsive to all but basic commands.

His first inclination was to find the nearest lodging and leave her to work the evil creatures blood out of her system. If he could have guaranteed her safety, there would have been no hesitation to do so. But he couldn't. Not without leaving Lynea or one of the others behind as well and everyone was necessary to success.

So, they were held to the necessity of dragging her along with them. No matter how severely she hindered their progress. He would find a way to resign himself to the need. To his surprise Lynea claimed the passenger seat before Aleece could.

"I need to discuss something with you." She spoke to the windshield, but he was certain the words were intended for him.

"OK. Go ahead." The others had settled so he turned over the engine and got their show on the road. In his rearview mirror he watched Naelah startle at the sudden movement. Her face remained uneasy as they bounced down the rough road.

"Megan woke me up in the middle of the night."

"She's barely awake now. Are you sure you weren't dreaming?"

"Absolutely. She claimed to have talked to Tyrone through some link formed by Sorche's blood." She turned to look at him as she spoke.

"Psychic type link?" He glanced at her to gauge her seriousness. This sounded like the build up to a joke.

"Yes. It's crazy right. But I keep thinking that Naelah claimed the blood is how Sorche exerts mind control. Then it doesn't seem so crazy."

"If the blood acts as a conductor for Sorche's mental influence then perhaps it is possible for it to link those she is connected to. Frankly, all of this sounds impossible even knowing what I've seen with my own eyes." Caneon rubbed the bridge of his nose between his eyes where a muscle twitched rhythmically.

"Where do we draw the line between what we know to be true and what Naelah tells us is true?"

"I'm unsure. Perhaps we allow the line to be movable. For now. One doesn't learn new things if they cling to tightly to the old ways. That doesn't mean we won't verify what we can." He was dubious about the new information as well, but it served no purpose for them to become overly suspicious. "Get some rest. We'll be at the airport shortly."

Naelah assured them she was capable of influencing the human mind to the extent others would fail to realize she was passing in front of them. This would allow her to board the plane and claim an empty seat. If it worked. He was dubious about that as well.

At the airport, Lynea dug through hers and Megan's luggage. She decked Naelah out in a floppy hat and sundress that brought her close to the human norms. Once her hair was contained in a bun and sunglasses hid her eyes she passed for the tallest, whitest human ever, but she passed.

Trenton and Drew scoped out the interior of the buildings while the women played dress up. With no choice but to put it to the test they divvied out luggage. Naelah leaned into the van where Megan was slouched in her chair. Caneon's view of the two was blocked. By the time he'd claimed a better angle Megan was revived enough to walk and talk and Naelah was slipping something into the shoulder bag she'd been given.

A buzz coursed through his body and settled in the pit of his stomach. There was no time to question what she had done to the girl. He put it on his vital information needed list. This alien was playing fast and loose with pertinent knowledge. He couldn't con-done that.

Megan looked like the dead risen but she kept it together enough to drag her own suitcase behind her. If it slid to the side and took out Drew's heels more than it should, no one said a word. At the counter they split up to book passage to their separate destinations.

As his companions diverged from the group to wait for their flight, he was taken aback at the flutter in his chest. Could it be possible he would miss them? What a foreign concept.

Aleece grabbed his elbow to pull him to their plane. They had been truly lucky to find an outbound plane with a connecting flight that would land them in Egypt tomorrow morning. It was already boarding. There was no time for melancholy farewells. Naelah had been true to her word. No one paid any attention to her.

The flight wasn't full, so she had no difficulties finding a seat. He purposefully pulled Aleece into a pair next to the window to give them some privacy. He aspired to gather her observations of what Naelah had done to Megan.

It proved to be a fruitless effort as Naelah situated herself directly in front of them. In the confined space she was practically sitting in their laps. Resigning himself to wait for a better time, he allowed Aleece to lead the conversation through various idle subjects.

The second flight was bigger than the first with even less chance for private conversation. Naelah was able to sit next to Aleece in the larger plane. This gave Aleece the chance to ask mundane questions about Naelah's life with the Aztecs. Had the alien woman been inclined to expound on details he might have found himself engaged. The reality was more in line with talking to a rock.

He let his mind wander down one of the various paths it always had on pause. Long ago he had concluded there were few people on the planet who were better company than himself. The process of landing and exiting the airport was uneventful.

After the jungle he found the desert sand a welcome change of scenery. His mother had dragged him here often as a child. Her digs in this dry land had ceased to be novel around the tumultuous age of thirteen. Most of his time spent with her became tedious around that age.

Open air markets passed by the taxi window with little notice from him. Aleece, on the other hand, was so entranced by the sights her head craned from side to side to catch it all. He grinned a little at the wonder on her face.

The hotel sat amid Cairo's busy streets. The McDonald's they could see down the street made Aleece giggle when he pointed it out. They had yet to exit the car when Naelah reached behind her ear and pressed lightly.

"We must return to the airport." Naelah closed the door she had begun to open and looked to them in expectation.

"Wait. We just flew almost an entire day to get here. Why would we turn around now?" Aleece was every bit as exasperated as Caneon.

"Lihah is being overrun by Dark Ones. She will not be able to hold her shields."

"Can we fly closer to where she is?" Caneon queried.

"No. We go to Molab."

"Why aren't we going to assist her?" Caneon was tired of the half explanations.

"She is dying. Her warning to anyone within communicator distance was an expenditure of the last dregs of her life essence. She gave much to ensure we heard it." Naelah indicated the still open door with her chin. A subtle command to close it that Caneon had no desire to heed.

"When she dies do Dark Ones become free?" He wasn't moving until his questions were answered.

"Yes. Which is why we must go. They will be locked onto my signal at any moment if they aren't already. There were seven trapped within her shield centuries ago. Even if several have perished, I will be significantly outnumbered. It's imperative they do not find us." Remembering what Sorche was capable of on her own, Caneon slammed the door shut.

"What about the people here?" Aleece pleaded.

"There is nothing we can do for them. We'll rally with the others and make a plan." He tried to console her, but the shoulder pat felt awkward even to him.

His nerves jangled around each curve in the road. Reaching the airport placed them in the open. He probed the crowd for giants with color changing hair. At least they would be conspicuous. It crashed into him that he was assuming Dark Ones and Valdan all shared the same characteristics. That was naïve. People came in all shapes and sizes.

Every face became a danger as they moved further into the busy airport. Pushing his way through the throngs of humanity, he spent less time than usual being considerate of others. They reached a ticket counter in record time. Two tickets were purchased on his abused credit card.

His heart didn't slow its erratic rhythm until he was settled into his window seat. There was no idle chatter as they awaited the plane's takeoff. Ascending into the sky was the only assurance they would have of safety. As the plane finally taxied away from the gate, Caneon glanced back at the terminal.

Standing at a window was the largest man Caneon had ever beheld. His frame topped seven foot easily. Silver hair cut close to his head still managed to shimmer and shift through shades of white and gray. Piercing emerald eyes locked onto Caneon's across the distance. Something slithered through his mind before the man disengaged. That quick he was gone from view.

Caneon wanted answers about what was now hunting him. Only one being could provide those. Turning to the women on his right he determined not to settle for less than the entirety of what he wanted to know.

"One of these Dark Ones was just standing at that window." He held Naelah's eyes as he stated the fact.

"We will be safe as long as the plane takes off." Her features were hard to read. Was she concerned at all?

"Good bit of information. Now we need to know more. How did you communicate with Lihah? How did the others track us to the airport? You said she's dead. How? What will they do now that they are free? Can they make you not see them?" He was sure there were more questions to be asked. This however was a good start.

"All Valdan have communication devices implanted before space voyage. It's procedure. The signal is only strong within a short range. I had mine on to contact Lihah before we breached her shield. She used hers to broadcast to anyone within the radius of her signal. That device is how the others tracked us to the airport. I was loath to terminate the connection until my friend was truly gone." Naelah turned away from them to stare into the empty seats across the aisle.

"How did she die? Did they kill her?" Life or death consequences trumped her need to mourn.

"The shield was being sustained by draining her life force. Sorche traveled to Egypt more expediently than we did. She must have shown the others how to push the shield. This forces the shield to draw more power. Sorche has been trying it for centuries but alone she was never able to push hard enough." Naelah continued to study the other seats as she recited facts.

"Can they hide from you like you hide from humans?" It was the scariest of all his questions.

"No." Signaling the end of their conversation the alien woman transferred herself across the aisle and closed her crystalline eyes.

"What do you think those creatures will do now that they are loose?" Aleece jumped in for the first time.

"Kill, torment, torture. Sorche didn't seem inclined to civility. I imagine her friends will take some time to learn the world they've been returned to. Once that goal is accomplished, I'm inclined to believe they will make a play for power. What that looks like I'm trying not to think about." Caneon took her hand and felt the trembling there. Squeezing slightly, he hoped his touch would bring her some comfort.

Aleece gave a valiant effort to her smile. It wasn't nearly enough. He leaned the short distance into her and placed a kiss on her forehead. Her hand came to rest on his cheek, so he tilted his chin down enough to examine her lovely green eyes.

The kiss she placed upon his lips was chaste and far too abrupt, but her lips had finally formed a smile as she pulled away. That was its own reward. Leaning her head upon his shoulder she closed her eyes in what he hoped was restful sleep.

His mind wouldn't find that respite. It was too late to quietly return the evil to its cage. Dark Ones were no doubt causing murder and mayhem at this very moment. Simple solutions were out the window. Resigning himself to the situation, he purchased the in-flight wireless and sent Drew an email. The others should be aware of how the situation had altered.

| 13 |

Chapter

Crisp air flooded Drew's lungs as he exited the charter plane they had booked in Anchorage. The snow-covered scenery proved impossible to ignore as he tried to navigate the stairs that had been rolled up to the plane. His left foot was nearly his undoing as it slid past his intended target and landed a second step down. Desperate to join the left, his right foot headed for the drop. Had Trenton not chosen that moment to exit the plane and grab his wrist, Drew's twisted body would have ended its journey in a pile at the bottom of the steps.

"Careful." Trenton's voice held an unmistakable hint of a chuckle.

Shaking free of his grip, Drew brought both of his errant feet into line on one step. His tread was deliberate until he was safely on level ground. The tarmac solidly beneath him helped to restore his dignity.

"Do you think the girls are okay in Anchorage?' Drew hadn't found a moments peace since they left the crappy motel.

"Yeah. No one knows they are there right? That's gonna keep them safe." Trenton's face didn't look as sure as his voice sounded.

"What if Sorche can find her because of the link thing?" Drew couldn't erase the picture his imagination had pulled up of them being torn to shreds.

"Didn't Caneon's email say she was in Cairo?" Trenton was headed for the terminal, leaving Drew no choice but to follow.

"Yeah." Drew was reluctant to let the logic soothe him. "We don't know how fast she can travel though."

"All that means to me is we had better get our butts in gear and find this guy. The quicker that's done the quicker we get back to our friends." Pushing the door open Trenton walked into the warm room with Drew on his heels.

"How do we find this Quelis guy anyway?" Drew was checking out the other travelers in the room as he spoke.

"No clue. Naelah said he lived within a day's travel of Anchorage. I figured it wouldn't be that hard to find a mountain of a man with hair that shifts color. That might have been short sighted." Trenton's head was swiveling around the room.

"What about a local guide? They should know who's who." Drew headed to a small desk labeled information with a petite Eskimo woman sitting behind it in uniform.

"Excuse me, ma'am. Can we ask you some stuff?" Drew realized as he came to a halt in front of her that she was close to his own age. Oops. The uniform must have thrown him off. He smiled sheepishly into her pretty brown eyes.

"Of course,…sir." Her emphasis of the last word came with a sly smile. Drew's face overheated.

"Excuse my friend, miss. We were hoping to find a local guide to show us around while we are here." Trenton cocked his hip onto the edge of the table as he smiled.

"That's a great idea. The winter snows are thawing. That can cause dangers a local would help you avoid. We have several options for you depending on how far from town you were intending to travel." Her face lit up as she smiled at Trenton.

"We were hoping to go pretty deep. Adventures the name of the game, right?" He chuckled as she giggled inanely. Drew felt like slapping her back to her senses. If only that was a real thing.

"Then you want Q. He's in the know for all the adventure you can handle. He might not take you on though. He's real picky about his jobs. You'll find him at Wally's Pub if you wanna give him a try. It's two doors down from the local hotel where I'm sure you're booked." She smiled sweetly as she passed a piece of paper to Trenton. Drew suspected the number on it wasn't the guides. It was hers.

"Thank you, very much." Trenton slipped the paper into his pocket with barely a glance. Was he that used to women giving him their numbers? Dude must be nice.

"Yeah, thanks." Drew headed for the door marked exit. He hoped Trenton was done flirting and followed.

"Slow up kid. You act like your pants are on fire." Trenton caught up with ease. Guess the girl wasn't all that interesting.

The street in front of them was lined with brick buildings out of some historical photo. Drew felt like he had stepped into a movie or a time warp. Walking down the sidewalk to the left they passed by a café and drug store straight out of the fifties.

"You think this Q guy is the alien? You know Q…Quelis. It's a pretty big coincidence." Drew was bobbing on his feet at the idea.

"Don't be stupid. Quelis is an alien. A..L..I..E..N…there's no way he's passing for human. Remember what Naelah looks like, shimmering hair? On top of that you think he's making a living among us as a wilderness guide in these backwoods. Like a technologically advanced being couldn't do better than that? Right. Besides there are tons of human names that start with Q." Trenton shrugged him off like a fly, but Drew wasn't convinced.

They had made Naelah passable to go to Egypt. Although she had looked stupid when he thought about it. Trenton was probably right. But it would be cool if it were that easy.

Two doors down was the hotel sign. Walking past that, they found a neon sign declaring Wally's Pub open, just like the girl had said they would. The entry door was painted a garish shade of green with a huge cartoon whale on it. The whale was jauntily holding a beer in one hand as he showed off the anchor tattoo on his other bicep. Kinda cutesy for an Alaskan bar, but whatever.

Pushing into the darkened interior Drew was momentarily blind. It gave him time to digest the smell of beer and peanuts riding the under-layer of vomit. Glasses clinked as bodies shuffled about the room. His eyes adjusting confirmed that the bar was incredibly packed for so early in the day.

Jostling their way to the bar, they claimed a couple of bar stools. Their packs safely wedged between their knees and the bar; Trenton signaled for the bartender. The man gave Drew the legal once over before offering up a coke and heading off to get Trenton's beer.

They used the waiting time to peruse the bar's clientele. Denim was the clothe of choice followed in a close second by leather. Most of the men looked as if they hadn't seen a razor since hitting puberty. The women stood out mostly due to their lack of facial hair. Anyone of them could have snapped Drew into pieces. Tiny pieces.

"How do we know who he is? They all look like backwoods guides up for a deadly adventure." Drew's head was starting to pound.

"I'll ask the bartender. He'll know who the regulars are." Trenton's voice was cocky. This wasn't Drew's normal scene, so he let it ride.

"What are we going to tell him we want to hire him for?" Drew was afraid of what men like this did when you wasted their time.

"Let me do the talking. I've got a plan." Trenton patted him on the shoulder as the bartender reappeared with a beer in hand.

"That'll be six bucks." Trenton choked a little at the price but handed over a twenty. "You can keep the change for a little information. We're looking for a guide called Q."

The bartender gave them a more thorough look over. Drew became certain the man was going to hand the money back when he signaled to a corner table with his head. Breathing easier, Drew turned to look at the table as the bartender walked away.

It was occupied by a lone man big enough to take on a grizzly. His matte black hair stood up in desperate need of a haircut and multiple scars marred the skin visible to Drew's gaze. Sapphire blue eyes rose to catch his. There was a momentary flash back to a pair of Amethyst eyes meeting his in an Aztec temple. This man didn't look like either of the Valdan they had met so far but Drew knew to his bones they had found Quelis.

"That's him." Drew reached to grasp Trenton's arm.

"I know. The bartender told us. Pay attention kid." Trenton spoke over his shoulder and Drew ended up with air in his fist as the older man moved towards the corner table.

Scrambling to gather his pack and his drink, he lurched after Trenton's back. There was no way to warn the other man they were about to talk to an alien not a human. Lead trickled into his feet the closer he got to the table.

Trenton was shaking Q's hand as Drew finally joined them. The Valdan looked comfortable in his seat and didn't rise to greet them. Drew could only hope that meant they weren't in imminent danger. How could Trenton not realize what this man really was.

"My name is Trenton. This is my associate Drew. We were hoping to engage your services as a guide. May we join you?" Trenton indicated two of the empty chairs at the Valdan's table.

"That won't be necessary. I was just leaving." The man stood and revealed his height for the first time. Drew figured the man came close to the seven-foot mark as he had to step back to comfortably look up to his face.

"Sorry to have bothered you." Trenton's voice had lost its cocky edge as his own frame was dwarfed. He took a step away from the table to clear the path.

Q moved with a predatory grace that had the other occupants of the room instinctively making way. He was out the door long before Drew could push his way through those same people. Trenton was struggling to keep up, but there was no time to wait for him. Using his smaller size as an advantage Drew weaved his way to the door.

Emerging into the sunlight sent pain lancing through his eyeballs. Ignoring the feeling, he searched for the largest blur moving away from him. Catching sight of what he hoped was the man to his left, he moved in that direction. As his eyes adjusted, he picked up speed. That was definitely Q.

Around two corners and past a store front he found the man lounging in an alleyway. Unsure if this was a trap, he slowed his pace as he approached. Looking back, he was disappointed to find Trenton was not behind him. Crap. Alone with an alien. He had not thought this out.

"You are one persistent guy. Other guides in town can take you wherever you want to go." Q shifted his hips to get more comfortable.

"No one else in town is Valdan." Drew watched the man's body go rigid. "We were sent here to find you. By Naelah."

"How do you know that name?" If anything, the explanation had served to stiffen the man further.

"Sorche escaped. She's gone to Egypt and helped others to overpower Lihah. Naelah sent us to find you. She needs your help." Drew took a chance and moved into the alley alongside the larger man.

"Why should I trust you?" Q's face glowered down at him.

"If she didn't send us, how else would we have found you?" Drew tried to casually lean against the wall behind him.

"Damn it. Come with me." Q pushed out of the alley. Drew spared a glance backwards for Trenton. The older man was not there. Guess he was on his own.

The Valdan's stride quickly left town behind. Parked in a clearing on the side of the road was an older pickup truck. Q strode up to it and jumped in. Fearing he'd find himself left behind, Drew bolted for the passenger door.

The truck was moving before he had the door closed. Shifting, he managed to pull his pack off his shoulder and into his lap. The road bumped and jostled them until his brain felt bruised.

Pulling up in front of the mountain man's cabin, Drew was once again reminded that he was alone with an alien capable of squashing him like a bug. Q jumped out of the truck and headed for the door of the cabin without looking back. Taking his courage in hand, he followed suite. At this point, he was already all in.

The interior of the cabin was surprisingly light and airy. Drew got the impression of wood and furs compromising the bulk of the furnishings and décor. His eyes were pulled to the open hatchway in the floor along the back wall. He recognized the blue glow emanating from it as the same one in Naelah's chamber of the temple.

Q was conspicuously absent from view, so Drew ventured to the hatch. His spine needed stiffening before he descended the ladder. His breath became trapped in his lungs until his eyes were low enough to see the room he was entering.

His scruffy host stood at one of the consoles lining the far wall. There was no stasis pod like there had been in the temple. Instead a screen filled the wall above the interface Q was working at. On the screen was a global map. There were red lights blinking at multiple points. His brain spun as it tried to muddle out the purpose of those lights.

"You're slow kid. Lives are at stake. Put some hustle in it." Q never took his eyes off the rectangular device he had sitting on the console next to him.

"Yeah. Sorry." Drew maneuvered for a better view. Both screens seemed to be streaming the same data. Best guess, he figured Q was downloading onto the more portable and way cooler looking device. Its clear screen was framed by a metal that almost looked like copper, but most definitely wasn't. "What are you doing?"

"Taking the important stuff with me. If Sorche is working to free Dark Ones we need to know where they are and how to get to them quickly. Where is Naelah meeting us?" Q glanced over his shoulder to pin Drew with his Sapphire eyes.

"At Molab's." Drew didn't dare give more information than that until he was positive he could trust this Valdan. "Why is your hair different than the other's?"

"Black dye." Q gave him the queerest look before returning to his work.

Drew knew he should back off, but how often in life do you get a one on one with an alien. OK so this was his second time. But he'd kind of blown the first one. This was his do over and he was making the most of it. Steeling his shoulders, he dived in.

"How do you know Naelah? Did you all live together before you came to Earth? Do you all have jobs like we do or are you all like jacks-of-all trades? Is there somewhere that keeps like the history of your people or something? What do you do if people figure out what you are?" Drew paused for breath as the taller man turned towards him.

"Are all of your friends as annoying as you or did I get lucky?" Q crossed his arms over his barrel chest. "I see no viable reason for Naelah to have chosen you. She must be in desperate straits, but I knew that when you said she sent you to find me. O.K. then. How I know her is complicated. We came here on separate ships at the same time. Of course, everyone has a trained skill. Stupid question. We have an official stored record of our history. No, I won't tell you where. We don't let people figure out what we are. That is the official limitation on questions. Now help me." Q strode across the room and grabbed a duffel bag off a shelf along the far wall.

"Fill this with clothes and food from upstairs. When that's done come back down here." The duffel hit Drew squarely in the solar plexus robbing him of the ability to speak. He suspected that was the purpose as he gulped for air.

Upstairs again, he didn't have to search hard in the immaculately organized rooms to find the items Q requested. The bag filled quickly. He didn't want to give Q another reason to call him slow. He took the time to pull out his tablet and send off a message to Trenton with a plan to meet back up at the bar later.

Downstairs he dropped the duffel next to Q's feet. The Valdan had finished with his alien tablet and was sliding it into a leather case which he deposited in a satchel on his hip. He reached across and placed his hand on the wall. A blue handprint appeared, pulsed three times and then the wall began to shift. The whole thing slid back and folded in on itself leaving bland wood in its place. Q's basement was cliché mountain man once again.

"Over here." Q grabbed the duffel and walked over to a spot in the corner with a strange circle carved into the wood planks. Taking his place in the circle he motioned for Drew to do the same. Goosebumps danced along his skin as he realized they weren't going back the way they had come.

His feet were barely settled next to Q's when light pulsed around the circle. Buzzing filled his head as his surroundings blurred into nothingness. His stomach dropped to his toes and his head expanded like a balloon. Disoriented by the conflicting sensations, he was scared his breakfast was about to make a repeat performance.

The light receded as his head resumed its normal size. Peering around he was able to make out a room with a stasis chamber in it similar to Naelah's. The walls here were roughhewn log chinked with stucco.

Q's hand released his arm alerting him that the man had been holding him steady. He wasn't sure enough of his stomach to vocalize a thank you, so he settled for a hand wave and a smile. Turning to his left gave him a view of a doorway leading into what looked like a front room with plush couches. He wobbled his way towards them only to be pulled up short by Q's hand on the back of his shirt.

"Easy kid, Molab will know someone has come through this Hub. It's safest if it's a familiar face he sees first." Q stepped past Drew to lead the way into the front room.

Standing at the kitchen counter with a 12-gauge shotgun leveled on them was the oldest looking Valdan Drew had yet to see. By human standard, the man appeared in his late fifties with shimmering white hair pulled back in a ponytail and ebony eyes tracking their every breath. The lines of experience etched proudly on his fiercely weathered face.

"Hail friend." The man's body softened as he recognized Q, but that shotgun never wavered. "Who is this you've brought uninvited to my home?"

"A friend of Naelah's. She sent him to summon me." Q stalked across the room and locked arms with the older man. The shotgun settled at his side with the embrace, but his eyes remained on Drew.

"Where would a human such as this have come into contact with our Naelah?" Molab's gaze judged Drew and found him less than desirable.

"Apparently the humans managed to bungle into her city." Q chuckled at their supposed incompetence.

"Actually, I built a device that used sound waves to disrupt the shield so that we could get into the city." Drew knew the second they both gave him their full attention that he should have kept his mouth shut.

"Did you really?" Molab sauntered over to the couches, took a seat on the edge, and motioned for Drew to do the same.

"Yeah. It wasn't a big deal." Drew tried to appear nonchalant as he angled around the nearest chair and sat down.

"That's technology beyond anything Earth will see in the next couple of centuries and you built a toy to disrupt it. But sure. No big deal." Q took a seat on the couch opposite Molab without his gaze once leaving Drew.

"It's not like I took it down. There was a hole we could slip through." Drew had an uneasy feeling it was time to undersell. "I couldn't even get us back out. Naelah had to do that."

"Before or after you woke her up?" Molab shifted menacingly on the couch. Drew's eyes darted to the shotgun left unattended on the kitchen counter.

"After..." Feeling the proverbial sands shifting beneath his feet, his heart wished for Naelah and the others to walk through the door.

"So, the humans have mucked things up for us. Again. Now you want us to clean up your mess." Molab shook his head irately. Ebony eyes flashed at Drew.

"Dark Ones are not humanities mess. Sure, we woke up Naelah and Sorche got loose but this problem started long ago when your people started preying on mine." Drew felt the heat flooding his face as he spoke.

"He's feisty. But also, right." Q chuckled. "The problem began with our species' depravity not theirs."

"Since we don't know how the blood consumption started we can't say that definitively." Molab crossed his arms over his chest and set his chin. Obviously, he wasn't open to debating the issue. Drew was fine with that. He felt like he'd tempted fate enough for one day.

"You truly believe they slipped their blood into Harcus' drinks or tempted Belnak to take a wrist just to see what would happen? That's ludicrous. You're holding to tightly to this. Ours discovered a drug and chased it's effects to the detriment of those they were supposed to protect." Q shifted forward. Drew was sure the alien was ready to pursue the argument but Molab turned his back to them and stared out the window.

Pulling out his tablet, Drew set to emailing Trenton. He needed to let the man know he wouldn't be making the meeting in Alaska, since he now found himself squarely in the middle of the Navajo Nation. The explanation of how he had come to be where he was, took longer than he had figured. When he raised his head after sending the email, Molab had exited the room taking the shotgun with him. Q sat quietly watching him.

"Where is Dexon?" Q asked.

"Who?" Drew was positive Naelah had never mentioned the name.

"Sorche's mate. He was trapped in the city with her."

"She was alone when we got there." Drew stated.

"Naelah hasn't mentioned him?"

"No man. Nothing." Drew's curiosity was clawing at his throat, but he was pretty sure Q had been serious about the no more questions thing.

Q closed his eyes to sleep or maybe think. Drew wasn't sure, but he wasn't going to interrupt and ask. Matter of fact he was determined to do nothing but sit on this couch and avoid attention until his friends showed up.

| 14 |

Chapter

The second the kids eyes glazed over Quelis left his perch on the couch. As harmless as the young human came across, years of living around them had proven they were wily creatures. He felt no guilt over inducing the boys trance. If Drew had been against the idea he wouldn't have been able to force the issue.

Molab was pacing in the kitchen. His mumbled complaints made him easy to find. It had been a calculated gamble to bring the human into the older man's home. Whose feelings toward the humans had soured greatly over the endless decades.

"Why have you brought this here? And don't feed me this line about Naelah. You broke with her centuries ago when she chose to stay behind and hold Dexon and Sorche captive." Ebony eyes scorched into Quelis.

"Well, maybe, that's why I need to do this now. If I had stayed with her there's a chance she could have held these humans out of the city. And the Dark Ones in."

"Or you both might have been overwhelmed. There is no way to tell. This device he talks about could be more than the toy we are assuming. The truth is the humans are advancing at a rate we can't control anymore. They were on the verge of finding us either way. In the meantime, you have been an invaluable asset on this side of the fight. Do not hold yourself accountable for sins that are not your own."

Quelis knew the older man was speaking truth. It soothed his frayed edges only enough to allow him to wait for Naelah and her human allies to arrive. No matter what the others believed, he would always know that he could have stopped this long ago had he only been strong enough.

"Why are we no closer to ending this?" He asked the question knowing there was no real answer.

| 15 |

Chapter

Megan walked the charred earth in search of Tyrone. Her fevered body lay drenched in sweat on a cheap motel room bed in the real world. This time around she was aware enough to know that. He had told her to fight and she was giving it a hell of a go. But she couldn't leave this world behind completely if it meant abandoning him to it.

No one deserved to be left in this nightmare. She had yet to encounter others along her trek. For a time, she had assumed they were the only ones here, but scurrying beings on the edges of her sight had put a lie to that. Whether they were human or not was indistinguishable. The furtive way they moved made the point moot, so she avoided getting closer.

Using her scorched hands to clamber to the peak of her current mountain assent, she was able to view the surrounding landscape. Her eyelids felt stuck at half-mast with no moisture to lubricate a blink. The perpetual squint caused her vision to double and triple as it worked its way into focus. To her right was a shape resembling a tree.

This oasis had presented itself multiple times already, only to dissolve as she approached it. Knowing better than to succumb, she shifted her gaze to the left. There sat a man on a rock not ten feet from her. He was dressed in a fancy suit and tie like her father wore to the office. The kind of suit that cost a normal person's yearly salary and screamed power player.

His smile was slightly lecherous as he gave her the once over. She couldn't imagine there was much to lust after in her current state, but powerful men can have very strange turn-ons. She had learned that at a tender age. How to fight back came much later.

"Who are you?" She moved to a rock mid-way to the man and sat as gracefully as she could manage.

"A friend." He moved his feet and Megan caught a glimpse of grass before it was burnt away. Taking a closer look, she realized the rock he sat on was gray, not black, and covered in lichen. Plus, there was no smoke or sweat covering his face or hands. Fishy.

"I've never met you before." She braced herself to play his game.

"No, but I know who you are. Sorche has sent me. To help you." He looked around in an obvious play at nonchalance. Her father would have scoffed.

"I don't want her help. I want to find my friend and leave. Full stop." Smoothing the fabric of her pants brought her attention to their sudden cleanliness. That was some trick.

"She can help with that too. In fact, she has a way you can both win. You convince Tyrone to give her full control and the two of you can leave this place. Easy." His eyes shifted to her shirt again. She resisted the urge to insure everything was adequately covered.

"Leave this place maybe. Have our lives back. No. A pretty prison is still a prison." Megan hoped she didn't look naïve enough to fall for something that obvious.

"Some things' just aren't negotiable. Others are. What do you want?" He licked his lips as he watched her. She fought the urge to flinch. No weakness.

"Nothing you have to offer. Go away." Megan stood quickly. Even at her diminutive height this left her looking down on him. She began the long sliding trail down the mountain.

"Maybe you'll be more reasonable after some more time here." He walked off the other side of the craggy mount like he was strolling a grassy hill. She watched him go over her shoulder as she continued her descent.

Hours passed while she slogged across the endless expanse. Her hope had exhausted itself when she miraculously caught sight of a lone man on the horizon. He stood surveying the landscape from a small cliff to her right. Closing the difference between them she recognized Tyrone's broad back. Tears would have leaked from her eyes had there been any moisture available.

"Tyrone." Her voice broke on his name. He turned at the sound

"What are you still doing here?" His forehead scrunched as he glowered at her

"I won't leave you here." Her chest was heaving as she climbed up to him.

"Now you care." He gave her his back as he resumed his study of the view.

"Right. So, let's find a way out of here. Together." She didn't understand his anger. Wasn't she here in hell for him? That should have bought her some good will.

"There is no way out of here. Even if I fought my way back into control of my body she has possession of it. I'm dead either way." His voice was steel.

"OK. We need to get your body back. I can tell the others that. They can do this." She clutched at his shirt sleeve, but he refused to acknowledge her. "Tyrone, stop being a quitter."

"Go away Megan. You have no clue who I am." He pushed off and soared through the air at least 20 yards before landing with a puff of ash. Megan's mouth hung open as she watched the feat. Now what? His long legs ate up the ground as he dashed away from her.

There was only one choice left. She needed to talk to the others. They would know how to fix this. But how did she wake up enough to deliver the message?

| 16 |

Chapter

Caneon steered the car down the long stretch of freeway with ease. Driving had always been a means of stress relief for him. Parked in his garage at home was a fully restored classic Porsche convertible that freed his soul while he was behind the wheel. The SUV they had rented at the airport was a poor substitute.

Aleece and Naelah slept while the miles flew by. The radio station pumped jazz into the interior speakers at an acceptable level for his passengers to maintain rest. His last desire was to have Aleece discomfited on his behalf.

They had reached Albuquerque in the early hours of the morning before the sun awakened. Jet lagged from zigzagging the globe, it hadn't taken either woman long to succumb to the lull of the car's smooth engine. The energy drink he had bought at the airport was sustaining his alertness just fine. Years of insomnia had trained him to function on little to no sleep.

The long stretch of road gave him ample time to reflect on all they had learned over the last few days. It felt like months had passed. His world had changed so completely. A nagging voice in his head insisted he should return to his library. Life was simpler there.

He wouldn't succumb to that desire. Nothing was more important than finishing what he had begun. No matter the discomfort it caused him. Glancing across at Aleece, he hoped she would open her eyes and smile at him. If only for the calming effect to his soul.

Light appeared on the horizon as the car's GPS alerted him to a change in route. 2.6 miles later he turned off onto the sleepy streets of Gallup, NM. There was a gas station ahead, so he pulled in to refuel. From here on in they would be traveling dirt roads. There was no indication on the navigation they would have another chance to obtain gas.

Both women stirred under the lights at the pump before resettling. He refueled quickly so they could be on the road again. Naelah had told them much about Molab on the flight and he was intrigued to meet the man. She said he had been one of a handful of Valdan who offered to spend stretches of time awake in the world to maintain contact with humans.

Because of this Caneon could only suppose the man would appear older than the other Valdan. After all, he was one of only two who was still alive after centuries awake. His sole purpose, to maintain a path for the Valdan to regain a place in the world once Dark Ones were dealt with, kept him close to humanity. He had chosen a place to live removed from them, in the heart of the Navajo Nation, so that he could maintain his secret origins.

Caneon expected the alien man to be as distinguished as Naelah. How he had managed to hide what he was from humans was a story Caneon was dying to hear. This man had to have witnessed some of the greatest moments in human existence. He was a cornucopia of eyewitness information not to be found in history books the world round. It was thrilling.

On his own world Molab had been a bit of a historian as well, according to Naelah. Caneon knew that despite their physiological differences the two of them would bond over this shared love.

Back on their way, it wasn't long before they were speeding down red dirt roads with a plume of dust billowing out behind them. He was eager to finally meet this other alien. The house they pulled up in front of was nothing like he had imagined.

This was a dirt hut. Literally. The walls were made of hand formed clay bricks. Straw could be seen peeking from the joints. Hand hewn logs poked from the tops of the walls with rough planks nailed along the top of them to form a front porch. The roof was made of rough planks as well. How did the man keep out the rain? Or the rodents?

Naelah exited the back seat as an older man ambled across the front porch. He was tall like the others with white hair shifting as the others did. It was contained in a queue at the back of his neck and flowed like shimmering silk to his waist. The man's face was darkened from the sun like the cracked clay he lived upon.

The two embraced on the front porch. For the first time since she woke, Caneon saw her body relax. This man was safety to her. He wondered about the relationship. The alien races longevity and stasis pods made deciphering these things impossible.

Him and Aleece hesitated to join the alien reunion as another man engaged with them. He was taller than the others with over-grown hair the color of dirty oil. His leather jacket and rough jeans made him someone they would have been hesitant to approach regardless. Naelah embraced him as well but the awkwardness translated even to the car's occupants.

Caneon would have sat in the isolation forever, but Aleece opened her door and he felt there was no choice but to follow. He could not abandon her to these beings before him. No matter how much his knees trembled as he stood. Naelah had been unsettling in her foreignness but bearably nonthreatening. These men brought home the danger of associating with unknown things.

On the porch the threesome turned to Caneon and Aleece as they approached. Having their eyes trained on him brought beads of sweat to his temple. He would tell Aleece they were from the heat if she commented.

"Molab, Quelis, these are Caneon and Aleece. My help mates for this journey. Please, welcome them." Naelah gestured to them as if presenting them as offering. Talk about creepy.

"Hey."

"Welcome."

The two men spoke at the same time. Their carriage was relaxed and casual to the point of being mistakable for human. Caneon felt his muscles unknot as they extended hands to be shaken like normal people. He fulfilled his part of the greeting with hope in his heart. These men knew how to work amid the world. They could be far more helpful than the inexpert woman he'd spent the last two days with.

The cabin's interior was much more sophisticated than Caneon had expected it to be. Breathtaking desert scenery was depicted in several paintings which shared space with pot shelves holding pristine examples of Native American pottery. He suspected that were these to be dated they originated from tribes that disappeared centuries ago despite their new appearance.

Caneon's perusal of the Native décor was interrupted when his eyes landed upon Drew. The kid sat composedly on one of the sizable couches centered in the middle of the room around a raw wood coffee table situated on a hand-woven Navajo rug.

"Drew." Caneon inclined his head at the youth.

"About time you got here." The kid's harsh tone was mitigated by the relief in his eyes.

"There is no possible way we could have arrived here any sooner than we did." Caneon informed him. Did the kid think they could have magically teleported? Were they going to search for unicorns next?

"Yeah. That's what you think." Drew stood. Caneon watched his legs wobble before they attained enough strength to hold him up.

"You've been watching too much TV. Typical of your generation." Caneon retorted.

"Where's Trenton and the others?" Aleece interjected herself into the conversation. Caneon was taken aback to realize the others weren't sitting on the other couches.

"Alaska." Drew seemed to have a thought strike him. He turned his attention to the device in his hands as kids his age tended to do at random times. Caneon dismissed him and went to obtain answers from an adult.

Approaching the three gathered in the kitchen area of the great room was enough to make his stomach churn. Forcing a nonchalance he never felt, he walked up to their group with confidence. They were deep in conversation and barely acknowledged him.

"We need to find the scientists. Even if they haven't accomplished their goal there should be progress." Quelis was saying.

"I've searched for decades. They hid too well. We need to target the Dark Ones that haven't escaped. Be proactive. There are modern weapons that could possibly have an effect." Molab shook his head setting wisps of snowy hair free from confinement. "There's little chance we'll find the hidden lab. Let it go."

"We need to look again. They have the best chance of having an effective weapon. Who would have better information?" Naelah asked.

"Maybe I would." Caneon inserted.

"How could you possibly know where Valdan had hidden their secret research facility?" Molab sneered.

"I've…we've been researching diligently for more than a year. We were able to ascertain the location of the temple in Mexico where Naelah was. I believe we may have clues to the placement of this facility in the information we've compiled at my home. If my assistant Megan were here, she would agree with me. Where is she by the way?" Caneon turned to each of the men in turn for an answer. He received nothing but blank stares.

"Megan, she's short. Black hair. Feisty. No? Neither of you know who I am talking about." Caneon turned to pin the young man with a glare. Drew had been in the process of joining them when he stopped dead at the look.

"I tried to tell you. Maybe if you listened to someone other than yourself once in a while." The kid muttered.

"Complain later. Explain now." Caneon worked to unclench his hands.

"Quelis here didn't want to talk to us. I had to follow him. Trenton went back to Anchorage to get Lynea and Megan. I emailed them." Drew's exaggerated hand gestures illustrated his choppy speech.

Caneon's face flushed as he fought to control his pique. A large hand landed on his shoulder.

"Easy man. He couldn't know I was gonna take him through the Hub. It's on me that his friends got left behind." Quelis stepped past him on his way to the back room. He passed through the archway without a backward glance.

Obviously, the man considered the conversation over. Aleece approached his side hesitantly. He tried to invoke an upturn of the lips for her. But it fell short. She reached over and grasped his hand. For the first time in his life he was glad to have missed the social mark.

Drew followed the dark-haired man into the far room. Caneon couldn't imagine what interaction could possibly go on between them. He hesitated to assuage his curiosity. Naelah and Molab were still occupying the kitchen.

"My home is the best place to go for information." Caneon stated emphatically.

"I've exhausted every database I could find. What makes you believe there would be new information at your home?" Molab's ebony eyes searched for the answers deep in Caneon's own but he wasn't going to back down.

"What do you have to lose, by looking there?" Caneon countered.

"Nothing but time." The old man stated with the arch of a snowy eyebrow.

"Where is your home, human?" Quelis asked from behind Caneon. He nearly jumped out of his skin at the man's voice. Primal instinct propelled him to face the predatory man. Fear sealed his lips shut. He very suddenly lost all desire to have this man in his home.

Drew reached around the large man and handed his tablet over. Caneon caught a glimpse of a digital map as it was passed. He had to restrain himself from darting across the room and knocking it out of the man's hands.

"I know of a Hub near there. We can go now. Everyone ready?" Quelis handed the tablet back to Drew nonchalantly.

"I will need a brief time to pack and prepare for my absence." Molab nodded at the other man before exiting the room.

Naelah took a place on the couch previously occupied by Drew. Aleece tugged on his hand to pull him over to the one opposite it. He had no compulsion to sit but he was loath to release her hand and remain standing. Once settled, his foot began to bounce off the floor in a spasmodic rhythm.

Drew perched on the arm of the sofa near Naelah while he tapped at his tablet. Whatever he was doing he was absorbed. Caneon was unsure if he should be angered or impressed by the kid's acceptance of their new reality.

"I've told Trenton to take the women back to Caneon's." Drew threw over his shoulder towards the archway where Quelis had once again disappeared. A grunt was the only response.

The silence stretched into spider webs tangling Caneon's thoughts. There was much that he wanted to know, but his mind refused to order any of it into reasonable questions. Aleece sat passively beside him entranced by a painting of a massive rock formation against a brilliant blue sky.

Molab entering the room jerked Caneon from his reverie. Time had obviously passed as the shadows now fell in altered patterns on the coffee table. How much he had lost was unknowable. Drew stood with the ease of youth slipping his tablet into his backpack in one fluid motion. A flick of the wrist later and the pack was on his back as he walked through the arch.

Naelah stood and followed Drew with Molab close behind. Caneon's mind buzzed with unasked questions as he dragged Aleece from the couch. She blinked sleepily at him while she gained her feet. They didn't have time for her to reorient. Caneon guided her into the next room. Quelis had already stated he had no problem leaving people behind.

The others were grouped inside a circle inscribed on the floor. A glow emanated from it as they awaited him and Aleece. Hustling forward they had barely passed the threshold when the light increased exponentially. His skull pulsated in his skin. He recited Beowulf to focus his energies.

The light receded as his stomach quivered. Forcing the contents thereof to settle, he ventured a look around their new scenery. Instantaneous transportation was reality. The walls around them were weathered stone dripping green algae. More natural than man-made they were none the less mostly square. There was a door on one side but otherwise he saw no openings.

The Valdan strode resolutely to the door. Drew trailed behind them on sturdy legs. Aleece was bent double next to him. Still fearing abandonment, he encouraged her to move. It wouldn't do to have her vomit, but they had no time to coddle her.

Quelis opened the stone door using the keypad next to it. A blue light flashed under his palm before the sound of rock grinding filled the room. Once they had cleared the doorway a blue light flashed around the jam and the door shut firmly behind them with nary a seam to betray its existence.

They climbed upwards over rocks and rubble until they emerged through a crevice into a ravine. The sound of a bubbling brook reminded Caneon he had failed to imbibe for hours. Reaching around he found his pack absent from its spot on his back. It was disconcerting to realize he'd left it in the car at Molab's home. There had been time. Why had he sat on the couch instead of retrieving it?

They left the rental there as well. He would need to send someone from the company to retrieve it. He supposed they would be willing to send the luggage to his home address for a fee. Where had his brain gone?

The group veered down the interior of the small canyon until they found a trail. From there it was a short hike to a parking lot. The trail head was clearly marked as one he had often traversed over the years. They were less than a fifteen-minute drive from his house.

"Caneon, hey. I didn't realize you were back from your vacation." The man talking was gangly in his khaki pants and sports polo. He was also one of Caneon's frequent hiking partners as they both agreed it was the closest either would come to team sports.

"I just arrived back." Caneon's head spun at the collision of two worlds.

"You just finish the trail?" His friend asked.

"Yes. Yes. It was an early start for us." Caneon ignored the other man's surprised look. Turning to his group he found himself standing alone. Behind the other man's back he caught a glimpse of copper hair turning onto the road.

"Could I impose upon you? I find myself deserted. Would you loan me your car? I'll have it returned before you finish your descent." The other man grimaced but handed over the keys. Snatching them, Caneon dashed to the older SUV.

Decorum aside he hastened to pick his companions up. There was a bit of a squeeze to fit all the oversized bodies into the vehicle, but they managed. Back at his house it felt like years had passed since he departed. He let the others in the front door before loading his mountain bike, so he could return the SUV.

"Want company?" Drew stood by the SUV with his hands in his pockets.

"Why would you leave the interesting company inside to ride with me?" Caneon wasn't sure he wanted the passenger.

"I wanted to pick your brain for a bit. About our new friends." Drew scuffed at the dirt under his sneaker.

"Suit yourself." Caneon wanted to get back to Aleece as quickly as possible. He threw the big vehicle into reverse the moment Drew's door slammed shut.

"Do we buy this whole good alien, bad alien thing?" Drew spoke to the passenger side window.

"Why would we not?" Caneon could see no possible reason for them to lie.

"It's all so black and white, you know."

"No, I do not know." Caneon put all his frustration into the words.

"People aren't like that. We can be both. Good and Bad." Drew stuck his fingernail into his mouth and began to gnaw. Caneon marveled at the kid's ability to develop a new bad habit out of thin air.

"They are not people. Technically we do not know what they are. Humanoid yes but not human." He felt it was of great import to clarify the difference to the star struck kid. "We must resist the urge to judge them by our standards."

"Yeah, yeah. I get it. Just seems like we aren't getting the whole picture." Finished with the first nail, Drew moved to the next one.

"You've seemed pretty enamored of our new companions. Why the sudden change?" Caneon resisted the urge to glance at the kid again.

"I dunno." Drew slunk down in his seat, stretching the seat belt to its limits.

Caneon made the right turn into the trail head's parking lot. Whatever was gnawing at the kid was going to have to wait. They had a trek back to the house still. Parking with haste, he removed his bike from the back then put the keys into the compartment for the gas cap.

"You'll need to keep up." He called to Drew as he mounted his bike.

"Sure, whatever man." Drew took off at a trot before Caneon could object to the slang.

Pedaling past the kid was one of the most satisfying moments he had experienced in the last few weeks. The wind rushed past his face as he navigated the familiar landmarks. Pulling into his driveway, he took the time to place his equipment back into its rightful places. Drew came huffing into the yard as he finished up.

"Shall we." Caneon indicated the front door. Drew waved him on as he walked the yard, hands on hips, chest heaving.

The one complication Caneon never anticipated was walking in to find a fourth large being sitting at his kitchen table conversing with the three he already knew. The man's hair fell in waves of golds and yellows as he turned and pinned Caneon with his onyx gaze.

Ascertaining he was face to face with a predator, Caneon arrested all unnecessary movement. It was a futile effort. His body double crossed him. The progression across the room was the worst betrayal Caneon had ever suffered. Tears leaked from his eyes as he fought to resist.

"DEXON!" Naelah's voice pierced through the yoke he found himself under. Slumping against the nearest piece of furniture kept his face from meeting the hardwood.

"Sorry." The blond man shrugged his shoulders like a child caught stealing candy. Naelah's frown showed no signs of leaving her face.

"What's goin' on?" Drew was outlined in the doorway as Caneon twisted to see him. He wanted to frantically motion for the kid to run, but his arms ached when he tried to move them.

"My brother was just about to offer his apologies to our friend." Naelah pinned the offender with her amethyst gaze.

"Of course." The chiseled man rose from his chair and approached Caneon. "I was unaware you were friend, not foe. My sincerest regrets."

Caneon jerked his muscles to attention as he slid backwards along the wall. It was retreat and he cared little who knew it. The smirk on the large man's face sparked what minuscule bits of pride he had left. Wrapping them tightly around his bruised body he drew himself tall and stood his ground.

His knees nearly caved as the other man stretched out a massive hand. Bracing, he extended his own to meet the alien man halfway. His limb felt unrealistically small inside the other's grip. Every effort of his body was focused on controlling the trembling threatening to overwhelm him.

"See, sister. I can play nice." Dexon's low chuckle vibrated through the handclasp and into Caneon's soul.

The second he was released Caneon put as much distance as he could between himself and the aliens. His life's dream was a nightmare he couldn't awaken from. Lynea's chair sat in its usual place near the front door. He sunk into it gladly.

| 17 |

Chapter

Lynea contemplated Megan's profile as they shuffled toward the airport terminal. The smaller woman had achieved a state of semi functional coma that defied the laws of medical science. Fever raged in her body, soaking the t-shirt she wore in sweat and leaving her eyes glazed and unfocused. Her pale skin had taken on an ashen tinge in the fluorescent lighting.

Megan's spiky black hair however, managed to look the same. Maybe it had always been bed head chic. Her thick goth makeup was worn off from the nights of fitful dreams. It was a definite improvement in Lynea's opinion, but she knew the younger woman wouldn't appreciate how young and vulnerable it left her looking.

She ate and drank if they told her to and that was a creepy amount of power to have over someone because she was running on auto pilot. Conversation went nowhere. Questions went unanswered. She mumbled semi coherently on occasion, but Lynea hadn't found meaning in it. She was left hoping Megan's ability to keep moving meant she was fighting her way back to health. It was a thin thread to hold onto.

In the meantime, Trenton had returned to them minus Drew. Lynea wasn't sure what she believed about his cockamamie story. He was adamantly denying it, but she was positive he had allowed Drew to be kidnapped by the alien they were supposed to be recruiting.

What a huge relief she felt when Drew emailed to meet up at Caneon's house. His being alive and well almost overshadowed her joy of going home. It had been too long since she'd laid eyes on her favorite faces. She couldn't wait to wrap her kids up in her arms. And serve Jared with divorce papers. Life was short. There wasn't enough of it to waste anymore with a cheating ass.

Megan had responded well to the news. If her blank smile could be considered well. Either way she cooperated nicely through the never-ending security measures. It only took one set of uncomfortable questions for Lynea to decide to defend her autistic niece. People gave them space after that.

Boarding the plane was uneventful. Trenton wrestled Megan's carry on so Lynea could concentrate on the young woman herself. Strapping her in, Lynea took the seat near the window. Trenton was left with the aisle. He glowered as passengers jostled him on their way past.

Mid-flight Lynea was zoned into a near sleep when a blood curdling scream broke from Megan's mouth. The younger woman began to claw at the seat belt still fastened around her waist. Trenton worked to hold back her hands as her nails drew blood from both of them.

Lynea reached to unbuckle the belt hoping it would settle Megan down. To her distress, once the buckle was free Megan arched her back in an attempt to break free of the seat and Trenton's confinement. His arms strained to hold her back as she lunged for the aisle.

Flight attendants came running at the disturbance. Lynea shouted over Megan's noises of protest trying to explain about the autistic nature of her niece. Uncomfortable looks passed between the man and woman as they tried to decide if they should intervene or not. The man looked ready to jump in when Megan went limp in Trenton's arms.

Lynea took her pulse as the male flight attendant raced to the pilot's cabin. Great. Now they would want to turn around or land early. What had made them think they could fly with her like this? Megan's steady pulse reassured Lynea as Trenton placed the young woman's inert body back in its seat.

Buckling the belt once more Lynea settled Megan's head at a comfortable angle. Trenton was charming the remaining flight attendant into complacency. He was rather talented at it with his rugged good looks and dazzling smile. She nodded understandingly before heading off to find her coworker.

"What was that?" Lynea leaned across Megan to hiss.

"Me getting the flight crew off our backs. You're welcome." Trenton huffed.

"Not that. I mean the screaming. What set her off?" Lynea glanced at Megan's still unconscious face.

"No clue. Did you catch what she was on about?" Trenton leaned in closer to Lynea as he lowered his voice.

"No. I was too focused on everybody else staring and pointing at us." They were close enough Lynea could smell his aftershave.

"She was sputtering about Tyrone's body. Were they a thing?"

"No. He wanted to be, but she paid him zero attention. Besides this is hardly the time she's going to be having fantasies." Lynea scowled at him.

"Good point. So why did she rouse from her stupor to yell at us about it?" Trenton scratched at his stubble as he spoke.

"Who knows. She's fevered and delusional. Even if there's a purpose to what she's saying there's such a small likelihood we would interpret it right. When she gets this blood out of her system, we can ask her what she meant." Lynea leaned back into her own seat. "Let's just get through the rest of the flight without drawing any more attention. We'll discuss it with the others once we're home."

"Agreed." Trenton place his head back on his head rest.

Lynea spent the remainder of the trip focused on the view outside her window. She couldn't wait to see her babies. They never let her call them that anymore, but no amount of growing up was going to make them anything else.

The first sight of her city set her nerves tingling. She decided then and there she would put Trenton and Megan in a cab then head straight home. He could get her to Caneon's house on his own. Lynea would meet them after she reunited with her kids.

At the curb, Trenton barely resisted the idea. He was on his way to the rendezvous with such small effort it eased her guilt. Taking a cab of her own she spent the time texting her kids with no response. She wasn't even sure why she paid for their cells when she could never get hold of them.

The front door was locked, which took her by surprise. They never locked the door unless they were on vacation. She had texted Lydee and Tanner several times from Alaska. There had been no mention of going away with their dad. She was going to be pissed if Jared had taken them out of town without notifying her.

Lynea unlocked the door and dragged her carry on behind her. Her other bags stood dejectedly on the front stoop. Someone would haul them in eventually.

"Lydee...Tanner. Jared?" Lynea yelled names as she made the rounds of the lower floor. No answer. Her carry on was abandoned at the foot of the stairs as she ascended. "Tanner." "Lydee." "Jared." Another round of shouted names garnered no response.

She opened each door as she passed, hoping to find one of her kids jamming away unaware with their headphones on. No luck. Her chest tightened as she searched for and found suitcases. The bathroom counters were still cluttered with essential grooming and personal hygiene products. Where was her family?

Returning to the first floor, she pulled out her cell and started dialing. One number and then another went unanswered. Dialing her husband's office was a desperate attempt to receive answers. The receptionist informed her Jared hadn't been in or called in two days. His personal assistant came on the line before she could hang up and begged to have him contact her the second he was found. Brazen tramp.

One thing Lynea was certain of was Jared's commitment to his job. If they didn't know where he was then no one would. Nothing on this earth would convince him to run off without covering his bases there. Nothing good anyways. Her pulse thrummed in her ears. Falling into a nearby chair she fought back the blackness threatening.

There had to be a reasonable explanation. Another round of calls to her family's cells resulted in nothing more than frantic voice mails. Needing to move she made her way once more through her home. This time she searched for clues, something out of place or broken, a ransom demand, anything. Nothing stood out.

Her head felt heavy on her neck as she strained to think of something she could do. Something that would tell her what had happened to the people she loved. Turning in slow circles her eyes refused to focus on the innocuous décor around her.

A tinkling jingle from the other room brought her back to the here and now. Rushing for the electronic noise she searched frantically, willing it to continue. There, next to the front door was Tanners backpack. Her fingers fumbled through the debris of a seventeen-year old boys' life. Amid the sweatshirts and stinky shoes, she found his phone.

The ringer was set as low as it could be. It was a miracle she had heard it. Making her way past the lock codes she was astounded at the number of texts and calls he had missed. The oldest were over 48 hours ago. Shortly after she had finished talking to him.

He would never have left this here. Something was terribly wrong. Her first call was to the police station. The officer who answered was very sympathetic until he had more information. Once he heard her husband was missing as well, there wasn't anything she could say to discount his theory that they had all gone off on vacation together without her.

She knew to her very soul that wasn't what was going on. This had something to do with what they had stirred up in Mexico. Her gut was screaming that it did. She shouldn't have called home until this was over. They were advanced aliens. Who knew what they could track?

Gathering her purse from the counter where she had dropped it, she let herself into the garage. Her crossover was parked in its usual spot next to Jared's. More evidence he hadn't gone anywhere on his own. Hopping in, she headed to Caneon's house. Her friends would help her find her family. She knew it.

Caneon's came into view the second her nerves reached their breaking point. Stretched beyond reason she pulled her crossover into his drive at an angle. The front tires veered onto his grass while she shifted into park and fell out of the car door. Her feet landed beneath her with moments to spare causing her to lurch forward as she caught her balance.

Her eyes registered Drew in the doorway but that wasn't going to slow her crossing the lawn. She didn't have time for niceties. He never even turned to see who was careening into the yard before she barreled into his back. Expecting him to give way, she was stopped in her tracks.

"Excuse me." She huffed. When that got no response, she proceeded to tug on his arm. "Drew. Let me in. I need to talk to the group."

He finally turned his head to look at her, but the minuscule movement of his body gave her no room to squeeze by. How had she never realized how solid this kid was?

"Lynea?" His eyes where unfocused and his voice came out slurry. Had they been letting him drink? One time she lets it ride in Mexico and all the rules get blurry. If she weren't so focused on her family right now she would stop to give him a lecture.

"Yes, it's me. Now move." She tried to push at his shoulder to create room, but he didn't budge. "Drew. Let me by." It felt like she was talking to a statue. He shifted on his feet finally giving her a glimpse of the interior.

A tall blond man took up the center of the tableau. Aleece stood in the doorway to the kitchen and Lynea glimpsed Caneon sitting in her chair on Drew's right. Naelah stood next to the table as if she had just stood, her chair toppled behind her. Two alien men perched opposite her ready to engage something.

"WHAT IN THE HELL IS GOING ON?" Lynea yelled the question over Drew's shoulder. The sudden noise seemed to break everyone free. It also brought the blonde's onyx gaze to bear on her. Pinned where she stood all thought fled her brain as she drowned in his stare.

"Lynea? Are you okay?" Drew was shaking her shoulders as he dragged her through the doorway. She shook her head to clear the fog.

"Yeah. I'm fine. I guess. Who is that?" She didn't dare take her eyes off Drew's to indicate who she was asking about.

"Naelah's friends. Quelis and Molab. She told us about them at camp. Remember?" He was looking at her like she was an addled old lady.

"Right. No, the other one." She could only focus on the one.

"Her brother. Dexon, I think." He shrugged his shoulders like it was no big deal but the look in his eyes was all warning. Had the kid always been this capable of subterfuge? Lynea was feeling like she had missed a lot of nuance with the people around her.

"Oh. She never mentioned a brother." It sounded stupid and inane even to her own ears.

"That is because I believed him to be dead." Naelah glided toward Dexon as she spoke to Lynea who hadn't realized they could hear her clear across the room. "He had just started to fill us in on how he came to be here among us when Caneon walked in."

Lynea could tell she was missing key pieces of information in that explanation, but her family's troubles had just returned to her. There was no time to listen to this man's back story, even if he was an alien. She needed to focus on getting her family home to safety.

"My family is missing." She directed her comments at Caneon for no reason other than it was his house.

"What exactly do you mean by missing?" He asked from his seat on her office chair. It took her longer than she would have liked to relay the information to his exacting standards. "I see."

"You believe the Dark Ones have something to do with your family." Dexon pinned her eyes when he spoke.

Unable to process, she resorted to a nod. Naelah moved to fill the space between them and Lynea found herself released. Moving so that he couldn't catch her again so easily, she focused on the alien woman.

"Can you help me find them?"

"Possibly. A more pressing concern is why they took them. Do others of your group have loved ones close by? People they have contacted as you did." Naelah made a point to lock eyes with each human in the room. "It is possible they are attempting to thwart us by taking them as Thralls."

The two men Lynea had identified as Quelis and Molab nodded along with Naelah. This was a tactic they had seen before then. In a war that stretched centuries, there was probably very little that had not been tried. Her drive to get her children back safely intensified three-fold.

"How do we get them back?" Lynea moved to grasp the alien woman's sleeve before thinking twice about it. Pulling her hand back to her side, she clutched at her pant leg in frustration.

"That is not a question I'm prepared to answer." Naelah's calm voice was wearing through the last of Lynea's composure.

"I'll go in and get them back." Dexon asserted.

"No, you won't" Four voices responded in chorus. Lynea was shocked to realize hers had been among them. She didn't want this person anywhere near her children and she certainly didn't trust him to bring them back safely.

"It's the only way. Sorche will be planning for anyone else." His voice rose as his sister continued to stare immutably.

"Your Mate will have planned for us. She will tear you to pieces the second she sees you." Naelah's shoulders flung back, she looked ready to throttle Dexon if he argued.

"I love you too sister, but you know I am the only one with a chance here." He leaned against the wall near him with smug delight.

"I can go." The alien who looked like a member of a biker gang spoke up.

"Why would any of the Dark Ones allow you in Quelis? Last I heard you were enemy number one." Dexon smirked at the other man.

"You've been locked away a long time. Things change. I have a way in." Quelis moved aggressively towards the blonde. His sapphire eyes sparking as his fists balled. Lynea eased her way toward Aleece. The other woman had remained strangely silent this whole time.

"I'm the way in." Dexon's teeth ground as he spoke. Lynea increased her speed.

"You are a disgrace to your Line." Quelis drew even with the shorter man, puffing his broad chest as Lynea reached Aleece.

"Calm, my friends." Molab pushed between the two men creating a buffer. "We're all on the same side now. Aren't we?"

The aggression ratcheted down at least two notches at the elder man's voice. Lynea stood quietly next to Aleece unsure of why she had felt such an urgent need to reach her. Glancing at her, she found Aleece smiling ruefully back.

A knock at the door had everyone trained that way. Drew was closest, so he walked over and opened it. Trenton stood on the step holding Megan's arm. Shame washed over Lynea that she had forgotten all about them. Megan was next to helpless and Trenton had proven to be less of a hero than Lynea had first thought him.

"Trenton!" Aleece rushed across the room heedless of who she might trample and threw herself into her brother's arms. He let go of Megan long enough to wrap his arms around Aleece.

Lynea was surprised to see Megan beeline for the golden-haired alien. It was the first time she had propelled herself anywhere in days. Not to mention her target was on the psychopathic side. It was a second's work to realize she needed to intervene.

Megan reached Dexon before Lynea could stop her. Cringing inside, she reached forward to grab the young woman by the shirt and yank her back. Only her hand was stopped before she could get that far.

Molab stood looking at her as held onto her. "Let this play out. Your friend has been infected. She should have passed through it by now. That she has not is a very bad sign. He has a better chance of helping her than you do."

Lynea couldn't imagine Dexon helping anyone, but Molab spoke logic so she was willing to give it a minute. With the full understanding that she would make someone pay if anything bad happened to her friend. She tried hard to convey that message with her eyes.

Shifting her focus, she found Dexon holding Megan's head lightly between his hands. The young woman had tilted her face up as if enjoying the warmth of the sun. Their eyes closed, they reminded Lynea of the meditation posters at her gym.

The picture was shattered when Megan started to jerk violently in his grasp. Lynea lunged to catch the girl as she collapsed. Holding her seizing friend, she glared ferociously up at the male she held responsible.

He surprised her by squatting down to tenderly smooth the hair from Megan's forehead. Her spasms eased immediately. Within moments, they had tapered away. He placed his hand onto Lynea's shoulder in what she thought was an awkward attempt at comfort.

"She's clinging to the remnants of Sorche's blood in her veins so that she can stay in the Twain. Her body is rejecting the effort. It's causing her system to shut down. She either needs to be purged or given more. It's your choice." Dexon's eyes contained nothing more than the facts he was stating.

"Why would she want to stay in this Twain place? That doesn't make sense." Lynea could see the honest concern in his face but her heart wasn't buying it.

"Someone named Tyrone. She won't leave without him and he can't leave until you all retrieve his body."

"How do you know that name? Who told him about Tyrone?" Lynea's head went on the swivel as she tried to find the culprit. Negative answers where all she received.

"Megan told me." Dexon smiled sheepishly. "Because Sorche and I have shared blood in the Mating ritual I carry her receptors in me and am able to communicate with her Thralls. Kind of. Your friend was desperate to share the information with someone and Sorche hasn't been able to override her will yet, so it was easy."

Lynea took a moment to gather Megan up off the floor and lead her to a chair. Anything to give herself a moment to put the pieces in place. Logically, if you ignored all the rules of science, or maybe if you expanded them, what he was saying could be true. If it was, what did they do about it?

| 18 |

Chapter

Drew wanted desperately to dash across the room and help Lynea with Megan, but he had seen firsthand what Dexon had done to Caneon. The idea of being someone's puppet hardened his heart. No matter how much that left him feeling like a cowardly jerk.

Shifting on his feet, he turned toward Caneon to find the man had finally vacated Lynea's office chair. It couldn't be the fear of Aleece seeing him weak that brought him to his feet. That had already happened. So, what had spurred the man to full height and posturing like he'd never been down?

Drew himself, felt like dropping to the floor and creeping out of the house. His mind was full of Trina and even his dad. If these creatures were using the people they love as some kind of shield, then he needed to find those people and protect them. Only, what if they were already taken? Then he needed this group to stand a chance of getting them back. His mind was splitting down the middle.

His backpack was propped against the wall where he had tossed it earlier. If he could get to it, his tablet would let him reach out to

Trina at least. But the tension in the room had his nerves screaming. A wrong move could detonate the whole thing.

Shifting to his left, he could see a path behind Trenton and Aleece, close to the wall. Using them as cover he slunk nearer his goal. No one even glanced his way. Taking heart, he slid along the wall at snail's pace until his foot was within range of the backpack. A quick jerk and he had the handle caught on the toe of his sneaker. A peek to make sure no one was watching, and he jerked the bag his way.

He had never done such a slow squat in his life and his legs burned but the zipper was finally in his grasp. Another quick glance and he was holding the lifeline in his hands. He reversed the squat as slowly as he had gone down while fumbling to turn the tablet on and silence it at the same time.

When he looked up one last time he found all eyes on him. Crap.

"What?" His best hope was to play dumb.

"What are your intentions with that device?" Quelis stalked across the room towards him.

"Nothing. Why?" Drew wasn't sure defying the muscular alien was a great idea, but it was for Trina.

"Really? Then why are you sneaking around? We can't afford for there to be proof of our existence." Quelis stuck his hand out in the universal sign for give it over. Drew clutched it harder.

"Duh. I'm not gonna tell anyone. I swear. I just wanna check stuff."

"Leave him be. It's harmless." Naelah spoke to Quelis from across the room.

"You don't understand the damage their internet can do to us. One overly ambitious youth and his toys is all it takes. Give me the device, kid." Quelis moved in closer to Drew, towering over him by a foot and a half at least.

"No." Drew's knees went soft as he struggled to hold Quelis' sapphire gaze.

"Don't be an idiot. Whatever your trying to do, it's not worth the risk. Give me the device and let's get to figuring out how to put the Dark Ones down." Quelis made a grab for the tablet that Drew narrowly evaded.

"I need to know if Trina is ok." He blurted as he put the tablet behind his back like a defiant eight-year-old.

"Who is Trina?" Naelah glided towards them.

"She's the girl he's enamored with." Caneon injected to Drew's irritation.

"I see. How will this device help you to ascertain her well-being?" Naelah's head tilted as she spoke.

"They use these devices to access their internet and communicate on platforms they call social media." Quelis stated factually. "We can't have him posting about this on those platforms. I can take the device. There's a minuscule chance he will be injured."

"I'm not going to say anything about you. You can watch over my shoulder." Drew's voice had turned to pleading.

"Use my phone to call her kid." Trenton reached into his pocket and pulled out his smartphone.

"Yeah, I don't think so. In fact, we are going to need everyone's devices." Quelis reached for Drew's tablet again as Molab grabbed the phone from Trenton's hand. Quelis didn't turn a second of attention to the contention that caused; his focus was solely on Drew. "Let's not make this a big deal."

Drew kept the tablet firmly behind his back, waiting to see if his friends where going to stick with him or cave to the alien's orders. Quelis shook his head and sighed as he advanced on Drew.

"Stop wasting time. Look." Dexon held a phone up for the black-haired alien to see. Drew couldn't decide if the Valdan had been carrying it the whole time or taken it from someone. It didn't matter. What he was showing them did.

Leaning forward gave Drew a descent view of the screen angled at Quelis. It showed a news report with the tag "Vampires terrorize downtown" in bold letters across the bottom of the screen. There was a lagging video playing.

Even with the bad lighting and the focus shifting constantly there was no mistaking the group of Dark Ones tearing into people on the sidewalk. Bodies were being flung aside like broken toys as the remaining humans stood transfixed waiting for their turn to be mauled.

Drew strained his eyes scanning faces for anyone he knew. Sorche's flaming hair marked her from the shadowy sidelines of a nearby building. The gratified smile on her face chilled him to his bones. Next to her stood Tyrone, gazing vacantly into the fray. A petite blonde shifted behind his broad shoulders giving Drew a fleeting glimpse, but it was enough. Trina.

Pulse racing in his ears, he snatched the phone from Dexon's grip. The alien made a halfhearted grab, but Drew was past them and halfway to Lynea already. Skidding to a stop by her side he placed the phone in her face. "Look."

Lynea reached up to steady the device. A tear slid silently down her face as she processed what she was seeing. Eventually she reached up and touched the screen with a finger. More tears followed. Pushing the phone away she turned back to Megan. "I can't watch that anymore."

"What do we do?" Drew didn't even know who he was asking.

"We find a cure." Caneon joined his friends.

"How do we do that?" Lynea's voice shook.

"The scientists. They were working on a cure. We locate them, and we obtain a way to stop this." Caneon reached over and placed an awkward hand on Lynea's shoulder. "We'll save your children."

Motivated by his own words, Caneon moved into the research area and started opening files. Drew's step was lighter as he moved to his computer bank with a purpose. Firing the system up, he drummed his fingers while the whir of electronic motors brought his workstation to life. Once the screen lit up, he began to type. Something on this web was going to tell him how to save his girl.

Out of the corner of his eye he watched Lynea approach Dexon. He was afraid to know what the two were talking about. Whatever they were up to, he was positive it was about Megan. She was looking worse by the minute slumped on her chair like a sweaty rag doll.

He forced his mind to put all of that away in a box, so he could focus on finding the scientists. He started his own private search engine looking for key words while his fingers pulled up pages to scan for relevance. He felt someone walk up behind him, but there was no time to turn and figure out who it might be.

Molab's white hair fell onto Drew's shoulder as the Valdan man leaned forward. This close to it Drew became transfixed by the changing hues of it shifting from purest snow through palest gray.

"This right here. What is this?" Molab's finger rested near the middle of the screen. The picture he was pointing at was an island off the coast of Washington that some conspiracy website had flagged as a new area 51. Drew explained as the Valdan shook his head enthusiastically. "Yes, this is it. I have seen this landmark in reports from the base."

"Are you positive?" Caneon was peering over Drew's other shoulder at the peaks visible in the background of the picture.

"I have excellent memory." Molab stiffened as he scowled at the librarian.

"Very well. We can narrow our research to phenomenon among the islands and coastal areas of the pacific northwest region. That will be helpful." Caneon managed to look down his nose at the impossibly tall alien male. Drew almost smiled.

Focusing his search with added key words, he narrowed in on an island grouping perched mid-way between the Canadian and American border. Molab pulled a cylindrical device resembling a fancy pen from his pocket. He pressed on the point and the thing split in half and moved outwards until he was holding a screen only slightly larger than Drew's tablet. His finger flicked to the side and an image appeared. From Drew's perspective he could make out water and a rocky coast with a mountain rising over the top of towering evergreens.

"This is the image from the report. I haven't received a new one since we lost the Canadian outpost. Quelis come tell me about this. You were there, were you not?" Molab turned the screen to give everyone a glimpse.

"I sent you that picture. It's decades old. We lost the outpost up there over 130 years ago. Man, it was a brutal battle to defeat the Dark Ones who escaped that day. Many valiant warriors were sacrificed in the fight." Quelis spoke as he joined them. Over the alien's shoulder, Drew watched Lynea and Dexon head for the kitchen. He couldn't think of more unlikely pals, but these where strange times they were living in.

"There was once a Hub near there. Is it still operational?" Molab scratched his chin as he stared at his screen. "My data is incomplete due to the time I spent in stasis. Nothing works like it should since I lost Carene."

"I know old friend." Quelis rested his hand on the other man's shoulder as both men's heads bowed. "We carry the fallen with us."

"Yes, we do." Molab placed his hand briefly over the other mans before shaking off the somber moment.

"There is one near the city of Seattle. I've had to move it several times as the city has expanded, but its functional." Quelis pulled his own tablet from its satchel. A couple of flicks and it shifted to show a topographical map. His hand clenched as several red dots appeared on the screen. "They have beaten us to the area. It doesn't look like they have found the hub yet, but it won't be long. We need to go."

"Just like that? Suddenly, we know where your super-secret scientific headquarters are?" Drew was a little let down that it had been so easy.

"No, child. We now have a region. So, we go there and work to pick up a signal before the Dark Ones find us and kill us. Nothing about this will be easy." Quelis smirked at Drew. Obviously, it was gonna take a minute before withholding the tablet was forgiven. "Gather your friends. Make sure you warn them of the danger. Anyone who isn't up for it should stay behind."

Drew rose from his seat at the computer to find Caneon was the only human left in the room with them. Even Megan was gone. He hadn't thought she was capable of movement. He headed for the kitchen to find it empty. Unable to imagine anyone hanging out in Caneon's bedroom, he skipped it before giving the rest of the house a top to bottom search.

Returning to the front room he found the Valdan, minus Dexon, huddled around the table strategizing. Caneon sat with his books splayed out on his desk. He was absorbed in a passage when Drew approached.

"Where did everyone go?"

"Huh?" Caneon glanced up with a look Drew recognized all too well.

"No one is here." He leaned in and lowered his voice.

"Where did they go?" Caneon swiveled his head as if he expected them to suddenly appear.

"That's what I asked you." Drew straightened with an exasperated sigh. Trying to get Caneon to pay attention to the world around him was a lost cause once those books were open. "I think they might have gone to do something stupid."

"Like what?" Caneon's eyes had drifted back to the page of the book.

"Like going and getting themselves killed trying to rescue people from Sorche! Would you stop with the book? Dude, this is real." Drew reached down and flipped the book shut fully prepared for the man to wig out.

"Hey...Sorry, yes. What can we do?" Caneon rose out of his chair as Drew's jaw hit his chest. Talk about old dogs and new tricks.

"You can start with telling us why you think your friends have run off." Naelah's voice over his shoulder had Drew dodging on instinct. Turning, he found all three Valdan standing within arm's reach. It was creepy unreal how quietly they moved.

"Lynea. Her kids are there...with Sorche. We saw them on the video. Then I saw her and Dexon sneaking off earlier. I have no clue why Trenton and Aleece would have gone with them." Drew used a shrug to cover his step backwards. It probably wasn't enough room to give him a head start, but his nerves felt better.

"Dexon would have played on her nurturing instincts to manipulate her into helping him." Naelah's shoulders fell. "If they confront Sorche head on, as he wishes to, they will all be killed. I have sacrificed too much for my brother to allow his death now."

"So, we rescue him. As always." Quelis' words were calm but the fists at his sides screamed bad history.

"Where was this video taking place?" Molab glowered. "We should go there."

Darkness surrounded them as they made their way downtown from Caneon's house. Drew stared out the window of the SUV at the town where he had grown up. It was far from perfect. He'd spent more time than he could count on dreams of getting out, but he hated the idea of it being corrupted by these twisted aliens.

The industrial neighborhood they ended up in was a couple of blocks from the washed-up brick building Drew had seen in the video. The Valdan wanted to walk the rest of the way so they could scout. As he stepped out into the night air, he felt a weight settle on his chest.

Screams could be heard in the distance. Knowing they could keep their prey silent and complacent if they wanted to, made those screams even more nerve wrenching. The shadows hung deeper and noises amplified in his ears. A crunching to his left had him jerking around only to find Caneon standing with his palms up.

The Valdan were gone from sight. During his dad's worst drunken benders, he'd never felt this vulnerable. Standing still seemed like a great way to become easy prey, so he trotted down the nearest street. Caneon could follow or not.

Seconds later he heard the scuff of feet keeping pace with him. Minutes passed before he worked up his courage to verify it was just his friend. Caneon met his eyes without missing a step. The librarian was far more athletic than Drew would have given him credit for.

They reached a crossroads and Drew darted to the left. He was letting his gut lead the way. Halfway down the block he spotted someone crouched in a doorway. No Dark One would be that fearful. Drew approached cautiously so he didn't spook whoever it was.

He inched close enough to make out details in the shadows. That was Megan's favorite shirt. She was propped against the brick doorway in a way that was clearly not natural. One of the others must have left her there. Why did they desert her?

His nerves seized as he dreaded finding she was dead. Having to check Megan's pulse was now officially the hardest thing he had ever done. Creeping forward with his arm outstretched, he was relieved to see the rise and fall of her chest.

She was sweating so badly rivulets ran down her face. His own skin warmed from the heat radiating off her as he pulled her into a more comfortable position. When her eyes popped open, he about wet his pants. Reeling backwards, he felt Caneon's hands steady him from behind.

"Drew?" Megan's voice was raspy as she whipped her head around looking for who knows what.

"Yeah. It's me. Are you ok?" He leaned in as Caneon crouched beside her.

"I...I don't..know. Where am I? Is this downtown?" Her eyes continued to scan everything around them.

"Uh. Yeah. You don't remember how you got here?" He reached out to check her forehead with the back of his hand. He wasn't sure if he was doing it right, but it seemed like how you tested for fever. Her skin felt cooler the longer his hand stayed put.

"No. I...We were in Mexico. There was a lady with flame hair. She was crazy scary....." Her voice drifted off as her teeth started to chatter.

"It's imperative we return to the car quickly. She requires warmth." Caneon reached down to help her stand, pushing Drew out of the way. "Can you walk?"

"I'm not sure." She wobbled as Caneon wrapped his arm around her waist. With her leaning heavily on him, they teetered down the sidewalk. Drew followed behind, watching her almost pull Caneon over twice before he stepped in. They didn't have time for this.

Taking her back to the car was going to waste enough time. Not that she didn't look like she needed to be somewhere safe and warm. She did. But Trina and the rest of their friends were still out there. The faster he could get her settled into a safe place the faster he could get to helping the others.

He scooped her up from behind before she could object to the plan. It was a testament to how drained she was that she let her head rest on his shoulder without a single protest that his manhandling was invading her space.

They moved quickly after that. Locked into the SUV he realized they were only marginally safer. It was a mighty big, stationary target more than a protective outer shell. Could he really leave her here with nothing more than Caneon for protection? Glancing out the window he watched the shadows shift in a nearby alley. Had someone moved down there?

Megan slumped in the middle row with her head leaned against the door. Drew couldn't tell if she was awake and didn't want to ask. Whatever the others where up to, she wasn't going to know about it. Endless questions would only create more tension in the car.

The shadows around them had taken on a life of their own. He was constantly shifting in his seat trying to see all angles. There was no way he felt good about leaving Caneon and Megan. No matter how much a part of him wanted to leave the confining vehicle and search for his remaining friends. The other part screamed the only safe course was to start the engine and drive as far as the gas would take them.

Time stretched out into breakable pieces. His resolve teetered. One minute he was opening the door and the next he was fiddling with the keys. Caneon tried to talk to him but his lack of responses kept that from becoming anything.

Finally, a shadow formed into a person in the alley across from them. He didn't even care if it was friend or foe. He turned the key and scanned the darkness for others. Molab's white hair shimmered in the lights of a nearby sign and Drew felt the air leave his lungs in a gush before his body resumed normal function.

The Valdan strode across the street, headed for the passenger side. He had Drew's focus so completely it was a surprise when

Trenton opened the back door and Megan almost tumbled out. Cursing, Caneon reached across the seats to pull her back as Trenton gave a shove from outside the vehicle. She lashed back at Trenton, taking him by surprise. Drew smiled when he heard the macho man yelp.

Megan let Caneon's pull slide her over, so Trenton could climb in. She pushed the matted hair from her face as she righted herself. A quick glare slid to the right before she settled in.

"Where are the others?" Drew knew that Trenton being with Molab meant the two parties had met up. He hated that being trapped in the dark car had left him out of the action.

"We don't know," Trenton growled.

"We were separated. A pack of Thrall's chased us down a side street. By the time we lost them and circled back the others were gone. So, we came here hoping they had returned." Molab scanned the area around the vehicle like he expected something to pop out of the dark. "We should make our way to the transportation Hub. It's imperative we locate the research post. The others will follow us to Seattle when they are able."

"You want me to leave my friends here. That's not how we roll dude." Drew's desire to hit the gas and run evaporated at the idea.

"That's what must be done. Dude. Your friends are nothing compared to the death toll these creatures will accumulate if left unchecked. All Dexon managed to do is stir them up. The imbecile." Molab was staring Drew full in the eye. He could feel a buzz in his head as the Valdan tried to push him to cooperate.

"That's not gonna work so knock it off." Drew glared at the man engulfing the passenger seat.

"I had little hope it would. That I tried should tell you how desperately we need you to do as I ask. The fate of humanity very literally could hang in the balance." Molab's powerful face implored Drew to listen.

"If we do this…and I mean if. Then you have to promise that we come back for them once we've found the research center. You promise?" Drew shifted in his seat, so he could put the car in drive before looking back at the big man.

"You have my word, kid. It should soothe you to know they have Quelis with them. There is no finer warrior among all our people. He was chosen to colonize this planet for that very reason. If there is a way, he will get your friends to the research post and there will be no need for us to return." Molab turned to the road ahead as Drew pulled out onto the pavement.

| 19 |

Chapter

Tyrone had stopped feeling the heat on his skin eons ago. A body becomes numb to that kind of pain after enough time passes. His lungs wheezed when he inhaled, and his eyes were sandpaper in his skull but that was par for the course. What he couldn't get past was the constant howl of the wind in his ears. Never ending, it raged against his mind like a banshee. Always there, always roaring.

Bracing against a jagged rock, he contemplated the visionscape before him. How long could he remain sane in this barrenness of dirt and ash? Was it worth continuing if his life was spent here? Megan had urged him to fight for his body. Like that wasn't something he'd already tried.

He'd been fighting as long as he could recall. Fighting to get an education no one thought he was entitled too. Fighting to stay off the streets and out of the gangs. Fighting to keep his mom taken care of and safe. Fighting twice as hard as anyone else to get half the reward. Maybe he'd used it all up. Cause right now he just wanted to lay down and let it go.

Hadn't he earned that right? Megan was asking for too much. What did she understand with her rich white family and their power? Nothing in her life had ever required a fight. She needed to get out of his business.

He could make her out on the horizon. Picking her way among the rocks looking for him like an overzealous babysitter. He stayed one step out of sight whenever possible. Maybe if she went long enough without finding him she'd leave this place like he'd told her to. Stubborn woman.

Between one blink and the next his world tilted. Literally. Rocks tumbled past him as he fought to hold to the one he'd been leaning against. Gravity went sideways as his world spun around him. His fingers bled as rock scraped layers of skin away. It was seconds before he felt the blood erase what little traction he'd maintained.

He was tumbling and twisting as he fell amongst the rocks. His head turned towards the horizon, searching. There were only more flying rocks and rivers of molten lava pouring towards him. Pain exploded behind his eyes, growing larger until his vision ceased. Silence reigned before emptiness took him.

His eyelids peeled open a fraction at a time. Several faces came into view, though his addled brain refused to give them identities. His stomach heaved and he jerked to the side to avoid getting its contents on his clothes.

Once he was sure there was nothing left to expel, he fell back. The faces were speaking to him now. He realized they had been for some time. Still searching for names, he stared past them into the beautiful night sky where stars shone cleanly against velvety black.

"Tyrone? Is that you? Are you in control?" The blonde to his left shook his shoulder and he finally gave her a name, Lynea. He smiled up at her.

"Man, we need to know who's driving this body." The Valdan near his legs spoke up. Tyrone was positive he would have remembered the guy's rock star swagger if they had met before, but something seemed familiar. His band of friends had been making new alliances. Could this alien be trusted?

"It's me." His voice cracked as it passed his lips. Had he fought his way back to his body or was this some illusion Sorche had thought up to torture him? "What happened?"

"We stole you." Aleece grasped his ankle as Trenton beamed over her shoulder.

"Where is Sorche? How did you get me back in control? Who is this guy?" He directed his questions to Lynea. She was the one he trusted most.

"Sorche is probably looking for us as we speak. This guy is Dexon and he put you in control. I have no clue how, but I'm desperately hoping he can do it again." Her smile at the Valdan man had all of Tyrone's warning bells blaring.

"How did you do it?" Tyrone pulled himself into a sitting position as he turned to Dexon.

"Sorche was my mate. We have exchanged mental bonding receptors. It allowed me to reach in and pull you out. So to speak. Yes, I can do it again, but it pisses her off, so I recommend we move before she finds us." He reached down, grabbed Tyrone's arm, and lifted him to his feet.

Suddenly upright, Tyrone fought for balance before Lynea stepped close and wrapped an arm around his waist. His pride took one for the team as he leaned a large part of his weight on the diminutive woman. Whatever he needed to do was preferable to facing Sorche.

Thank goodness every step had him moving more on his own. The group's pace picked up with each block they passed. Eventually, they were moving at a good clip. Aleece and Trenton ducked into an abandoned building without looking back. Him and Lynea where right on their heels with the Valdan taking up the rear. Down a hallway, they entered a doorway on the right. Inside, he found them hunched near two windows facing the street.

It was the first time he registered the handguns they had at the ready. Had they been out this whole time without him noticing? Usually, he would have clocked them right off the line. He needed to get his head in the game.

Pushing free of Lynea's support, he made a sweep of the room. The walls were brown from caked on dirt, and papers littered the floor. An abandoned table covered in broken bottles wobbled on three legs against the far wall. From his viewpoint he could make out graffiti on the wall across the street through broken window-panes.

Voices carried on the stale air. He strained pointlessly to make out words. There was no way to tell if they were Thralls or other humans looking for safety. Lynea moved to a position near Aleece where they could both see down the street. He longed for their viewpoint. He shifted his body closer to Trenton. "Why did you guys come after me?"

"What do you mean? You wanted to stay with her?" Trenton gave him the stink eye.

"No, I just got to thinking I was probably not the only one she had. I know Megan was in there. I saw others sometimes. Why me and not one of them?" Tyrone scuffed his sneakers on the trash littering the floor.

"After we saw you all on the TV, we came to confront Sorche. She sent you out to hunt us. It kinda made you the easiest target." Trenton met his eyes before turning his attention back to the view of the street.

"Gotcha." Tyrone tried not to feel deflated that his friends had saved *him* only because he was the first one they found. Free was free after all.

"I've got to tell ya, man. I was glad it was you. We need all the help we can get, and you've always been a great asset in a fight." Trenton flashed him a quick grin. Tyrone couldn't decide if he was happy with the compliment or pissed that the man was trying to run game.

Dexon glanced their way from his station by the door. When Tyrone made eye contact the alien nodded at him once. Had he overheard their conversation? Despite his time with Sorche he knew next to nothing about these aliens. He needed to fix that.

His body was feeling back to normal by the time he made it to Dexon's side. Resisting the urge to scrutinize every detail of the larger man, he tried to act casual. He was pretty sure he hadn't pulled it off when the Valdan chuckled under his breath. Fine, straight to the chase.

"What's your plan? Do we even have a plan?" Tyrone folded his arms across his chest.

"Survive. That's as far as I've gotten at this point, but it's usually a solid plan." Dexon swiveled his attention from the hallway to Tyrone.

"Perfect. Would you like to add details?"

"Your lady friend there seems pretty adamant we find her kids. Sorche has them. The plan was to send me in, and I bring you all back out. Didn't work. The second she felt me close she sent the hounds to find me. A.k.a, you." Dexon switched back to staring down the hall. "If I thought for half a second she would send those kids out, I'd send you back and wait to find them."

Tyrone didn't know if this guy was blowing smoke or what. He seemed sincere, but really he was an alien. How can a human understand what motivates a creature like that? More importantly, why would something that could take control of a human being care about them? It didn't play.

Once someone had power, they didn't give it away. They sure as hell didn't use it to take care of the folks below them. Not in Tyrone's experience.

"I'm sorry to hear about her kids. Could I walk back in and pretend I'm not free?" Tyrone wasn't even sure he wanted to volunteer for something like that.

"You got balls. No, that's not an option. She knew the second you broke free. I had to shake her world up to knock you loose. Not a chance she missed that." Dexon's words let Tyrone release the breath he hadn't realized he was holding. The Valdan went rigid as a board.

"What is it?" Tyrone tried to look out the doorway only to find it filled with Dexon's shoulders. "What the…?"

Aleece and Trenton were trying to keep an eye out the window at the same time they stared at Dexon. Lynea made her way across the room and tried to force her way past their Valdan sentinel. He didn't even acknowledge her pushing and pulling at him.

The thud of heavy footsteps reverberated in the hallway. The humans braced for a fight. Aleece and Trenton had their guns trained on the space despite Dexon blocking it with his body. Tyrone pulled Lynea over and flattened her against the wall behind him before finding his fighting stance.

He was prepared for everything except Dexon's shoulders relaxing as he stepped aside. A massive man with ebony hair and a biker's wardrobe came through the opening. The humans in the room relaxed a notch. When the sapphire eyes met his, Tyrone felt every muscle tense. Alien.

Another Valdan followed the first. This one with white hair shifting through the shades of snow and ice. Lynea stepped around him to greet them. His nerves on high alert, he managed to catch their names and little else. A beautiful woman glided into the room, copper hair floating around her. He averted his eyes the second she turned his way.

"How did you find us?" Lynea directed the question at the woman, Naelah.

"I can locate my brother within a certain distance. We share a blood bond." Naelah looked down her nose at the human woman. Tyrone disliked her immediately.

"Do you have a ride out of here? We got cut off from our vehicle." Lynea acted like she couldn't see the alien woman's uppity BS.

"Drew is waiting with an SUV. It will not fit us all, but we can make alternate plans from there." Naelah turned like she expected them to follow. To his horror, they all did. Like little ducklings.

He wanted nothing more than to run the other way, but that way brought him back to Sorche. He couldn't do that again. Pushing his bile down, he mustered up the courage to join his friends.

They cleared the building and an entire block before they saw the mob headed their way. Sorche's Thralls had found them. He turned to head back only to find another group behind them.

"Any suggestions?" He turned to the group he was forced to rely on.

"We split up. Regroup two blocks to the east and three to the north." The man with the snow hair, Molab, tapped Trenton and Lynea on the arm before the three of them turned into an alley on the left.

Dexon grabbed Aleece and Naelah followed them to an alley across the street. Left with Quelis, Tyrone indicated he would follow the Valdan's lead. The burly man leaped straight up onto a fire escape. His foot knocked the ladder down for Tyrone to climb. The breath of a Thrall was hot on his neck as he grabbed hold of the lowest rung.

Kicking back with his foot, he felt the familiar thud of hitting a human body. Before he could release his hold and prepare for a real brawl the ladder was soaring upward with him hanging on for dear life. He almost knocked loose when it came to a jarring halt at the top of its run. Quelis used his arm to brace as he transferred onto the landing. Then it was a breath stealing sprint up the stairs to the roof.

Never in his life had Tyrone had a desire to roof jump. That was for crazy movie stunts and urban acrobatics. Too bad because that was exactly what he found himself doing. He could only hope the Valdan understood the limitations of a human body or he was going to end up splattered on the asphalt.

The world rushed past him, as he soared above the lights, sending blood pumping through his body. Even if he never saw the daylight again, he was gloriously happy to be free. This was what living was about. He let go of the rest and reveled in it.

They raced through the night for an eternity before Quelis found an open roof door and went through it. Dashing down the stairwell, had Tyrone feeling trapped. He couldn't wait to feel the night air on his skin again. They burst through a door into a dead-end alley. A man huddled behind the trashcan. Two Thralls stood at the open end of the alley peering down the street. Exchanging a look, Quelis and Tyrone raced stealthily towards them.

The Thralls turned at the sound of their feet. Tyrone suspected it was only his feet they heard. He was already in motion as the Thrall twisted around. His fist connected with the man's nose sending blood spurting into the night. The man tried to rally but the first blow must have messed with his vision. His fist swung wide. Tyrone stepped into the opening and laid an upper cut/ jab combo in the sweet spot. The man dropped like a rock. Textbook perfect.

Quelis was looking at him expectantly as he bounced on his feet. Right, he was the slow one. Wiping the slap happy look off his face, he scanned the alley to find the man behind the trashcan gone. He fell in behind the Valdan and they took off down the street. Two blocks over they turned to head east.

Tyrone hoped Quelis knew where he was going because his own sense of direction had become nil. When his fearless leader darted into an alley way, he never thought twice about following. A small group of panicked people fled past the entrance behind them without stopping. He turned his head to watch them with a desire to help, but there was no time to pull his companion back. They emerged on a side street blocked by abandoned cars.

They found a chaotic scene with bodies lying across hoods and tossed on the street like garbage. He moved to the nearest to check her pulse. Nothing. The next was only a few inches away and he could see her chest wasn't moving. He stuttered to a stop even as Quelis hood jumped into the next alley. Flashes of something skittered through his mind like shadows afraid of the light. Had he been here? The him that *she* had controlled.

Looking down the road his eyes told him there was nothing moving but a desire to find someone alive rose up in him. He couldn't live with the idea that he stood here and let these people be massacred around him. Forgetting Quelis, he made his way further along the street and into the carnage.

A cry came to him from the macabre scene. It could have been a cat or metal in the wind, but his mind screamed 'baby'. It became vital that he find the child. Scrambling through the obstacle course, he followed the sound as it wafted from first one direction and then another. He passed the same car twice without being able to pinpoint the origin.

A hand on his shoulder stopped him cold. He had become so focused on the sound he had lost track of his surroundings. Turning his head only enough to use his peripheral vision, he was relieved to find Quelis standing there and not the flame haired monster herself.

"Do you hear it?" Tyrone was becoming afraid the noise was a trap she had set to lure humans in.

"The baby crying?" Quelis' head swiveled left to right as he tried to watch all the angles.

"Yes. Help me find it." Tyrone could feel the eyes of predators on him, but he couldn't leave a baby behind.

"Why?" The other man's head tilted to the side as he waited for an answer.

"What do you mean why? Because it's helpless and we aren't."

"Humans are so emotional. It's over here." The hulk of a man led him to a minivan crashed into the front window of a nearby store. The driver's door hung open, but no light shone from within. The wail became louder as they drew nearer.

Tyrone stumbled on the rubble as he reached for the button to open the sliding door. It opened on a whoosh and the crying stilled. In the seat opposite he could see a carrier strapped into the seat. A piercing howl erupted from its depths. He slanted his body across the interior of the van to push the release button.

Free of its base the carrier lifted easily, but the awkward angle he was laying in made it a painful stretch to right himself without dumping the baby. Back in an upright position he was not amused to find Quelis chuckling at him behind his back.

The diaper bag for his rescued baby was sitting on the floorboard. He handed the carrier off to a shocked alien, so he could retrieve it. The look on the aliens face was ample payback.

"We should go. This little one needs shelter and food." Tyrone slung the diaper bag over his shoulder after retrieving a full bottle. He shook it quickly before handing it over.

Quelis held the bottle in one hand and the carrier in the other like either could explode at any second. Tyrone was tempted to leave the big bad Valdan to figure it out himself, but that wouldn't be fair to the baby. He retrieved the bottle then turned the carrier to peek in at the little one inside.

She was adorable, but all babies are. He figured she couldn't be more than two months old. Her face was scrunched and red from screaming, but the second he popped that bottle in her mouth she transformed. Instant angel.

Smiling, he tucked her blanket more tightly around her and flipped the cover over the front of the carrier. No way was he letting her catch a cold after she had survived a car crash and a massacre. He placed the handle of her carrier over his forearm, tucked it up like a football and looked to his companion for direction.

Quelis' eyebrows probably couldn't move any further up on his forehead. Shaking his head, he ran a hand through his disheveled hair before shrugging and loping off. Tyrone kept pace as best he could without jostling his passenger. He was relieved the other man slowed to accommodate.

They had to be nearing the rendezvous point. It felt like they had been running for hours. A blonde woman came barreling out of a doorway and right into their path. He thought they had a Thrall on their hands until she turned his way. Even with the frenzied look in her eyes he recognized Lynea.

The fear there had him searching for a pursuer, but he found none. Where had Trenton and Molab gone? Why was she alone?

"Lynea." He called her name as she moved away from them. Maybe she didn't recognize him in the badly lit street.

"I need to find them. They called me." She waved her phone at him as she took off down a side street. His need to protect the baby warred with his desire to help Lynea find her children. In the end she was an adult who could take care of herself.

"Do we follow her?" Quelis asked from where he had stopped. "The others will probably have gone on without us by now."

"And drag the baby into more danger? No. We need to get her somewhere safe." He started down the road they had been traveling.

"Where exactly do you think is going to be safe? Now that the Dark Ones are breaking free around the world?" The Valdan hadn't moved from his spot.

"What do you think I should do? Leave her here in the streets to die? Do you people even have children?" Tyrone turned his back on the alien. He would find his way out of this maze by himself if need be.

"I wasn't implying we abandon her, only that we do not abandon our fight because of her." Quelis's sapphire eyes bored into Tyrone's mind. "Our people can have children. We understand their value and still have the ability to apply logical assessments."

"Doesn't change a thing. I'm leaving. Feel free to follow Lynea if you want." Tyrone shook free of the mesmerizing gaze and took off at a trot. It was no surprise to feel the absence of the alien male. Glancing back at the empty street only briefly, he steeled his nerve. "Don't worry little one, I've got this."

The night felt darker as he made his way among the deserted buildings. Sounds were louder, shadows deeper. More than once he crossed to the opposite sidewalk to avoid an imaginary threat. There was no such thing as being too safe.

The wail of sirens welcomed him as he crossed into the light. A barricade had been placed across the road. Police cars sat sideways behind it, lights spinning. A uniformed man swept forward with gun drawn yelling for Tyrone to get down on the ground.

"I have a baby! There's a baby!" He yelled as he moved to hit the ground without dropping the carrier.

He made it down without bullets blazing past him and only then did he allow his muscles to relax. A little. He was surrounded by officers jostling to handcuff him. Rough hands pulled him to his feet. Over his head words like "alien sympathizer" and "Vampire lackey" flew around. They didn't know what to call him, but they knew he was bad.

Only he wasn't and he knew he couldn't explain that to a group of people who had no desire to hear it. They had seen him standing next to the Dark Ones. No words were going to convince them he hadn't been in control.

He was shoved into the back seat of a cop car. A couple of officers jumped in the front and they were pulling away when he caught a glimpse of an EMT with the baby. She was safe at least. Whatever happened to him, he could rest easy with that.

The police station was overflowing with bodies when they pulled up. People streamed in escorted by the city's finest and cops streamed out to arrest the next law breaker. It looked like the seedier element was using the chaos as an excuse to run wild.

He was shoved through the crowd by the burlier of his two new friends. With his hands behind his back there was no way to shield himself. He would wear the bruises for days. It wasn't the first time.

Inside the building was standing room only, with a line winding from booking out into the hall. It was gonna be a long night.

"Fill out this form and leave him with us. Tonight, is all about streamlining. We need warm bodies on the street." A gruff older man handed a clipboard to the smaller officer standing with Tyrone and wandered off. The two uniforms looked around before starting on the paperwork.

Tyrone tuned them out as they took on the task. He wasn't about to help them. He refocused when he caught sight of flame colored hair out the grated windows. His mind took a step outside of his body for a second as he flashed back to the soul charring landscape he'd been trapped in. He wasn't going back there.

Twisting to the side, he used the officers' distraction to ratchet away from them. He was running down the hall full tilt when the front doors blew behind him. He could feel the whoosh of air and shrapnel flying past. Using the sound as motivation, he moved faster. He needed another exit.

Like an answer to prayer, he spotted a neon sign pointing to just that. Turning the corner without his hands almost took him down. Bouncing off a nearby wall had him back on his feet and sprinting towards the next sign. He took the next corner with more care. Down a short stair well and he found his way out.

Blasting into the cool air set an alarm to screaming. He figured they had too much on their hands, dealing with Sorche, to come looking into a misused exit. The street to his left was a mass of screaming and running so he headed right. As the noises faded, his mind moved to his next problem. He needed his hands free.

There was more than a good chance she had followed him to that station. Running around with handcuffs on made him a dead man. To get his bearings, he needed to calm his nerves. That was a feat all on its own, but this was his neighborhood. He knew where every store and shop was if he could just slow down long enough to use his brain.

Scanning his memory gave him three options. He headed to the closest. A block and a half later he stood outside the neighborhood hardware store. The window was broken, and the door stood pried open. It felt wrong to walk into the already plundered shop, but this was life and death.

Inside, he found the owner standing next to the shattered cash register. Someone had thrown it to the ground and taken a sledge-hammer to it. The drawer hung open, empty. Luckily, the old man appeared physically unharmed.

"I'm so sorry Mr. Miller." Tyrone could see the tracks running down the man's cheeks. This business barely stayed afloat on a good day. "I hate to do this to you, but I need a saw. I'll pay."

Mr. Miller looked up as he wiped his cheeks. "There wouldn't be much point in that now. Over here."

Tyrone followed the man's stooped shoulders through destroyed displays and ruined merchandise to the back of the store. He turned with embarrassment, so the older man could see the cuffs. Only, the older man didn't start to saw away. He chuckled a little. Like people do when something's too bad to be funny.

"Come back to the front, son." He made his way over the debris to the front counter. Reaching underneath, he opened a drawer and pulled out a set of keys. "These are what you need." He motioned for Tyrone to turn then worked the small key until the cuffs popped loose.

"Why do you keep handcuff keys, old man?" Tyrone was having a hard time picturing one of his neighborhood heroes as a secret villain.

"My son left them here awhile back. I've been meaning to return them." The older man deflated onto a stool behind the counter. "Go now. Whatever put you in those cuffs is surely following close behind you."

"Thank you. Really, I'll come back as soon as I can and help you clean up." Tyrone rubbed his wrists as he backed away from the man. His heart wanted to stay, but he knew that Mr. Miller was right. Sorche would be there any minute and he couldn't bring her into this man's store.

"Be safe, Tyrone."

He heard the old man's words as he made his way back into the night. He wished there were a way he could follow the advice, but life hadn't offered him that choice. He was less than a block from his apartment, where his mama lay fighting cancer. He longed to check on her.

When she sent him off to Mexico neither of them had planned for it to last this long. His mind overruled his heart. He was not making Sorche a trail to the most important person on the planet.

Was his only option to go back and find Quelis? He wasn't even sure he wanted to continue this fight. His heart was ready to find somewhere to hide. But how did he live with himself if he didn't do anything to try and stop Sorche?

| 20 |

Chapter

Sea spray soaked into the collar of Caneon's shirt where it peeked above his rain poncho. Molab had insisted each of them put one on before boarding the boat. Personally, Caneon felt like they should have life vests, but there was no arguing with the Valdan male once he rested those obsidian eyes on you.

Immediately afterward, Molab and Drew had angled for the captain's cabin leaving Caneon, Megan, and Trenton on deck. They had been at sea for hours, circling the islands one after another. Trenton had already emptied the contents of his stomach over the rail multiple times.

Caneon didn't bother to hide the enjoyment that brought him. No one was paying attention anyways. Megan had curled up in a pile of ropes and closed her eyes. He assumed she was sleeping.

Molab had sworn he could sense the island once they were in range. To Caneon if felt like they were calling a lost phone and waiting to be close enough to hear it ring. Only the phone was invisible and located in the middle of a bunch of other phones floating aimlessly on the ocean.

Caneon had long since decided there was no secret island to find. They were wasting their time. He would have expressed that opinion to the Valdan if he had thought it would do any good. Instead they were resigned to endless circles until the gas ran out.

Going back to shore was a nonstarter. After leaving the Hub, they had barely made it through Seattle alive. The chaos that had been threatening at home had blossomed into full on mayhem there. Thralls ran those city streets in packs rounding up humans for their Dark masters.

Drew kept talking about the others joining them. It was a fool's dream. Their friends would never make it through that war zone. Caneon wasn't going to be the one to pop that bubble.

He was watching the waves slap against the hull when the boat veered hard to the left. They had a word for that, but it slipped his mind. Sailing had never been a past time he favored. Water and books never mix well.

They settled into a straight course that headed out into the open waters. Perhaps Molab had also come to the realization that they were chasing wild geese. If so it made sense to head away from shore and then turn south or north to find a safe landfall.

He was astounded to find the rate of speed they were traveling at decreasing. There was no good reason to stop in the middle of nowhere. There was no hope for it. He was going to have to brave the alien's den and insist on being informed.

As he turned to leave the rail, a shimmering began in the air just off the bow. Like tiny fireworks going off in the middle of the day, they burst open then fizzled as they fell. He was scrutinizing one such trail when he realized the boat was still proceeding forward. He watched the hull and deck disappear before his very eyes as he inched his way backwards.

The boat was making better time than he was as the sparkles came ever closer to his toes. Taking a breath, he gathered himself to take the plunge. Unless he was willing to dive overboard, there was nowhere to go but through. His step forward propelled him onto the other side of the phenomena.

Before him was an island like he'd never beheld. It lacked the softened edges and natural lines that man can never quite reproduce. Instead it featured sweeping waterfalls and foliage unknown to him. Birds of radiant color swooped over head as the boat drew closer to shore.

A crystalline pier jutted out into the water. Its fluid lines disguised it so well he would never have spotted it where it not for the people standing on it. They ranged in age from toddlers to teetering old men. There couldn't have been more than a hundred, but they packed the pier and spilled over onto the beach.

Behind them a road could be seen winding into the tree line. He wondered where that led for a brief spell before his eyes were drawn back to the crowd. They neither cheered nor shrunk away. For all intents they seemed to have no reaction to the strangers arriving on their shore.

Some of the children milled among the adult's legs, as small beings do. The waning distance between them revealed details that lead him to believe these were not entirely human beings. A pair of truly Amethyst eyes set in a human face. Shades of copper in brunette hair. Impossibly thin bodies with alien grace, yet unremarkable features.

The Valdan and the humans could reproduce. It was a revelation he had not prepared himself for. Which was ridiculous in hindsight. Of course, the possibility was there. They were close enough to humanoid after all.

Shaking his head at the shortsightedness he'd been using, he stared in fascination at the island they were about to embark upon.

Tropical palms grew alongside evergreens, both reaching into the cerulean sky. The undergrowth was packed on top of each other so densely it was near impossible to identify one bush from the other. Wildlife crawled, flew, and climbed wherever he gazed.

The hull of their boat came smoothly to rest alongside the pier. Hands caught the ropes Drew and Megan tossed down to them. Before he could make his way over to help, the boat was secured to the pier and Drew was dropping a plank into place so they could disembark.

Molab dragged Trenton to his feet as Caneon waited for the others to make their way onto solid ground. It wasn't long before it was his turn to walk the plank per se. He moved swiftly across the unstable area. No use dawdling.

None of the native residents greeted them. The movement of bodies and the waves lapping against the boat were the only sounds. They shifted only enough to leave room for those coming off the boat before resuming their regard.

Molab came across the plank with Trenton plastered to his side. The human man looked like he had been ridden hard. Sweat slicked his hair to a face rendered a ghastly shade of green. His legs wobbled as Molab pulled him along and Caneon could see a tremble in the hand he had draped around the Valdan's waist.

A male stepped from the crowd of onlookers. He was taller than the others by at least a foot with human bulk. His blue eyes shone a little brighter than Caneon was used to seeing and his blonde hair moved through all the sun kissed shades of a surfer.

"Greetings. We welcome you to Sanctus, Molab the Beholder. I am Gerus the Greeter. What brings you to the atoll?" The man bobbed forward in what Caneon believed was a bow.

"You as well. Thank you for receiving us. Who has charge of Sanctus?" Molab returned the bob to a lesser degree.

"That would be Entaya. She currently endeavors in the labora-tory. They have been making headway with the latest version of the serum. I can act as guide if you would be so inclined." Gerus seemed eager to please the Valdan. Flash backs to the moment Caneon met Dexon pinged through his head. Were these people here of their own free will?

"That would be lovely. We will follow." Molab moved to do just that as Gerus turned and headed down the road Caneon had glimpsed from the boat.

It seemed they were to walk and Caneon worried about Tren-ton's ability to make the hike. The green had faded somewhat, but he leaned on Molab with no less intensity than before. Clearing the bodies pressed around them was easier than he had feared. They all took the exchange as a finish to the proceedings and most ambled off in various directions.

Some kept pace with them either in front of or behind their group. Others disappeared into the underbrush like it swallowed them whole. He watched two boys jump into the trees and shimmy up to a series of bridges so camouflaged they had escaped his notice. Aware of them now, he spotted others traveling along the elevated paths.

His eyes were so occupied with what was above him they failed to notice the rock lodged in the dirt road he trod. One foot came to a sudden halt. A quick shimmy brought his feet back in time with-out a loss of dignity. Lucky.

Rectifying his almost fatal error, he returned his gaze to the path they traveled. They were entering the tree line when the road un-der their feet turned to a solid material he couldn't identify. It was smooth like marble without the shine or slickness. Gray in color, it suggested frozen storm clouds.

Ahead of him, Megan and Drew were discussing what it could be. He watched the young man take a surreptitious picture with a smart phone. Where had he obtained one of those? Megan perhaps. Caneon didn't believe anyone had ever searched her.

She seemed to be recovering from her ordeal. The color was in her cheeks. Although that could be attributed to her lack of cosmetics. Without the paled skin and dark eyeliner, she looked fresh and young. A shower in the motel they had rented on the road had left her short black hair to wave naturally around her face. He preferred it to the normal spikes and clumps.

Beyond them, Molab seemed at home here. Even with Trenton leaning on him, there was a lift to his shoulders that spoke of ease and dignity. Caneon found himself pondering on the world the Valdan had left behind. If he obtained the chance he would very much like to hear about it.

All thought exited his mind as they came out of the trees. Spread before him in the valley was a town much larger than he would have estimated this island could hold. Built of the same material as the roads, the buildings climbed to the sky with rope bridges connecting the upper levels to each other and the trees surrounding them.

Running through, around, and sometimes under the buildings were roads with carts of roughhewn wood, trundling along them. Pedestrians crowded the edges, in some places leaving little room for the carts to pass. Store fronts occupied the lower levels.

As they made their way, he caught site of small cafes and social areas. Interspersed among those were shops hocking everything from homespun cloth to technical gadgets he could only guess the use of. Drew would no doubt be headed straight for those the second he was set free.

They seemed to be on the main thoroughfare headed straight through town. From his, albeit brief, look as they came out of the trees there didn't seem to be anything on the other side. Caneon's intestines clenched ever tighter as they passed farther towards their unknown destination.

The smiles and waves passed back and forth between Gerus and the citizens did nothing to ease his condition. Trusting strange people required skills he wasn't sure he had. His footsteps dragged him farther from the guide with each building they passed. Had he not been equally afraid of being alone in this town of hybrids, he would have cut and run for the boat.

They passed the last man-made structure with Caneon far back from the main group. So, he had the unfortunate experience of watching them walk into the jungle and disappear from one step to the next. Hide and seek of the highest order, only he had lost all desire to seek.

Standing less than a stride from the spot he was now considering the point of no return; he fought an internal battle. Half of him yelled stick with your friends dumdum! The other urged prudence and caution. A third voice appeared from nowhere pushing him forward. This voice was not his own.

Digging his heels in did him no good as his legs were no longer obeying his wishes. He searched frantically for something to grab. A branch or beam would do nicely, but none appeared. With no recourse to stop it he found himself stolidly stepping past the point.

Everyone stood looking at him as he breached the shield. He could see that's what it was now that he was on the other side and staring at an elevator set incongruously in the jungle undergrowth. His face was easily twenty degrees hotter than average as he faced their looks of impatience. Sure, make fun of Caneon. That's what they all do.

"Well. Let's go." Caneon snarked at them when they didn't immediately turn to the elevator.

"Are you okay, dude?" Drew stepped towards him, then retreated quickly under his withering glare.

"I am perfectly fine. Shall we stop dawdling and resume our...whatever you call this." Caneon fought to keep the wobble out of his voice as he spoke.

Drew conceded with his hands up, then turned to be ready to board the mysterious elevator. Caneon watched them all turn, and the doors opened before he allowed his shoulders to slump. What a fool they must think he was.

The elevator was crammed full. Being last in gave him the benefit of being able to stand as close to the doors as his body could manage. It didn't cease all the personal touch, but it did allow him a modicum of control over it.

Unlike his entrance into the elevator, his exit was swift and without reservation. He strode into the lobby as if he had a single clue as to where he was going. Since he didn't, it was prudent to stop on the far side without entering the hallway. There was only one so he could have continued down it confidently, but his ego wouldn't let him for fear he would strut right past the correct door.

He stepped to the side to give Gerus enough room to regain the lead. While waiting for all parties to file past, Caneon took in the utilitarianism of the lobby. It was done all in gray with walls, floor, and ceiling made of the mystery material. The two chairs placed opposite each other along the walls and the cube tables that sat next to them were midnight black. Not a flower or nick-knack softened the area.

Caneon watched Trenton move past him without the aid of Molab's arms. The green had gone, but his skin tone matched the lobby's walls entirely too well. A few more hours on solid ground and he'd be fine and dandy. Maybe he would decide to live here rather than face the return journey. That could be a bright side.

Feeling a smile twitch at his lips, he took up the rear of their little parade. This time he ensured his pace matched the others impeccably. There would be no second chance to scoff at him today.

They were less than thirty paces from the elevator when Gerus took a sharp right. By the time Caneon had rounded the same corner, the others had gathered in the room. All eyes were focused on the enclosure encompassing the majority of the far wall. He recognized what it was from the room where they had found Naelah.

The woman within this room had hair to rival the ocean waves and eyes of Opal. Unlike Naelah, she was fully awake and interacting with the workers from a massive central chair. They moved to and from various consoles tapping keys on one then scurrying off to the next.

"Madam Entaya the Analyst, may I present Molab the Beholder and his entourage." Gerus bowed far lower than he had previously then backed away with an overly dramatic flourish of his arm.

Caneon had never been anyone's entourage before. Truth be told, it was far less glamorous than it sounded. Molab stepped forward to occupy the place Gerus had vacated. He refrained from the dramatic gestures at least.

"Entaya, how pleasurable to enjoy your presence once again. We come seeking news of the progress you and your colleagues have made." His bow was so slight as to almost be nonexistent.

"Welcome you are. We have made great progress, but I despair to inform you it has come at great cost. I am the last of us. Time has required the sacrifice of much energy to maintain our shields and power. It gladdens me to lay my gaze upon you. I had feared we would have no means to disseminate the vaccine and no hands to wield the weapons." Entaya tapped her fingers on the arm rests as she spoke.

Caneon was unsure if she was working controls set into the chair or simply expressing nervous energy. He simply lacked the ability to read body language. Focusing on something he could interpret; he turned his attention to the words scrolling across a nearby screen in Hebrew. They were population averages of every city on the planet.

"We would gladly be of service. First though, I require a guest's place to sleep and food for me and my people. It has been a long journey." Molab inclined his head towards her.

"How discourteous of me. Gerus shall arrange for such. Return here once you are rested and we will discuss the details of our progress." She inclined her head and then dismissed them with a glance.

Gerus waited by the door to implement her instructions. They filed after him with a little less pep than when they had entered. Caneon felt his stomach growl for the first time in days. When had he eaten last? This morning. Drew had brought around granola bars and water on the boat.

That realization was a trigger for his body to recall all its miscellaneous aches and pains. He trudged along to their rooms with little sense of his environment. Eyes barely holding half-mast, he glanced up as Gerus opened a door and motioned him into it.

His first stop would indubitably have been the bed had his sense of smell not caught the mouthwatering aromas wafting from the table where a feast had been laid out. A spark in his brain roused him enough to trek across the room and obtain a seat.

Filling his plate was effortless as everything appeared appetizing. Cleaning it required only slightly more exertion. Stomach satiated; he made his way to the bed where he let the fatigue have its way with him.

Light blazed its way through his eyelids with the intensity of a million suns. The pounding in his ears was only slightly less intrusive. Caneon reached for a pillow to cushion the effect as his mind processed.

There had been no alcohol with the meal. Why did he feel like the mother of all hangovers was crushing his will to live? Was there something else causing his discomfort? The door opened so he ventured a peek from under his plush protection.

Drew came skipping into the room like a cheery tornado. He was carrying a tray with something that smelled like eggs and bacon on it. Caneon's stomach did a happy dance, confirming his theory. Hangovers always left him lacking an appetite.

"Hurry up lazy. We have things to do." Drew set the tray on the table that should have been holding the remains from last night's meal and wasn't. Caneon's pulse picked up at the idea that someone had been in his room.

"Why are you so happy?" Caneon fought his way free of the blankets. The world tilted as he moved. He sat on the edge of the bed holding on to steady.

Drew shrugged at him before pouring coffee into two mugs he'd set out. The smell galvanized Caneon into action. He fought through the vertigo and made his way. Sitting was a relief. He grabbed a plate off the tray and set to work filling it.

"Did you wake up feeling…off?" Caneon couldn't let go of the feeling he was missing something. Like the real cause.

"Nope. Woke up excited to see what Entaya has for us. I'm thinking this is it. You know. Where we flip the script and kick some Dark ass." Drew's exuberance was catching. Or maybe it was the full stomach. Either way Caneon found his energy returning.

After he took a few minutes to clean up and a few more to finish a second cup of coffee he was ready to follow the kid anywhere. They made their way through hallway after hallway. They were uniformly utilitarian with their gray walls and black doorways. Caneon was never going to be able to navigate.

"Do you know where we are going?" If he couldn't tell them apart how was Drew doing it?

"Yeah. This is the way we came down last night." Drew glanced over his shoulder to grin before moving on. "Don't you remember?"

"No. I was exhausted. I'm fairly certain I sleepwalked from Entaya's chamber to my room." Caneon was adding that exhaustion to his list of strange happenings.

"Hmm. Weird. So, I'll show you the trick to it later. Everything's marked." Drew pushed a code into the door he'd stopped in front of. "This is it."

Caneon didn't have time for more questions as the door slid open to reveal a room full of people. Molab, Trenton and Megan were there along with Gerus and several others like him. This was not the room Entaya's chair dominated despite Caneon's expectations.

A large black table occupied the center of the room. Standard conference chairs surrounded it, waiting for those in the room to cease mingling and sit. Caneon feared they had been waiting on him and braced for the scorn filled eyes to turn his way.

"Hey guys," Drew lifted his hand in greeting as everyone turned their way. "Who we still waiting on?"

The wall directly opposite them blinked twice. Gerus tapped a pad on the table and a picture of Entaya appeared. She watched benevolently as everyone took a place at the table. Caneon found himself near the door, sandwiched between Drew and Molab. The Valdan man had naturally acquired the seat at the head of the table directly opposite Entaya.

"Greetings. Thank you for joining us." Entaya inclined her head and the others in the room returned the gesture. Caneon and his friends fumbled to emulate the movement. Gerus and his associates showed no reaction to the awkward jerking of heads.

"How may we assist you, Madam?" Gerus posed the question from his perch directly in front of the screen on the left. Caneon surmised the seat Gerus was in would have sat at the end of the table opposite Molab had he not moved it to see the screen.

"Your attention will suffice for now. I must explain our situation to Molab and his entourage at this time." Entaya's lips twitched and Caneon got the impression she was holding back her emotions. "I will save us all the time it would take to recount the many failed programs we pursued. Suffice it to say we have covered much ground to reach our destination. The timing of your arrival is precipitous."

"You mentioned a vaccine and a weapon last night. I applaud your success." Molab tapped his fingers on his leg under the table as he spoke.

"I did. We have cultivated a vaccine by isolating the proteins within human blood that transform the Valdan physiology. The vaccine can subtly alter the DNA of those cells in such a way as to prevent them from interacting with Valdan blood. This renders the human blood ineffective for the purpose of the Dark Ones without harming the human." Entaya was to the point. Caneon appreciated that. "Through various trials we have discovered the most effective dispersal method to be the human water supply. Three to four days of consuming the treated water and the effect will be complete and permanent."

"Feeding on them would no longer give the Dark Ones any type of enhanced abilities. That is good. You wish us to take the vaccine out into the world and disperse it?" Molab leaned back in his chair.

"That is correct. We were planning to send our descendants, but your arrival has mitigated that risk." Her lips quirked as she glanced at Gerus.

"Descendants? Procreation with native species is strictly forbidden. You are aware?" Molab glanced at Gerus before capturing Entaya's eyes with his own. "How do you plan to explain this when the council reviews reports?"

"They would have to come for us to receive those reports. Do you truly still hold to the belief they are planning to rescue us? Do not be naïve my friend. We broke protocol long ago and they have abandoned us to the consequences there of." Her face was filled with such loathing and pity that Caneon even picked it up. He couldn't decide who it was directed at. Molab? The council? Herself? All of the above?

"That may be, but it does not release us to act as we wish without concern. As soon as the shields fall, your progeny will be exposed to the world. What then? Did you consider that when giving in to your baser instincts?" Molab's fist pounded the table as he spoke. Caneon had never seen him so fervent and moved his chair closer to Drew, just to be safe.

"You are not the one to pass judgement on us. Your right to do so was forfeit when you left the council to act as recorder for this excursion. We have had centuries governing ourselves with nary a word from the council. There is no call for you to appraise the laws we enacted in that time. Continue to live as you see fit and we will do the same." All facade of calm had left her face as she spoke. There for the room to see was her defiance and passion. It lent a wild aspect to her features.

"Calm yourself!" Molab's voice raked over the room. "There is no need for such displays. I will not act against you, for now. You will eventually be required to take responsibility for these creations despite your protests. That's all we'll say on the matter. How many water ways must be treated to be effective?"

"All of them. The treatment cannot be diluted too far, or it will become ineffective." Entaya worked to steady her breathing as she spoke. "There are operational transportation Hubs around the world. Many of those are near target areas. We need only access the transportation Hub outside of Seattle to give us the ability to reach a large percentage of those we need. For the rest we will use subs launched from the ship."

"Why not use these subs to get to all of them?" Drew cut into the conversation with a disregard for proper etiquette that only the young have.

"They require large amounts of energy to operate. We do not have those kinds of reserves. Besides the Hub is a much more efficient means of transportation." Entaya fought to hide her annoyance with his impetuousness. Caneon recognized the look because he'd worn it often.

"Seattle's transportation Hub may no longer be accessible. We were chased to our boat by Thralls. The Dark Ones have taken the humans by surprise. I imagine that will not last and they will mount a defense soon. We can only hope it will be effective. At this moment Dark Ones control the area we would need to travel through. I do not believe it is possible to follow your plan without great casualty. What is your secondary option?" Molab had yet to relax the fist he held still on the table.

"There is a transportation Hub within the ship. It is operational but we cannot use it and power the shield at the same time. We will be exposed." Entaya scratched at the base of her throat.

"The saltwater will protect us from immediate attack but you're correct that our position could be compromised. Is the ship capable of moving the island without tearing it apart?" Molab raised an eyebrow at her. "If so, we raise the shields once more and relocate."

"It is likely we will be unable to raise shields once we drop them." She scanned every face in the room making Caneon squirm in his seat as she passed him. "As Molab knows, that takes a considerable surge of power. The island can be moved but without a shield there would be little point." Entaya was telling Molab something with her eyes but Caneon couldn't interpret it.

"Tell us of the weapon." Molab's fist had unclenched only to have his fingers press into the wood so hard his work roughened knuckles were white against his brown skin.

"It is a serum that, once introduced to a Dark One's system, will temporarily nullify the effects of the human blood." Entaya's lips clenched as she waited for Molab's reaction. Caneon wasn't the only one who jerked when Molab's laugh burst into the room.

"Only a scientist would call that a weapon. Oh, goodness…that is truly funny in the worst sort of way." Molab shook his head as the last of the chuckles passed from his lips. "Do you imagine they will hold still for us to inject them? How short sighted. Perhaps we can use dart guns. How long until it would take effect?"

"Five to ten minutes on average." Entaya's cringe told Caneon she had failed to take that into account.

"That is an eternity in a battle situation. There could be possibilities as a coating for our weapons, were we able to speed up the reaction time. Is there any likelihood your scientists could accomplish such a thing?" Molab was tapping his fingers as he stared at an empty corner.

"Probable, given enough time. The situation you've described implies we don't have that time to spare." She looked off screen and nodded to someone.

"We will move forward with the vaccine. It will lessen the amount of blood and Thralls available to them if nothing else. For the sake of winning this war you will have to sacrifice your safety here. I regret that but fail to see an alternative." Molab met her eyes through the screen. A battle raged between them before she lowered her gaze. She nodded once before the wall returned to just being a wall.

Caneon's breath froze in his chest. They had no weapons and only a mediocre solution for resistance. Molab and Entaya were engaged in an alien power struggle. Last but not least, they didn't have the power to enact any of their plans. All their eggs had been in this basket. Following blindly where the Valdan led had cost them dearly. That couldn't happen again.

| 21 |

Chapter

"We shouldn't go in without scouting ahead." Quelis' words echoed through Lynea's mind in torturous loops. If she had listened, they wouldn't be chained to a cement column in the middle of a dank basement. Why hadn't she listened?

Because her rush to reach her children had clouded the reasoning part of her brain. The one that would have told her it was a trap. Every word Quelis uttered had fallen on deaf ears. She gave him credit for following her in even though his centuries of experience had him seeing things for what they were. It would have been smarter to leave her to her fate, and she wouldn't have blamed him.

Her kids had been stationary in the middle of the decrepit apartment when she pushed through the door. One look at their blank faces was all it had taken for her to recognize her own stupidity. The hole opening in her chest had consumed the little time she might have had to run. Thralls swarmed from every direction until even Quelis couldn't fight them off. They had pumped something into his arm with a syringe until his thrashing stopped.

It had taken four of them to carry his limp form into an adjacent building where they rode an elevator into the basement. The throbbing in her cheek was enough to keep her complacently following along. She was no fighter.

Hours passed, sitting on the floor, chains wrapping her to the column from hip to chest with Quelis' dead weight pulling them taut. Her ribs had been rubbed raw by the time he regained consciousness. There were a few excruciating minutes where he tried to break the chains and the pressure on her lungs as she felt her ribs flex had her thinking he might pull them straight through her. Her groans of pain had stopped his struggles.

The pulling had loosened some of the links. Just not enough. He'd spent hours trying to break individual links from his side alone. If she hadn't been there, Lynea was certain he would have been free. Her discomfort kept him from using his full strength. Had Sorche planned it that way?

Lynea had tried to apologize, and he had grunted that it wasn't her fault. She didn't believe it any more than she believed she was going to live through this. Her inability to draw a full breath through the invisible weight sitting on her chest had her fearing the worst.

Quelis was prepared to escape the first time their captures came in. She felt the tension in the chain as he readied. The guy with the food was followed closely by a guy with the kind of scary gun you see in army movies. There was no way she was dodging that many flying bullets. That might be an okay way to end the despair of failing her kids, but she didn't think Quelis could survive the onslaught.

He must not have thought so either since the chains relaxed and he didn't fight when their hands were released enough to eat. Lynea scarfed the food as quickly as her breath would allow in case they decided to take the sandwich back. Sliced ham had never tasted so good to her.

Sandwich polished off, a third man came and escorted her to the bathroom. He left the door open but turned his back to her. She didn't waste a second on modesty while taking care of business. She was shoved back to the column where they pulled Quelis up and took him to the same restroom. It was a surprise when he returned without a fight. She thought that was his chance.

They fell into a routine after that. Long periods of nothing, then eat, bathroom and repeat. The pressure on her chest eased as the time passed. Hope for enough time to recover began to ebb its way into her mind.

Quelis wasn't much of a conversationalist so she filled the time with her own voice. She covered the highlights of her life without him telling her to shut up. That included her kids greatest moments. Even without his putting the brakes on her jabbering, she eventually ran out of things to say.

Now they rested. A lot. Quelis didn't seem to need as much sleep as she did, or his alien soldier training had taught him how to stay awake. He had all the qualities of a kick ass fighter. She really hoped he wasn't going to die down here trying to save her, a middle-class housewife from the suburbs.

The dank smell of wet concrete warred with that of their unwashed bodies by the time the door opened to Sorche. She had left them to rot way longer than Lynea had believed she would. Perhaps, she'd thought the time would break them. If so, she'd underestimated Quelis by a long shot.

"My how the haughty has fallen." Sorche circled them at a distance that ensured they couldn't have reached her even if the chains were to break. Several bulky men stood ready with guns behind her. Maybe for that very reason.

"Come a little closer and we'll talk about who's fallen." Quelis growled at her.

"I think not. There's so much I need to get done. We'll have to put those games on hold until later." She leered at him as her tongue darted between her lips. "Right now, I need some information. You give me that and I let you and your little pet go free. Unscathed…mostly."

"What could we possibly have to offer you?" Quelis was refraining from following her as she moved out of his line of sight. Lynea dipped behind her hair as the woman tried to catch her eyes. She wasn't falling into that trap no matter how irritated she was to be called a pet.

"Tell me where the research station is. That simple. Make it easy and I'll throw in the woman's offspring. Still breathing." Sorche stopped playing chase with Lynea's gaze and moved to level her gaze at Quelis. It was a good thing because the mention of her kids had snapped Lynea's head up.

"You've miscalculated. As usual. We wouldn't tell you that, even if we knew." He growled at Sorche as she stepped closer. Lynea could see on Sorche's face they weren't going to convince her they didn't know where it was.

"Oh, Quelis, we both know that lying isn't going to get you anywhere. You will tell me now or I will break you and you will tell me then. I prefer the second option, but I'll let you take the first. That's how generous I am." She moved close enough to run her fingers over the chain binding him.

Lynea felt the flex as he fought to be free. Her chest ached as the metal pushed on already constricted bones. The tight feeling that had lived in her chest since Quelis had woken, spread and engulfed her until her only concern was her need to breathe.

Gasping and gagging as the chain loosened, she fought through the black curtain engulfing her sight. Quelis was yelling an impressively imaginative series of cuss words at Sorche who laughed delightedly at every suggestion.

"Time among the humans has improved you, old friend. I find myself regretting my choice. Dexon hasn't turned out to be the Mate I had believed he would be. I blame it on his straight arrow of a sister. She ruined him. And us." Sorche lost herself in whatever path her mind had wandered. Shaking her head, she continued. "Too late for that now. Done is done. I'll give you some time to think about my request."

She walked over to the door and gestured to the man standing next to it. When he opened it, Tyler stepped through. Lynea choked down a sob at the sight of her son's bruised face.

"Tyler. Look at me. Tyler. It's me. It's mom. Resist her. Tyler. You need to fight her baby. Fight! Her!" Lynea's voice gave out as Tyler stared dumbly on.

"While you decide, I think I'll entertain myself." Sorche backhanded the boy before gloating over at Lynea struggling for her sons life against the chains. "Don't worry mama, I'll take good care of him." She caressed the side of his face with a sneer as Tyler turned into her hand like a kitten seeking warmth. Lynea's fingers bled where they pulled at the chain binding her. He never once glanced her way as Sorche led him from the room. Lynea's roar of frustration rattled off the walls as the door closed her and Quelis in.

| 22 |

Chapter

Megan stood as the conversation, if you could call it that, between Molab and Entaya came to a close. She had ended up on the far side of the room from the men. Not that any of them had noticed. Since they had found her slumped in that doorway she'd felt like nothing more than a piece of baggage they had to cart from place to place. It was exhausting.

She couldn't blame the situation entirely on them. Her body had only been ill for a few days, but it felt and looked like years' worth of deterioration. She had never rocked the runway-model thin look before. It wasn't as cool as people made it out to be. Her cheekbones could cut someone, and last night she had counted her ribs-through her t-shirt.

On top of that, the world had spun on its axis while she was out, so it was taking her a couple of breaths to catch up with the goings on. Her friends were scattered to the wind or trailing behind pompous aliens. She wasn't sure who was where at this point. The truth was, she wasn't much good to anyone right now.

Which was probably the reason the men were choosing to relegate her to the background. She was tired of it. As the only fully human woman on this island slash spaceship she deserved to have a say. Right?

"What now?" She didn't bother to direct the question at anyone. Let them figure out who should answer.

"We get the vaccine ready to ship." Molab turned from his movement towards the door. "Once it is transportable we will lower the shields and go through the Hubs to deliver it."

"Right. I caught that. So maybe my question should be. What then? What comes next?" Megan tapped the table to punctuate her thought.

"We will see how effective the vaccine is and then formulate a plan." Molab leveled his onyx eyes at her.

"So, the plan is to sit here exposed, and hope for the best? That doesn't seem smart. Entaya should never have agreed to this." Megan made her way around the table by pushing people aside. Molab's eyebrows raised.

"She had little choice. Even without my seat on the council, I hold more authority than her." He motioned for the last couple of people between them to move.

"This is her island. How can you possibly out vote her?"

"Explaining that would require a history of my people that you do not possess, and I do not care to extrapolate on. Suffice it to say, I do." Molab turned once again to head for the door.

Megan found herself with little choice but to follow. That didn't mean she had to do so quietly. Her days of being a silent puppet were through.

"Who will be sent to distribute the vaccine?" She wiggled her way between Caneon and Drew to be at Molab's elbow as she spoke.

"I imagine Entaya has several able-bodied persons who will be assigned that chore." Molab didn't manage to mask the annoyance in his voice.

"Great. I want to go with them." Megan had made the snap decision to be an integral part of everything going on. No matter how crazy it seemed.

The look on the Valdan's face was insulting to the extreme. He clearly deemed her unfit for the mission. Too bad. She was done with him and his alien kind. All that mattered to her was saving humanity.

"If you desire to join them, I will inform Entaya." Whatever he had seen on her face must have convinced him. Good. Megan broke for her room before he could change his mind.

Hours later, her room had become a self-made cage. She had assumed for some stupid reason that someone would come get her so they could work together and prepare to go on their mission. Too many movie montage's obviously.

Now, she was left with the debate raging in her own head. Did she leave the room and wander aimlessly through the halls hoping to find the Hub or the Lab? Go or stay. Get lost or left behind. Everything had a risk she wasn't willing to take.

Her mind spun in on itself until her chest hurt from the constriction. It was impossible. When the knock sounded on her door, she rushed to it like a drowning man to air. Yanking it open, she found Drew on the other side with his arm upraised.

"What?" Her voice was clipped. He wasn't who she had hoped to see.

"I thought you might need a guide to the Eatery. It's midday and you didn't come down for lunch." He smiled sweetly at her and guilt ate at her heart.

"Yeah. That would be awesome. Thanks." Now that he had mentioned food, her stomach rumbled. Closing the door behind her, she moved out into the hall.

"The symbols on the plaques up there tell you where you are." Drew pointed up towards the ceilings where there were indeed plaques mounted at the tops of the walls. He handed her a thin sheet of plastic material with symbols printed on it. "This is a code for them. It'll tell you what they mean so you can get from one place to the other."

To illustrate his point, he reached over and used the sheet to show her how they needed to get from here to the eatery. She would have preferred a map but figured it wouldn't take too long to get the hang of the alien coding.

Drew let her lead the way through the halls. She only got them lost once and was able to reroute and get back on track without his help. By the time they made it to the room that looked like a huge food court she was confident she could make her way around without help.

Inside, he helped her navigate the ordering system. There was no money exchange system here. Everyone was entitled to a meal, so it was a matter of choosing between preferences and allowed portions.

Very little of what ended up on her plate looked completely normal. Then again, none of it looked totally foreign. At the table, she was more excited to taste it than scared. Drew dug into his plate with gusto, wiping away the unease.

By the end of the meal there was only one truly horrible flavor combination. No matter what planet you come from blackberries do not belong in egg salad sandwiches. Other odd combinations like diced oranges in rice could be adjusted to.

"Do you know what's going on with the vaccine distribution?" Megan was regretting her earlier decision to leave Molab's side.

"Not really. Molab's not a big sharer. He's holding some bad feelings towards humans. I don't think they really have it ready to go yet." Drew was looking longingly at the food counter. Megan wondered if they allowed seconds for growing males.

"So, it could be days before we go?" She was dejected to hear that. At the rate the Dark Ones could turn Thralls, every minute was precious.

"Yeah, I guess." Drew got up and headed back to the counter. Megan debated waiting for him to fill up, but the reality was he could go back again and again before that happened. Her time was better spent finding Entaya or Molab and getting real answers.

Waving goodbye to Drew, she headed out of the Eatery. It was a challenge to her new skills, but she managed to find the tank room where they had first met Entaya. The room was twice as active as it had been the day before. Megan almost retreated rather than brave the bustle of bodies.

The beautiful Valdan woman sat on her chair answering questions and directing activity. When her opal eyes landed on Megan, she waved her over. The others made way as she crossed. Megan tried not to notice the whispers and side glances drifting her way. She went lots of places where her look caused a stir. That was the point. This was the first alien one.

"It's come to my attention you desire to join our delivery teams." Entaya gestured to a spot next to her throne where Megan assumed she was supposed to stand.

"Yeah. I want to be out there helping." Megan didn't expect this alien woman to understand so she wasn't going to waste her breath with a long explanation.

"Forgive my rudeness but you don't seem up to a strenuous activity such as this." Her hand waved regally from Megan's head to foot.

"I'll get the job done. Don't worry about me. I'm tougher than I look." Megan set her shoulders. This Valdan would be the next in a long list to be proved wrong.

"Very well. It is your fate. Understand that my people have been instructed to put the mission first. Should you fall behind they will leave you."

"Understood." Megan had expected nothing less at this point. Whether they called themselves good or evil, every alien she had met to this point was cutthroat to the core. All that mattered was she got to go.

Standing in the Hub later that evening, anticipation bounced around the room. It hadn't taken days to get things together like Drew had told her. They weren't making a full out assault like she had hoped either. Three targets. That was all they were hitting tonight. Three targets.

The intention was to see how the distribution system worked in these three areas and then calculate for a wider dispersal. Megan was afraid they were being too timid with their approach. Once they left tonight, the shields would be offline, and their position compromised. The downscaled objective meant they would keep minor cloaking abilities intact.

It was better than nothing but only slightly. The compromise felt like it had put them into a dangerous middle ground that threatened to cost them everything while giving them nothing. Too late to change the game plan now. Assuming anyone with power would even be willing to.

She was in the first team to leave. They were headed for London, England. She had never been so that was kind of exciting. The Dark Ones in that part of the world hadn't broken free, so the vaccine was being distributed as a preemptive strike. They were the control group. And the team least likely to see action.

The second team was headed to Giza, Egypt. Nearby, Cairo was overrun by Dark Ones and their Thralls. It was a dangerous mission and she had fought to be on that team, but the answer had come back a hard no. She was going to accept the loss...this time. Anyone on that team was taking their life into their hands.

The third team was headed to their hometown. She knew Molab had chosen that target specifically in the hopes of clearing a way for Quelis and the others to reach them. Megan was all for seeing Sorche get her ass handed to her, but it was a mission she wasn't up for quite yet. Not that she would ever admit that to anyone. She had the excuse that it was going to be just as dangerous a mission as Giza. 'No' to one meant 'no' to the other.

The Hub here was fancier and way larger than the ones near home and outside Seattle. Probably because they didn't need to disguise it as anything else. A set of concentric circles radiated out from the center of the room ending a few feet short of the walls. The room itself was the size of a basketball court if they were made round.

The inner most rings began to glow and radiate outwards as the time for transport grew near. Porters in gray jumpsuits directed everyone into the glowing rings and Megan could feel the vibration throughout her body. It increased to the point of discomfort long before the porters had everyone situated and left the area. Finally, the glow became steady and the now familiar sensation permeated her cells.

When normalcy returned, she was standing in a back alley in what she could only assume was jolly old England. It was day here. Cool. The smell of rotting vegetables and old urine overwhelmed her nose and she happily moved with her colleagues into the wider thoroughfare.

The roads were narrower than back home and the buildings closer together. She enjoyed the feeling of age and history. Scuffs in the walls and roadway a testament to the millions of travelers who'd proceeded her.

Two blocks over and down another alley they descended a set of stairs and encountered a metal grate. A younger man with sprouts of purple hair stepped past her and cut the lock with a hand-held laser. Pushing the gate open, he motioned for her and the others to enter.

She clicked the light disc they had given her with her gear and descended into the waterways. It was a fifteen-minute walk in the dank murky tunnels before they reached the first aquifer. Dumping their payload took them half that time and they were off to the next drop spot. Two hours later, they emerged into the dusky light successful.

The guy with the purple hair used his laser to weld the gate shut once again and the party returned to the alley way. Megan wasn't sure how their team leader knew which was the right one, but it began to turn blue when he pressed the right series of bricks. Assured they were in the right place, she settled in for the return experience.

Back on the ship she felt the letdown of adrenaline unspent. Traveling to England in an instance was always gonna be cool but their mission had been the equivalent of a science expedition. Not so exciting.

The other teams would have better stories to tell. Those would be worth hearing. It would be hours before they returned though. She wanted a shower and a nap while she waited. Molab was next to the door standing vigil.

"Where are Caneon, Drew and Trenton? I want to fill them in before I head to bed." She yawned as she waited for a direction to head.

"They have yet to return."

| 23 |

Chapter

Tyrone paced the confines of his front room. Two days of evading Sorche as her bond with him faded had culminated in his return to an empty apartment. Where his mama had gone was a question he had no answer to. And he had tried to find that answer.

The apartment was cleaner than he had ever seen it. The worn furniture was sporting a fresh coat of polish and minus some stains he had believed permanent. Whoever had come through had been way more thorough than the underpaid nurse he employed.

He feared Sorche had come for her but why clean the house? Why take a woman losing a battle with cancer? Her only value would be leverage. If that was the plan there should have been a message. *Come back to me or your mama gets it.* He hadn't found anything like that.

So, where did he go from here? It made no sense to dash around the city aimlessly, and he couldn't leave without her. The only option he could see was find the others and take Sorche down. That way everyone would be safe.

Flag on that play being- he didn't know where the others had gone. He had checked Caneon's house several times, hoping someone would show up. Eventually, he'd left a note taped to the door. Cell reception had become unreliable now that Sorche's goons were leading bands of Thralls on rampages through the city.

It was the craziest thing he'd seen. These unbonded idiots were aligning themselves with the Dark One in a bid for power. Evil is evil. You don't make it your ally. You can't trust it to keep its word or treat you right.

Afternoon was fading. It would be night soon and the goon squads would be out rounding up anyone they could. Sorche had brought in other Dark Ones. They worked with the goons to sort out those who were sent back for Dark uses, and those who were enthralled and left to continue their lives to maintain a semblance of order.

The Dark Ones were smart enough to keep some of the modern conveniences in place. Who doesn't like running water and electricity? Being highly advanced and all, he was sure they knew better ways to produce everything, but it had to be faster and easier to maintain what was already going on. At least for now.

They had no desire to hold onto our governments though. News media either. Both were under constant attack. He got most of his information from the news stations like CNN and FOX who had switched to web broadcasts only. Traditional TV channels had gone off the air.

They weren't given a lot of choice. The Thralls kept an eye out for reporters on the street. Tyrone had watched two separate feeds where reporters and crew were viciously beaten to death while the camera was picked up and operated by a Thrall. Sorche wanted everyone to know what would happen to them should they be caught.

Web reports verified that politicians and government employees who tried to show up for work received the same treatment. Tyrone skimmed past the videos of those. He didn't have the stomach for it. Sorche was a twisted woman. He didn't need any more evidence to prove that.

He needed to be on the move again. There was no telling what sick torture she would have for him if she were to find him. A duffel sat on the floor next to the front door. Inside were clothing and personal items he couldn't stand losing. The feeling of a last goodbye kept creeping over him no matter how many times he pushed it off.

The sky began to darken over his neighbors buildings one last time before he picked up the bag and left his home behind. Back into the fray for him. Sorche was going to pay for everything she had taken.

He made his way out the side door into the alley as the last of the light faded. The dark would give him cover as he made his way through the urban landscape. There was no clear destination in his mind when he started, but he found himself turning at this intersection or that, like his inner GPS had been programmed.

The building in front of him stood two stories tall. It was cliché villain hideout stuff. An old warehouse with dirty windows and an air of disuse that no one in their right mind would go into alone. He knew it wasn't Sorche's lair. Who or what had drawn him here? The only reason he hadn't resisted the pull was his desire for revenge.

He was debating the risks involved when a familiar strawberry blonde stuck her head out the door. Aleece smiled crookedly at him before retreating into the building. He assumed that was the only invitation he was going to get. His head swiveled to check both ways before darting in after her.

Inside, there was a smaller area walled off from the larger warehouse. Someone had lived there once as evidenced by the worn-down bed crammed into the corner. Dexon reclined on an old leather couch like it was designer while Naelah perched on the matching recliner as if it might bite her.

Aleece had alighted cross-legged on the sturdy desk. She indicated the office chair that had been pulled around to the side near the couch. He dropped the duffel near the door and took the seat. He still wasn't sure about these two aliens, but he trusted Aleece and so far she showed no sign of being controlled.

"Who brought me here?" He shot right to the heart of it.

"That would be me." Dexon raised his hand with a schoolboy smile. "Leftovers from pulling you out of Sorche's hell."

"Why did you wait until now?" Tyrone figured it was kinda crap to leave him hanging all this time.

"I've been trying for two damn days. You've been blocking." Dexon leaned his head back against the couch rubbing his temples. "You've been one big old headache, man."

Tyrone didn't know what to say. The guy was obviously playing for an apology. Like he was going to say he was sorry for blocking out an alien intrusion into his mind. No freakin' way! "Sorche has been tracking me."

Dexon sat straight up like a lightning bolt had jammed down his spine. "Is she still?"

"No. I lost her yesterday. Sat in a park for two hours with no blocks on just to be sure before I went home to my mama." Tyrone worked not to let his emotions cloud his voice.

"Good. Good. This place is crap, but I'm not wanting to find another one right now." Dexon relaxed back into the broken cushions. "Now, let's figure out how we get to Seattle."

"What? Seattle?" Tyrone was getting used to this particular alien causing him mental whiplash, but that was over the top. "Why would we want to travel halfway across the country?"

"There's an island offshore from there that the Valdan have a research facility on. We need to get there." Aleece's smile was softened by the sympathy in her eyes.

"Why? "Tyrone hated feeling left out of the loop.

"They are working on a cure. Or they are supposed to be." Naelah spoke to him without looking at him. Nothing dismissive about that.

"Great. Let's go." Tyrone was tired of playing defense.

"Just like that?" Dexon was back at attention.

"Yes. Just like that. We work out the details on the road. Sitting around here isn't going to make anything easier." Tyrone pushed out of the chair.

"Very well. We go." Dexon stood and the others followed suite.

A midnight blue crew cab truck was parked in the back bay of the warehouse they were in. Naelah lifted a suitcase into the bed and headed for the seat behind the driver as Aleece opened the driver's door. Dexon claimed shotgun leaving Tyrone with the cramped seat behind him. This was going to be a *fun* trip.

Stuffed into the space given him, he hoped his knees were digging into Dexon's back. The second he thought it, he shifted to the side as best he could so they would avoid pressing on the seat back. No matter what he had been through with these people his mama had raised him to be polite.

The high road has the better view, she always said.

His lower back began to ache as they reached the suburbs. Shifting to the left, his knee bumped Naelah's. A quick jerk had him back on his own side. He recognized the area around Caneon's house with relief. They must be stopping by there before heading out. The chance to stretch his legs would be welcome. Maybe if he were lucky, he could talk Aleece into letting him drive.

She didn't turn into Caneon's subdivision though. The road she took led towards a hiking trail Tyrone had frequented once or twice. It was a nice trail, but the road ended there. Why would Aleece be headed that way?

Reaching forward, he meant to tap her shoulder. Another vehicle came out of the dark and slammed into the side of their truck before he managed it. His hand flew sideways and ricocheted off Dexon's head. Aleece fought for control of the truck as the other larger vehicle rammed into them again and again. The front tire slid off the road and lost traction in the gravel.

Aleece jerked back towards the road as the other truck plowed into their back tires. They spun round and Tyrone lost track of the other vehicle as he fought to hold onto his dinner. The next collision came from the side sending them rolling off the road.

Bodies butted against each other in the cab as they were thrown around. The truck came to rest with the wheels in the air. Tyrone was laying on the roof with his ankle lodged above him between the seat and the console. He could feel blood sliding down his skin inside his pants. Naelah shifted to his left knocking into his bruised ribs.

Reaching up to wipe the sweat from his eyes, he was caught off guard as they were struck again. The truck slid over rocks and twisted as it knocked into smaller objects until it was shoved into something large enough to stop its momentum.

The sound of an engine revving accompanied the screech of metal as the door he was leaning against began to cave under the pressure. Dexon moaned in the front seat. Tyrone twisted to escape the flexing panel. His trapped foot was holding him back. Blood flowed harder as he yanked at it trying to break free.

Voices yelling in the background increased his anxiety. They were coming to finish the job. He needed to get free. Now. Regardless of the long-term damage, he forced enough space to wrench his leg loose. His foot was numb and his ankle throb. It was a bad combo, but he was free.

The door next to him was never opening again. He worked at the back window until it slid free under his sweat and blood slicked hands. Reaching forward he jostled Aleece. She didn't move. Dexon grabbed his arm and pushed him away from her.

Turning to the other man, Tyrone caught a tight shake of the head. He knew what that meant. But he was stubborn, and this was Aleece. She was sweet and kind. He reached for her again. The alien didn't know everything.

Dexon pushed him away again with a grimace and started to climb between the seats. Tyrone could see several large gashes across the man's face and torso, and he was cradling his arm to his chest. They could argue later. The voices were coming closer.

Pushing himself through the tiny back window was no easy feat. He lost more than a few inches of skin, but the motivation was strong. On the other side, he knelt in the cover of the truck bed and pulled on Dexon's good arm to pry him free. Naelah crawled from the opening seconds after her brother cleared it. Tyrone was shocked to see tear tracks on her cheeks.

Dexon used hand signals to lead them clear of the wreckage. Crouched behind a bush they watched a group of people swarm from the forest onto the truck that had hit them. Whoever had been in that truck must have fled because the doors stood wide open. Dome lights spilled into the night illuminating the people investigating.

Tyrone noticed the odd coloring of them almost immediately. At first he thought he might be in shock and imagining things, but no they really were some kind of human alien hybrid. He wasn't sure if that put them on the side of the angels or not. Then he saw Caneon.

Relief washed over him as he realized they were working with his friend. Finished with the empty vehicle, the group approached the blue truck and Tyrone ran for the driver's door. He couldn't let Caneon find her without warning.

His twisted foot gave beneath him five yards out. The pain of it pushed a cry past his lips the likes of which he'd never expressed before. People came running at him from out of the night. Fight or flight reflexes kicked in, and he was mid swing before it registered in his mind. A man sprawled in the dirt to his right while another clutched at his midsection to the left.

Tyrone forced himself to sit on a nearby log as people retrieved their friends and retreated to a wary distance. Dexon and Naelah remained in the dark. He searched for them on the fringes of the light without even a shadow to tip him off.

"Tyrone? Is that you?" Trenton broke from the crowd milling around him.

"Yeah, it's me." Tyrone's heart dropped to his toes. "Good to see you, man. I thought you took off with Molab."

"I did. We found the island and a cure. Kind of. Caneon and I came back to help distribute it. And find you guys." Trenton came to sit next to Tyrone, and he couldn't help but want to shuffle away from the guy.

"I was in the blue truck there when we got hit. My ankles pretty messed up. Sorry about the whole swinging at people thing." Tyrone rubbed his head as he did his level best to avoid the other man's eyes.

"Was anyone else with you? I know everyone got split up there in the city. Any chance you found Aleece?" Trenton moved closer on the log, eating up the space Tyrone had managed to eke out.

What more could he do? Drag this out until it was so horrible they could never speak again? That wouldn't be fair. It was time to be an adult and do the thing nobody ever wants to do. "She's in the truck."

Trenton turned toward the blue truck like it was materializing in front of him. Someone had turned on the other trucks headlights. One was broken and the other shown at an angle into the sky. It created enough light to see the outline of her head in the driver's seat.

"I'm so sorry, man." Tyrone wanted to say more. Something comforting or helpful, but his mind refused to offer anything up.

Trenton walked to the truck on tilted legs. Twice the crowd around him kept him from falling over branches and rocks in his path. The door had been pried open by the time he arrived. Tyrone knew the moment Trenton was sure it was Aleece because the man collapsed onto the ground. Every muscle ceased to function at the exact moment. It was creepy as hell and heartbreaking to watch.

Tyrone looked for Caneon. He had to be feeling this, but whatever he was going through it was being done in private. Or Dexon and Naelah had hijacked him and he didn't even know yet.

The throbbing in his ankle was incentive enough to stay firmly seated as Trenton's new friends took care of Aleece's body. They were careful not to touch her directly as they wrapped a black cloth, pulled from one of their packs, around her. Then she was laid carefully on the ground, close to where Trenton was leaning against a tilted tire.

The leaders of their group carried on a huddled conversation Tyrone couldn't hear from his perch. He tried to read Trenton's reaction, but the other man was wearing a million-yard stare. They had to be deciding whether to finish their mission or take care of her body. Was it even their responsibility?

Tyrone's head was pounding. When did that start? He wanted to lie down and close his eyes like he hadn't wanted anything in a long time. Looking at the log next to him, he started doing mental calculations, deciding if he could lie on it without falling off. He was leaning toward yes when a tall man with gray hair approached him.

"Can I help you to stand?" The man couldn't have been older than twenty-five and the gray was changing color. Hybrid.

"Uhm. We goin' some'ere?" Tyrone could hear the slur in his own words.

"To get you medical care." The man helped Tyrone to stand without putting his weight on the injured ankle. Fully erect he found the world spinning slowly like a carousel ride.

"Thank oo." Tyrone did his best to keep the line they were walking straight but the ground kept moving.

When his gray-haired friend helped him into a cave, he didn't even question. It was a tricky, trip and catch yourself, situation through the short tunnel before they hobbled into a small room. There were already several people inside waiting. They took a spot in the middle as a light filled his vision.

The spinning became unbearable. He clung to the only point of reference he had. His gray-haired companion. The man said something, but Tyrone couldn't make it out through the pressure in his skull. His legs gave way as a buzzing absorbed his focus. It ate away at his brain until there was nothing but the horrifying noise. Then it was gone, and the light faded.

Taking in the area around him he saw Molab first. The white-haired alien stood imperially near the door with his arms clasped in front of him. His expression changed little as he took in Tyrone's bloody state. It was hard to look more condescending than when they had first met.

"TYRONE!"

A whirlwind hit him from the side before he could turn to see who it was. His gray-haired companion hadn't released him yet, and that was the only thing that kept him from going down. The sudden movement sent his stomach contents on the climb. He lurched away from the arms entangling him into the bucket an anonymously helpful person had left nearby.

"Oh Crap. I forgot about that. I'm so sorry. I shouldn't have jostled you. Are you okay?" Megan whirred around him with an energy he wasn't up for.

"Megan. Beck ovf." He made his way as far from the bucket and its contents as his mangled ankle would let him. In the bright lights of this alien room, he could see the torn and bruised skin way too clearly and his brain had taken to banging its own thunderous beat inside his skull.

Gray hair was back with his helpful arm to steady Tyrone. He was moving down the alien hallways with no idea where they were going, and it didn't matter because the guy had said medical something or other back on the log. Megan trailed behind like one of those yippy little dogs people kept in their purses.

He wanted to be happy to see her. Later maybe. Or maybe not. So many things had happened since they left Caneon's house for Mexico. He wasn't the same guy with the stupid crush on the girl who was never going to see him.

They entered a room with beds and monitors his muddled brain could still identify as medical equipment, even if they looked like sci-fi movie props. Tyrone tried to push backwards out of the room when a woman with orange hair approached. Gray wouldn't let him, and one footed he couldn't gain the purchase he needed.

The two hybrids impelled Tyrone onto one of the beds without a full-blown panic attack, but his heart rate was sending all kinds of alarms beeping. The woman with orange hair moved out of his eyesight and his body relaxed. Gray hooked him up to the last of the machinery in the bed while Megan hovered nearby.

"Aleessse.?" Tyrone needed to know what was happening with her and Trenton.

"She's being taken care of. As is Trenton." Gray spoke quietly as he adjusted a sensor attached to Tyrone's forehead.

"What's wrong with Aleece?" Megan moved closer to the bed. Gray glanced at her then Tyrone with the question written all over his face. Should they tell her?

"She diied." Tyrone wouldn't make the other guy do his dirty work. "In the wrethck."

"She's dead?" Megan's eyes welled as she grabbed his hand. He squeezed her fingers in the best version of a hug he could. Whatever the bed was doing, his head was starting to clear. He watched giant tears spill from Megan's eyes as she stared into the corner of the room.

Tyrone realized for the first time that she wasn't wearing her usual Goth makeup regimen. Eyeliner and makeup yes, but not the layers of it in black and red. She looked younger, more vulnerable. He reached across to cover her hand with his other one.

"How did you wreck?" She was looking at him again.

"Sorche sent someone to run us off the road." He was relieved to hear the words come out clear. "She must have been able to track me after all."

"How did you get free?"

"Dexon." It was his turn to look off into the corner. He didn't want her to see the guilt. It should have been Lynea's kids who got free.

"I need to go check with Molab. I'll be back. You're in good hands." She smiled at him and he let go of her hand reluctantly. The lady with orange hair was lurking around here somewhere. He knew she wasn't Sorche, but his mind wasn't listening to logic on this one.

"Let me know what Trenton is going to do, for Aleece. As soon as you know. Please." Tyrone pleaded with her.

"Of course. I promise. And I'll see if Drew's back. He went to Giza to distribute the vaccine. He'll be so excited to find out you're here." She smiled again and this time it reached her eyes.

Once she was gone Tyrone let his own tears fall.

| 24 |

Chapter

Caneon walked into the dark forest with no assurances as to where he was headed. A sense of peace and confidence availed him of the knowledge that he was going in the correct direction, so he continued on. Someone was waiting for him out there. He was aware of that and he trusted whomever it was.

That was far less information than his mind would normally require, but today was extraordinary. For some reason he couldn't currently pinpoint. Perhaps the person he was meeting in the woods would elaborate for him. Even more reason to hurry along.

The voices behind him had faded long ago, but the darkness didn't carry its usual malevolence. His thoughts were able to sort themselves in the quiet stillness of the night. Crickets chirping and branches rustling around him served as white noise to the inner voice.

It soothed him. Washed away images of strawberry blonde hair stained red. Green eyes fixed beyond him; no one residing there. Of peaches and cream skin faded to shades of ash. His heart could not see those things again and again. So, he listened to the voice.

It whispered. Soft and sweet. Like a friend, lost for a time but returned to him and excited to reconnect. He'd had a friend like that once as a child in Egypt with his mother. The reunion had been magical. Like finding himself all those years later. It was a shame they had lost touch after that.

Water splashed under his feet. He should have leapt over the small stream. It was a miscalculation on his part. Not the fault of the person waiting for him. His memories had distracted him. That was not a mistake he would allow to happen a second time.

Turning to the left, he focused back in on the direction he should be traveling, and his thoughts faded. Whomever was waiting, they could deal with it all. He only needed to get to them, and every other concern could fade away. He need not feel it ever again.

Breaking free of the tree line brought him face to face with his salvation. His first inclination was to run into their arms, but the voice that wasn't truly a voice urged him to show some decorum. So, he restrained his impulses and came to a stop directly in front of his new-found savior.

"Caneon. How are you tonight?"

"Not well. Thank you for asking. How do we proceed?" Caneon tried not to let impatience color his voice. He didn't want irritation to cause them to renege on their promises to him.

"First things first. We have a lot to do and very little time to do it in. Follow us."

| 25 |

Chapter

Lynea was relieved to be free of the weight across her chest. One of Sorche's Dark flunkies had come in and waved a medical disc over her ribs yesterday. It eased the band of pain that had settled there but he obviously chose not to heal her completely. Quelis said they should be suspicious Sorche repaired anything.

When the goons came to bring them out of the basement, she knew they were about to find out the price for the generosity. Her legs protested the extended hike up through the buildings stairwells. Whatever laid at the end of this little journey, wasn't going to be a picnic.

Quelis' plodding steps sounded in rhythm behind her. She wasn't alone and that was something. His silent company had become a pillar of strength. What if Sorche took that away? Would she sell out the human race?

Tyrone's return meant there was hope for her beautiful children to be free again. What cost was she willing to pay for that freedom?

The enslavement of the entire world? Would that even gain them anything? To be free of Sorche but trapped in a world where her and her kind ruled would still make them slaves.

There was a wall she kept ramming into when she told herself she had to leave them in Sorche's grasp. It just wasn't in her to walk away from them. There had to be a solution. A way to save them all. If she could focus, she could find it. She knew she had it in her.

The burly men who pushed and prodded her around refused to give her time to contemplate the solution she needed. They were constantly in her space. Keeping her distracted with their mere presence.

A shove to her shoulder sent her through a doorway she hadn't been paying attention too. Stumbling forward, she fought to gain her balance. Had her hands been free this would have been easier to accomplish. Years of yoga paid off as she used her core muscles to right her center.

Standing at the other end of the room was the woman she least wanted to see. Sorche. Searching frantically, Lynea found neither of her children's faces amidst the crowd packed into the area. There was a medieval feel to the whole proceeding as Sorche's goons paraded Lynea and Quelis down the narrow aisle left clear by the crowd.

Sorche had failed to erect a throne but she was definitely holding court. Lynea was appalled to find that the eyes of the courtiers meeting her own weren't enthralled. These people were here of their own free will. Pledged to the alien woman without mental persuasion.

A cheer rose up as Sorche raised her hand to the newcomers. She almost seemed as if she expected them to kiss her knuckles. Lynea was not doing that. The goon behind her shoved extra hard as they neared that outstretched hand and Lynea ended up kneeling below it.

Pressure at the nape of her neck kept her from lifting her head. The cheers of the crowd escalated, sending chills down her spine. Her heart sped in her chest until she thought she might faint at the nasty woman's feet. Wouldn't that be wonderful.

"Enough, Sorche." Quelis' voice cut across the noise.

"You seem to be misinformed. I am the one who says when something is enough." Sorche spoke softly but the words carried a poison that pricked at the skin.

"You wanted something from me. If you harm her, you'll never get it." His voice carried steel.

"The time for bargaining is past. As is your usefulness. I have gained what I need by other means. You are irrelevant." Sorche sneered at him as she danced a small dagger lightly between and over her fingers. "She at least still has a use for me. As her children did before her."

Lynea's body shook as the import of Sorche's words seeped through her mind. There was only one other use the alien would have for pets, as she called them. Squeezing her eyes tight to hold back the flash of nausea, Lynea braced for the plunge of the knife.

This was the way it should end for her. Now that she'd failed to save them. Tears dripped from her nose unheeded. She no longer cared what this creature or her followers thought.

"You've found the others?" Quelis shifted, jangling his ankle cuffs.

"They will be in my control very shortly."

"That's not a yes. You still need a backup plan in case this other thing falls through." His voice sounded lower to Lynea. She wished he would stop arguing so they could get this over with.

"Look at you trying to convince me I need you. How pathetic. I assure you I have everything in hand." She laughed, but it didn't sound as confident as before.

"Very well. We'll be taking our leave then."

Lynea didn't have time to process the statement before the weight on her neck was gone. Standing upright, she was propelled through the crowd by Quelis' large frame. His ankle cuffs were gone, and he moved the two of them swiftly to a side exit.

With his free hand, he broke the chain on her handcuffs leaving them dangling from her wrists, and she realized he'd already done the same to his own. They moved down a long alleyway with him mostly carrying her weight before he stopped to break her ankle cuffs loose.

Free to move, they took off at a run leaving Sorche and her twisted court behind them. Lynea allowed the air moving past them to dry her flowing tears. If Quelis noticed them, he chose not to acknowledge it.

Two hours later they slowed, and she was following his back on auto pilot. He could have run off a cliff and she would have gone over the edge right behind him. No questions asked.

When he stopped in someone's back yard, she had no idea where they were and no inclination to figure it out. He opened the door and they walked into a familiar kitchen. He had taken them to Caneon's house.

It was probably as safe a place as any. Sorche had no real use for them. She might hunt them down for the pleasure of killing them, but right now her resources needed to be focused on keeping that antidote from getting out. They had time before she would come.

Lynea wandered listlessly into the living area. Dropping onto Caneon's outdated couch used the last of her energy. If only her mind would turn off and stop with the what ifs. Letting her head drop back, she fought to shut it all down.

Footsteps pulled her from her fugue sometime later. Forcing her eyes open, she found Quelis standing in front of her awkwardly. His eyes darted to the table across the room and hers followed suit. Two bowls sat on the nearest corner with steam drifting up into the air.

"I made us soup." As declarations went it was obvious.

"I'm not hungry. Thank you." She tried to smile at him. It was sweet that he had tried.

"You need to eat anyways." He reached down to take her hand. She tried to jerk away but found she wasn't fast enough to avoid his grip. "It's chicken noodle."

He pulled gently. She wanted to resist but the energy required was beyond her reserves, so she let him lead her to the table. He had her in a chair and pushed up to the table in no time. Taking his own seat, he smiled encouragingly at her before taking a spoonful.

"After we eat you should shower. It will help you feel better to get the last few days grime off you."

Lynea realized he must have done so already as his hair shined. She shifted uncomfortably as she wondered how bad she smelled. Maybe the hot water would help ease the ache in her bones. He was watching her expectantly, so she lifted the spoon to her lips.

"We need to talk about our next steps." He stared her down again, until she took another spoonful. "I think we should stick to the original plan. Hub to Seattle and then boat to the island. The others must be looking for us by now. I found a note from Tyrone on the front door. He left a phone number to contact him, but no one answered."

Lynea shoved another spoonful into her mouth as he continued to talk. How did she tell him she didn't want to go anywhere? Her fight was over now that her reason was gone. Her spoon scraped the bottom of her bowl. She'd finished her soup while he planned.

"I'm going to go shower now." She stood abruptly catching him mid-sentence.

"Yeah. O.K. I would recommend you use the one in Caneon's bedroom." Quelis began clearing the dishes as he talked.

"Thanks." Lynea dragged herself to the master bathroom. She wanted the alone time as much as the hot water.

She was amazed at the luxury Caneon had splurged on. Marble and nickel created an oasis of cool class fit for a spa. Jets of hot water massaged her aching muscles while she let her tears flow from the ache in her chest.

Everything was lathered and rinsed before the water turned cold, but just barely. Drying off with Caneon's towels was the equivalent of using a throw blanket. They were huge. She welcomed the extra coverage as she contemplated her grungy clothing.

No way was she climbing back into those rags. They weren't fit for anything but the little trash bin where she deposited them. Maybe Caneon had sweatpants or something in his room she could borrow until she got home. The thought of going back to her empty house nearly dropped her.

Walking out into Caneon's room, she found Megan's suitcase open on the bed. Quelis must have brought it in while she was showering. She didn't have the energy to decide if that was creepy or thoughtful. They weren't the same size, but a deep dive brought up an outfit that would work for the short term.

Clad in a thread bare concert T and a pair of jeggings that fit like capris, she faced her companion once again. He was sitting on the couch swiping through his version of a tablet. When he saw her, he smiled.

"Great, you were able to find something. I wasn't sure her clothes would fit you. She's very small."

"Yes, Megan is tiny." Lynea pushed a piece of hair behind her ear self-consciously.

"It's like someone forgot to feed her as a child." He shook his head scornfully. "Neglectful."

Lynea found herself relaxing at the obvious disgust on his face. He didn't think she was a giant compared to Megan's petite frame. Jared would have. Had Sorche killed him as well? Tears leaked from her eyes anew.

"I'm sorry. I didn't mean to offend you. Here, sit down." Quelis half stood and grabbed her hand, dragging her to the couch with him as he sat back down. Settled on the cushion near him, she felt stupid for breaking down over Jared.

"It's fine. Really, I'm fine." Lynea swiped the tears from her cheeks.

"I'm sure you're not. How could you be after what's happened?" Quelis' fist clenched on the couch arm. "I failed you and your children. I can never atone for that."

Lynea's gaze jerked to his face. Why was he chastising himself? He'd done nothing but try to help her.

"Quelis, no. You didn't fail us. Sorche did this. If you could have saved us you would have."

"I could have saved you and the boy. That night she brought him. I took a calculated risk that she would bring the four of us together. It was a mistake." He met her eyes squarely as she absorbed that he was telling her he could have been free at any time.

"You could have left us all behind and saved yourself."

"That was never an option."

"Why the pulling at the chains? Didn't you know it was hurting me?"

"I had to test them to know how much force it would take. And yes, I was aware of your pain, but it couldn't be helped. I needed to know if breaking them would kill you. That would have been coun-terproductive. I had decided your odds of survival were pretty high by the time she came to see us. But some of it was for show. I stu-pidly believed that the more vulnerable she felt I was the more likely she would be to bring both children, to taunt me."

"I would be lying if I said I didn't wish you had saved us that night. To at least have Tyler...but then I would hate myself for leav-ing Lydee. We can't play 'what could have been'. It won't get us any-where." Lynea reached over and placed her hand on top of his. His fingers relaxed under her own, finally. "Thank you. For what you did."

Lynea closed her eyes as the tears leaked from them. She couldn't watch him as she mourned. It was too much. He pulled her into his arms, letting her lay there long after the salt had dried on her cheeks and her sobs had quieted.

She woke later to find herself alone on the couch. Since she hadn't looked at the clock in forever doing so now was pointless. Stretching to work the kinks out of her back, she searched the house for Quelis. He wouldn't have left her alone and vulnerable.

Finding the house empty, she headed into the back yard. He was there practicing what looked like highly complex martial arts moves. Sitting on the back step, Lynea watched the graceful movements play out from one pose to another. When he caught sight of her, he came over and joined her in the sun.

"We should be going soon. Sorche will come here eventually." Quelis glanced over at her.

"I'm not going with you. I want to go home." She met his eyes and looked away.

"She'll find you there."

"Don't take this the wrong way, but maybe I'm okay with that." Lynea trained her eyes on her feet.

"You only think you mean that." He placed his hand on her arm. "I felt the same when my Marrola died."

"Who is Marrola?" Lynea turned to meet his gaze.

"My daughter. She was young. Just older than your children but not yet an adult. Adventurous and stubborn. Like her mother. She thought she could dare anything. There was an accident with a racing vehicle. She died instantly." His eyes never left Lynea's as he spoke. "I was so furious at everyone and everything that had put her there. I joined the first expedition that needed a soldier leaving our home planet."

"Did you leave a Mate at home? Your daughter's mother?" Lynea found herself filled with questions.

"No Mate. I'm a soldier. We rarely are chosen as anyone's Mate, but our genes are valuable. Women will ask us to father their young. Veia, that is Marrola's mother. She is an educator Mated to a legislator. They tried several times to have children before she came to me. It was an honor." Quelis shifted closer to the handrails as he spoke.

"It sounds like a lonely way to have children. I'm sorry you lost her. No parent should bury their child." Lynea placed her hand on his knee as she felt a tear trickle down her cheek.

"Excuse me."

Lynea and Quelis jumped at the unexpected voice. Ratcheting their heads to the left, they locked onto the group of three people standing at the edge of the yard. Dressed in jeans and t-shirts they could have passed for everyday people on the street except for one small thing. They were obviously alien hybrids.

The tallest stood at close to seven feet tall and the shortest no less than six. One had metallic green hair with blonde highlights. Another sported aquamarine eyes and a tiny nose. The third was so slender she would forever be told to eat more and the orange highlights in her hair had a lively look no dye could accomplish.

"Who are you?" Quelis deftly put himself between the three and Lynea before she had a chance to protest. Not that she was going to.

"We were going to ask you the same thing." The man with the metallic green hair took point. His blonde highlights moved in the light the same way Dexon's did.

"I'm Lynea. This is Quelis." Lynea spoke from behind Quelis for safeties sake, but she couldn't see the harm in them knowing names. Last time they checked, the one people Sorche wasn't working with was hybrids.

"Thank the stars. We've been looking for you. I am Naba. We were part of a group sent from the lab to disperse the vaccine into the city's water supply. After what happened to Aleece, the three of us were sent to find those of your group who hadn't been accounted for."

"What happened to Aleece?" Lynea came out from behind her protector for the answer.

"She was killed in an automobile accident caused by Sorche's followers."

Lynea grabbed for Quelis as her knees buckled. Another loss piled on. How many more could she carry before the weight crushed her? His arm came around her waist and brought her up against his side before she could collapse. Finding strength in his, she shored up her legs beneath her.

"We should go." Her steady voice surprised even her. Quelis questioned her with his eyes, but nodded assent to whatever he found on her face.

"Yes, we should." Naba motioned towards the side yard and they followed him out.

A hybrid vehicle waited at the curb and Lynea took a moment to appreciate the irony as Naba got behind the wheel. It was a tight squeeze for so many large beings, but they managed. Finding her body squished up against Quelis' she felt awkward about it for the first time since they had fled Sorche's lair.

Luckily, the drive was quick. They piled out at a local hiking trail. This must be where the infamous Hub was located. She couldn't wait to experience it for herself. Free of the car's confines, her bashfulness disappeared. When Quelis set off down the trail, she was right beside him.

She didn't see the attack coming out of the underbrush. Quelis probably could have avoided it easily, but once again he decided to protect her by jumping between her and an attacker who dropped from a branch above them. This was going to have to stop. She needed to learn that martial arts stuff he was so good at.

Focusing in on the threat at hand, she reached down and grabbed a fallen branch. Swinging as hard as she could, she brought it round on the goon headed her way. It glanced off his shoulder barely slowing him down, so she reared back for another swing. This time she managed to bash him in the head causing blood to flow.

He was nowhere near out, but she'd made him cautious. Swinging again and again, she didn't give him room to move in closer. It was keeping him at bay, but her arms where starting to burn. This wasn't going her way. She could hear struggle around her and knew there wasn't anyone to come to her rescue. Why hadn't she been taking those self-defense classes Jared had been foisting off on her for years?

Her opponent stepped left before lunging right and she barely knocked him back out of her personal space. He was leering at her now. The heavy breathing was probably giving her away. Yoga hadn't prepared her for extended cardio.

Then the man's face went blank. Swiveling to the left and right, Lynea searched for Sorche without taking her eyes off the man. Why had the alien woman taken her own goon over as a Thrall? Why wasn't that Thrall attacking?

Everything fell into place when Lynea locked eyes with Dexon. He fought on the edge of the clearing engaged with two of Sorche's goons, but he gave her a little wave.

Lynea wasn't sure how long Dexon could hold the man. She knew he didn't have a world he could keep them in like Sorche did. With that in mind, Lynea grabbed a rock and knocked the man over the head with it.

It wasn't fair sportsmanship by any means, but she needed to know he was out of the picture for a bit. Quelis and Naelah were moving towards her as a new wave of bodies came out of the tree line. Sorche wasn't going to stop and she could keep throwing people at them. Literally.

Lynea watched Naba disappear up the path towards the Hub. His companions lay broken in the clearing. She hoped he made it home to let the others know what was happening here. Too many stood between them for her group to make it. She turned and ran for Quelis and Naelah.

They reached Dexon as he finished the last of his opponents. Lynea couldn't help feeling that he'd played with them a little. There was a darkness in him that shown through no matter the light he tried to project.

"Follow me. We've found a hidey hole." Dexon veered to the right as he flung the words over his shoulder.

Pushing her body to its limits, she still trailed behind them. Had they not been waiting for her; she would have missed the moment when they dipped into the cliff wall and disappeared. She walked through the door Dexon was holding and into a room far beyond human evolution.

The walls shone softly, illuminating the space in a calming light. Symbols flashed on screens mounted into the walls with interfaces placed directly below them. In the far corner a table and benches were crammed next to a rumpled bed. Dexon hustled over to them. A quick interaction with the interface and they folded into the wall and floor seamlessly.

"It's an observation outpost." Quelis wandered the room inspecting screens. "I didn't know we had one in this region. Was it ever occupied?"

"Naelah knew of it from her time as planner. Apparently, it was never activated. Lucky for us since it's fully stocked. We can use it as home base to plan our attack against Sorche."

"We're all going to cram into this one room?" Lynea couldn't keep the strain out of her voice.

"No. The outpost has several rooms off this one. A central kitchen and living area as well as several bedrooms. This is the watcher's room with a rest bunk for whomever is on front watch. I'll show you the entirety of it while Naelah catches Quelis up." Dexon smiled his most charmingly as he offered his arm old world style.

"Thank you, but I'd like to be caught up as well. I think from here on out we all need to be on the same page." Lynea dug her heels in.

"I agree. She should stay." Quelis nodded at her.

"Very well. Let us begin." Naelah sighed.

| 26 |

Chapter

Megan drug her feet on the return trip to the infirmary. It hadn't slipped past her that Tyrone was less than enthused to see her. Their shared time in Sorche's hellscape had done damage. She longed to repair it but wasn't sure that was possible.

It wasn't going to help anything that she had to deliver more bad news. He'd endured so much. She was worried this could break him. Putting it off as long as possible seemed like the only move in her play book. So, she shuffled down the corridor at snail speed until her conscience popped off.

He was sitting in there all alone waiting for her return. As much as she didn't want to bring him this news, he didn't deserve to be left in limbo. Kicking herself in the ass, she picked up her pace. She could do this.

Breezing through the doorway, she stopped short of the medical bed. Tyrone was crashed out, snoring in a soft cadence. Barone waved from the corner, sending his gray hair into movement. Megan tiptoed around the bed to join him.

"No need to move quietly. We've been jostling around for the last hour and he hasn't registered us at all. We healed his wounded body then we gave him a light sedative for his anxiety. Teelie was making him jumpy." Barone gestured to a clear partition where Megan could see the red-haired tech working in a lab area.

"Will he be asleep for long do you think?" Megan wasn't sure if she was grateful for the reprieve or not. She'd worked up her courage once. It was going to be harder to do it a second time.

"It's hard to tell. His concussion was pretty severe. There was significant swelling as well as bleeding. Had he been left to human care there would have been lasting damage. Our intervention has healed that, but the process takes energy. He'll need time to recover."

"Can you tag me when he wakes?" Megan was still getting used to the communication device they called a PEC. She felt bad leaving, but there were things to take care of and he didn't need her while he was like this.

"Of course. I'll let you know the second he's conscious." Barone smiled boyishly, reminding her his hair lent an age to him he hadn't earned yet.

"Thanks, I'll owe you one."

Megan let her mind run through her to do list as she traveled the halls to Entaya's lab. Between Aleece's funeral, Caneon's disappearance, and Lynea getting cut off and stuck in an outpost, her friends were keeping her busy. Not in a good way.

Entering the Valdan woman's busy lab always made Megan feel like an intruder. Today was even more hectic. Once the Giza team went missing, it was all hands-on deck. Molab and Entaya stood shoulder to shoulder at a console near the back wall. Megan made her way to them.

"We can't narrow down on any of their trackers?" Molab's voice was a low rumble as Megan approached. "What if we dropped an extender cube outside the Hub? Would that give us enough of a range boost?"

"It's possible, but I'm reticent to send more personnel to Giza. There could be Dark Ones waiting for them upon arrival." Entaya tapped her fingernail on the display as she spoke. Megan didn't think the alien woman was aware she was doing it.

"I would be willing to take that risk." Megan watched the two larger beings jump at her voice.

"Megan, we didn't realize you were there." Entaya inclined her head in greeting as she made room for Megan to join their conversation.

"I didn't mean to startle either of you. Sorry. But I'm serious. I'll take the risk. For Drew." She peered up at their faces expectantly. Jeweled eyes stared back at her without a flicker.

"Should you be captured it would be a tactical disaster." Molab shook his head as he continued to access her. "Although, your time with Sorche may give you an advantage. I've found it impossible to influence you since. It leads me to believe you've developed a resistance to us at the very least. Perhaps even an immunity. I had hoped to test it when Dexon returned."

Megan was less than enthused to find out he was planning her future as a lab rat. Even if it did mean proving she couldn't be controlled by aliens ever again. That was something she could embrace wholeheartedly. If it was true for her then it was true for Tyrone. She could enjoy giving him that good news.

"Tyrone is healed. I'm sure he'll want to go with me. For Drew. If I'm immune or whatever then he should be too." Megan was practically bouncing at the idea. Finally, she was going to get something good out of that ordeal.

"We have little choice. It's less than ideal but yes we will give you and your friend clearance to place the extender if he chooses to go with you." Entaya turned back to the display, dismissing Megan.

The high handedness rolled right off her back as she made her way out of the room. Barone still hadn't signaled that Tyrone was awake. There was time to stop by and see Trenton, but she was going to be quick.

He was eating alone in his room when she entered. The lights were low, leaving everything in a state of gloom. When she sat next to him at the table, she could see he'd moved the food around on his plate more than put it in his mouth. His eyes were swollen and blood shot when he finally looked up.

"What did you need Megan?"

"Just checking on you. Can I do anything?" She reached to touch his arm, but he jerked away.

"Can you bring my sister back?" He sneered.

"I wish I could. Aleece was amazing. Smart, funny...beautiful. Too young to have been taken from us." A tear slid down Megan's face as a memory of Aleece laughing flashed through her mind.

"We never should have gone with you guys. If we had stayed in Phoenix." He pushed away from the table to pace the room.

"We all have things we would do different. IF we could. I can't stay long. Drew and his team are missing in Giza. I got permission for Tyrone and me to take a range extender through the Hub. They hope it will give them enough power to lock onto their trackers. I just wanted to check and see if I could help you prepare a service for her." Megan watched his back as he wore a groove in the floor.

"They have her body stored in a cryo something or other. There won't be a service until I can bury her next to my parents. I was told they can keep her that way indefinitely. I want in on your mission." He stopped pacing to drill her with his eyes.

"Wait, what?"

"Giza. I want to go."

"You just lost your sister. I don't think this is the best time to go running off. I'm sure they can get you to Phoenix." Megan was having trouble catching her thoughts up.

"Phoenix has been infested. Haven't you been watching the news? Dark Ones are popping up all over. This water thing isn't going to cut it. I need to be fighting." He started grabbing his gear before Megan could decide either way. Since there was little chance she could stop him on her own, she followed behind when he left the room.

"Tyrone's in the infirmary." Turning to the left, Megan lead the way.

They came through the doors to find the medical bed empty. Searching the room, Megan found Barone and charged right over to him.

"You were supposed to let me know the second he woke up." Megan did her best to look intimidating from two feet below his face.

"Calm yourself. He's changing his apparel. I sent a tag." Barone held up his own PEC to show her the proof. Checking hers, she realized she'd missed it. Her settings needed to be changed, so she heard the thing go off, but she had no clue how to do that. One more reason they needed to get Drew back.

Tyrone came out in the baggy pants and tunic like tee that the hybrids preferred. It looked good on his muscular frame. Very martial arts chic.

"Hey." She wished her brain had come up with something better than that to start.

"Hi. Trenton. Man, I'm so sorry." Tyrone extended his hand, pulling the other man in for an embrace once it was accepted. "Aleece was special to all of us."

Megan was shocked to see tears leak from both men's eyes before they abruptly released. She averted her gaze quickly to give them a private moment. The sound of clearing throats was her signal it was clear to resume the conversation.

"Drew is missing." Megan had planned to ease into it, but now that the moment was here her brain lost its tact. "Molab and Entaya have a mission for us to drop an extender in Giza to give them better range and lock onto their trackers."

"We can't catch a break." Tyrone looked like someone had punched him in the gut.

"It gets worse. Caneon disappeared after the crash. Quelis thinks Sorche has him and will use him to find the atoll we are hiding in. Lynea got cut off from the Hub. She's holed up in an outpost near home." Megan tore the band-aid off as fast as she could.

"Damn. Tell me that's all you got." Tyrone ran his hand over his head.

"There's nothing we can do about that last bunch. We can help Drew. Let's go do that." Trenton's voice trembled more than Megan would have liked, but she agreed with his sentiment.

"OK." Being the reigning expert of the group, Megan took the lead to the Hub.

Molab was there with a box about two foot by two-foot square. Made of a smooth black material, Megan couldn't see any seams or closures. Molab handed it to Tyrone while scowling at Trenton.

"Where do you think you're going?" He rumbled down at the hostile human.

"With them." Trenton growled back.

"You're a liability."

"Deal with it." Trenton pulled the box from Tyrone's grasp and moved out to the middle of the light rings.

"We'll keep him safe." Tyrone threw the words over his shoulder at Molab as he joined his friend.

Megan decided it was better to follow without comment. Molab sent them or he didn't. She had no sway on his opinion. Relief filled her when the lights started to pulse.

People in gray jumpsuits hustled forward carrying backpacks and guns. The men happily accepted them. Megan took the box to free their hands. She'd never trained with weapons. They'd be more accurate than she would.

"The extender will activate itself once you set it outside of the Hubs rings. Return immediately. Do not do anything stupid to jeopardize this." Molab's words rang across the room to them as the world began to vibrate.

Megan braced herself for the now familiar buzzing sensation. When the world settled again, she was standing in the shelter of a sandstone cavern. Light discs flickered to life near the ceiling as sand drifted down into the empty space.

They were going to have to leave the room to set the box outside of the Hub rings. With firearms at the ready Tyrone and Trenton took the lead with Megan following behind. They pressed against the sides of the opening ready to fire out should an ambush be there when it opened.

Megan pushed in the code to open the door and stood as far out of the line of fire as possible until they gave her the all clear. It was a tense moment as the door slid open with all eyes straining for the slightest movement.

Fully open, it revealed an empty hall trailing into the dark. Trenton pulled a light orb out of his pack and sent it sliding into the unseen. When that failed to unmask hidden enemies, they breathed a little easier. If the Dark Ones had taken Giza, they hadn't posted troops at the interior of the Hub.

"How far out do we need to place this box?" Megan was all for getting this done and getting back, but she wanted to make sure it worked. If they were too far underground to get the range they needed, it did Drew no good.

"I vote we get to a surface area. Cell phones and Wi-fi need open air. So, should this." Tyrone was looking at Trenton who nodded agreement.

"OK. Let's go." Megan gestured to the doorway and the two men took the lead.

Following them down the gloomy hallway, Megan felt her legs tremble a little more with each step. A ball formed in her stomach and twisted until she could feel it rising up her throat. The outer door came into view as her courage stretched to its thinnest.

She nearly wet her pants when the door began opening before they reached it. Trenton and Tyrone took up positions on either side of the hall but there was nothing to hide behind. They were exposed to whoever came through. Friend or Foe.

A large frame filled the door taking far more room than a human would. Megan felt the air move as the men forming a wall in front of her braced to fire. Trenton kicked the light orb and it slid over to blind the intruder. As the tension built to crescendo Megan caught a good look at the man's shimmering blonde hair and almost sapphire blue eyes.

"Gerus! Don't Shoot! It's Gerus. He's one of us." Megan pushed at the muscles around her, clambering to breach the moment before it turned deadly.

"Megan?" The hybrid male stepped forward. Others followed behind him once he cleared the door leaving their companions outside to guard the opening.

"You're safe." Megan was still holding the black box as she pushed her way through the arms and legs her companions kept placing in her path.

"Yes, we are. It was touch and go for a moment, but we seem to have persevered." Gerus made it within striking distance of Tyrone and she had yet to get past her companion. Glaring up at the man, she pushed through his latest obstacle with relief. He had the nerve to shrug at her as he shifted out of the way.

"Entaya sent us with a range extender so we could track you. We thought you were captured." Megan held the box up as evidence of her story and he lifted it easily from her grasp.

"That won't be necessary, but I appreciate the gesture. We should get inside quickly though. I would like to seal the Hub." He gestured towards the hall. His men slid past them until the door was once again closed. "Drew has chosen to stay behind with Tonamas. He believes he can be the most help there. If you would like to join him I can arrange for an escort. Otherwise, I would prefer to fill you all in when I tell our story to Entaya and Molab."

"I'd like that escort." Trenton spoke decisively for a man who had no details. Megan expected Tyrone to join him, but he shook his head no when she looked his way. Gerus called back one of his guys and the two were gone just like that.

She resisted the urge to grill Gerus all the way back to the island by trying to figure out why Tyrone was returning to the atoll. He'd made it clear he was over whatever crush he'd had on her, there was no one else there, and he was less than enthused with the Valdan. Man of mystery, your name is Tyrone.

Standing outside of Entaya's lab for the second time in twenty-four hours, Megan felt fatigue pull at her. Adrenaline was only going to carry her so far. She hoped Gerus wasn't one of those speakers who droned on until you wanted to poke something into your ears to make it stop.

The room was the emptiest Megan had ever seen it with less than a dozen people working the monitors and machines. Entaya and Molab sat at a table near the center of the room. Normally it was covered with equipment and work debris but tonight it sat cleared of all but two cups.

Gerus moved round the table to take Entaya's hand as she rose to greet him. Her smile was warm and full of relief. He took the seat next to her as the others fanned out around the table near them.

Megan jostled to make sure she ended up in the seat next to Molab. He wasn't her favorite person, but she was positive he wouldn't be left out of any details. Tyrone bumped her elbow as he sat in the seat next to her.

"Tell us where you've been and why you've returned without members of your team." Molab directed the command to Gerus in his low voice.

"We encountered resistance in Giza. Thralls had been planted near the water supply. They knew of our plan before we arrived. There was an altercation. They must have signaled to Dark Ones nearby. We were quickly outnumbered. Things looked dire. Then Tonamas showed up." Gerus' lack of details had Megan clenching her fingers. Come on.

"Captain Tonamas?" Entaya interrupted.

"I'm unsure. He didn't identify himself by any designation. There were several Valdan following him. They defeated the Dark Ones, and once we explained our mission, helped us distribute the vaccine." Gerus leaned back satisfied with himself.

Megan found she had more questions now that she'd heard his story. Who was this guy who had saved them and why? Did he have a better way to fight the Dark Ones? Gerus said they had defeated them? What did that mean? Could they learn to do it? She wanted to ask all these questions and more, but it felt like the wrong time. The vibe in the room was off.

Everyone sat in silence waiting for Entaya or Molab. Scanning their faces, Megan was having a hard time deciding what she was seeing. They were radiating fear and distrust which didn't make sense. Hadn't they just found allies? The prolonged silence made her uneasy.

"Who else was with him?" Molab's voice was a welcome break to the tension.

"He has dozens who fight with him. I didn't get an accounting of their names." Gerus leaned forward, placing his hands on the table.

"Dozens? How many? Where did they come from? Where does he house and feed them?" Molab leaned forward as his voice whipped across the table.

"Fifty fighters maybe more? Not all of them pure blooded. He didn't give us exact numbers. That's why Drew stayed behind, for more information. Tonomas uses the Hub in Giza to gather them from around the world to be trained and armed. Now that he knows we exist he wants to align with us." Gerus met Molab's glare with an impressive amount of confidence.

"What's the big scary deal? He sounds like someone we should be embracing and you're acting like we've met a new enemy." Megan had thought she was prepared to have Molab's focus on her until it was. The weight of his gaze had her prepared to shrink under the table.

"Captain Tonamas was one of the first to become a Dark One. He led their forces to defeat us time after time. The man has a brilliant mind for strategy. The battle to imprison him and several of his most devoted followers in Egypt was bloody and brutal. It was also a great turning point for our side." Entaya spoke softly to the room. Megan could see the exhaustion creeping into her eyes.

Megan felt like she had been fighting for her life forever and it had only been a few weeks. How must Entaya and the others feel having seen this war drag on for millennia? Megan couldn't comprehend the weight of it.

"I understand why you wouldn't want to trust him. That's one hell of a history, but I trust Drew. If he says this Tonamas guy is the real deal then we should go with that." Tyrone leaned casually on the edge of the table.

"You've spent most of this engagement under the thrall of one of their more powerful fighters. I'm not sure that qualifies you to have an opinion here." Molab snarled derisively.

"Perhaps it does. He has a firsthand look at the inside of Sorche's mind. We never managed to free any of their Thralls before. That is a skill that Dexon brought with him when he reverted. And he did revert. This is all new territory Molab and we need to explore it." Entaya pushed herself up from the table. "I'll not sit around here and discuss it endlessly like politicians. He's offered his aid and I am going to take him up on it. If you want to stop me, beholder, you will have to do so physically."

Megan watched the alien woman glide out of the room with her blue hair cresting around her. She felt like applauding her exit. That was probably over the top, so she kept her hands firmly clasped in her lap.

"It looks like we're here for the long haul. Want to help me find a room?" Tyrone's voice floated down to her from where he stood next to his chair.

"Yeah. Of course. I know just who to talk to." Megan stood up and was surprised to find that she did know just where to go and who to talk to. When had she gotten dialed into the hybrid community and why did it feel like the first place she ever wanted to call home?

| 27 |

Chapter

Drew watched Trenton enter the room with mixed feelings. The last thing they needed right now was a macho standoff. Tonamas was all alpha with the -follow or get the hell out of the way- attitude that entailed.

It had taken Gerus and Drew days to convince the alien man they could be useful allies to his cause. His first inclination after saving their butts and finding out they worked with Molab had been to send them back home while he and his men distributed the vaccine.

There had been a lot of smooth talking required to change his mind. Gerus had proven himself a valuable asset. The hybrid could probably sell sun in the desert. Still, he'd utilized every bit of his skill to convince Tonamas they had other things to bring to the table once the water was treated.

Now, they stood on the tipping point as they waited for Gerus to convince Entaya and Molab to see the value in the exchange. Drew knew from firsthand knowledge how stubborn the weathered alien could be. He was hoping Entaya would soften him.

There was a lot to be said for Tonomas and what he could offer. He had built quite the resistance up. They were using a family compound as a base. The owner was a single man named Amun whom they had influenced shortly after breaking free. The amount of influence exerted was never clear.

Drew had felt bad about that until he found out about the hidden gun cache that came with the property. Every reason that might be here was shady as all get out. He had yet to meet the other human, who stayed in town, but it all felt like a karma thing.

The center of operations was set up in the football field sized dining room. The heavy wooden tables running perpendicular to each other were covered in maps, books, and laptops. Drew had claimed his own section of one in the farthest parts of the room. By five years old he knew that the quiet corners were the safest places.

Less than an hour of being here and he'd realized the alien sized beings jostling through the room had no sense of personal space. There was a bruise from an unattended elbow slowly turning yellow on his forehead to attest to that. So, he had to weave his view through the bustling bodies to get clear sight of Trenton's arrival.

His friend didn't seem to notice him nestled away as he swept the room. There were a lot of people between that door and his spot, so Drew took the chance to get a read on the other man. Something was off.

Trenton was lacking his usual swagger. His shoulders hunched as he followed a hybrid through the room. Drew recognized him as one of the soldiers sent with Gerus to the island. It was way too soon for there to be a reply.

Curiosity pulled him out of his chair and across the room as sure as a string on his sleeve. He met the incoming group where they had stopped to talk to Tonamas. The conversation was intense as the leader of this group was introduced to yet another intrusive human, as he liked to call Drew.

"I did not invite you here." Tonamas scowled at the human as well as his escort.

"I am *sorry* to intrude. I was under the impression you were looking for soldiers to fight the Dark Ones." Trenton puffed his chest and met the aliens eyes boldly before letting his gaze slide to meet Drew's.

"You believe you can be of assistance with that, human?" Their leader's laugh brought everyone's attention to the center of the room.

"Us humans drove your people into hiding. Don't underestimate what we can do." Trenton wasn't fool enough to let Tonamas take his gaze, but Drew could see him wrestling with the urge.

"I will give you that your numbers are daunting, but only until they turn you. After that, you're a liability we cannot afford to have."

"There are some among us who cannot be turned. Do they have value?"

"Is this possible? I didn't realize the vaccine was capable of such a change. Is this how you've acquired the ability? I was under the impression nothing had been tested on the island out of concern for the hybrid population." Tonamas turned to meet Drew's eyes with a question he didn't have an answer to.

"They hadn't tested it when we left. It could have happened after." Drew felt ridiculous throwing out the non-answer, but he didn't have anything better. Tonamas continued to stare. That wasn't going to force a different answer, man.

"How did I not realize before?" Tonamas finally broke eye contact to look back at Trenton.

"What?" Drew felt suddenly like a kid at the adult table. He hated that.

"I can't push you. You have been accommodating. Why? Was this a trick?"

"What are you talking about? There was no trick. I've been diplomatic. That's all." Drew's frustration grew as he processed the implications.

"He's not the only one." Trenton jumped in to snag the leaders attention. "They think that once someone has been manipulated and then freed from the control they form some kind of immunity or at least resistance to the mind control."

"Entaya is researching this?"

"She just started but yea." Trenton smiled cockily at the alien. Drew was relieved to see the other man hadn't completely lost himself.

"Interesting. There are facets to this we had not considered. How have Drew and these others been freed from control?" Tonamas pinned Drew with his eyes like he could peel the answer from beneath his skin.

"Dexon has been able to help us with that. It's still a work in progress but we're optimistic." Trenton was laying the charm down now that he had an audience.

"The rumors are true then. He lives. We believed Sorche would scourge him once he turned from her ways."

"She's trying her hardest. Naelah is doing what she can to keep him alive and in one piece." Trenton leaned his hip into the table.

"I felt her when she came to Cairo. There was a human male and female with her. I tried to reach one of them. To pull her back. The man almost let me in but the woman...she was strong of mind. It is rare to find a human so sure of oneself as to leave no cracks. I would like to meet her again. She is a soldier we could use in this fight."

"That would be Aleece. I've never thought of her as a fighter, although she did shoot Tyrone once. She's Trenton's sister so I'm sure we can arrange something. Right?" Drew turned to the other man to find him standing white knuckled and ready to bolt.

"That would be hard to do. Sorche killed her." The words worked their way past his teeth and dropped at their feet.

"Oh, hell. I didn't know. I'm an ass." Drew felt trapped by his own stupid mouth. He wanted the details. He wanted to feel the pain coursing through his chest. He didn't want to make this anymore horrible than he already had.

"My condolences. The loss of such a soul is truly a sorrowful thing. You are welcome to join with us in our fight. I have a council with my lieutenants I must attend. Perhaps, later we can meet to discuss Entaya's findings on this immunity." Tonamas dismissed himself, leaving Drew staring helplessly at the friend he'd just hurt.

"Let's get you a place to sleep. We're pretty full up around here but there's an extra bed Gerus is no longer using in my room." Drew took to the hall with only a peek to be sure Trenton was following. It was no accident that he stayed far enough ahead of the other man to make a conversation uncomfortable.

Inside the bedroom, he showed Trenton the empty bed and waited patiently while his friend took a minute to look around. There wasn't much to see between the sparse furnishing, lack of décor and crappy view out the only window. Feeling helpful, he pointed out the bathroom two doors down from their room.

"You don't have to stick around kid. I can figure this all out on my own." Trenton spoke from his spot in the hall.

"Yeah, I know. I just thought maybe you'd like a tour or something." Drew bumped his fist against the wall repeatedly.

"If that comes with side looks and pity face, I'll take a hard pass."

"My bad. No looks. Promise. When you feel like it, maybe you'll tell me what happened?" Drew pushed away from the wall and shoved his hand out.

"I can live with that. When I'm ready." Trenton shook his hand once before dropping it and motioning down the hall.

Drew stopped by his workstation to grab his PEC before they headed out. It wasn't something he used often but he didn't dare go long without it. If Tonamas decided he needed him this was the way he'd call.

"What's that?" Trenton was pointing at the handheld device when Drew turned.

"They call it a PEC. It's an acronym for private electronic communicator. I've found they aren't really imaginative at naming things. Mostly it's a dumbed down cell phone." Drew stuck it in the pocket not already carrying his smartphone and headed out the door.

Along their way, he showed Trenton the makeshift mess hall, and the bunk room where the other men slept before taking him outside. The compound sat on enough land that you couldn't see a neighbor on any side.

The aliens had set up a shooting range on an open area away from the house. Anytime a new member joined the group the first thing they did was teach him or her to shoot. The bullets didn't have as devastating an effect on the Dark Ones as a human, but anything died if you shot it enough.

None of these older creatures were excited to receive their human gun. They grumbled about lost technology and togs. One of the men had explained to Drew that a tog was a small arms weapon that shot pellets of energy. Apparently, depending on the pellet it could be a stun gun or fatal as they come.

Every fiber of Drew's body wished there were a tog he could get his hands on but the Valdan council had ruled that colonizing ships go without them. They were issued defensive weapons like personal body shields and frequency emitters instead.

According to Drew's source, it was all due to a riot on one of the early colony ships. The crew had been slaughtered by their own weapons and the passengers had landed on the wrong planet. Chaos and war had ensued when the indigenous people didn't take kindly to visitors.

It was part of the reason the Dark Ones had managed to gain the upper hand in the original war. Nobody on the good guys team had been armed. Unless you count spears and arrows. Drew didn't after watching Sorche fight.

On the opposite side of the buildings there was a makeshift death-defying obstacle course. They made their way over to find it full. That didn't surprise Drew. It was always that way. In the dead of night, you could come out here and find people running it.

"Dedicated." Trenton braced with his hands in his pockets as he watched the bodies swing, duck, dive, and jump.

"There's always someone adding something to it. To make it harder or whatever. See the barbwire at the top of that far wall. Wasn't there yesterday. They're way proud of how difficult it is." Drew tried to mimic Trenton's pose, but he couldn't find his balance.

"I can see why. Maybe I'll give it a go when it's not so packed."

"Good luck with that." Drew was done looking at the crazy people bleeding for nothing. He headed back to the buildings. There was work he could be doing if Trenton didn't want to come.

"Hey, wait up. This tour ain't covered everything yet." Trenton fell into step with him easily. Everything the man did came easily.

"Over here is the armory." Drew turned to the left and headed to what had once been a pool house. Inside, a guy sat casually on a crate with his arms crossed on his chest. He eyeballed them as they entered but Drew knew his only job was to make sure they didn't take anything without permission.

"Hot damn. This is quite the collection." Trenton was already across the room checking out the guns lined up in stands.

"Tonamas says this war is going to last awhile. He figures now's the time to gather our resources. Before the Dark Ones know what we're up to." Drew repeated the spiel he'd been given when he first saw the room.

"He's gonna need more than one room if he's looking at all-out war."

"This is only one of several safe houses around the world. He likes to train new troops here and then send them on to the other places. When they go they take guns and supplies with them."

"You sure know a lot about this guy after being his guest for a short time." Trenton glanced away from the guns to raise an eyebrow.

"I like to know things. So, I make a point to find them out. Big deal." Drew shrugged as he moved out of Trenton's sight line.

"I wasn't criticizing kid. Just making an observation."

Unwilling to continue the conversation, Drew decided the best option was retreat. If he wanted to be interrogated, he'd go home and visit his old man. Outside again, he headed back to the main house. It had been too long since he'd checked his computer anyways. His probes might have found something while he was wasting his time playing tour guide.

| 28 |

Chapter

Blood dripped onto the floor at Caneon's feet. He wasn't sure it was his. Parts of his body had gone numb. Was that the onset of shock or were they gone?

He struggled to remember how he had come to be in this hell, but the images slammed into each other and fragmented ever smaller. Melding into the cries of pain resonating around him where the voices of his past.

Whispering to him. Run. Be free. She's not helping you.

He believed them. Sometimes. Then he would fight and struggle and scream. His voice was hoarse from those times. Then she would come.

She smelled of flowers after rain. Sunshine on a meadow. Lightness and beauty. Her hands soothed his skin until the stinging stopped, and the burning was no more. She was goodness and grace in his torment.

And then she was gone. Leaving him alone to the dark. For a time, there would be fragments that coalesced together again.

Stretching to the limits of his chains he could see out a window. It was covered in mesh and trash but occasionally the sun would filter through. Shining through the detritus like stained glass. Then he would remember Aleece. Beautiful, strong, wonderful Aleece.

Not like at the end. Before. On the plane or in the jungle. Light on her face, a smile touching her lips. Soft kissable lips.

And he would see Drew. Annoying, brilliant, youthful Drew going where he didn't belong. Courage and bravery.

Or maybe Megan. Doting, devoted Megan with her horrible makeup and hair. Her spirit to wear them proudly. Rebelliously. So determined.

Then the pain. Always the pain. Over and over the pain. And the fragments would go. No more friends. No more light. Only the numbness and the blood.

| 29 |

Chapter

Tyrone stood on the sandy shore of the atoll looking across the waters at the smoking mainland. Buildings burned twenty-four hours a day. Great billows of smoke poured into the skyline like factory stacks. Their sources passed word that Sorche had brought her armies to Seattle. They were advancing on Sanctus.

It would be a matter of days before her armies found a way to the atoll itself. Boats were not as plentiful as they might have been a few weeks ago but they were there. She would fill them with her Thralls and the Dark Ones who followed her. Then her flotilla of death would search them down despite their cloak.

The Hub was still functioning. The flame haired horror had tried to use it.

Entaya had locked it closed after the first wave had broken through. Too much blood had been shed to put that wave down. All entryways, doors, and hatches had been sealed shut in case they found a way to hack the lock. Nothing was full proof.

When they had encountered Gerus in Egypt three days ago Tyrone had been so sure they were on their way to victory. Sorche had snatched that from their fingertips. She was becoming horrifyingly tedious that way.

Seattle had been vaccinated. They had managed that victory before she came. She wouldn't be taking new Thralls from the people living there. Turning from the smudged skyline, he headed back to the war rooms forming in the atoll below his feet. News that she was on her way had galvanized the hybrids.

He made his way through the depths of the ship, dragging his heavy heart along. How else could Sorche have found them but by tracking him? This death and destruction were once again falling on his friends heads because they had saved him.

"Tyrone, have you seen Molab?" Entaya's voice in the hallway pulled him from his dark thoughts.

"No. I was returning from the surface. He was supposed to be meeting in the conference room. He had a video call with Tonamas. If you'd like I can take you there." He tried to fight the urge to bow to the tall woman and lost.

"That would be lovely. I find the walk to be monotonous." She took his arm as they strolled along. "How are you fairing these days?"

"Uh. O.K. I guess."

"I worry that you've taken on too much with the experiments Molab has pushed on you." Her hand wrapped tightly around his arm was a reminder of the strength in her slender frame.

"The experiments were my idea. Anything I can do to help stop Sorche. And they've been worth it. Barone was able to find out how we got our immunity. The brain gets electrically rewired when Sorche or a Valdan takes over and that creates a new pathway. When you break free you burn the pathway. Sear it in a way. After that happens it's fried so bad there's no way to use that pathway and get control again. For most people that should be enough for the brain to reject any further attempts to rewire it." Talking about the progress they've made makes him eager to get back to work.

"When the Dark Ones first turned we searched for ways to stop them. Why didn't this show up then?" Entaya mumbled under her breathe.

"Molab says that human beings are always evolving. Every generation is more attractive, smarter, taller. Whatever. So, all those hundreds of years ago the human brain was more malleable and less likely to fight suggestions. Easier to manipulate."

"Your species has become intelligent enough to be on the cusp of no longer being prey. A couple more generations and we might not be able to control you at all." The gentle wink takes the sting out of her words as he gapes at her. "I see the validity of Molab's theories even if I find them condescending."

"Him and Barone think they can find a way to fry the pathway manually. With a mental impulse or something. If they could do that, her Thralls would be free. Forever. It would take Sorche to her knees."

"That would be a grand weapon indeed. I sincerely hope they succeed. Be wary young man. You've set your sights on Sorche and there's no doubt she's formidable. That by no means makes her the most sinister thing out there." Entaya turned at the swooshing of the conference room doors leaving Tyrone to shake free of the ominous words.

Sorche was the only one who had set up an army and come forward to do battle. She was the enemy they needed to fear. Anything else was jumping at shadows in the dark. He didn't have time or energy for that.

"Without access to the Hubs we can't move close enough to be of help." Tonamas spoke from the large screen mounted on the wall. Tyrone watched from the doorway as the silver haired alien stared

Molab down. "If Dexon and his group could unlock one, preferably the Seattle Hub, that would be useful."

"As I've already relayed, there are only four of them. Sorche will undoubtedly have those Hubs heavily guarded. The risk is untenable when there's a high chance you won't arrive before she departs the shore. For the time being, you are out of the fight." Molab glowered at the screen from his position near the head of the table.

"So, you've said, but I see no alternative where you triumph against her alone."

"We are working on several strategies at the moment. Rest assured she will not take this ship without a heavy cost." Molab's hands clenched behind his back. It was the only clue Tyrone had that Molab wasn't as confident as he sounded.

"You aren't comprehending the situation, beholder. She can't take Sanctus at all. If she attains control of that ship she can leave this planet. Do you fathom the damage if she takes her blood sucking addiction into the cosmos? If it looks like you will succumb then someone must destroy the ship." Tonamas is practically frothing.

"Be assured Captain. Precautions have been taken." Entaya's sensible voice cut through the male tension like a silken knife.

"Of course." Tonamas bowed slightly to her before the screen went black. It made Tyrone feel a little better to see he wasn't the only one who did that.

"What does that mean?" Molab had turned all his frustration onto his co-leader.

"Exactly what I said." She stared him down with her opal eyes.

"Don't play your games with me. I need to know in case something happens to you in the fight."

"There are fail safes should that happen. Have no worries. All is planned for." Smiling benignly at him, she left the room. Tyrone loved her style when it wasn't directed at him.

Megan caught up with him on his way to the labs the next morning. They had both been helping develop the weapons to break people from Thrall. Her smile was fleeting before she fell into step with him. The companionable silences were nice these days.

He wasn't sure his feelings for her were gone, but they didn't carry the intensity of before. This new friendship they were developing was something calmer, more equal. He liked that.

Barone greeted them at the door with the swimmers caps they wore during their sessions. The hard-plastic dots stuck to the inside dug into his scalp, making it a joy to wear. Teelie, the assistant, had explained that each of the dots transmitted specific information back to the medical analysis equipment. The explanation didn't make it any more comfortable.

It wasn't fashionable in any way. He still had to stifle a laugh when he saw Megan with hers on. No matter how much she had loosened up, she wouldn't appreciate the joke. They had learned a lot with them, so it was worth the indignity. Barone swore they could have something to use against Sorche by the time she landed. Tyrone hoped that was more than a false promise.

Just in case, Tyrone spent the time he wasn't in the lab practicing his MMA skills. One way or the other, he would be ready. She wouldn't make a victim of him again.

Megan grabbed his hand pulling his mind back. Turning to her, he was thrown by the look of shock on her face. He'd missed something.

"What?"

"Didn't you just hear Teelie?"

"No, I zone her out anymore. What?" He was getting sick of asking the question already.

"There are bodies washing up on shore. Lots of bodies." Megan's face was white, and her voice shook. She still hadn't let go of his hand.

"Bodies? From Seattle?"

"Yeah. We should go talk to Molab." She was already removing her cap while pulling with the hand she still had captive.

He rushed to get his own cap off before she yanked him down the halls wearing it. Leaving it discarded on a lab table, he took notice of the empty room. Barone must have followed Teelie out immediately. Good thing Megan cared enough to shake him out of his self-absorption.

Down the hall they hurried, dodging others rushing to wherever they needed to be in this crisis. The closer they got to Entaya's command center the more cramped the halls became. Ten feet from the door it was a matter of pushing their way through the barely moving bodies.

Some people shifted aside as they realized who was prying at them but most stubbornly held their ground. Tyrone traded places with Megan, using his bigger body to force a wedge between people that she could slip through. There linked hands kept them connected in the jostle.

Inside the room, there was a small niche they slid into near a console on the wall. From their vantage, they could see Tonamas' face on one screen and Quelis' on another but their focus was drawn to the center screen. On it were multiple live feeds of the atoll's shores on the mainland side. Bodies piled up as the waves pushed them in and left them behind like stacked driftwood.

More ominous were the ones floating on the ocean as far as they could see. The shear mass had turned the tides red. Waiting for their turn to be taken by the waves and placed on the beach to be found. Tyrone could hear Quelis growling at Molab that this was Sorche's response to the vaccine. When she found she couldn't turn them or feed on them, she slaughtered them on the shoreline and sent them. A message.

Tyrone's stomach heaved. He pushed it down. He should have known she would do something like this. Sorche was not the kind of creature to react in half measures. Who would know that better than him? He should have done something to stop this.

He wanted to leave the room, but the number of bodies pushing into it made that impossible. Standing pressed into the corner behind Megan, he used her as a shield from the enormity of the death toll weighing on his soul. Those people's deaths were on him and the team who had poured that vaccine into the water supply.

Molab, Quelis and Tonamas discussed offense, defense, and retaliation as if they were planning a football game strategy. Cool and calm like bodies piling up on shore was no big thing, they put forth plans and shot them down. Switching things up with statistics and probabilities until they could all agree on an attack. The ship always came to the forefront. She couldn't be allowed to leave this planet behind.

Tyrone had already figured out from Entaya that the ship wouldn't fly. Centuries of sea water and earth life had deteriorated it beyond the point of launching. He wasn't sure why the males of the Valdan didn't understand that. Had she not shared the information? Or did they fear Sorche would find a way to repair it?

Eventually on screen, hybrids covered in innocent blood carried the bodies off the shore. Tyrone could see from his viewpoint they had been savaged before she threw them away. The inhumanity of it broke his heart.

He'd become familiar with Hybrid burial practices as Aleece's body had been processed. There were very distinct and beautiful rituals in place for the handling and burial of their dead. Had those on the beach been family to the hybrids they would be treated differently. He knew instead they would be taken to a furnace to be incinerated.

Strangers were viewed disparately. They were simply refuse from the sea. Outsiders to be disposed of as quickly as possible. The sheer number of them wouldn't deter their new hybrid friends from protocol. When he first discovered the practice, he convinced one of the men who usually worked cleanup crew to keep identification from any bodies they found. It was a crap shoot whether he'd do it with this many coming in, but Tyrone could hope.

They watched the bodies come in and be hauled away. The people in the room circulated in and out as they went about the preparations Molab was putting in place. Tyrone and Megan waited for the crowds to thin enough then made their way to a place near the throne and found chairs.

Megan confiscated a Valdan version of a laptop and went to work. She had set up an online web ring to communicate about the Dark Ones movements. Her and Drew used it to keep in touch with the safe houses as well as other people setting up their own havens around the world.

Tyrone was proud of their efforts to build something to fight the terror Sorche had unleashed. It was more productive than anything he had managed.

Lynea was manning the outpost and staying in contact with Sanctus while Quelis and the other Valdan went to do recognizance. Tyrone was happy to see her looking strong and confident. Her losses had turned her into iron.

Needing to do something, he flipped through the alien books sitting in front of him. They were ship manuals someone had pulled out. The pages were a foldable plastique and he could zoom in on words or diagrams when he wanted. It was interesting reading, too. He already knew how the air filtration system worked.

Barone had returned to the lab to push forward on his work. Tyrone decided he would be more help there and pushed away from the table. Megan looked up like she might join him, but he waved her back down. What she was doing was more important right now.

The walk back to the lab was no less crowded. People were scurrying around with packs and boxes of who knew what. Entaya had definitely set plans in motion without filling Molab in. There wasn't anything to do about that.

Barone was bent over his workstation when Tyrone walked in. It almost made him feel bad when the gray-haired doctor jumped.

"Can I help with anything?"

"Not really. It's down to the testing stages. I'm not even sure how to do that. There aren't a lot of humans hanging around here and hybrids can't be controlled."

"Do we dare open the hub and let Thralls through?" Tyrone shuddered remembering the last time.

"It may be the only option, but I don't think Entaya or Molab would give us approval." Barone shook his head as he held up the small device for inspection.

"How does it work?"

"You place it on your finger with the disc inside your hand along your palm. After that, all you have to do is touch a Thrall. The device creates an electrical impulse from your brain to theirs overriding and blocking the pathway Sorche has created. In theory." Barone demonstrated the proper way to wear the device before turning it over to Tyrone. "This one is for you. We'll know how effective it is the second you try it."

"What will happen?" Tyrone looked at the ring the same way he looked at spiders.

"No idea. The whole reason I would love to test them is so I could answer that question. These may be successful, knock them out, or kill them. I can only guess without trials."

"Are we okay with that?" Tyrone had killed enough people lately. "I'm not saying I won't fight because I will. It's just that I'm not sure I want to use people as guinea pigs."

"I don't have any better options here. If it makes you feel better, the only people these will be tested on are going to be intent on killing you." Barone shrugged before returning to his work.

Tyrone stuffed the device into his pocket before heading to the gym. The only place the world made sense. Pounding on the bag, he fell into a rhythm that let his brain shut down. Left, right, left, left, right. Back and forth until sweat dripped from his body.

Showered and enjoying the sweet exhaustion he only got from a great workout, he was pleased to find Megan outside his room. She was sitting against the wall by his door with her laptop open next to her.

"Hey. Whatcha doin?"

"Tyrone. About time. Where have you been?" The way she snapped that laptop closed just about cracked the screen. He was tempted to head back down the hall.

"In the gym." It seemed like an obvious place for anyone who knew him, but he tried to keep the duh out of his voice.

"For two hours?" Her huge eyes carried surprise.

"Yeah. It's a thing I do. What do you want?" He didn't need her judging him. They'd done that enough already.

"Entaya came to find me. Sorche is coming." She pushed into his room right on his heels. Care to wait for an invite?

"Yeah, I know that. We all know that." He waved his hand over the sensor to bring up the lights and moved to the table.

"So, get your stuff together. Mine's packed. It's sitting in my room so I can grab it to evacuate." Megan's words had morphed into a speed that left him longing to catch his breath.

"We're evacuating? She's here?"

"Not yet. But Entaya says she wants all non-essentials off the atoll now. Sanctus will be mostly empty when Sorche gets here. Did you get your device? Barone gave me mine. Everyone gets one before we go."

"She's giving Sanctus to Sorche? Molab said we can't let her have it! Does he know about this?" Tyrone was up from the table and headed for the door before Megan could catch him.

"Wait! Tyrone. No. Don't go to Molab. She doesn't want him to know." Megan's legs were little, but they moved fast. She caught him by the arm about five feet down the hall. "Stop. Please. Listen to me. She has a plan. There is no way she would put the hybrids in danger. We need to trust her."

"Why would I trust her over Molab and Quelis? They both agree we need to keep Sorche from having this ship." Tyrone wanted to rip his arm out of her grip, but there was something in her eyes that held him still.

"Trust me. I know that's asking a lot, too. I haven't always been good to you, but please. Go with me. This will work out. Tyrone?"

Rational thought told him to go with his first instinct and find Molab, but he let her pull him back into his room. There wasn't much to pack. The clothes the hybrids had given him and a few personal items he'd gathered all fit in the rucksack he'd found days ago in a storage room.

Ready to go, he followed her down the hall to her room a few minutes later. She had three bags stacked near the door. He shouldered the biggest one and they made their way further into the depths of the ship.

He had assumed they would head for the surface, but his choice to trust Megan was solid. In for a penny, there was no backing out now. The deeper they went the more curious he became and the more company they had.

Twenty minutes after departing their rooms, they came through a doorway into a cavernous chamber. A solid floor ended halfway across where three large submersible type vehicles sat in a watery opening.

Hybrids moved up ramps into open hatches in the side of the subs loading boxes and sacks alongside people. It was a somber group moving quickly through the process as everyone filed into the room, stopped at a checkpoint where it looked like they received an assignment and then boarded.

Him and Megan took their place in line and waited. It was a quicker process than he had ever experienced in a human queue. At the front, they found that Megan had a place to go and his name was nowhere on the lists. Entaya hadn't planned on including him.

He tried not to take it personally as he urged Megan to follow their luggage and get on the ship without him. That was proving impossible. Eventually, one of the hybrids in charge of moving things along came to check on them.

A quick explanation had Entaya on Tyrone's PEC asking him to join her in the throne room. He tried to use that to get Megan onboard the sub. No luck. She followed him every step of the way back. Entaya met them in the hall.

"Dear Megan. You were not supposed to pass on the invitation you were given." The rebuke though mild had Megan's ears turning pink. "I'm afraid at this point there won't be time to get you onto the subs headed out of here."

"I understand, but I wasn't going to leave my friend behind." The color in her ears faded as her chin came up.

"No one was ever going to leave this young man anywhere. I needed his assistance to pull this last part off. Still do. Follow me." Her hair flowed behind her like waves crashing as she moved down the hall.

Megan looked to him for guidance. That was fair. When he had followed her, they had ended up in a huge pickle. About time she recognized he had a brain and could make rational decisions. There was only one choice here though. Entaya held all the cards when it came to this ship.

| 30 |

Chapter

Lynea ducked into a burned outbuilding to avoid the pack of thralls coming down the alley. She had lost Quelis a couple of blocks back when a group of survivors had been flushed out of a high rise by Sorche's minions. He had made a stand to buy time.

She'd wanted to stick with him, but he gave her a mental push to be gone and she decided to steer the survivors to safety rather than fight it. That was her job, and she was getting damn good at it. Even if it still felt wrong to run off and leave him.

He'd growl at her if she did anything else. Which was helping to break her of the instinct to go back and try to 'save' him. As if she could. So, she'd gotten the group to Naelah and Dexon. They would take them out of the city and steer them to the sanctuaries Tonamas was setting up. This group had been small, only five including a child.

None of the groups they had helped had ever been large. Maybe fifteen people at most. But the numbers were getting smaller as

Sorche and her companions rampaged the area. The kids were the hardest for Lynea.

Now, she made her way to a high point. He always went there when they needed to rendezvous. Which was every time he took her out. She wasn't at a point where she could keep up, yet. Her new training regimen meant one of these days she would be. That would be the day they stopped putting her on lookout duty.

Seeing an inner staircase that appeared intact, she made a stealthy run for it. Two flights up she stopped to listen for followers. In the absence of sound, she counted herself safe and made the rest of the trip to the roof top.

Crouched low like Quelis had taught her, she worked her way to an outer ledge and used her binoculars to scan for him. He was three roofs over. Signaling with the mirrors they kept for that, she let him know where she was and waited the thirty seconds it took him to make the jumps to her side.

"Took you long enough." She gave him a side smile as she continued to scan for enemies.

His chuckle was the only response she was going to get. He took off for the next roof and she knew he wouldn't wait for her. Pushing her body to its limits kept her on his heels. She couldn't wait for the day she didn't need to work so hard.

He made his way down a fire escape and onto the street. Even though he preferred the roofs, they weren't safe now that Sorche and her hordes had torched the city. There were too many unstable buildings waiting to crumble at the littlest provocation.

The alley they landed in was covered in soot and ash like the rest of the city. Lynea looked away from the bodies discarded haphazardly. No one was trying to deal with them anymore. It wouldn't be long before the stench of decay set in.

Quelis darted to the left. She was quick to follow as they made their way through the nearly unrecognizable streets of Seattle. Rubble from fallen buildings littered the blacktop next to bombed cars and broken bodies. They wove their way over and around the debris as quickly as they could.

The sun was sinking. It was bad out here in the daytime, but night brought out the darkest of the souls that had followed Sorche. A side effect of prolonged overindulgence in human blood was a sensitivity to sunlight. So, the most sadistic favored the deepest blackness.

They reached the truck as full darkness fell over them. Jumping in, Lynea tried not to feel cowardly when she shut the door with a little more force than necessary. No one was going to blame her for locking it the second it was closed either.

"Were there fewer of them today than last night?" Lynea asked the question even though she knew the answer.

"Yes." Quelis' jaw was clenched tight enough to crack his molars.

"Does that mean they've headed to the atoll?"

His silent stare out the windshield was all the answer she needed. The mass murder on the shores early this morning had been all the warning Sorche was going to give. Lynea's whole body shook re-membering the blood-soaked beaches and piers left behind in the aftermath of massacre.

She had made Quelis take her as close as he could, to see. It was stupid. There was zero chance anyone had survived that. Instead, she had found crimson stained sneakers and teddy bears amid the refuse to vouch for the children among the dead. Pieces of bodies washed back this way as the tides turned. No human soul except herself to mourn.

After vomiting up what breakfast she'd eaten, she had insisted they go straight to work finding survivors. Those who had escaped Sorche's mass round up. Seattle was emptying of its last lost souls. She was hoping to help as many as they could find.

There hadn't been enough to wash away the blood she felt on her hands. Sorche wouldn't be free if they hadn't gone on their little expedition. These people, her children, would be living their lives if she hadn't been looking to put a little excitement into her own.

Quelis reached across and placed his hand on hers. She hadn't realized she was crying until she felt his touch. Using her free sleeve, she wiped furiously at the wetness on her cheeks. It was past time she stopped falling into this weakness.

Her tears couldn't bring anyone back or make a thing better. Fighting was the only thing that could help them now. It was the only thing she could do to set right what she had done wrong. Bracing her shoulders, she pushed the air out of her lungs before drawing in a fresh new breath. She could be strong enough for this.

"Can we help them? On the atoll?"

"I don't think so. I've talked with Molab and Tonamas. The consensus is Sanctus will stand or fall alone. We should try to coordinate with Tonamas to rebuild and fortify."

"So, we're going to open up more of the outpost network."

"Yes. With a mixture of humans, Valdan and hybrids working together." He took his eyes off the road to meet hers for just a second.

She broke the contact to focus on the scenery blurring beyond her window. It was less complicated than the man sharing the cab with her. Life had moved so fast since she left for Mexico. She needed time to stop and think.

They came up on the cliff and moved right through it. She'd lost the thrill at seeing it dissipate around her as they cleared the shield and entered the underground garage. Shifting away from Quelis, she was out of the truck and headed for the interior of the outpost at a steady clip.

He wouldn't follow until he'd checked in his weapons and gone through a sit rep with the others. She'd have at least a thirty-minute head start to make it to her room. Plenty of time to make sure she was dead asleep with lights out when he came by.

| 31 |

Chapter

Megan felt the fire in her muscles as she pushed them to move. Entaya had kept them at a steady pace down previously sealed corridors for the last thirty minutes. So much for thinking she knew her way around the ship.

The Valdan woman was proving to Megan that she hadn't been allowed to explore even a fraction of it. That wasn't some grand surprise, but it was a disappointment. For some stupid reason she'd thought this woman trusted her.

Tyrone wasn't good company. He was still pissed that she hadn't gotten onto the sub like a good girl. It didn't matter that he was trying to protect her with that move. Why couldn't he see that she wouldn't buy her own safety with his?

Maybe he could and it didn't matter. She might need to face the fact that she'd never mend things right with him. That was a bitter pill to swallow. One she wasn't prepared for yet. There were still cards to be played because it turned out this man was a lot more important to her than she had ever admitted.

When they got through this she was going to tell him that. She was going to tell a lot of people things she hadn't. These walls she'd built weren't keeping her safe. They were keeping her alone. She had family to clear the air with. Guess it was time to do that.

Lost in her thoughts, she came up short as Tyrone stopped abruptly. Leaning to the side gave her a good view of Entaya opening a vacuum sealed door with a hand pad next to it. The whoosh of air signaled its release. Tyrone stepped to the side for the women to walk through.

Megan trailed behind Entaya trying hard not to feel like an uninvited guest. Which she was, but that wasn't something she wanted to dwell on now that she couldn't change it. She rubbed at the goosebumps that popped up on her arms as Tyrone sealed the door and fell into step behind her.

Through a short ante chamber, they entered what looked to Megan like a control room. She could make out consoles on the pedestals throughout the room. The glowing screens lining the wall to their left flashed views of the atolls' hallways, rooms, and beaches.

Entaya moved to the right where she opened a sliding panel with her palm. Inside was a clear exoskeleton. Megan moved closer as the Valdan pulled the pieces of the suit out to inspect. Motioning Tyrone over, she placed them next to his corresponding body parts before laying them on the table like a bizarre game of dress up.

"These should fit you nicely. Megan and I will monitor from here. If you would disrobe they will mold better to skin."

Megan wanted to turn and watch the screens. Curiosity kept her eyes pinned to the suit. She had to know how it worked. Tyrone's movements out of the corner of her eye told her he was doing as Entaya asked so she kept her sight line above the waist, mostly. Not that it was entirely necessary since he kept the fun parts hidden behind his hands.

As Entaya placed the suit onto Tyrone it solidified to a pearly material. Clear crystal shot through it where Megan could see his dark skin glowing faintly. With all the pieces in place a clear film formed over his face then appeared to meld with his features. When he didn't gag or choke, Megan let her own breath out.

"You shoot your weapons using the interface built into the gauntlets. There are tactile controls in the gloves that will interact with the visual read out. We don't have time to give you a full training on all aspects of the suit. I regret that I didn't have the foresight to begin with you earlier, but I had truly hoped this wouldn't become necessary." Entaya reached up and touched a space on the back of the helmet that turned green. Tyrone's' body stiffened and his head slammed back so hard his teeth clacked.

"What did you do?" Megan moved to help.

"Started a program that will push the knowledge he needs into his mind. Ideally we would have days to run it. We do not. He will get what he can. Sorche is here." Pointing up at the screen, Entaya grimaced.

Megan was torn between the need to see her enemy arrive and her desire to keep tabs on Tyrone. Sorche won. The fire haired woman stood aboard a tugboat at the pier. Every surface of the boat was crammed with her makeshift militia.

Goons and Thralls fought to stay onboard as they jostled each other. The difference between the two was obvious as you watched the anxieties play across the faces of those who were still allowed to feel and think. The Dark Ones smattered among them stood out like scare crows looking over the flock.

Thralls jumped to the pier the second it touched the bough and caught the ropes thrown down. They were still tying off when their leather clad leader made the leap herself. She sauntered her way to land as her people disembarked.

Megan was so focused on the tugboat she almost missed the other boats as they beached and threw ladders over the sides. Sorche marched on the village with an actual army. Megan prayed everyone had made it out.

Her eyes sought another camera until they found them. A detonation in the midst of their ranks took her by surprise as much as them. Entaya pushed buttons and crowed at her side as another blew farther back.

"Did you do that?"

"This ship isn't without its defenses. If Molab had been willing to listen he would have known that." She winked an opal eye and Megan found herself smiling. "We may not win, but we'll make her question the cost."

"Can I help? I'm not a hacker like Drew, but I know my way around a computer, and I've become fluent at reading your language."

"Take over this console. It's already set to go." Entaya moved to switch places. Megan picked up the gist of it pretty fast.

No matter how many she blew up they kept coming. She tried hard not to look at their mom sweaters and skinny jeans as they flew amongst the debris. Sparing a glance at the shores she saw more ships waiting for a chance to get close enough to unload. Where had Sorche gathered all these people from?

"She's found the elevator." Entaya's voice was clipped as she drilled the console in front of her with her fingertips. Nothing they did was enough to turn the tide.

Lasers shot through the crowd near the elevator cutting through flesh with ease. Megan could see them mounted on what had only appeared to be trees nearby and knew Entaya had activated them.

Sorche stepped out of range while pushing her Thralls to keep prying at the doors. It wasn't long before they opened.

As she stepped inside, the fiery haired alien smiled up at the camera. Megan shoved away from her console as she felt the woman's touch slither across her mind. She could see a group of hybrids waiting for the doors to open inside the ship.

She smiled as she imagined them shooting into the confined car with the alien trapped inside. The bullets flew as the doors opened and the Thralls rushed out. To Megan's horror the hybrids were overwhelmed as Sorche's people appeared to register no pain. They never slowed, only stopped by death.

Sorche exited the elevator as if the encounter had never taken place, stepping on the hybrids bodies like fallen pieces of trash. Megan returned to her console, working furiously to find whatever pitfalls or traps she could to slow the steady march.

Movement behind her signaled Tyrone's return to the fight. Entaya wasn't at her pedestal when Megan glanced that way, so she had to assume the Valdan had something to do with that. There were more important things to focus on.

The elevator traveled up and down the shaft at a steady pace spilling enemy troops into the ship. Sorche and her minions cut down every hybrid who came near them. Megan fought to catch them off guard with the ships defenses, but the alien woman evaded them every time.

She watched two separate hybrids try to use Barone's devices to return the Thralls to free will. Each time ended in immediate death for the Thrall. A weapon, but not the kind they had hoped for.

A screen in her peripheral caught her attention. Tyrone cut through a corridor making his way toward Sorche, his stride fierce in the alien armor. She took hope that he would be the one to put their enemy back where she belonged.

Entaya had yet to return to her pedestal. Megan took a second to look around the room. She spotted ocean hair gliding out a back door. As tempting as it was to investigate, she couldn't leave now.

Turning back to the screen, she focused on helping the hybrids stay alive. Tyrone was doing a great job of clearing a path for himself. The armor must be enhancing his strength as he knocked people out of his way like dolls.

Twice she caught flashes of light as he pointed toward Thralls. She couldn't wait to pick his brain about those weapons later.

The hybrids she was helping took most of her attention. But there was always a part of her aware of the alien woman. Sorche was homed in on something. Megan recognized the look on her face.

Two hybrids trapped in a dead-end hall pulled her away from that screen. She used a hidden laser to give them an opening on their left then watched as they slashed their way to safety through it. Usually, they would return to the fight but these two beelined for an empty path.

She watched them make their way farther from the fight as she tracked the other hybrids. It didn't take long for a pattern to emerge. They were all moving away from the enemy. Someone had called retreat.

Her gaze was pulled to where Tyrone strode deeper into the enemy lines. No one had pulled him back. Or he wasn't listening. Watching the screens, she could clearly see now that he was Sorche's target. The other parts of the ship filled with her army as all resistance ceased.

Megan didn't waste her time searching the retreating defenders. Wherever Entaya had gone, they likely were. All that mattered to her was the man on a collision course with the deadliest creature she'd ever met.

"Megan. We are required to leave now." Entaya's voice jarred her to her bones.

"I'm not going."

"I'm afraid you don't have a choice this time, dear." The Valdan had drifted closer to Megan's perch at her console where she was entranced with the two beings squaring off. Entaya reached around her to push some buttons and the small screens morphed into one large screen.

Megan could see the determination on Tyrone's face as his body braced for battle. He raised his arm and the light she'd seen earlier shot out. She watched in wonder as it expanded in a wave, rippling across the room until it drilled into Sorche.

The Dark One slammed into the wall behind her before regaining her footing. With a smirk she walked back to the space she'd just occupied and shook her head. "I hadn't expected you to face me like this Tyrone. It's a bit of a waste. I'd hoped she'd send Quelis or Dexon as her champion."

Thralls moved to encircle Tyrone as their leader spoke. He stepped quickly to the side and slapped his palm to the side of a man's head. She wanted to scream through the screen that the device would fail. He was wasting his time.

The man fell to the ground unconscious. But not dead. Megan could see the rise and fall of his chest. What was different? Had it worked this time? There was no time to know as Sorche went on the offensive. She came across the room at a run. Her and Tyrone were exchanging blows between one blink and the next.

Megan forced herself to breathe as Sorche pushed him ever backwards. He twisted to the left and swept sideways with his leg, catching her by surprise. Her ankle twisted, forcing her to withdraw or lose her balance. Tyrone took the space to rain down blows of his own.

Entaya was so close, Megan pushed out with her hand to get personal space and the world started to tilt. She watched Sorche come up under Tyrone with a blow that sent him flying across the room as her own world began to fade. Entaya's voice floated above it. "I promised him you'd go. So, you'll go."

| 32 |

Chapter

Tyrone strode down the corridor with purpose. He wished he had been able to talk to Drew, but he trusted Entaya to pass on his message. As much as he trusted her to take care of Megan. Now, it was time to keep his part of the bargain.

He could feel Sorche somewhere ahead of him like a beacon. He embraced the bond for the first time. Calling for her.

Thralls tried to get in his way, but they stood no chance. The suit reacted to his commands like it was part of him. The agonizing shock Entaya had given him must have put him in sync with it.

When he needed a weapon to fire, the display highlighted his arm. He lifted it, and a light wave shot out so quickly and powerfully he almost didn't brace for it. There wasn't time to be awed by the power as he engaged minions charging out of a doorway.

Two against one would have tested his skills before. Not now. He dispensed them in a blur of kicks and punches that lacked his usual precision. Entaya should have given him time to train with this thing before she sent him on this suicide mission.

People kept throwing themselves into the fight. He tried to find a time to use the device Barone had given him, but they refused to come one on one. His reactions were instinctual, and they were down before he remembered his intentions.

Finally, he found Sorche. She'd surrounded herself with Thralls and minions ready to take him on. He wasn't surprised. Her need for blood and gore was boundless, but she never took chances when she could stack the deck.

Here she was. Ready to fight him. Taking advantage of having the first blow, he raised his arm and fired the light wave. She flew into the wall with such force he felt the vibration through the floor. Before he could gloat, she was brushing herself off and returning to her spot like he hadn't fired.

He moved closer as she yelled across the room. Something about Quelis and or Dexon and a waste. His brain was too busy processing strategy to lose time on an old trick meant to get into your opponent's head.

He watched for body language that would tell him she was ready to pounce as her people encircled him. One of the Thralls moved close and he saw a chance to turn the tide. Grabbing the Thrall, he slapped his hand upside the man's temple.

A buzz like the zap of a battery ran up Tyrone's arm and into his brain. The man fell unconscious onto the ground. Rage rolled off of Sorche at the same instant. Did that mean the man had broken free?

There was no more time to worry about it as Sorche sprinted across the room. He met her midway with fist upraised. The blow was enough to set her back, but it didn't stop the swing she sent from her left. It connected with his ribs sending a rush of air from his body.

Pulling breath back into his lungs, he swung at her kidneys with his right and landed a blow that threw her counter punch off. He dodged to his right and evaded her fist. He couldn't avoid the kick she swung into his knee.

The armor took the brunt of the blow, but he lost his balance. A roll to his left put him out of range of the foot she sent flying at this head while he was down. He popped back up behind her where a Thrall took a swing at him with a chair.

He sent the man flying away from the fight but lost track of Sorche. She landed two blows to his kidneys before he could turn. The speed of his back hand nailed her across the face, sending her spinning away while he put his feet back under him.

She came back with renewed vigor. Blow after blow hitting his body and his face with savage intensity. He stepped back to get his hands up, then back again to find room to move. She gave him none.

His arms ached from the continued onslaught. Never in his career had an opponent kept at him like this. Desperation ate at his confidence. Gritting his teeth against it he swept his leg out. She was so focused in she missed it.

Her ankle rolled under his foot as it made contact. She swung away as she fought to regain balance. There wasn't a second to fail. Pushing into her space, he delivered punches to her body like sledgehammers.

All of his weight thrown behind each swing caused the impact to rattle back into his own body. But he didn't stop. Over and over he pounded at her. Memories flashing through his mind. Paying back every pain she'd inflicted on his world since the moment they'd set her free.

The upper cut took him without warning. He went flying through the air as Sorche smirked through bloodied teeth. When his body hit the wall, it didn't stop. It cracked and crumbled around him as he flew into the next room.

Landing on the floor amid the rubble he fought to breathe. He'd felt this before. At least one rib was broken or badly bruised. There wasn't anyone here to wrap it for him. The thought had barely formed and the suit increased pressure around his midsection. Handy.

Sorche advanced on him as he wrestled free of the debris. He didn't make it to his feet. She reached down to grab him by the front of his suit only to find there was nothing to grasp. He used the moment to bring his arms under her and fire both light waves into her midsection.

Her eyes went wide as she was lifted away from him by the double blast. She flew out of the hole he'd made and into the next room. He fired at her three times more while she was in the air. Missing once but nailing her the other two.

She landed in a heap at the far side of the large room. Her Thralls advanced on him. He used the device on his hand wishing Barone had given him two. Bodies fell left and right. He hoped they would rise again with free will, but this stage of the game left him equally okay with them staying down for good.

The flame haired she-devil was pushing off the ground by the time he finished her crowd of defenders. He could see the pain he'd caused in her jerky movements. He smiled at that. Karma and all.

He didn't give her a chance to get all the way right before attacking again. His blows landed to her head and ribs while she fought for balance. Her arms came up trying to deflect but it wasn't enough as he pounded his anger out.

"How have you managed this?" Her question came as her body collapsed at his feet. "You are human."

"Your kind will learn not to underestimate us. We aren't prey." He grabbed her by the arm and wrenched her to her feet. He needed to get her to one of the cells the suit was identifying on his display. Then Entaya needed to know not to blow the ship.

| 33 |

Chapter

Drew walked into the center of operations with his nose in his tablet. His PEC had summoned him here more than half an hour ago, but he'd been deep in communication with one of the safe houses. They were full to bursting with hybrids and humans. The Valdan that Tonamas had put in charge there was begging for food, supplies, and money to build additional rooms.

This was becoming a problem with the refugee network as they worked to set it up. Too many of the people that ran to them came with nothing. That included clothes and money. Parts of the world were still running like normal. If they could find a cash infusion, supplies could be bought.

In the places where scavenging was the way to get it done, he was hearing complaints that there weren't enough people trained to be out on the dangerous streets. So, now he needed to convince Tonamas to set up training centers for humans. Or send people who were trained to these safe houses. It was a logistical nightmare.

He needed at least two more sets of hands. Megan was helping from the atoll, but she'd been impossible to reach for the last 24 hours. When the Hubs were up and running again, he needed to bring her here.

"Drew!" Tonamas barked from in front of the communication screen.

"What?" Drew hadn't realized he'd beelined for his desk in the back corner.

"I called for you forty-five minutes ago. Tyrone wished to speak with you."

"Oh. I didn't realize. Yeah. Let me put this down." Drew set the tablet on his desk before making his way through the maze of tables and chairs to Tonamas. "Right. So, where is he?"

"There was no time to wait. He had to go. I'm sorry." Tonamas looked to the floor before returning his gaze to the screen. "Molab will explain."

"Explain what?" Drew scrutinized the white-haired alien.

"Tyrone is a brave and valiant human." Molab stood tall in what appeared to be a control room packed with hybrids. "Sorche attacked the atoll. We fought her with every weapon at our disposal. There came a point when we realized we would be unable to defeat her."

"Your friend is right now fighting Sorche on the atoll so that we can get far enough away from the explosion." Entaya stepped onto screen, crowding Molab over.

"He's what? How does he get off?" Drew was fighting to put the reality of their words in order.

"I'm afraid he doesn't. She's too crafty and she draws others to her. We need to ensure she is there when it explodes. The only way to do that was for him to volunteer to keep her engaged." Molab was clearly trying to look sympathetic. "If it makes things any better, there is no way he won that fight. Even with the suit Entaya gave him. She will have beaten him very badly."

"Makes things better? That he was beaten? No, it doesn't. What's wrong with you? How long? Until?" He couldn't say it. They had just gotten Tyrone back. He hadn't even seen him in person yet. There was no way he was ready to say goodbye. Why hadn't he answered his PEC when it went off? He could have talked the stupid SOB out of this plan. Out of trusting these two.

"Any minute now. We are about to pass the trigger point. Once we are beyond that, the bomb will automatically detonate." Molab turned to watch a separate screen.

Drew moved to a side console and pulled up the feed from Molab and Entaya's ship. It was a simple hack with how interconnected the Valdan technology was. The atoll was clearly visible.

He made out an uncountable number of boats crashed into the shoreline and smoke pouring from the treetops all along the skyline. His chest rose and fell, rose, and fell as he waited.

A message flashed onto the console below the picture.

She's been neutralized. DO NOT BLOW THE SHIP. Barone's device works. Thralls are waking up free. Tyrone

"STOP THE SUB! DON'T PASS THE TRIGGER POINT!" Drew leapt to the side to get Entaya or Molab's attention on the other screen. "The message at the bottom of the screen. Look at the message. Tyrone won!" Drew's lungs heaved as he searched their faces for a reaction, any reaction.

"Did you hear him? We don't need to do this." Tonamas growled.

Sanctus exploded on the screen to his right, catching him unaware. His chest nearly exploded with the shock of sound and light. Fighting for focus, he reached behind himself for a chair and fell into it. Why hadn't they stopped?

"What did you do? He had her down! You saw the message. I told you. I told you to stop. He could have been saved and you killed him anyways!" Drew's voice broke on the last of it. Silence echoed off the walls.

He was sure they could have pulled back in time. He'd seen the specs on those subs while he was on Sanctus. Had they valued Sorche's destruction over the cost of human life? That was a stupid question. Of course, they had. They were Valdan.

| 34 |

Chapter

Megan roused at the sound of Drew yelling over a speaker. Why was he so insistent? Sitting up, she looked around the crowded control room of what appeared to be a sub. What was Tonamas saying they didn't need to do?

Entaya and Molab stood on the far side near a screen bank. She could see Drew and Tonomas on a midsize screen to the side. On the biggest one dead center was Sanctus. She was horrified by the sight of smoke pouring from the treetops and ships listing around the shores.

An explosive burst of light and sound permeated the screen as the sub rocked violently. She grappled for a handhold as she was thrown to the floor. Her head bounced off something hard as she was jostled every which way before the waters settled. Intending to confront Entaya, she pulled her battered body up off the bench. Her brain struggled to process.

That could not have been Sanctus blowing up! Tyrone had been on Sanctus. Entaya had made her leave him there. Entaya liked Tyrone. She couldn't have left him to die. Entaya wouldn't have let him die. He wouldn't have left her alone to deal with this world. Because he loved her. That was always going to be true right? That he was going to be by her side?

Warm trails made their way down her cheeks as her heart accepted what her mind wouldn't. He would have stayed behind. To save them all. Knowing he would die. That's why he made Entaya take her by force. Sobs shook her until she was left with no choice but to sink back down onto the bench. The will to fight washed away.

Her person, that she loved, was gone. He had given himself to save her and so many others. The sub was filling with cheers and congratulations as the hybrids realized Sorche was dead and her army with her. We had won. Why shouldn't they celebrate? Most of them had never known the man who had died for them.

They gave her plenty of space as she made her way off the bench and out a hatchway. She had no clue where she was going. It didn't matter. All she needed was to be away from their happiness.

Finding an empty room, she dodged into it. There was a neatly made bunk suspended from the wall. She made sure the door was secured behind her before falling into it.

Curled in on herself, she remembered everything she could about the man she'd taken for granted for way too long. Tears soaking the pillow below her head, she wouldn't let her mind turn off until she'd burned it all into her memory.

Eventually, the fog of grief took her into blessed oblivious sleep.

| 35 |

Chapter

Drew rushed across the pathway to the outbuilding where Megan was staying. She'd gotten here two days ago with Entaya and Molab's group, but he'd barely had any time to talk to her. Getting everyone settled had been a full-time job.

That was the whole reason he had set this meeting. To make sure he took a minute off to mourn with his friends. And now he was running late because Gerus had caught him on the way needing to talk about the hybrids getting better rooms. As far as Drew was concerned, they could suck it up and deal.

Nobody was enjoying the forced cohabitation. He was working on getting them moved to a different site. There were two sites with open space, one in Arizona and one in Sweden. Both of them were human only right now but mixing in the hybrids should be good for everybody. They needed to learn to live together. They were in this together for the long haul.

Unfortunately, the Hubs had been knocked out of sync by the blast on Sanctus. If only Entaya had seen that coming, she might have thought that was worth the risk of not blowing the place up. He pushed the bitter thought aside. Nothing good was going to come of it.

So, he needed to find a way to move large groups of people around the globe. Or go crazy sharing space with the entitled aliens who chose to let his friend die. He was trying to see that from the big picture, but it was hard.

Walking up to the door, he knocked twice to let them know it was him. Trenton opened the door with a drink in his hand then stepped aside with a grand gesture. Megan sat on a small futon to the right of the door. She was wasted away and the ghostly pallor she wore these days had nothing to do with make-up.

"Hey. Good to see you." She rose from the futon to give him a light hug and peck on the cheek before sinking back down.

"Right back at you." He wanted to hold her longer, maybe transfer some of his strength over, but he was afraid to break her if he grabbed to hard.

"What's happening up at the big house?" Trenton took a seat in one of the chairs on the left of the small room. Drew followed suit as he thought about how to answer that question. He hadn't told either of them about the message from Tyrone the day of the explosion. It was eating at him to share it, but he was afraid it might fracture the alliance they were building. They needed that alliance to rebuild this world they had shattered.

"Barone thinks he can get the Hubs running soon. Another week, maybe two at most. He says. I'm not sure he isn't just being diplomatic about it. We could be waiting months. Dark Ones are popping up all around the globe. Tonamas says they are coming forward to claim power. He thinks his people can handle them. We'll see." Drew shifted uncomfortably in his chair. "How are the training sessions going?"

"Pretty good. The group I'm in with is pretty hard core. Koldac says we will be ready to fight within the month. If Barone comes through with the Hub that means we'll be deployed soon after. I'm ready to get back out there and kick some Dark ass." Trenton grinned. "Now that we took down Sorche, it's just a matter of rounding up the stragglers and we get this planet back."

"Aren't you going out to help settlements with scavenging and defense?" Megan leaned forward.

"Yeah. Of course. But that doesn't mean we won't get to take down Dark Ones too." Trenton shrugged.

"Maybe. Don't be so eager to get into a fight." Megan fell back wearily. "I'm thinking I'll go find my family once the Hubs work again. Or maybe I won't wait. Are planes or trains running Drew?"

"Some. Mostly military. Tonamas has reached out to them. There's a tentative alliance forming between the Valdan and the US. He's hoping they will help him negotiate similar terms with the rest of the world. I can probably get you on a plane state side if you want. Moving one person isn't so hard." He searched her face, unsure if he felt good about sending her across the world on her own.

"You can get me to New York City?" She perked up for the first time since he'd entered the room.

"Sure. There hasn't been a lot of Dark activity there so it would be simple. When do you want to go?"

"Soon. I need to see them. It's time to stop running from my past. When I've settled that I'll come back. There's so much that needs done. It's going to take all of us to put right what we broke." She smiled sadly at Drew.

Looking at her, he knew they had broken themselves right along with the world. Hopefully, they would be able to fix that too. "Has anyone heard from Lynea?"

"She's helping Quelis and Dexon get the settlement network across the US set up. They are starting with ones close to Seattle so they can help the refuges there first, but they hope to move across the states quickly. I was kind of hoping I would get deployed where they are, so I could work with them again." Trenton shrugged as he picked up his forgotten drink from the table next to him.

"I was hoping they would at least be joining us on a video call." Drew couldn't explain the depth of disappointment he felt. "What about Caneon? Anything?"

"We've searched with everything we have, but the world has become a vast and easy place to hide in. Wherever he's gone, I don't think he wants to be found. Until he's mourned Aleece properly, I don't think we'll see him." Megan's voice had grown tired again.

"We will see him again. Each other too. Tyrone and Aleece would fight for that if they were here. Since they aren't, it's our job to do it for them." Trenton raised his glass in a solo salute then downed the contents. "I need to get going. It's chow time. Then back to training. See you guys around."

Drew was pulled to his feet and into a rough embrace. Just as he adjusted to it, he was set free and Trenton moved on to wrap Megan into his arms. She wrapped her arms around the other man and held on like she hadn't with Drew. He had to wonder about that. Shared grief?

With Trenton gone, the conversation fizzled. Drew couldn't seem to move away from the awkward silences. Knowing there was a list of things for him to do that was getting longer by the second, he decided it was time to go.

"Megan. I'll let you know when I get you a flight to NYC. If you need anything else just let me know. I have my PEC." He stood to head back to the operation center. Tonamas needed him.

"Could they have saved him?"

"What makes you ask that?" He dreaded her answer as much as he wanted a confidant.

"I heard you yell and Tonamas talking. Before. It's taken me time to replay it and piece it together." Megan pinned him with her eyes.

"Does it matter at this point?" He hated himself for saying it. "He's gone and placing blame won't undo it."

"Since when do you tow the party line? Tell me." Megan drilled him with her stare.

"So you can stir up trouble? Who does that help? Go make peace with whatever family you can. Maybe find out what happened to Tyrone's mom. He would've appreciated us doing that. Then put this war behind you and leave it there. That's what I'm doing." Drew made sure he was out the door before she could come at him again. He knew her well enough to know she would get the answers she wanted eventually, but not from him.

She'd stirred up the gunk that he usually let settle to the bottom of his mind. All of those lost on Sanctus. Tyrone had said Barone's device worked. Trina had to have been there. Had she been Thrall or free when it blew? How had Sorche found the atoll so quickly? The cloaking should have kept it safe for months. Had someone been working with Sorche? The mire swirled round his mind, but he fought for the clarity he needed.

Back in the main house he was bombarded again by the needs of those Tonamas was responsible for. He loved every second of it. Helping to set the world back on its feet was better than delivering pizzas any day of the week.

| 36 |

Chapter

Caneon forced his eyes open at the sound of feet hitting the concrete floor his body was pressed against. Pain drowned out the ability to care who was coming. They would hurt him. Or they wouldn't. It didn't matter anymore.

He only liked to see their faces. His one perverse way of clinging to hope. Maybe he would see sympathy. Just one time. A glimmer of something. And then they would help him escape. Maybe.

Blankness greeted him as he met the eyes of the men who dragged him to his feet. His shredded pants offered no protection for his knees as they scraped on the ground when his legs refused to hold his weight. It never slowed them.

Down the damp corridors, they drug his half lifeless body. He mustered his reserves to manage the winding staircase only to find his shins banging the treads as they hustled upwards faster than he could lift his wasted muscles.

Somewhere along the way he ceased to try. What was the use? They were most likely taking him somewhere to dispose of his body. His usefulness was fulfilled now that he had betrayed all that he held dear.

There was no semblance of a man left in the shell he allowed to be dragged through the last set of doors and deposited onto a cold marble floor. The smell of flowers after rain drifted to him. It had been an eternity since he'd caught even a touch of her unique aroma.

Glancing furtively around, he searched for the woman who carried him through the darkest hours of torture. She remained allusive.

An oversized weathered man held office in the large room. He sat opposite Caneon behind a large ornate desk from a bygone era. Bodyguards in gray suits stood to each side of his rail thin shoulders. His piercing eyes dominated his face.

"It is good to finally meet you face to face Mr. James. I feel that I already know you so well but let me introduce myself. My name is Harlan Burrows. It has been many things over time, but there is no one left alive who calls me anything else. I do hope that you've enjoyed my hospitality." The sound of his hacking laughter echoed into the corners of the room before dying out. "My daughter tells me you were a model house guest. I appreciate that. Sethena, come out darling and say hello."

She appeared from the shadows like a magic trick as Caneon struggled to push his body upright. The desk was the only piece of furniture near enough to lean on and he didn't dare touch the old man's property.

Her sunlight hair shimmered around her graceful features in a choppy cut that ended at her chin and framed her jade eyes. If it weren't for the black leather jacket and ripped jeans Caneon might have mistaken her for a pixie.

He had convinced himself long ago she was a hallucination brought on by blood loss. To see her standing before him almost broke the tenuous hold he had on his sanity.

"Father." She addressed the old man with an edge of scorn he had gotten used to hearing when Trina talked. "What do you need of me?"

"Sorche has fallen." Harlan stated it like the implications were clear and she acknowledged it without question. That scared Caneon more than anything he'd been through lately.

"I'll prepare the contingency plans." She came around the desk and latched onto Caneons arm with a strength that belied her size. He was following her down the hall before the questions in his mind could find their way out of his mouth. "Don't ask."

"What?"

"Your questions. Don't ask them. I won't answer and we'll waste time arguing about it. Do what I tell you when I tell you and you might stay alive. Become a nuisance and I'll leave you in a ditch. Are we clear?" She stopped on the front terrace long enough to drag him eye to eye with her.

"Yes." He wasn't a stupid man, and her sincerity was written all over her face.

"Good. Now, get in the vehicle. We have a world to dominate."

Shasta Jordan enjoys all kinds of stories, especially fantasy and sci-fi. Her love of writing bloomed while growing up in a small ranching community in northeastern Arizona. There she honed her ability to create the worlds she now thoroughly enjoys sharing with you. She resides in Florida with her husband, 4 of her 7 children, a cat, a dog, and an infinite number of lizards. When she's not crafting stories about otherworldly beings, she can be found helping other author's bring their stories to life with her editing skills.

Lightning Source UK Ltd.
Milton Keynes UK
UKHW020649010221
378044UK00015B/1730